I Kill Rich People 2

I Kill Rich People 2

a novel by Mike Bogin

Avasta Press
Seattle, WA

Additional information: www.MikeBogin.com

Cover design by Tony Goedde & Kelsye Nelson
Interior design by Kelsye Nelson

ISBN-13: 9780984911035
ISBN-10: 0984911030

Published and manufactured in the United States of America

First Edition: 2014

This story comes completely out of my head.
All factual elements in this story were derived from readily-available,
publicly-accessible websites. Absolutely no secure or confidential
information has been cited.

This country is so much better than its government. We all know it! What happened to our democracy? Why has it gotten so bad? Most people want the same basics: to feel safe and to have a fair chance of a better life. But our votes don't seem to change things.

We can't elect people to improve this country; not from inside, not anymore. We can only elect the puppets, some willing, some not, while billionaire puppeteers rule over us.

Our world is not wrecked! We are not zombie hordes set on devouring one another!

But the people will awaken. The rich have made themselves easy targets. When we recognize what is happening we will be their worst nightmare.

We are a million to their one.

We can take this country back in the blink of an eye.

- Captain Samuel Hall
United States Army

CHAPTER ONE

Vibrations rumbled through his guts. His insides coiled with springing intensity; all thoroughbred, anxious to burst out of the gate and do what he was put on this earth for. *Your mission, your skills, your will. All you.*

"We've been flying through here the last five nights," the young specialist shouted through the engine roar into Spencer's headphones. C130s and Chinooks had been making regular night runs all along their current flight path in order to get his ass in there without raising suspicion. "Burning all that gas to cover for you."

The kid kept moving his lips, only nothing resembling words came across. Inside the dim cabin Spencer could hear only THUD buhROOM THUD buhROOM THUD. The huge dual-rotors whirred; their methodical thumping churning into him from sternum to tailbone.

A dry wind blasted over Spencer's weathered face. He flipped the protective cover to check his wristwatch. *Fifteen minutes out.*

"Getting the Taliban down there used to the pattern," the kid continued excitedly. He had never seen anyone dropping solo deep into the Badlands. The sergeant, his one passenger, wore Airborne, Rangers, and Special Forces patches; a Tower of Power. Without realizing that he was doing it, the kid's hand was magnetically drawn to the desert-brown Barrett 50-caliber rifle. Spencer's fierce glance singed the kid like he had touched a hot stove.

He smiled sheepishly but Spencer's snarl remained. Spencer stabbed a stiff finger and pointed toward the far end of the helicopter's long cabin. The kid got the message. *Get the fuck away.* The kid served one function: give the five minutes to drop alert.

Below, blackness. A uniform sea of absence that hid ten thousand unknowns with one thing in common: a raging intent to kill him. Above, a billion dazzling stars; electric, alive, stretched wide across the soft moonless universe. He could reach out and embrace it. With one easy step he could rise up and lose himself within that infinite beauty.

Jesus. Get on routine!

Routine was everything. Routine kept him alive.

Routine. Review the drop zone photos, targeting site(s). Target identities.

Day old drone photographs. No pickup trucks and no mortars indicated inside the mud walls. Pick-up 1, alternate 2, his cover zone if everything went to shit. He had four hundred meters across open ground to the only outcrop offering any cover. Four hundred meters at full run to make it. Barrett, ammo, water. Fuck the rest. Four hundred meters down to a few boulders rising twenty feet above the plain surrounding the village.

He could make it, if they really had no trucks. He could hold them beyond range for a while with the Barrett, if they had no mortars. Lots of "ifs", but "ifs" go with the job. Ifs and death.

Nothing new there… you live with death; yours, the men around you, and the targets; you eat it, sleep it, breathe it. You need to get one with it, bring it inside. When you start making plans, you look forward to living, then you're paralyzed. Finished. Time to get the fuck out.

Spencer had packed his own chute, bagged ammo, and run through his checklist twice hours before he ever stepped up from the landing bar into the helicopter. *Routine.* He ran through it again in his head. Six gallons of fluids, split two-thirds and one-third between main pack and the ankle bag. Barrett in hand, 45 Colt in the ankle bag. The Barrett was about separation. The Colt was about keeping a handle on fate. No capture. Don't get shown around the world on some grainy Taliban video with your head being hacked off.

He left that thought trailing into the darkness.

Routine. One hundred twenty rounds. MREs for two days eating. One fourteen-ounce emergency meds kit. Two locators, neither of which he hoped to use; the Afghans down there, living in their mud hamlets, could be scanning signals faster than the U.S. Army.

Night-vision goggles brought the pack carry-weight total to seventy-one pounds. U.S. forces were losing the night vision advantage. More night raids coming from their side. Only six months ago, Night-vision goggles on the Kabul black market had been worth twenty RPGs or ten Kalashnikovs. Intel now pegged the price point at half that amount, plus they were taking Afghanis, the local currency, in payment. *Fucking Pakistan; bringing Chinese product out to the Tribal Areas then straight into enemy hands.*

Any fighter watching the fly-over with night vision capability could plug him twenty times before he touched the ground.

He left his body-armor in camp; it had no practical value and he had been on the job too long to get any gain from illusions. Under his army-issue camouflage, the clothing was his own: a Northface fleece and REI Polartec. Adding the Barrett and the additional forty rounds of ammunition in the ankle pack put 130 pounds onto his 190-pound frame.

He flipped open the cover and checked his watch again. Eleven minutes out, by his estimate, to some no-name village somewhere east of Garmsir, Shit Storm Central.

Just get there already. The waiting always fucked with his head. Over 200 drops and nothing changed. Always that one confused blink when he always wondered…what if? What if he didn't pull? What if he just let it happen, if he became one with the moment? Could he fly? *The seductress.*

"You'll thump down dead like a sack of potatoes," he shouted aloud, smacking himself back to focus. *They will strip you naked so some ready-for-Paradise asshole can wear this uniform on to get close to our guys before he blows his vest.* They would put their fucking hands on his Barrett and use his weapon to fire on U.S. positions.

"Sergeant?"

The Specialist was back; he had been sitting on his heels and watching Spencer.

Spencer tapped at his watch cover and shook his index finger toward the cockpit. At five minutes out, he would begin pre-jump routine, checking how the pack was riding, snugging down the Barrett, making certain that nothing was loose and that no points would come through to jab him upon impact. Jumping at under 400 feet. No room for imagination. *Just pull the chute.*

"Three minutes," the Specialist signaled, holding his fingers in front of Spencer's unshaven face.

Spencer jumped up, angry. One important job, just one, and the kid had fucked that up. Five minutes! Now he had three minutes, not the full five that he needed. No margin to open a pack and make any last-minute shifts. He slung the heavy load onto his shoulder and passed his arms inside the straps. Two magazines carrying forty-fives dug at his side just above his left kidney, but there was nothing he could do about that. Not now.

He was still testing and re-closing the heavy Velcro strap that cinched the ankle pack when the red hatch bulb above the slide-door lit up. Spencer reacted fiercely, pointing at the light Before the Specialist understood what was wrong, Spencer unstrapped his helmet and slammed it against the fixture. The young Specialist stared in disbelief.

Bad fucking training. The kid didn't know better than to leave a red light on in an open jump door for thirty seconds.

The stiff-moving wind rushed coldly into the open doorway now. Spencer began counting down. *Get past it.* It was either that or throw the kid out the fucking side.

Twenty-nine, twenty-eight, twenty-seven. He blinked once on the GPS; the moving red circle was coming nearly into alignment with the fixed green drop location. His right hand moved to Pledge of Allegiance and closed on the rip-cord handle. *Just pull the fucking chute.* Seven, six, five, four, three, two.

A green light flashed inside the cabin as he launched himself into the black night. The huge helicopter was above and away, its deafening roar diminishing.

The night air now washed softly across his face. The pack no longer pulled, the ankle pack felt like nothing.

Pull the fucking chute!

Jumping at 400 feet leaves no time to enjoy the sensation of floating downward. He had to check his chute lines, saw the black outline ballooned above him cleanly, and then he landed, slamming hard. He used a multi-point roll to offset the impact.

The Barrett's muzzle dug into soft dirt. Spencer sprang to standing position and reached for the night vision goggles. A uniform bright green flickered on, with orange crosshairs and metric depth measures replacing the black darkness.

No movement evident, nobody coming out from the mud perimeter with guns ready. Even the dogs were silent, disinterested. His transportation still rumbled, blinking off into the distant night.

Spencer dropped the main pack and pulled to collect his chute. He tugged only a few feet of cord before feeling resistance. The chute had closed over the one nasty, dwarfed tree in the entire area. Two-inch thorns snagged at the black fabric. The tree was a product of the harsh terrain, suited perfectly to survive alone.

Charlie Brown and the kite.

The chute had to come down. At sunrise, what remained invisible in the moonless night was going to flag for his position bringing on every jihadi from miles around. Leaving it flapping there in the morning, it would look like a giant black flag saying, "come and get me." He told himself that his extraction team would be in position out there, but even if they were poised and ready, they could never get close in time to cover his ass. He had to either abort now and use the night to make distance on foot or strip it down off those fucking thorns.

Get it done.

Spencer pulled and ripped at the billowing fabric with both arms. His mind wandered to bad shit as the long ripping noises he was making sounded out into the moonless darkness.

Superficial cuts and jabs kept nicking away at both hands. The cuts he could handle. But a thorn pierced beneath his fingernail and deep into the knuckle. A nasty toxin instantly aggravated sensitive nerve-endings, scalding him and quickly swelling the finger thick as a turnip.

Get centered, calm it down. He knew that the veins in his neck were enlarged without needing to touch them. *Throttle back the adrenaline.* MOB. Mind over body.

Using his tarp-blind to cover a short burp of light, Spencer identified his first-aid pack. A second flash, one blink longer, to locate the Neosporin and cortisone. *Worthless.* Nothing. No effect whatsoever. Morphine was his only other option. *Use morphine, scrub the mission.* Waste two weeks of flyovers.

Once the Strykers showed up he'd get no second chances. If he called in to get evacuated, his targets would scramble for Pakistan and chill out in the tribal regions. Failure. *On him.*

His body was his tool and the tool wasn't working for shit. His dexterity was dropping. Clarity and judgment could be going, too. He ran a self-check exercise: place (three kilometers west of Marja, South Helmand, Afghanistan), time/date (03:11 hours, 5 October), target (primary = male Taliban, 19, just under six feet tall, severe facial scarring along right side). *Check.*

"*Your person is the property of the United States Army. This army has gone to great effort and expense to train you, to equip you, and to support your mission. When your mission is compromised, it is your duty to return that army property that is your person to this man's army in the best condition possible.*" Special Forces training echoed in his ear.

Bullshit. He was clear, he thought, but it was ego, only ego was weakness and he could not square up to that. Right thinking meant weighing all the options, including aborting, only he was never adept at assessing failure.

His evac-A location was a mile west, out in the open hardscrabble. Any movement at all fired excruciating shots up his arm and straight into his heart. *All from a fucking thorn.* But pain was just another test; he could take pain. All day long. *You trained for that.* Working past pain proved who he was. Tower of Power, he reminded himself, and then he reached out, squeezed down on the fucked finger, stared down the red-eyed demon and smiled. His finger was the instrument he needing to have working, doing the job.

He turned to a field fix; Spencer fumbled at the fly of his pants and then pissed down his left forearm arm and again down his right, working in the fluids and rubbing briskly palm to palm and between his fingers. Maybe urinating on a sting is an old wives' tale, maybe the relief was psychological, and maybe the toxin was short-lived. *Fuck it.* He felt some relief.

He was in focus again; back on operational assessment. No more drift. Pulse returning to 56 BPM. He hydrated, took a deep breath and blew it out, and then he picked and yanked back the shredded pieces of chute cloth, embracing and savoring every long ripping noise that sounded across to the village dogs.

Signs of light were showing over the eastern mountains when he was finally able to dig in his position. Now, with the morning, Spencer spotted small scraps that were still left hanging, but at least he hadn't left a giant black billboard right above his shallow shooting blind. He broke an Adderall and swallowed half, then dragged a long sucking gulp from the nipple tied into the electrolyte-enriched fluids he carried.

Spencer grabbed for his binoculars then recoiled. A shock of pain zinged from the bad finger into his armpit. It was an angry red now, and in his way.

In the dim blue morning light, beside the village a young child was opening the crude shrubbery gate of a livestock pen. A muezzin wailed out the Morning

Prayer from the single brown brick minaret at the center of the village. A herd of about thirty goats that the little boy released were instantly attracted by the remaining bits of cloth fluttering on the thorns. White, tan, some tiny goat kids, some larger billy goats with dramatic, magnificent horns twisting out more than a foot on each side of their heads moved in single-file directly toward his position. All that he could do was to hunker down beneath his cover in preparation for bad shit and watch out a narrow slit, gripping tightly around the Barrett. He dragged his ammo close alongside, wishing momentarily that he had an old-fashioned BAR instead of the bolt-action weapon and then patting the Barrett to apologize.

Spencer smelled the goats' musky wool as they moved in close. The smaller ones made exacting targeted leaps onto the thorny limbs and took tentative nibbles before one goat devoured a scrap and the others quickly followed to clean the bush completely bare. They were cleaning up after him. Their movements were blending away spots where he had disturbed the ground; anyone looking out after the herd would be unlikely to spot the exposed foot-high mound hidden beneath the mottled tan-and-gray cover tarp.

He held the tarp's ends pinned beneath him, but the air was stifling. He considered kicking up the Barrett's bipod legs to bring in air but dismissed the idea. *Amateur bullshit.* Stay focused. *Hydration discipline.* He needed to consume a liter each half hour. Forget that and the legs go first, right when you need to move.

The chilling nighttime breeze was long gone. When the sun arched into full view above the jagged eastern mountains, the temperature rose fast.

Shadows shining through his camouflage cover cloth wove patterns everywhere while the irrigated fields just outside the village burst into rich greens and warm morning gold.

One of the goats rained crap down onto him from above. Then, just like an epidemic of yawning, one goat after another joined in the shit storm, hitting his cover like warm hailstones. He couldn't care less; it was funny, just as long as the dogs and villagers kept their distance. For any solid shooters, he was 400 meters inside the range. It would take him twenty seconds at a full gallop over open ground to get beyond rifle fire. Running was not an option. If it came to fighting from this placement, accuracy and experience were the only advantages that might save his ass. Intel had said that the village had no mortars; this time, intel had better be worth a shit. If they fixed on his position with mortars, putting the Colt to his brain was about as good an option as running away.

Fuck!

The biggest billy goat sniffed along the edge of the cover tarp only inches from his face. *Jesus. Don't fucking chew my cover.* He tested his regular grip on the Barrett and tried to ignore the animal. No good. The finger was worse. He was forced to roll his left shoulder and cup with his thumb and middle finger to keep the painful index finger out and away, clear from touching anything. Breaking routine.

He could hear the mantras of a dozen trainers: *"Improvisation is overrated. Routine methods produce intended results. Routine brings you back alive."*

Two clicks might bring in the Strykers. Play the percentages. *Abort!*

Outside the main village walls, scrawny dogs yawned awake and moved carefully around the periphery of bearded men wearing pakols and lungees on their heads who squatted drinking tea by the morning fire with their baggy pants hiked up along their thighs. Spencer raised the bipod and drew in a deep breath of air before putting his eye to the scope. The billy goat straddled the Barrett's long rifle barrel.

"Got you."

His second target, a middle-aged Pashtun wearing a dirt-white lungee around his head, a long red-haired beard hanging down to his chest, strolled out to greet the others.

"Asalamo Alikom."

"Walikom Wa Salam."

The men shook hands. Red-beard thanked them but waved away the offer of tea.

Ten o'clock position. He looked left as a gaggle of women with their heads wrapped in chador passed deep red and rich blue rugs over a stiff clothesline then smacked at them, raising puffs of dust off their forked sticks with each strike.

Ahead of him lay open furrows of red soil tilled by donkey and by hand. He saw concrete culverts and steel water gates along the irrigation channels. Somebody had to have brought those in. Without reliable diesel supplies, the work was done by hand; tractors were of little use, even if the village might have afforded to buy one. *Helmand Province, ground zero for the world's opium supply.*

Get out of here, Goat!

Spencer reached out to thwack at the back of the goat's leg. Instead of retreating, the creature bleated and turned toward the hide, angrily trusting its horns beneath the tarp until Spencer finally punched its nose. That sent it running.

Provided that his Comsys worked and the Predator was where it was supposed to be and his extraction vehicles didn't run into an ambush or an IED and intel was correct that there were no mortars in the village, provided that all of it was perfect, then he was home free. *Cake.* The Strykers should be waiting in the wadis and gullies four miles to the north and west to come in and extract him. Upon confirmation of target, he was to contact them by sat-phone. Three targets, and then hold off whatever firepower that the 200-person mud village could muster from behind the walls, wrap it up and hop into an air-conditioned rig. Piece of cake. Only, he and anyone else with half a brain knew that one man and a Barrett 50 weren't going to hold off that whole village. These were people who had already lasted through two generations of continuous warfare. This ground had seen three thousand years of violence between families and villages and tribes. Piece of cake? Piece of shit, just as likely. But thinking you're dead and living is only a short vacation makes the work easier.

Lifting his mini-scope to his right eyeball, he scanned the fields outside the walls in search for his primary target, the bomber. Miller had briefed him that Red beard and the mother, the whacko parents, were helping their son plan to blow himself apart. Something there should have tipped him off; no parents help their children commit suicide. But he wasn't questioning, not on that level.

Despite the cover cloth, the Barrett's tan muzzle was radiating heat up the barrel. His palms slowly baked; he had to lift his face away from the rifle to wipe sweat out of his eyes. Spencer began his micro-exercises as both a discipline and a distraction; starting from his toes and working all the way up to his neck and out to each arm, he tensed every muscle once, followed by four quick contractions, and repeated the routine another two dozen times.

The finger hurt like a motherfucker. Spencer stored it and moved past the pain. His right hand touched the ammunition. Picking up one of the nearly five-inch-long bullets, he imagined the warm heft of the cylinder in his palm before thumbing it into the magazine. Without looking, he touched again up and right, adding the physical memory for exactly where the next round was awaiting his fingers, and continued loading until his primary mag was filled. He always loaded his one-mag immediately prior to mission-fire. That routine was as important for centering himself as his breathing. His one break from standard was using his opposite hand to open first the end cap on the Leupold Mark 4 scope and then the eye-cap, avoiding touching anything with the tender finger. Balancing right and left hemispheres was important and it was too often overlooked, but this time he had his left shoulder rolled uncomfortably to compensate for the fucked-up index finger.

Then he spotted his primary. His muscles clenched, on point from jaw to toes, before he steadied his breathing, leaned into the Leupold scope, and relaxed his finger along the trigger. The intel coming from Miller, Spencer's "lead", proved to be on point. The teenager had on the same red Manchester United FC t-shirt he was wearing in the briefing photos. His features were caved-in all down the right side; no jaw or cheekbone, one side ghoulish and on the other a handsome kid. The whole of Afghanistan, captured in a face.

Even without the distinctive red beard, the elder man's hooked nose and deeply set green eyes would have been a clear match. The woman with them was covered entirely in her chadri; Spencer had to identify her by association with Manchester United and Red-beard.

He made one subtle sweep until the targets were in frame, and then adjusted the sight to clarity. Three-hundred-sixty meters.

He switched his sat-phone on and popped twice, waited, and then popped twice more. He could already have taken the targets—one by one he ranged them in the crosshairs. At this easy range he had no need to compensate for wind or distance—but he held to the discipline, waiting for the response chirps. *Forty solo missions.* You respect the routine.

Where the hell was his counter? *Strykers need to get their thumbs out of their asses. Respond already!*

One chirp. Two chirps. *Right.* They had the signal.

"OK boys, let's wrap this up and get on home."

The three, father, son, and the black-clothed specter, routinely strolled out into the field, straddling the furrows out toward the irrigation culvert's water gate. The elder walked first, followed by the primary, with the mother hopping her way along. The kid stopped and used his toe to flip up a donkey turd, then soccer-dribbled it on his Pumas a half-dozen times. Spencer popped twice, waited, and popped the sat-phone three times, signaling the Strykers to move in fast.

The mother lifted her burqa, exposing her sandaled feet, and mimicked soccer-boy's dribbling skills before she side-kicked a pass toward her son. The turd broke into dry bits when he caught it on the toe of his shoe. The father held his head down and walked fast, both hands folded behind his back. He forced soccer-boy out of his path atop the furrow until they turned, moving out perpendicular to the farm rows. Every time the woman leapt from one furrow to the next, she passed in front of the soccer kid, bringing both of their heads into a single crossing frame. Spencer considered the pattern. It brought a little challenge into his routine. Could he take out the bomber and the woman with one bullet?

The three were well out into the field, 200 meters beyond the brown mud walls. Looking back later, he would see how none of it added up, but at the time he couldn't add right. He was thinking on some level about two busloads of Afghan Army recruits. Gunmen kneeled them down in rows and blew their brains blown out. Why was he thinking about this? Why did his brain go there? Mission drift…it was like closing your eyes just for a second when you're dog-tired behind the car wheel. That's the second that gets you killed.

Three quick chirps back from the Strykers. Three minutes out. *Thank Christ for that.*

Spencer locked onto his targets, framing his focus like Olympic ski-jumpers melding minds and bodies to their skis in facing down the 100 meter jump. He became an extension of the Barrett.

The weapon is perfect. Be at one. Make perfection.

He inhaled from his fingertips, his eyes, from the ridges along the tops of his ears. His right eye caressed the hot rubber fitting of the Leupold.

The kid zigged and zagged, dancing his feet around imaginary opponents.

Spencer centered upon the bright red cloth between the bomber's shoulder blades, but held, timing his fire to the woman's leap. BRASS. Breathe. Relax. Aim. Slack. SQUEEZE. Her feet landing on top the next furrow and his shot converged just as Spencer had choreographed it within his mind's eye. The dime-round fifty-caliber bullet burst through her skull, lifting her body off the ground and sandwiching the woman to her dead son. One strike. *Both.* Spencer enjoyed a moment before shifting slightly to bring the turban and beard to center sight. The man turned and immediately roared his pain and anger. Spencer let him live a minute longer.

Fuck with the U.S. Army. This is what you get. Take it in.

The older man dove down into the shallow furrow, but he remained ludicrously exposed. Spencer centered on the eyes, watching the rage bulging out from red, burning burning eyeballs. Then he did something that Spencer appreciated. He didn't try to run. Instead, he managed to pull the AK out from under the kid and rose up screaming, wildly spitting a spray of bullets on full-automatic until he emptied the full mag. When he was out, he shook his fists above his head and screamed.

Spencer let him empty the weapon, let him rage, all the while breathing in, centering his shot. Hindu love-tap. Right between his bulging red eyes.

Three kills. Confirmed. A day's work done. *Exhale.*

The goats stood entirely still, every one of their heads twisted with eyes locked onto him when he stood. Spencer turned and glanced behind him. The Strykers looked to be about two miles out, hauling ass and kicking up a dust cloud.

A return round coming from the mud walls popped up dust a foot in front of him. He lifted the heavy rifle and shifted his eye back to the Leupold while, typical to amateur shooting, two more bullets hit wide, landing way off center at a ten-foot spread. The shooter's ragged head showed eight inches above the village wall to compensate for the AK-47's long, curved magazine. Spencer squeezed the trigger and the head disappeared concurrent to the stiff recoil. Two more dark shapes showed over the wall. Spencer dispatched them in quick succession, and then scanned the village and the top of the lone minaret. Nothing more moved, except for the goats hustling back to their pen, complaining noisily.

Spencer scanned. Not a dog or person in his sights. He replaced the barrel-cover, dropped flaps on the Leupold scope, removed the magazine, cleared the chamber, and slung his weapon across his back with practiced efficiency. He had already accounted for his supplies, checking and double-checking ammunition, binoculars, mini-scope, night vision goggles, sidearm, and the obvious, his Barrett.

When the Strykers came in the firing from the village was already over with, but that didn't stop them from coming in hot, strafing cover-fire that sent chunks of mud exploding off the village walls.

Spencer towed his pack down low and walked out, keeping the thorn tree between his back and the village walls and swaggering forward with casual nonchalance through the thick dust they kicked up as the incoming Strykers slowed. An extended arm reached out to him. He locked his grip around the other soldier's wrist and felt a tight grip wrap around his own wrist, and then he was pulled inside the cool, air-conditioned cavity.

Spencer looked over the swollen finger. A black line showed through his fingernail, surrounded by deep reds and purples where the thorn had penetrated a full inch under the nail and into his knuckle. A corporal riding with him in the back reached over, taking hold of Spencer's hand, and turned it up and down again to get a decent view inside the dim compartment. He didn't like the look of it. Reaching down beneath the bench he was seated upon, the corporal retrieved a field emergency medical kit, opened it and fished inside until he located lidocaine. He motioned for Spencer to stick out his left hand and sprayed it wetly on all sides. He put back the kit and closed his eyes afterward.

With their turret gunners working fifty caliber guns in tandem, the Strykers drove out to the fields to the bodies Spencer had dispatched just minutes before. Two-man relays jumped from the vehicles, quickly snapping black body bags lengthwise on the ground and rolling in bodies while the gunners loosed short bursts that put out the clear message that anybody who wanted to keep his head had better stay off the walls. Spencer and the corporal lifted their own legs clear when they heaved the first heavy sack into their Stryker, landing the contents with enough momentum to slide the woman's body over the metal floor. The next one was bagged and shucked in by a second pair of hands. The first pair dropped in the third and lightest bag, then slammed the rear gate shut again. The corporal stuck in ear buds and closed his eyes, seeming unbothered as his helmet banged off the steel wall behind him. Neither one of them said a word. Their Stryker, on point, moved out instantly. The trailer, the second Stryker watching their backs, loosed a last burst from the fifties as the unit jerked through gears, making distance from the village.

Spencer's heels thumped against the body bags for the next forty minutes while they bounced across twenty rough miles. Tears dripped over his cheeks; he attributed them to the adrenaline dissipating through his system.

CHAPTER TWO

The Strykers removed Manchester United and the old man and woman from their vehicles before they ripened. Spencer waited through five long hours, resting his head on his knees with the body bags fifteen feet away from him until somebody finally boxed in a helicopter to lift him and his stinky cargo back to base from 2nd Bridge 2nd Division Stryker's forward position. The bags were left stewing in the heat, where they had ballooned with gasses by the time they were loaded into the chopper. Even with his head stuck out the open doorway, the sickly sweet stench was inescapable.

Right after landing Spencer made straight for his tent. *Towel and shower first, then shuteye.*

"Fuck!"

Outside Spencer's tent, Miller's "translator" sat squatting on his heels, his chin low beneath his pakol, the Afghan cap he wore pulled down over his eyebrows. Spencer instinctively loathed the man. The Afghan would never look him in the eye. He was a snake, not a fighter. The man's loyalty was to the money Miller represented, period.

A half-emptied bottle dangled from Miller's loose wrist. The drinking was nothing new, but this was the first time that Miller was flopped inside Spencer's tent drunk before noon. He had his muddy canvas boots on, too, one on Spencer's sack, the other rested on top of Spencer's guitar case. Spencer kicked Miller's boot to the side and toed his guitar case deeper beneath the cot.

Miller wasn't Army, which made for a loose, undisciplined hierarchy. Their relationship was tentative at best.

Neither saluted.

"Take a drink," Miller slurred. He reached out the bottle and sloshed a long splash of the Johnnie Walker Blue Label onto the tarp floor. Spencer stared as the whisky soaked into the canvas, leaving concentric rings of wet dust on the floor of the tent that was more home to him than anyplace else that came to mind.

Spencer pulled his shirt off over his head. Ripples defined every movement across his taut, lean musculature. Miller thrust the amber liquid toward him again. Spencer turned away before peeling himself out from his pants. In his skivvies, he stared down at Miller, who remained kicking back on the one place where Spencer might have sat down to unlace his boots.

Miller rested the whisky bottle against the receding hairline on his forehead. "Boy Scout," Miller griped. "Jesus Christ Almighty, have a fucking drink!"

Between the swollen finger and close to thirty hours without any shuteye, Spencer's only reaction was to shift his stance, bringing the fifty caliber's long barrel hanging from his shoulder to point straight at Miller's face. The weapon was covered; safety and scope caps on, chamber cleared, but Miller's eye followed the menacing line of the weapon. Spencer's silhouette stood outlined against the intense daylight outside the tent.

Miller drew back the outstretched Scotch whisky, followed, after a pause, by Spencer racking his weapon.

"Fine," Miller agreed. "Fuck it." Miller swung his boot off Spencer's cot. "Debrief at 4 o'clock, back here," Miller ordered, then he rolled out from the cot with his bottle in one hand, cup in the other.

That's 16:00, asshole, Spencer thought.

There was a written zero-tolerance policy for alcohol on base. That was one more thing Spencer disliked about his handler; the way Miller treated rules like they were all a joke that didn't apply to him. Miller didn't even bother to hide the bottle inside a bag. Every time Miller got into a bottle, he was bound to mouth off and cynically snark at everything. Always acting like he was something special, like he knew the score while everyone else around him were order-taking idiots.

Poisonous loser bullshit. Real soldiers were giving sweat and blood to handle tough duty and Miller talked like they were all chumps. But Miller moved through debriefs faster than any intelligence officer Master Sergeant Jonathan Spencer, MSJS, had ever seen. Drunk or sober, Miller synthesized ground photos and aerials, troop movements, supply chains, tactical models, and complex scenarios on the first pass, holding them inside his head in a three-dimensional picture that he was able to examine from every angle. He knew every technology, he knew the personnel, and he knew topography and weather data even and what outpost was going to get a fly-in from a visiting congressman. If a local Afghan Government official was killed anywhere in his district, Miller knew who would be taking his place. Well before any announcement was made, he was already shifting chess pieces in his head.

Spencer's assignment was to support Miller, but there were no rules dictating that Spencer had to like the man or his behavior. MSJS trained, maintained, sustained; he achieved the stated objectives again and again. That was the job. The three bloating bodies spoke for themselves. Whatever decisions or policy choices his army or his Commander-in-Chief set forth, he was there to execute on them. The information and the knowledge to evaluate was beyond his pay grade.

Spencer moved outside into the sunlight to examine the damaged finger. It remained double its normal size. Not ballooned like before, but it could not go without repair. Still, that could wait until after a hot shower and a trip to the mess tent. Other than a cold MRE with the Strykers and one granola bar, he hadn't eaten since 18:30 the night before.

He climbed the metal steps in his flip-flops, opened the shower stall inside the portable trailer, and glanced around, feeling good that the first shower stall he picked was freshly cleaned. He left the hot water splashing against his eyelids for minutes, then lifted his head and felt the spray against his throat and neck, all the time forcing the images that passed inward through his scope to wash past. *One direction. When you look through your scope you locate targets. You dispatch targets. It's a one-way baffle. The shit goes out, never in.* The black-covered mother he dispatched was only the third woman he had ever shot. A mother playing with her kid. *Fucking war.*

You shouldn't have done it, shooting both together. It didn't matter that the fresh Afghan recruits were shot down one by one by the roadside; there was no excuse. He scrubbed hard, but no amount of scrubbing would clean away how he had made a game out of it, how he killed them with one bullet.

Full soap dispenser. That was good. Plenty of hot water, red dirt flowing down the white shower walls, swirling, past the stainless steel screen, and down the drain. But the one finger ached at even the slightest touch. Spencer shampooed his scalp then turned off the hot water and left the water on cold, or, rather, the lukewarm temperature that was as cold as the water ever got at midday. Running along his back and shoulders, he lifted his arm up into the spray to scrub his armpit. Spencer felt a tiny, penetrating burn running along the latts. He made a mental note of it, turning just enough to check whether there was a tear. No. Just a pull. He recalled thinking that he had landed poorly when he jumped; the Barrett added thirty-one pounds and it was his fault for not front-balancing it during descent. He had no excuse for allowing an injury that was preventable.

He walked in his underwear straight to the medical tent after the long shower. He learned something there; who knew about Plant Thorn Synovitis? Puncturing the knuckle could easily have left him with a localized form of arthritis if he had ignored maintenance and toughed it out instead. A shot of antibiotics later, along with a bottle of naproxen, and Spencer felt satisfied that he had made good decisions. He entered the mess tent having missed the regular lunch so instead of pulled pork and a French roll, he got a PB&J and an apple. Fair tradeoff. *Maintain the hands, the tools of the trade.*

Inside Spencer's tent, Miller was flopped-out; a snoring ball of drunken sweat, half on Spencer's cot and halfway out. Spencer looked on and wished that he could have turned in Miller to the Duty Officer for drunkenness. Miller was an asshole, but Spencer was no rat. For better or for worse, he and Miller were an autonomous operation. Once a week, on average, Miller appeared with a translator in tow. Miller arrived by helicopter when he could, by convoy when he had to. IEDs scared the shit out of him.

Miller's stomach heaved, his throat swelled, and his mouth opened wide, looking like he was about to puke. Right on Spencer's cot. It looked painful as he choked it back, but then he rested and went back to snoring.

Spencer stripped and cleaned the Barrett while Miller snored. Right after he finished, he looked at his cot with Miller still on it and his bullshit alarm went off.

"Hey. Wake the fuck up." Spencer lifted his boot heel and rattled the cot. "Miller!"

Miller awakened contorting his dried-out mouth and tongue, initially looking for the Scotch before squinting to see Spencer across the tent seated on the floor.

"Enough! I earned so down time! This is my place. Get off my bed!"

Miller opened the bottle then took a sustained swig from the last dregs.

"Ten months going from one shit pile to the next one," Miller griped. "Pricks won't even give me a permanent helicopter."

"Its way past 1600 hours," Spencer shouted, this time rousting Miller and pulling him into a sitting position then holding him upright, shaking at him until his glazed eyes stayed open.

Miller's cheeks puffed like a blowfish, and then he exhaled and took in a deep breath, blinking as he centered his focus.

"What time is it?"

"21:15. You slept through third mess."

"Doesn't matter. Got Commissary food on dry ice if I want it." He shook his face to wake up then held his balding skull in both hands. Shaking was bad.

Spencer added, "Commissary food and $200 whisky."

"You don't know anything," Miller wheezed.

"I know that drinking that way the body can't regulate temperature," Spencer warned. "You can go from sunstroke to hypothermia in the same day around here."

"Whisky won't kill me." Miller twisted his neck and worked on getting focus. "Out there's an IED with my name on it. I'm going to get blown to shit. Those mangy fucking mongrels out there will licklittle bits of me off a metal carcass. All for some piece of shit war in this piece of shit place. Fuck."

Miller's speech slowed, but beside that and the occasional misstep and quick recovery, Miller generally held his liquor. Not this time. He tipped back another gulp, blew the alcohol out over his tongue and lectured on how "the U.S. is going to leave here and the sand will wipe away our footprints just like that."

He snapped his fingers. "Another dirty forgotten little war... we shit ourselves until we die and then nobody knows or cares that any of this ever happened."

The translator, Afif, appeared behind Spencer and began to boil tea. Spencer smelled him before he turned around. Afif had the dank mushroom smell of decay.

Spencer seldom liked the smell of people; gun oil and graphite, sawdust and nitroglycerine were his cologne. Miller's scent was acrid, a vinegar-sour stench of lies.

"Does he have to be here?" Spencer griped. Outside the wire, they went with the territory, but inside base, Spencer felt he had the right for some relief from these skulking types.

"Don't worry about this one," Miller assured. "He does what I tell him. No more Pathans. Done with them. It's always the same with Pathans… they'll take the money, but they're guilty about it. Always on slow boil. One day they blow up and cut your throat."

"Tell him to stay in front. I don't want him behind me."

"I've tried Tajiks, Hazzari, too, Miller continued, ignoring Spencer's comment. "Afif is Ismaili."

"Ismaili?" Spencer asked.

"Shia, from Badakhshan Province way up in the northeast. Best brand of go-fer. His kind has got no place to run. If he goes into China, the Han kill him, or if they don't, the Uyghurs will. He can't run over to Pakistan like any Pathan and hide with his cousins. The Pakis will cut his nuts off then listen to him howl for a couple days before they chop off his head.

"I own his ass."

Miller pressed the heels of both his palms up to his temples. "Jesus. Let's get through this. Right now if somebody cut off my head, it wouldn't be so bad.

"Report, Sergeant. Tell of your mighty accomplishments!"

"Extraction better this time out?" Miller asked. All of Miller's special assets were at the mercy of other units to get in and, especially, to get out again.

"Yes sir." Spencer paused. Miller wasn't his superior officer; Miller wasn't even military. The "sir" was automatic. But nothing in the job description said he had to babysit drunks, especially a chickenshit civilian pissing and moaning because the big world might not be so pretty. It wasn't entirely clear that Miller was CIA, either. Miller and his Afghan interpreter showed up, Miller delivered target orders. Miller returned, Spencer debriefed, Miller hit the Scotch.

"Correct coordinates. GPS working for a change," the sergeant continued.

Spencer nodded and began. After nineteen years in, he was usually on autopilot at end-of-mission debriefs. "Successful drop at 03:00 hours, thank you 82nd Airborne." He held up the swollen finger. "I managed to drop on the one thorny bush for a mile around.

"Dug in at position 400 meters outside the village," he continued. *Routine.* "Confirmed Strykers at staging point ahead of extraction. Three targets sighted 06:45. Three targets neutralized 06:58. Extraction 07:05, along with remains. That and waiting around for hours to get me back with the rotting skunks."

"I need more detail on this one," Miller insisted. "Full report."

Spencer continued, still on autopilot. Orders-missions-debriefs and systems-maintenance in between. Manchester United, his mother, his raging father. Bloated body bags all smell the same, sickly sweet repulsion.

"Correct coordinates," Spencer narrated. "GPS was working correctly for a change." Targets were located. Mission completed. Remains retrieved, as ordered. Extraction uneventful. Strykers laid down a few short bursts, 60 rounds, estimated. Kept the rest of the village behind walls. They picked up an Apache that kicked up a dust storm over the village while the Strykers moved out. Good packed earth on the return so they kept off the roads on the run back here.

"Targets?"

"Like I said, mission accomplished." Spencer finished speaking and eyed Miller, who pulled a tablet computer from his satchel, turned it on, and squinted with one eye until the photo display came into focus.

"Positive ID? All three?"

"Like I said.

"They're bagged. In the mobile morgue. Look for yourself. The two males, absolutely. Can't ID the woman, not with her always covered head-to-toe in chadri and burqa.

"Can I have my bunk now?"

Miller tapped his laptop and opened the video. Taken from ten thousand feet, it keyed on Spencer and all three of his three targets. He sat there, squinting, until suddenly snapping to attention like he was watching the team driving for a touchdown in the fourth quarter.

"Oh shit! You didn't!" He ran his finger across the bottom of the screen and held the computer excitedly out to replay it so Spencer could watch with him. The scene showed the soccer player and his mother flopping over simultaneously.

"One shot?" Miller questioned, perking up enthusiastically. "Motherfucker! A two-fer!"

Spencer turned his eyes away. It sickened him now, hearing Miller's excitement. When he was lying in the dirt alone, with a village of hostiles a few hundred meters away, it wasn't nearly as bad. Taking a target with one shot is a decent way to kill and a decent way to die. A fair exchange; clean and organized. Not dirty and chaotic, not like a bomb. But he should not have done that, made his duty into a game.

Miller stared down at his courier satchel where it was lying on the floor beside the cot. On a whim, he snatched it and flipped it upside-down, snapping the wire closure and shaking the bag. A cascade of $10,000 stacks of bundled $100 bills tumbled over his chest and around his sides. He patted the pile and began shrieking a hyena-like crazed laughter.

Snatching up a bundle, he flipped it at Spencer to catch and hit Spencer's midsection. Spencer let it fall on the tent's canvas floor.

Miller leaned over, looked at the money, and his tone changed. "Take a taste, Sergeant," he told Spencer aggressively. "You earned it."

Afif, the translator, instantly poked his head inside the tent. Even in the dimming light, Spencer saw Afif's eyes lock onto the bills. Afif shifted his yellow jackal eyes up at Spencer, his hard glare communicating volumes—a man who sold out to the invader, a man who turned his back on his tribe, his village, his clan; no translation necessary. Spencer closed the tent flap in front of the Ismaili's face. Men like Afif needed money; without money the Pathans would chop through his ribcage and tear his heart out the second he was beyond the American protection.

Spencer snarled "You pick that shit up and get it out of here. I'm not touching that. " *The money? That was not OK.*

"Evaporation," Miller insisted. "Lost in transit."

Miller moved tens of millions in cash money as part of his regular routine. After the first IED rattled him to the core, he pilfered two $10,000 bundles, figuring his life was worth a lot more than that, and then he waited anxiously for four weeks and almost peed himself when he had to stand before that same governor. Nobody even hinted at the missing $20,000. After that, Miller repeated the approach at another drop and then another, and before long his cut was a regular commission. He had funds moved into Luxemburg, in Macau, in Uruguay; he even had amassed $80K in Guinea Bissau. Aid money, capital projects, narco funds… it all spent the same.

"Pick it up and get it the fuck out," Spencer repeated. His tone made it clear that he wasn't going to say it again, but that had no effect upon Miller. "That's none of my business," Spencer growled. "I do the job, that's it."

"You don't like me much, do you?" Miller observed offhandedly. He looked around, vaguely remembering how he had a bottle somewhere.

"Get off your high horse," Miller grumbled. He threw a second bundle in Spencer's direction. "It's shrinkage. Goes with the territory."

Spencer watched Miller patting around, finally locating the bottle between his legs.

"Is this all a joke for you?" Spencer asked Miller. "Do you stand for anything?"

Miller's bloodshot eyes wandered up to Spencer's face. "Just what do you think you stand for?" Miller challenged.

"I'm a soldier. I serve this country."

"Afghanistan?" Miller teased.

"You fucking know what I mean!" Spencer reached out his boot and flicked the bundle soccer-style back at his handler. Something about the physical action made him recoil. *Manchester United.*

"It's only money," Miller chortled. "You think you're better than me? You're not better than me." Miller's fingers found the bottle. He gulped the last two fingers then wiped the back of his hand across his angry mouth. Miller sat up and grew rigid.

"Sergeant, don't sit so tall in the saddle. I pass orders to you and a dozen more killers. Not one of you motherfuckers ever said 'no.' You want to be here!" Miller griped on. "Do you even know how fucked up that is? No, not you, 'cause you're the Spear Point, the Warrior." Miller ran his fingers through his thinning hair, and then swept up handfuls of cash just to let them drop again. "I'm twenty-nine years old. Did you know that? Twenty-nine. I look forty!"

His eyes fixed on the bundles where the two had tumbled to the canvas floor.

Spencer eyed his Barrett but kept it together. "Don't get me involved," he warned Miller, who acted like he could care less.

"Nobody trusts an honest man," Miller scolded. "Oil or no oil, Sergeant, this whole place is a profit center. None of us would ever be here if it wasn't. Spending trillions on a no-win war for a place where armies had been going to die for two thousand years? Come on. Give me a break."

Spencer hovered above the cot and Miller, looking down through the comb-over at Miller's sunburned red scalp. The thought flashed, just for a split second, that he could reach out and snap Miller's neck.

"I am not involved."

Miller went back to scrolling through sat footage and drone views, but reached down to the $10,000 bundles of cash. His fingers rubbed and caressed the bills before he reached them out, holding the money toward Spencer.

He directed Spencer to "take the money, Sergeant." This time it sounded more like an order than a request.

Spencer lifted his hands in the air, refusing even to touch it.

Miller's face twisted. The veins thumped in his neck.

"Everybody takes a taste, Sergeant," Miller insisted. "It's the way it is."

Spencer didn't budge.

"Spencer, you're an idiot", Miller grumbled, rocking forward until he could swing his feet onto the ground.

"Boy Scout," Miller told Spencer, phrasing it as a toast before taking a last pull from the bottle.

He made an effort to stand then gave up.

"Get me a sandwich," he yelled out to the translator, who was positioned, kneeling, just outside the tent. Miller was obviously agitated, both at Spencer's refusal and at having drunkenly run off his mouth. This was more than a contest of wills.

He focused toward Spencer with one eye open. "What do you think you do, Master Sergeant?" Miller asked.

"My job."

Miller spit up slightly then he spat in Spencer's direction.

"Your job. And that is?"

"Killing the enemy."

"Ha!" Miller halted himself, lifted the bottle to his lips, and then looked at the damage he had done to its contents.

Miller's chin dropped to his chest. He began expostulating with his hands alongside his voice. "Sergeant, there's you and there's the real world. Here is how the real world works. Somebody somewhere in this fucked up place pisses off somebody else, and then one names the other as a Taliban insurgent. That's our first tip. Tip number one. Then that guy, the bastard who pointed first, he goes and he gets one of his thousand cousins to contact us and that cousin names the same person. Tip number two. Next cousin, next tip. Three tips and we have a winner! Three tips, the Haji goes on the list, and you get a target.

"Some of them must be Taliban I suppose," he continued, shaking his head, "but mostly it's one Rag Head trying to get some other Rag Head's farm or there's some other shit between them that has zip to do with you and me or the war. Anyway. Bang, three tips, name on a list, they give me the name, I find the closest one of you guys, you blow his head off, and, *hakuna matata*, it's the circle of life."

Miller reached for a cigarette and patted himself down to find his lighter.

"Not in here," Spencer snarled. "Smoke outside."

"Jesus. Blowing people's heads off is OK, but a little second hand smoke…" Miller made another effort to get upright, managed to swing himself into a sitting position and slowly shoved bundles of cash back into the courier bag.

"Money," Miller announced, with the conviction of a drunken sage. "Money, money, money," he repeated. "Widgets. Guns, heroin, God. Everybody's selling something." Miller rolled toward Spencer and glared through a bloodshot eyeball. "Mister high and mighty Zen warrior, Master Sergeant. So full of yourself." Miller poked his finger in the air pointed generally in Spencer's direction. "Take the fucking money."

Spencer shook his head.

"The Russians hate heroin," Miller explained, waving his hands to emphasize that Spencer should wait, that it was going to make sense. That he really should take the money.

"The Russians… the Russians share their border with Afghanistan. Afghanistan grows 80 percent of the world's opium supply. Do you know that we used to spray the poppy fields, but that's all stopped? Opium. Heroin. Big profits. Four billion a year in foreign sales, their one and only export product until we leave and the Chinese come in to mine away their resources. Karzai makes billions, the farmers don't hate us, and we flood heroin in to fuck the Russians."

Miller tried again to fish out a cigarette before Spencer leaned forward to snatch the pack from his hands. He glared. "Hell, you want to eradicate the opium, you bring back the Taliban. Best narcotics cops in history. Karzai's brothers want to run everything, except maybe not every district lets the brothers fix the market price for raw opium. So some farmer, say, wants to run a cooperative in his village and get a better price than Karzai pays out. Karzai or the brother has the cousins call in three tips, the farmer gets on the list, and you and I get tasked to blow him up.

"Sorry. That's too messy for you, Sergeant. You don't blow shit up, you 'eradicate the target.'"

Miller pressed himself up out of the cot with bottle in hand, saw again that it was empty, and flung it at his translator outside.

"But it isn't clean," he went on. "It stinks. That stink is dead bodies. It comes off people. Somebody got pissed off and now they're rotting meat. You did that. Own it."

Miller rocked himself upright, held out his arms to get his balance, and then spun himself around like a whirling Dervish.

"Ninety-nine bottles of beer on the wall," he sang out sarcastically. "Take one down and pass it around, and then there's ninety-eight more.

"It's all just bullshit," Miller explained. "None of this makes any difference. Take the fucking money. We're going to leave here and it will all go right back to shit. Karzai will move to London or Paris or buy a penthouse in New York City. It's markets, Sergeant. Commerce; everything else makes zero sense; the second you put a pin in it, this war pops like a great big balloon.

"You've got eyes, don't you? The United States spends trillions so the big boys back home and here get to make their billions. Me? I'm just scraping this little tiny crumb off the bottom of the pie pan. It's evaporation, barely a commission.

"Americans don't turn down money. Military contractors sell $60,000 Toyota pickups and five-dollar sodas. Colonels and generals get seven-figure paychecks.

"Take the fucking money," Miller urged him. "Are you a fundamentalist or are you a righteous American capitalist? It's money. When it's there in front of your face, you fucking take it! Do you really believe you can conduct yourself honorably? Really? And I saw the Blessed Virgin on the TP when I wiped my ass this morning! When the whole thing put together is a puss-ridden tumor, there's no honor. Take the fucking money, Sergeant. Pick it up."

Spencer stared blankly at the clean, crisp bundles, lying green like Kryptonite. A slide show history began to snap through his head, a zombie army of 131 dead targets that threatened to break through the walls of his psyche. All the training that he had done, all the exercise and focus and precision that sustained him; still shots of faces penetrating through the lens of his scope; all dead, but coming alive in a ruminating rotation.

Bullshit! You did your job, the job you've been trained to get done.

Money doesn't sustain grunts humping 120 pounds across mountainsides, going solo sixty miles inside tribal areas. Money meant zip out there.

"Take your dirty money and get the fuck out of my place."

Miller looked over the prefab shelter with disgust, grumbled something incoherent, rocked himself upright, and then scratched at the air to find a wall before stumbling out of the tent.

Spencer was tired enough to sleep for days. He knew he had to recharge, but every camp noise kept him awake and thinking into the night. The container was pierced, it wouldn't hold water. The only way to fix the hole was to stop guys like Miller. Could he kill another kid on Miller's orders?

Miller awakened inside the back of a Bradley. He stretched out a furry, dehydrated tongue then reached underneath his stomach for what was jabbing his insides and came up with a wrapped bundle of new one-hundred dollar bills. He studied them until his eyes cleared, and then random snippets from his drunken ramblings came back to him. He stumbled out the Bradley's rear hatch into the black night air. Through the darkness, he tried to make out the outline of the tent where Spencer was finally lying asleep on his stomach.

"You fucking idiot," he grumbled through a brutal hangover.

"Best case scenario if he talks, they transfer my ass." That would be it for handling the cash. In small increments he had amassed nearly $600,000. Thanks to his big mouth he might as well have handed the key to Spencer.

"Crap." The crime wasn't taking the cash; his bosses were probably taking a hell of a lot more themselves. Putting the spotlight on the skimming? *That* was something else. *That* was a capital offense. His ass would get capped and nobody would ever think twice. Miller decided that the Boy Scout was going to talk. He would disappear in a shallow grave.

Miller gripped his knees and hovered over Afif's sleeping mat. He fumed alcohol into the tribesman's dark face; it was pouring out with every whispered order. He tugged a bundle of bills out of his shirt, felt its weight and then stopped himself from handing over the entire wad. Three bills were enough. Miller peeled off twice that, began to count it into Afif's rutted palm, then gave up and crushed it in as Afif's fist closed around the money.

Miller reached his hand over his own mouth, the universal sign for silence, and then pointed toward the wide-bladed steel dagger ground down from a Soviet bayonet that the Ismaili always carried at his hip. He missed and nearly fell forward before Afif caught him by his elbow to keep Miller upright.

"Kill him. Quietly."

Afif's turbaned head nodded. He understood.

Across the camp a Humvee fired up and headlights came on. Miller looked up then back. Afif and his knife had disappeared into the night.

The Ismaili lifted his loose trousers and squatted down outside Spencer's tent, with only the canvas between them, listening to Spencer's steady, undisturbed breathing rhythms. He withdrew the blade and felt his thumb along both edges. He would have honed it ahead of time if he had been killing a sheep. But cutting into a sheep's woolen throat is harder than a soft and bare American. The tribesman held the blade out from his body, choked his right-hand grip against the hilt, and crooked his wrist so the blade and his arm formed a vee. He pulled backward, practicing the motion of ripping up through jugular veins and carotid arteries and the crunchy resistance of windpipe cartilage in between. Wrist tight, right arm pulling up. Pressing his left hand down on the back of Spencer's head while the knife plunged and he yanked back.

Afif left his worn-out shoes outside and timed his entry to the gusts of wind ruffling the canvas. His yellow eyes were accustomed to the dark. He could make out the shape of Spencer's legs stretched beneath the covers, stepped over the sergeant's huge size thirteen sand-colored boots, and stood with his thumb against the hilt of his knife at the head of the cot.

Spencer's ribcage rose and fell again as his lungs filled and depressed. The odor of decay drifting on Afif's breath made Spencer stir in his sleep. Every vertebra along his spine stood out clearly beneath the taut skin. The Ismaili froze, watching and listening for Spencer's deep even breathing to resume. Spencer's fatigues hung above the cot, three stripes up and down and the white-faced Airborne eagle.

Afif flipped the knife so that his right thumb covered the butt of its handle, moving the blade into a stabbing position. His target was a two-inch circle left of the spine and just below the rib cage. Stab and lean in, driving the steel edge up into the heart. Down and push. More like killing a horse than killing a sheep or goat.

He shifted, spreading his legs to support his choreography, then lifted the blade and pillow and steeled himself.

Like a 2x4 slamming into Spencer's ribs, the blade stuck there, all blunt force into bone. Spencer's entire frame contracted. Afif's full weight smothered him beneath the pillow. Spencer felt the sharp blade's point moving, tearing a line down his back, through nerve-endings. Then a new, sharper pain surged deep inside; Afif had found unresisting soft tissue and plunged in the blade all the way to its hilt.

The agony surged into Spencer's eyeballs. He rolled toward the pain, snapping and sweeping back his right forearm, thrashing instinctively, and the pain soared again, intensifying as the tribesman pulled back the blade to stab again toward Spencer's chest.

Spencer lifted his blanket and stretched it out between his fists, meeting the knife as it was plunged for the kill. Spencer twisted Afif's entire arm in the heavy cloth and rolled. His attacker's shoulder socket popped out of joint. The blade dropped on his belly and fell to the tent floor.

Flashlight beams darted around the room. Spencer's eyes swam as the interpreter's face showed, brightly lighted just inches away. His cot collapsed under the weight of the soldiers diving on top of them. Spencer was unaware of his own shouts and of the five-foot bloody arc spraying the tent walls from his severed renal artery.

"You dirty motherfucker," Miller screamed. Before anyone could react, he jammed his pistol barrel into Afif's prominent nose and fired. An ear-ringing explosion of warm liquid, grit, and muck blew six feet around. A medic yelled something. Spencer felt hands turning him over. He imagined his hands gripping around the squared bars of a field stretcher.

"Get off me," Spencer thought. *Leave me alone, let me stand up. I'll be OK. Only I need to stand up.*

Pressure applied against his back.

The sweet, rusty, familiar stench of blood.

Being lifted. He reached his right hand around the stretcher's rail, feeling the heat coming off its utilitarian square steel. A chopper motor. The screech of metal sliding on metal then the door clunking shut. Nothingness.

Four days in Bagram. Landstuhl, Germany, after. Where they took his kidney.

CHAPTER THREE

Spencer transferred stateside on a stretcher. His complete belongings consisted of a light blue hospital gown, one blue toothbrush, and an army-green baseball cap. No Barrett. No guitar. He told himself that his weapon and his music were waiting for him; the mission was getting back to combat readiness. From the second day in Germany, he ignored doctor's orders to relax and give his body the time to heal, and began a strict regimen of micro-exercises from toes to his waist and neck to his shoulders; hours of them. Once the intravenous drips came out he mouthed pain medications beneath his tongue then dumped them out the window. At Madigan, he tried a squat exercise and ended up feeling something tear. But now the sutures were out of his back, he was ambulatory, putting on weight, and already planning to be into more intense workouts. Behind his bed, the window looked down into the open quad where groups of broken men, half of them in wheelchairs, sat around and chain-smoked together. Spencer fought being lumped in beside the gimps. He didn't belong.

The poor bastards would never be soldiers again. Some were missing limbs, others looked fine except that TBI's, traumatic brain injuries, had robbed them of their abilities to process thoughts or to speak or to make it through a day without uncontrollable seizures. If a chair was set down hard on the linoleum some of them would dive for cover. Any loud noise could freak them out.

Spencer eyes scanned them when he shuffled through to the bathroom. Some had noses gone, some minus an arm, two in wheelchairs with air where both legs were gone, one with concave voids, no eyes, with both forearms ending in bandaged stumps.

I'd chew a bullet, he thought.

Estimated wait time before his Medical Evaluation Board and final Physical Evaluation Board was out to nearly four months, meaning that he was stuck there with the gimps. He had a singular purpose for his time: to come out of there physical fit; better than ever before. In four months, he was going to overcome anything they put in front of him. *Keep it together and get back to what you were trained to accomplish.* Only Major Davies, the female psychiatrist running the floor, just wouldn't leave him the hell alone.

"Master Sergeant Spencer, I can't force anyone to attend group counseling sessions, but psychological fitness is equally important.

"Sergeant," she warned him, "isolation is a sign of depression and I consider that your unwillingness to support your fellow soldiers in their own recoveries is a serious malaise."

When Spencer offered no response she put it more simply. "Participate in Group or I'll write you up, Sergeant. You receive a negative psych eval and I guarantee it will impact your PEB."

Her message was loud and clear. *Attend or face a shitstorm.*

Major Davies spoke in group using a practiced calm tone that sounded like a bad infomercial with a touch of Southern Baptist tossed in there. She sounded to Spencer like any of a hundred Southern black women around where we grew up in Virginia. Strong women, always ready to lead the congregation, looking for "Amen" and "Praise the Lord." Only the major had been on the job too long. The evangelist had left the building. Spencer quickly learned to tune her out. He would show up, but that was all. Nobody was going to turn him into one of *them.*

Spencer wanted to run out of the room. He should not have been there; his presence was like leaving a weapon out in the rain. It was irresponsible and wasteful. When he got back to business, he didn't need that stuff in his head; none of it added to his capabilities.

Major Davies, all five-foot-three of her, sat there bursting out of her uniform like a sausage in the frying pan, one part doctorate in social welfare, part cheerleader, part hardened no-bullshit realist. "We've all been told and trained to be tough; we stick our heads down and work through the pain when it gets hard. But when you've been through stuff that is never going to make sense no matter how many times you put it through your head, that doesn't work so well, does it?

"All the toughness in the world won't bring back your arm or your leg and toughing it out won't make you a better son or brother or husband or father because it isn't just you; the people who love you don't understand and just won't get it no matter what. So don't drag them through your being tough. Behind all that toughness, it's scary. We're leaving something we know and going out into the unknown. What we're going to do here, together, is to acknowledge our fears and to identify and embrace new opportunities. There's not a man here who is fully equipped right now to look into the mirror and see his own potential. But I see it in you and I'm going to help you bring it out. So let's do it." She put her hands together and started the group of them to 'clap it out'.

"Can't decide if I'm going to become a court stenographer or a film editor," the blind guy offered, deadpan. He raised his stumps and held them together in a handless mock prayer.

"Won't one of you righteous individuals please help me?" he mocked. Spencer had a hard time looking at the man.

"From recruitment to basic right through to every deployment all we hear, Major, is 'us,' 'we,' 'together,'" Captain Sam snarled. "We and us, plural; team, squad, unit, company, battalion, division. 'We're only as good as the guy next to us.' 'That soldier next to you, ahead of you, behind you, we're there for one another.' All 'us,' all fuzzy warm togetherness. And then we get shot or we get blown up or worse, we get it in the head where nobody else can see what's wrong. Then nobody fucking says anything about it being 'us' anymore. One split second and then it's all 'you and you and you and you 'cause the army is all done with 'us'. We're on our own and we are fucked.

"Tell me, Major, why don't you talk about 'us' now? There are two and a half million of *us* who served in Iraq and Afghanistan. You tell me, you really think we need to ask for anything? All we need is to stay 'WE' and WE can take what WE earned."

The major was standing up and puffing, with her giant boobs looking ready to burst the fabric barely holding them contained.

"Captain, we have a lot of material to cover in this section and you have been through the entire program before," she told him, rigidly pressing herself to maintain her icy even tone, "so I'll ask you to refrain from interrupting." The man was an officer! What kind of officer crushes morale? His injuries didn't alter his responsibility to offer leadership.

"Material. I've heard it, remember? This isn't my first rodeo. Major, these men have all been in combat. I've been there, too. Have you? Tell me that. Where did you fight, Major?"

Major Davies glared at the captain; she kept steady and calm, but Spencer could see that the captain had struck a nerve. Major Davies sent a text. 9-1-1. Two orderlies rushed down the hallway trailed by a nurse who hustled to uncap a syringe.

Before they could inject the sedative, Spencer sprang to his feet and lifted the captain up off his seat.

"Major," he told her, "I'll take the captain out for a walk." He put his body between the captain and the orderlies.

"Cap, I got you," he whispered. "Come on. Now."

He hooked his arm around the captain's forearm and choreographed his movements. His body wasn't fully there, not enough to be reliable. Not yet. Fighting two meant disabling blows, the sort of violence that they wouldn't walk away from.

He stared at both orderlies, his eyes conveying that they were the ones in trouble.

"Do they have sedatives?" Captain Sam asked Spencer.

"Affirmative."

"Major, I'd like to take that walk," Captain Sam told her. He told Spencer to "walk slowly until we get a pace together and try to tell me what's coming up, stairs and curbs especially."

Spencer did as ordered. The orderlies parted without intervening.

As they walked toward the double doors at the top of the ward, Spencer wondered what made him get involved. Why would he risk screwing up? He was onto the home stretch. Bagram to Landstuhl, Landstuhl to Madigan, Madigan to Walter Reed, Walter Reed-PEB-Afghanistan.

Group made the men feel small. None of them were small, but they went along. Only the captain didn't go along. Before that, Spencer had added it up, but it was just like the captain said. The army was always about working together right from the first hour of basic training; now personal responsibility was all they ever talked about. Now they were making guys who are already down feel like they ought to be grateful for everything the military was doing for them and not the other way around. Captain Sam saw what was coming, how the MEB and PEB processes weren't about a soldier's future; this was all about pencil-pushing actuaries getting the grateful nation off the hook with the cheapest settlement they could get away with. Major Davies worked for that machine. Everything coming out from her mouth was filtered by it.

They took the elevator down to the ground floor without talking. They headed east out the rear entrance toward the flat grassy sport fields where Spencer thought the captain could walk on his own without any obstruction.

"Sergeant, I apologize for taking you away from therapy." Those were the first words the captain ever spoke to him. It might have been the first time he had heard any captain apologize about anything.

"Not a problem, Sir," Spencer replied, sounding upbeat. The reality was he'd take fresh air over Group any day. "I'm just killing time until they get me through Physical Exam Board and I get back to Afghanistan."

They were coming to stairs; Spencer told the captain, who asked him to stop at the top of the stairs and then take them one at a time.

"Tell me when we're on the last step before flat ground."

Spencer felt the pressure on his shoulder increase and prepared himself to straight-arm the captain if he tripped going down, but they made it successfully without incident.

"I like what you said, Sir," Spencer admitted, surprising himself when the words came out of his mouth. "About how we don't need to ask for anything."

"But you're going back?" the captain questioned.

"Yes sir."

Captain Sam stopped and turned, squaring his shoulders toward Spencer. "You've been deployed. You know these wars are bullshit," he said. "But you want to go back there?"

"Affirmative."

"Affirmative what, Sergeant? That the wars are bullshit or that you want to go back?"

"Affirmative."

Captain Sam raised his stumps as if his missing hands were still attached to help him get his mind around Spencer's statement. "You've been there. You know we can't win. We're not accomplishing a damned thing. But you want to go back?"

In motion, his mind worked clearly. Standing there in one place his thinking was like digging a hole at the seashore, with every wave caving it in upon itself. Spencer started walking again.

Spencer assessed bluntly that "Out there I am an Olympic gold medalist and an astronaut. I know what I am supposed to do and I know how to do it, with precision. I know my job, I do my job, I get it done. There I am the real deal. Here… I'm nothing."

Outside of the army what would he be doing? He had asked himself the question plenty of times. Not a single response painted a picture in his head.

"It won't last forever, the war. You're going to have to find a new normal sometime."

Spencer shook his head, not that the captain could see. What would he do, pull Romex for Jack; maybe someday learn how to install a service panel?

"What's happened to you?" Captain Sam asked, relieving him of the toxic thought process of writing out a new and lesser life.

"Green on blue, Sir. Got stabbed." Spencer thought about additional details, but what he said was all that really mattered.

"And you're OK now?"

Spencer took them between the buildings heading east toward the playfield. The captain moved easily; it seemed like everything that wasn't missing was working fine.

"Yes Sir. Down a kidney, but you only need one. I'm lucky." Spencer hesitated. "Sorry Sir, not meaning anything by that." They were into a wide path now with no obstacles for a hundred feet. MSJS stopped and considered that there had to be an easier way to walk. He decided to try.

Reaching across his chest, he took the captain's forearm and let it down to Captain Sam's side. "Captain, we're in a wide open spot. I'll let you know different if anything comes up. You're good to walk on your own." Spencer sensed that the captain needed to be challenged.

Captain Sam hesitated, reluctant to try, but made four tentative steps before he was veering off at a forty-five degree angle, heading straight toward a maple tree. Spencer caught his shirt. He needed to rig up some type of harness to tie them together so the captain could correct himself if he started going in the wrong direction.

"Talk to me," the captain said.

"Sir?"

"Jesus, Sergeant, talk! You talk to me and I'll know where you are."

Spencer looked around for something to say. "We're on grass now," he told him. "It was just cut."

Captain Sam smiled and agreed. He could smell it.

"Talk to me if we get near obstacles and we're good, I think." He used his forearm to brush off MSJS's grip on his shirt.

"Family?" he asked Spencer.

"Just my dad. I'm not married. You, Sir?"

"Yes." The captain was married. Kids, too. A couple of little girls.

"That's good, Sir. You must be ready to get your PEB, too, and get home to them."

"Would you saddle your wife and kids with me?" the captain responded. I'm a 200-pound infant who can't ever be potty-trained.

Spencer had no reply. What can you say to that?

"I didn't think so," Captain Sam answered for him. "Not going to happen, Sergeant. I guarantee it."

"Sir, can the Major do that, have you injected?" The captain was making trouble, no doubt about that, but sedating him like he was going nuts?

"The Major is doing precisely what her job description says to do, ticking every single box. She's an idiot. She's not helping these men.

Nobody is afraid of lost limbs. We can take that challenge just like taking the next hill. Those things go with the job."

The look on the captain's face said that Major Davies might as well have been spitting dog turds.

"I can hear it in their voices," he continued. "Every minute they've lived as soldiers has been mapped out, morning to night. They knew who they were, where they were, what they were supposed to accomplish, and exactly how to do it. Just like you said. They don't know anything now. They face a huge blank unknown."

The captain was never going to pour maple syrup over a rock and call it breakfast, that was for certain. Respect.

"The Major knows what's next. These men will get in front of a bunch of trained negotiators using actuarial tables saying just how little this grateful nation can get away with paying for a foot or a hand or an ear or an eye."

Now is exactly the time for 'we' and 'us' and banding together and that's the last thing they want us to do."

*****

"I'll make you a deal, Sergeant," Major Davies proposed. "You don't want to attend Group and Captain Hall can't seem to resist interfering. Captain Hall hangs onto being bitter. That's poisonous here and I can't allow it. Run it right out of him, Sergeant. Like my mother always said, 'a tired mouth is slower to talk back.' Everyone in this facility means to do well and we are doing our best. If you agree to be responsible for the captain rather than attending group time, barring any reason otherwise, I'll agree to write a positive psych eval toward your PEB."

Spencer was startled by the major's outstretched hand. Major Davies' tiny hand was tight, efficient, and shockingly firm. Spencer agreed to the deal not just to get out of Group and not to underscore a psych evaluation, either. On their walk, Captain Hall explained how he was never going to receive prosthetics. Walter Reed determined that without sightedness prosthetics could never function. But maybe, Spencer hoped, he could help Captain Sam get some hope, maybe, and maybe see his way to going home. That prospect gave him purpose, something more than killing time.

The following day, Spencer started by rigging a harness that allowed Captain Sam to trot and then jog on the flat east playing field. He was sprinting within a week, with Spencer dragging behind because he couldn't keep up. Spencer was built for endurance, not long-legged flat-out speed. When he sprinted, Captain Sam kept his elbows in tight to his sides; his body moved in perfect synchronicity, like a well-oiled machine.

"You don't just run, not like that," Spencer panted, tugging at the captain to stop before he collapsed behind so the captain would have to tow him like an anchor.

That was the first time Spencer ever really saw the captain smile. "400 meter high-hurdler, Cornell," he said. He was like that, always talking about politics and people in general and hardly ever letting on about himself. Cornell. ROTC took him to college. Economics and History.

*****

"Here," Captain Sam told Spencer. "I've got us something."

He reached into a bag slung over his shoulder and came back up with a newspaper clamped between both his wrists.

"Washington Post," he said. "Let's read it."

"Sir?"

"Let's find a cool place to sit down and read the paper."

Spencer went to the front section and looked over the headlines.

"What do you want me to read?" He was reluctant at first, but it wasn't too bad once he got going. Back in school he had been a good reader.

They moved through the paper fast. Most of the time, Captain Sam seemed to be satisfied by the first couple lines from most of the articles. Sometimes he would paraphrase the whole piece just from the headline and then have Spencer read it out loud. He was always right, too, calling it "predictable filler."

"Skip to the editorials," he asked Spencer.

After reading the titles, Captain Sam asked Spencer to read the whole editorial out loud. He read it. The words weren't especially challenging.

"What do you think?" Captain Sam asked.

"What do you mean?"

"I mean what do you think of what she's saying?"

Spencer hesitated. "I thought you wanted me to read it to you," he finally responded.

"You read it to me. Thanks. So what do you think? Do you agree? Do you disagree?"

Spencer protested. "I didn't think there was going to be a test."

"What test? I'm interested in your opinion. What do you think?"

"I don't know," Spencer grumbled. "Let me read it again."

He started rereading aloud when Captain Sam cut him off. "You can read silently."

"OK."

When he was done reading, the captain listened to Spencer's opinion, but it didn't stop there. That was where it began.

"Why do you say that?" the captain wanted to know. "That writer has a Ph.D. Do you know something she doesn't?"

"Sorry."

"Don't be sorry! She's a total ass!"

Spencer breathed a sigh of relief and laughed.

"Why do you think she'd write something like that?" Captain Sam asked him.

"It's her job, I guess."

Now the captain laughed. "Yup. She's syndicated in something like 200 papers across the country. For that crap!"

*****

After that, they started reading the paper every day. Right after their runs. They listened to news programs, too. Fox. CNN. MSNBC. They talked about what was in the news and even what wasn't there, too. Captain Sam asked a lot of questions about what Spencer thought that the news channels were trying to say. "Why do you think they chose that story? Was it fair? Did it make you think about all sides of the story?"

He would go further. Deeper. "Do you think the writer, or the newspaper, or maybe the company that owns the newspaper wants you to think a certain way? Do they want you to think at all? What are you seeing on the screen? Are there differences between reading a story and hearing it on the radio and seeing it on TV? What do you think about that?"

"Captain," Spencer said one time, "Enough already. There's all these agendas out there. I get that. But it's tiring always questioning everything. Captain, you can't question everything and run an army. I'm getting through my Physical Exam Board, I'm going back, and I'm going to do what I get ordered to do. Chain of command."

"So if they tell you, you just go and do it. Jesus! 'Mine is not to reason why, mine is but to do or die.' Jonathan, you weren't even twenty when you went in. How was your mind even formed? Listen to me!" the captain said. "It's not OK to be this empty vessel and leave it to the army to fill you up. That's not OK! You build a life by questions, by opening up to ideas and opening up to people. Don't take other people's ideas. Not mine, not anybody's! Question! Challenge them! Formulate your own opinions."

*****

Spencer threw himself into improving every tiny factor in the captain's daily functions. The captain had been at Walter Reed for six months; in a week, Spencer had him washing and feeding and dressing himself. He made up two elastic cuffs and covered them both with strips of heavy-duty Velcro. He wrapped more Velcro around spoons and forks and around a scrub brush for the shower, too. He put patches of the stuff along the hips in a pair of sweat pants so the captain could pull up his own pants. Spencer was like a one-man rehab center and Captain Sam got into the spirit as he could accomplish more and more. But the toilet remained a challenge.

"What if you had a bidet," Spencer asked the captain. "You sit down on the toilet, do your thing, and go through a quick car wash and blow dry. No need to find somebody to help, you just go like everybody else."

"Sergeant, just because something exists and makes sense has nothing to do with the army. You know that."

"It doesn't hurt to try," Spencer told him. He already had the information for a bidet downloaded and printed out. $400 on Amazon.

Spencer was already used to Captain Sam's knee-jerk negative reactions. But the idea had Captain Sam thinking. Spencer could see it on his face; the deep lines were standing out on his forehead. They were making progress.

Spencer approached the major with the idea for Captain Sam's bidet. She provided him with the forms to put the request into writing. He looked at the sheaf of paperwork; it looked like enough work to fill a week.

"Major, how long will it take to get a special requisition through approval?"

"There are five toilets servicing eighty men on the ward. That is already beyond capacity. It won't get approved, Sergeant, but it is your right to submit the request."

Spencer kept his cool. "Adding the bidet seat allows Captain Sam to use the toilet by himself, but it won't stop the rest of us from using the toilet. A grown man deserves to be able to take a crap without calling somebody to help. Right at the very top of the Patient's Bill of Rights it says we have the right to respect and dignity. Can't you cut the red tape?"

"Sergeant Spencer, you have the forms."

"Major, they're sending him books in Braille every two weeks. Is he supposed to learn Braille with his elbows? It's completely safe, UL-rated, and there's an outlet in reach of the cord. I'll buy it with my own money and install it myself."

"Sergeant, fill out the forms."

*****

The SFAC, Soldier Family Assistance Center, kept getting TTOs for the captain's wife, Alice, and the girls. They flew them in and put them up at Mologne House. Captain Sam had no discretion if and when his wife was coming up to the ward, but he refused to go down to the third floor, knowing very well that children couldn't come up with her. Under-fourteen not allowed, for their own good.

Alice gave Spencer more background in a few minutes than the captain ever told about himself. "I married him for his big heart and his mind. He still has those. If he wasn't so damned stubborn, we could figure out the rest. Sergeant, Sam and me, we can figure this out. I'm strong. The girls are strong, too. Help him get past worrying about us so much. We're going to be OK. OK?"

Spencer found himself listening to Alice the next day, too. Captain Sam had wanted to become a teacher, "possibly even a college professor." Every so often he would let slip that he had a dream of teaching at West Point.

"But then he fought in Fallujah. After that, everything changed. He called it their Alamo. Fallujah wasn't all IEDs and hit-and-run attacks. Sam said that they held their ground. Insurgents with small arms and homemade bombs fought the best-trained army on Earth to a standstill. They had no food and no water and still they fought. One night he had his unit translator write out a note saying 'God respects all brave men.' Sam taped it to a carton of MREs and somehow got the carton with the note over to the insurgents.

"He wrote me that not a single shot was fired at his unit for the next 24 hours. But then what he did got up to brigade and his colonel found out and went ballistic. He threatened to have Sam court-martialed for aiding the enemy. Can you believe that? Right there, right in the middle of the battle," she said.

"It was OK to kill them, but showing the enemy a little respect? No way. All the talk about winning hearts and minds. Right. Didn't matter that the shooting stopped. The army couldn't let it happen. Sam's immediate superior at battalion intervened, thank goodness. The major told the colonel that Sam sent over pork rations to attack their morale. So he got out of it, but he wasn't the same. Not after. He'd had it with the army."

She looked around her at the ward, at the posters on the walls and the shiny linoleum and nurses trotting along in their scrubs, and sighed. "He'd be whole and home if they had court-martialed him," Alice added.

He got it. About the MREs and the note. After that, Spencer found himself listening more deeply and more often when the captain spoke. Talking, too. A lot of times he thought that about the tribesmen in Afghanistan, fighting on guts and belief. No satellite photos. No drones. No air support. Sleeping under rocks on freezing windswept hillsides. Eating only the food they could carry, if there was food to be had.

The captain was right about a lot of stuff. But he was wrong about Alice. Alice and the girls deserved a chance, too. Only nothing he could say could convince the captain to think about going home.

*****

Captain Sam never did talk about what happened. His eyes. His hands.

After a long run, four miles Spencer figured, Spencer held the water fountain handle and Captain Sam sucked down about a gallon and then put his face and his head under the spout.

East of the hospital and rehab buildings a huge hundred-year-old oak tree became their favorite resting spot. The two of them cooled off after runs in the shade of its long limbs. Spencer lead Captain Sam up to the trunk and the captain pressed his back against it and slid down until he was sitting on his butt at the base. He drew up his knees and closed his eyes.

"How did it happen?" Spencer asked quietly.

Captain Sam recalled it in vivid color but Spencer wasn't certain that he was going to say anything.

"I'm four hundred yards out, above and away from the action," Captain Sam explained, finally opening up. He never said where, but Spencer didn't interrupt to ask.

"I was observing and reporting back to battalion. I can see everything from where I am. There were two jihadi jackrabbits with AKs waiting behind a half-wall. My four-man recon patrol was moving right at them. I couldn't raise them. Communications crapped out. All I could do was watch."

"You didn't have a sniper?" Spencer challenged. Hell, it was only four hundred yards.

"No, no sniper. Christ. They had to have had a spotter somewhere, because these two waited until my guys were inside twenty yards and then they stuck their rifles around the wall and loosed a couple bursts. No aiming. Teasing. They took off running and it was on. Marty Seagull, my platoon sergeant, Jaime Estavez, his corporal, this little Guatemalan who was always playing guitar and singing songs in Spanish, and two specialists. They were sucked in hook, line, and sinker."

Spencer thought about his own guitar. He hadn't seen it since the medivac to Bagram. He wondered a lot about where it had ended up, but he said nothing.

"Do I wait for the Black Hawks?" the captain continued. "No! There's an M11647A1 there so I jump in and floor it like I'm Bruce Willis. I should have waited, but these are my guys and I'm watching them heading out to get themselves killed. So, of course, what happens? Ragheads lured the little fish to bring in the big ones. Completely predictable bullshit. I chased their chumming right into an IED that blew the six-ton Humvee flying twenty feet in the air."

Sprinkles of these pictures dropped through the captain's mind like tiny fragments from the IED. Shards of plastic had stuck like porcupine quills into the mush where he had always had eyes. He knew they were destroyed. Knew instantly. But he didn't even know his hands were gone, not then. He knew only bandages.

It took a month before he could piece words into sentences.

"Almost 5,000 Iraq-Afghanistan soldiers have lost feet and legs," Captain Sam told him. "But IEDs and mines blow upward. They either kill you or blow off your lower limbs. Just 280 upper limbs have been blown off or amputated. Through the whole of Iraq and Afghanistan both. If they counted by the limb, I'd be a shy one percent of that total. I may be the single casualty in the entire military with both eyes and both hands gone. A freak event. They don't even have an official designation; I am rated an 'MLD,' Multiple Loss Dysfunction. Sounds like mild, doesn't it, 'MLD'?"

"Did you save your guys?" Spencer asked.

"Yes. Estavez came home a citizen. That's something, I suppose."

"Damned right it is! That's valor, Captain."

"A silver star for hands and eyes? It's stupid, is what it is. Dumb-ass trade-off. That valor you're talking about, that 'be all you can be' BS that makes us go across the globe, is marketing. We should be turning our guns back on the chickenshit greedy assholes who sent us there."

"Four men are breathing 'cause of you, Captain, and that is a fact. You did that."

"We fought a rich man's war," he said, "fought by everyone except the rich."

Spencer let it in one ear and out the other. Captain Sam ranted a lot.

"Jonathan, I know you want to go back. Would you tell me, please, what are you going to accomplish? You and me, our families, the guys who fought beside us, our kids and their kids, killing and dying and getting fucked up and burning through trillions of dollars for Iraq and for Afghanistan. Trillions! For what? Trillions in public debt dollars that rich assholes turned into billions in their own private cash. They're real life people living in mansions and flying private jets. They cost me my life and I don't even know who they are! That pisses me off! Why don't we have a government that tells us that stuff? Explain that to me, would you, 'cause I want to know!

I want my girls to be able to afford college. That money could be student loans, money for veterans, money for roads and bridges and curing diseases," the captain said.

"Shouldn't we at least know who they are? Rob a bank, go to jail. Own a bank, rob everybody.

Nobody ever looks into the really colossal crimes happening right in plain view, Jonathan. I know where I'd start looking. If I still had eyes I'd start with two angry old bastards worth billions who get off on playing this country like a fiddle with all their bullshit institutes and behind the scenes string-pulling. Follow the money!"

"Why don't we get a couple soft-serve ice creams," Spencer suggested. "I've been thinking how I can set up your strap so you have it on your own. It'll be good."

"Jonathan, I'm talking about this whole country and you're wanting ice cream."

"Yup. It's hot out."

*****

Two days later, under the big oak tree, Spencer framed his own idea: if they were "wounded warriors," then shouldn't they be reconnecting with the warriors inside them? They had wheelchair basketball. Why not martial arts? Teach krav maga. Teach stick fighting. Show a guy with no legs how to crush through a pelvis with one blow. Spencer had the captain stand up and worked him through the basics: balance, centering strike energy, elbows/forearms/knees, straight kicks. Throat, sternum, pelvis, knees.

After a half hour he had the captain energized, animated and positive.

A krav maga program would work alongside rehab and vocational counseling, Spencer suggested to Major Davies. "Help the men feel powerful again, then maybe writing resumes and applying for jobs, the stuff you keep pushing, would be easier, too. "

"Resources are limited, number one," Major Davies responded. "Number two, these men need to fit in, not get instruction for how to act out." She said that getting them thinking like warriors was a form of cruelty. Their war was over.

"Major," Spencer argued, "they're truly scared of the war that begins when they leave here."

Captain Sam tried telling the major "You get us into Group and you say we need to support one another, but then all we talk about is how each one of us is going to handle it after we're out,

"All that advice about staying away from booze and drugs, about breathing and counting to ten and not hitting our wives and our kids… that's all about staying small. You don't get it. You can't make a man a warrior and then take it away without putting something strong into that black hole. Demons breed in that hole."

She closed like a steel vault. Spencer saw it. Captain Sam felt it and heard in her voice that they were wasting their time.

"Captain, we were talking about krav maga," she briskly reminded him. "I am forty percent over capacity. What we can achieve is small steps, and without cooperation we won't even achieve those. Keep it clear, finite, and fixed in the achievable and I'll work with you, but knowing how to fill out a job application will help these men. Teaching bar-fighting tricks won't."

"I'm talking about really supporting one another. About organizing," Captain Sam yelled back. "But you can't talk about that, about real change. That's rocking the boat.

"Your attitude is nothing new, Major. Governments have been afraid of veterans for three thousand years. Two millennia ago, Julius Caesar was taking stolen land back from rich Roman senators and giving it to Roman army veterans. The vets earned it, but the Senate stabbed him to death."

"Captain," Major Davies griped, "you need to stop this appeals nonsense and go home. Go home and organize all you want.

"What are you doing here? Appealing your PEB. You have full benefits for life? Don't you realize how ungrateful you are acting? How many men would kill for the benefits you won't accept!

We have a program in place here. It doesn't include martial arts, or bidets, or Julius Caesar either. Go home! That's your reality. Final. Period."

*****

Captain Sam pressed his back into the tree trunk and pulled his legs up to his chest. Get him talking politics and he wouldn't stop talking, but mentioning even the idea of him having a home or any future with Alice and his girls and he snapped shut like a bear trap. Spencer caught how he always turned away; even without eyes, he was looking somewhere else.

"Look at what you're able to do, Cap. You're dressing yourself. You're feeding yourself. You run my ass into the dust. Couldn't you maybe just give it a chance at home? You can read books on tape. You can still teach or do radio. You can run and dance and tell the girls bedtime stories. Dude. Yeah, it sucks, but get out and do the stuff you keep talking about. Hell, run for Congress!"

"Congress!" Captain Sam scoffed. "What, so I can do nothing just like the rest of them? So I can play the north pole-south pole charade like corporate-owned Democrats and Republicans? Red states and blue states both made to look a thousand times more different than they really are. Money isn't red or blue, it's green. I can see that and I don't have eyeballs."

"Then go and change it," Spencer urged. "You say corporations are killing more people than wars. Go after them! You say billionaires are buying our democracy. Go after them!"

"Jonathan, do you ever listen to anything I say?" Captain Sam shot back. "The American Legislative Exchange Council alone writes a thousand times more legislative bills than any elected politician. One lawmaker against that is like a ditch digger up against a bulldozer! Besides, I'm blind and I have no hands, or did you fail to notice?"

Spencer got nowhere trying to change the subject. Ranting about politics again. Captain Sam even floated a crazy idea that every vet who was going to kill himself anyway ought to put on a suicide vest and take out a bunch of rich people with him.

"One vet every hour," Captain Sam said. "That would change things."

Spencer laughed it off. "We don't get 72 virgins, Cap. Our guys don't off themselves to get to Paradise for jihad. Besides that, how would you ever reach them? Take out an ad in Stars and Stripes?"

*****

While the two of them were sitting on the grass, sweating and breathing hard after a two-mile run, eight laps around the track, they talked.

"We are either warriors, teachers, nurturers, or healers," the captain told Spencer. "Whatever other title or rank we have is just splitting hairs. We're one of those or we're nothing, just taking up space.

"This country has three times as many billionaires now as when you, YOU, first went to Afghanistan. Eight hundred new billionaires. How many of them are warriors? Teachers? Nurturers or healers? They're thieves!"

Man, I've been a warrior for a long, long time, Spencer thought to himself. Don't tell me that we're all being used, that the wars were for nothing, that they were about money and nothing else. *I don't want to hear it!*

What he wanted was to get his PEB done and to get back to his real life. In Afghanistan.

He was meant for war. He knew that. Sitting on lawns had his mind was drifting to the soccer kid in his red Manchester United shirt. He was thinking about him too much, and about Miller, too.

Captain Sam asked him point blank "Are you going to find Miller and kill him? Is that why you want to go back?"

Spencer never gave an ounce of energy to imagining revenge, but if that was how the captain could make sense of his plans, that was ok. Captain Sam, a great man, and that piece of shit Miller were actually on the same page about the war, but Spencer never told that to the captain.

How could he explain that he was made for what he did, that what he brought to the table and a million dollars worth of training went into a purpose?

He, MSJS, might well be the best in the world at what he did. The missions were fact, objective proofs. That was something. That had significance.

In the quiet of the night he also sometimes asked himself what else did that say about him, that he was better at war than anyone else he had ever seen? It did stuff to him, to his insides. There were periods he couldn't take a crap for weeks. His insides were too tied up. He could have taken the bus down to visit or had his dad drive up; Jack was only two hours away from Walter Reed, but that never happened. From Afghanistan, he couldn't make himself call Jack, not even to say he was OK. Life outside war was what was really scary. How fucked up was that?

"Just 85 people in the world have more money than the lowest 3.5 billion people," the captain continued. "The more the rich take, the faster everything falls apart. They can't justify that, Jonathan, not even if they own the Supreme Court, the government, the police, the intelligence services, and everything else. Which is exactly why the rich are consolidating power. They know they can't take everything and then expect to hold onto it for long. But they can't stop themselves.

The captain continued: "Jonathan, consolidation is the one fundamental flaw of tyranny. When the people fight back, and they will, concentrated power also concentrates the targets. There is no changing things from the inside! We are supposed to be one man, one vote, but that's over and it's not coming back. Oligarchs, all over this planet they're strangling democracy like boa constrictors.

"You don't talk to snakes. You cut off their heads!"

"Captain," Spencer suggested, "let's get you dictation software so you can write your ideas down by saying them out loud. Just talk into a microphone like you're talking to me."

Captain Sam should have been talking to a microphone. He certainly wasn't listening.

"They wiped out Occupy in one coordinated night," he went on. "Swept it out of existence just like the Chinese wiped Tiananmen Square.

But people won't take getting poorer forever. Hard work either brings the reward of a better life, or things are going to bust loose. We're right back in the same fights we had in 1789 and 1889 and 1932, only this time the bad guys are winning!"

"Whoa. Cap, bring it down to scale, OK? Look at a regular day. You could cook the girls' breakfast. I know you could! You could work on the telephone and organize vets. It's all good, Cap. That's the smarts I have. The politics is your thing."

Mission planning and procedure were in his wheelhouse, not politics. Yes, mission success required knowledge. Intelligence-gathering. You keep the enemy on his heels, keep him guessing, make him look over their shoulder because he knows you're coming but never knows when or from where. But politics? *Jesus, shoot me now.*

"That's not OK," Captain Sam screamed at him. He set the back of his head against the tree trunk, leaned forward, and banged it back hard.

"You have to be into politics!" He was about to smack his skull a second time when Spencer grabbed his feet and pulled him away lengthwise on the grass.

Captain Sam rolled away from the tree trunk onto his side and curled up. "I can't remember their faces," he sobbed. "I can't picture my own girls." He really wasn't thinking about politics at all.

Spencer placed his hand on the Captain's forearm and looked away, past the manicured lawns, toward Wisconsin Avenue. What could he say? At Harmony Church, in sniper training, they said don't think about faces, you push them down. If they came back in your dreams and you couldn't stop them, then you stop yourself from sleeping.

One time, in 2004, he rotated back to Benning and then he stayed up for six weeks straight. It can be done. It's just different. He pushed them down, but it tied his bowels in knots so badly that he didn't crap that whole time. So he didn't eat much. You can make yourself do that, too. He stayed hydrated and drank cans of Ensure.

He stopped talking to people. He spent two weeks inside a dark bedroom wanting all the time to be back in Afghanistan, back on familiar ground.

Now, he just wanted the damned PEB squared away and to be back in Afghanistan.

He wasn't married and he didn't have kids and the captain had both and the captain didn't even give them a chance to be together as a family!

*****

"Captain, I am a doer. I get my mission; I get my mission squared away. Men like me; we're trained to get the job done," he said. "You, you've got a mind and a voice and a lap the girls can sit on and the parts you have all work fine. Step up, Cap. It will be different, but it can be good. Alice wants you home. I can't say that. Nobody wants me to come home."

Captain Sam didn't say anything. Spencer reached out and stroked the captain's head, once, then let him be. The blind helping the blind. What the hell did he know? Jack, his dad, went through the motions of living but Jack was a harmless zombie. Half the time he ate his dinner out of a can without bothering to heat it.

He thought about being 39 years old and never having a real girlfriend. *How different was he from Jack?*

"At least when Jack was thirty-nine, he still had Mom," he said aloud.

He thought about Mercy again. Mercy, who lived next door and helped with the house after Mom went on chemo. After her mom's boyfriend started "getting weird," Mercy stayed with him and Jack for a year. She was trying to stay put to finish high school and then she was moved in, just like that.

The mom's boyfriend came around the first night. Jack walked him back off the porch. Spencer watched out the window. He must have been fifteen then. The guy was wearing an undershirt with no sleeves. He had tattoos and a mustache. He started to point at their house and tried to walk around Jack, but Spencer's dad got in his way every time. Then he walked away a few steps. He turned around and stared, but then he left and stayed away. That was cool. He liked remembering that. Jack stepping up. He liked remembering Mercy.

Sometimes she cooked. Her food was bad. She wasn't very good at cleaning, either. But with her there the house came back to life. Mercy was two years older. He liked her smell. Like cheesy sweat and flowers. Patchouli.

She taught him to play the guitar. She always had time for him. They practiced for hours, usually sitting on her bed. Her red-blonde hair was everywhere; she used to brush it away a hundred times until she finally raised her arms and pulled it back into a bushy ponytail. She had thick hair in her armpits and freckles all over her shoulders. He wanted to just reach out to feel the weight of her breasts in both his hands.

Every year, usually around Christmas, she still kept up. He never heard from anyone in his high school, but Mercy always came through even when he didn't write her back. She'd had enough of cities; she said the last time she wrote to him. She had a farm now, in the southwest corner of West Virginia where the coalmines were all played out. She was raising sheep, or maybe goats, to make her own cheese. No more getting up to wear stupid outfits to go into some office. He tried to picture the place. He tried to picture Mercy twenty years older.

*****

The major stayed off his case. No more telling him about "dissociation" or that his intention to return to Afghanistan as soon as possible was "regressive" and "symptomatic of significant psychological wounds." She no longer expressed a "profound level of concern" about his "reintegration into civilian life habits." *Jesus.*

During their mandatory five minutes of "social behavior measurement" she explained how "You're beginning to relearn the basics for communication between people and not ranks." Apparently people can talk, just banter. "It isn't wasteful or weak, Sergeant. It's another way to bond. Combat isn't the norm," she said.

"Between people, the norm is day-to-day conversation, which leads to fitting into a social unit and to forging healthy relationships."

That was how he was going to fit in with the world "we hope to live in" rather than an environment dictated by threat and terror and hurt. "Afghanistan," she said, "the war," was "an artificial context." He needed to get to know his real self. She urged him to remember the kid who used to lie down on the grass and watch the clouds go by. That unstructured joy was what they were are fighting for. (He never knew that one.) The war was going to be over. He was going to have to learn to fill his days himself, no more orders, to find out what he was good at doing and what he liked to do and then go do it.

Spencer nodded agreeably. That came easily now. He was squatting four hundred pounds in twenty-rep sets. Free curls, too, ten legitimate reps at fifty pounds each arm. He was clocking his run east across Bethesda, around Congressional Country Club, south to the river, then back to Walter Reed north through Little Falls Park, eleven miles, in seventy-four minutes. He could zip through twenty chin-ups and one-arm twenty push-ups. Going on for thirty-nine years old, but he was ready to go head-to-head with any Navy Seal. One kidney? No problem. He was getting faster, too. Not as fast as Captain Sam on those giraffe legs of his, but measurably ahead of where he expected to be.

"Race you," he challenged the captain. They could sprint now without needing to tie themselves together. Captain Sam could feel the painted lines on the running track. If he missed and moved across lanes, Spencer shouted "left one" or "right two" and Captain Sam adjusted to keep himself in a center lane.

"Four laps. First to a mile."

The captain won by thirty meters, but Spencer was still smiling.

"Three times a day, more," Captain Sam admitted to Spencer afterward, "I just want to annihilate the world. But you, Jonathan, you're always cool. Like, nothing ever gets a rise out of you. It's amazing. God, I hate that about you!"

"You think too much."

"How many people did you shoot? 131? You didn't hate them, but you looked down a scope and blew their heads off. How do you do that?"

"It wasn't all head shots," he responded. "Seventy percent were center torso."

He wouldn't say so, but Spencer had nightmares sometimes. Other times, when he felt the rumble of helicopter rotors, he got this weird shiver that ran from his neck down to his ankles and just for a second he didn't always know where he was. He always manned up, but it stayed inside his guts, poking.

"One time a couple years ago, in Khost, there was just one squad of us in this little outpost set up in the middle of a big open square," Spencer told Captain Sam. "We had concrete anti-vehicle barriers set up a hundred meters out, but except for those were pretty lean, sandbags and razor-wire. We had a tripod-mounted .50-caliber machine gun and a Bradley on our backside with the 25mm cannon, but the chain gun on the Bradley was the main thing covering our butts. Anyhow, I remember that it was hotter than hell. I was inside this one sandbag room that was our quarters, our mess, supplies, everything, sacking out, sweating mainly, no way anybody was sleeping. All of a sudden there's this noise, like a roar, getting louder. I don't remember if somebody called me or I just came outside to see and there must have been thousands of people moving out of the covered market and stampeding right at us. They were packed in so tight that all they could do was just pour forward like a churning wave.

"From behind six feet of sandbags this one specialist, good guy, from Iowa I think, he had the fifty, he just didn't know what to do. Nobody looked like they even had guns, but if he didn't fire, there was nothing to stop them from douching all of us. Vehicle barriers, sandbags, and razor wire were never going to stop that mob. They were way inside 100 meters. There was zero time to call in help. We couldn't even move to radio HQ. We're talking close," he said.

"People were screaming. I scanned through my scope and there were these flashing reflections. I kept looking there until I could see a clear picture. It was one man, long beard, sandy turban, faded black jacket. He had two swords and he was killing everything, men and women, dogs, goats, donkeys, slashing into the crowd, stabbing and driving them forward as they tried to get away. They were too packed together to avoid him; I don't think they even knew exactly where he was.

"The lieutenant and Iowa kept looking at all those people and at one another, not knowing what to do. I sighted down and his red eyes were bugging out while he kept slicing with those swords. So I set to fire and blew his head up like a melon. He still moved forward two or three more steps, still swinging, before he dropped."

Captain Sam couldn't quite figure out why Spencer told him about that. Was he proud? Was he proving that something he did served a purpose?

"What happened after that?" the captain asked him.

"The crowd tore and kicked at his corpse until some men took the swords and hacked him into pieces. We got evacked out of there before dark to diffuse the situ before anybody decided to turn on us."

"Why did he do it?"

"We heard later on that his son set out to blow up some Afghan government official. He never made it past the outer compound. Detonated his vest. The father watched the martyr video and he just lost it, started killing people, animals, everything. Went through the souk leaving hacked bodies and blood trailing behind him. I don't know that he was thinking about the outpost or us at all."

"And you're OK? It doesn't get to you?"

Spencer shrugged. "It's what I do. What I was trained for. That time I know I saved lives."

Captain Sam thought he knew about heroes and warriors. No soldier thinking about offing himself was ever going to wait for a rich guy to come along so he could take a billionaire out with him. It didn't work that way, not in real life. Guys killing themselves weren't thinking about jihad against the rich or anybody else. They were like the guys on the ward, so scared that there was nothing else out there for them that they pulled the plug just to stop being scared and useless and chugging back pills and liquor. Veterans were never going to rise up. Soldiers get orders and follow them. That's what you do. Why would soldiers trained to obey orders suddenly start to question the social order?

"Well, you're starting to question, Mr. Tower of Power," Cap said. "You're never going back to working for anybody like Miller."

"We're just talking, Sir. I get my Physical Evaluation Board then I'm going back into combat. Maybe not working for Miller, only doing what I'm trained to do."

"Jesus, Jonathan. I told you. You can't be some empty vessel and leave it to the army to fill you. Man up! The military doesn't make you into a person. Life does! Have you ever been in love? Have you ever made love to somebody you love?"

Spencer understood the army. Understood what was expected. Exceeded expectations. These other things were a foreign language and he didn't have the words.

"I don't know if I could be good at that," he finally replied.

"So you fail!" Captain Sam shouted. "Hell. Experiment! Make mistakes. Fail! You get up, dust yourself off, and you try again. That's how we figure it out. Haven't you ever wanted to get yourself a deep-throated Harley and just take off for the open road? Try something different?"

"The army always has a place for me. I perform."

"You perform. They can depend on you. Tell me something. What if the army ordered you to fire on Americans?" Captain Sam challenged him. "Are you going to do it?"

"That's stupid."

"Really? Stupid? Add it up."

Captain Sam rattled off statistics. Two million, three-hundred-thousand men in prisons and growing. Did Spencer know when the numbers started shooting up? Exactly when incomes stopped growing for regular people and all the increases started flowing to the rich.

"Coincidence?" Sam asked.

Police stopped carrying revolvers and moved to semi-automatics (MSJS pictured S&W 38s and 9mm Glocks). SWAT teams got started and kept growing at the exact same time prisons added more and more solitary confinement cells. Every major police department has armored vehicles, helicopter assault training, tactical weaponry, and commando squads. There were drones over U.S. cities.

"Coincidence? Captain Sam pressed.

"Jonathan, crime is going down. Pretty soon 9/11 will be a generation behind us. But those things don't seem to matter. The government still listens to our phone calls and reads our email. You think that's a coincidence? Really?

"This government isn't America. Not the Democrats and not the

Republicans, either. Jonathan, this was a great country once and we can be great again. We're great when regular people thrive, when next year is better than this year and when our kids do better than we do ourselves. That's when we believe again. It's never going to happen with a government doing what the rich want and putting blinders on everyone else. We let them corrupt everything and turn us into a nation of greedy parasites. We're heading toward a police state and you can't wait to go right back to fighting bullshit wars for bullshit reasons. Wars on the other side of the planet that we can't ever win!"

The veins stood out along his neck and across his forehead when the captain got all worked up. Spencer liked him too much to tell Captain Sam how crazy he sometimes sounded. Like he was talking about Pakistan or something, not America. Besides that, the captain didn't know the first thing about recon, mission procedures, tactics, or anything else that goes into turning words into actions. All the planning and training and discipline in the world wouldn't help sight-down on a billionaire who is smart enough to lay low and hire disciplined security.

"The banks brought down this economy and nobody went to prison, Jonathan. Nobody," the captain said. "That's fact, that's not opinion. If we don't start going in different direction, if we don't let regular people have a real chance to live better lives, to educate kids, to get ahead, then it all falls apart, the whole apparatus we fought for. How many people die then, when we sit back and wait for that to happen? You know how you shot that guy with the swords? You saved lives by killing that one guy. Would you kill a hundred people to save this country?"

"Captain, it doesn't work like that. Once people know they are targets, you might get to one or two and then the others run for deep cover. You sound a little wacky. For real."

"So what, you wouldn't even try to rattle them, to put up some resistance? As long as we keep thinking as individuals, they keep winning," Captain Sam explained. "It's the 'you' thing, exactly what Davies does in Group, telling us to think about our individual futures. None of it is about supporting one another. The only reason it's Group is they won't pay the money for one-to-one counseling! You make an Oklahoma City-size truck bomb; drive it outside their next billionaire's club meeting. You do that and this country starts working again." Then he went off on the Koch brothers.

Then Spencer smiled. "Captain, you and I both know we were just shooting the shit, right? Nobody is going postal."

Captain Sam was deadly serious. "We can't stop them in the courts. We can't do it in Congress or in the media. So stop them with fear."

"Jesus, Cap, how do you, of all people, talk about bombing?" Spencer disagreed. "Don't talk about that, you hear me. Not even shooting the shit. And what's the major supposed to do, sign up the guys for an invalid army? We're going to hit the streets with M16s and wheelchairs?

"Tell me about your daughters," Spencer suggested. "Do they do well in school? What sports do they play?"

Captain Sam scowled.

"Captain, you're not going to change the world, but you can do things for those girls. But first you have to believe you can be a dad. You try to fix the big stuff because you think you can't fix what is right in front of you."

"Right in front of my eyes?" Captain Sam thrust the scarred, hollow voids toward Spencer's voice.

"You know what I mean."

"You sound like Major Davies."

"Agoraphobia is a natural response to acute stress and anxiety, Captain. Top-down processing is consistent with belief-biased effect and chunking dissimilar data into schemas as a result of cognitive dissonance."

"Fuck you," Captain Sam laughed begrudgingly. "You're smart, Jonathan. You try to hide it, but you know that, right?"

"Why wouldn't I?"

*****

"Jonathan, if you didn't go back to Afghanistan, what would you do instead?" the captain asked.

"But I am going back. That's what I'm built for. One of these days I'll be at Benning, getting set to deploy. I'm not disappearing, Captain. I'll phone you. Really. You're not getting rid of me so easily."

"But what if you didn't go back?" Captain Sam pressed him. "What's your fallback, your Plan B?"

Spencer shrugged. It was a stupid question.

"Humor me. The war won't last forever. If you weren't going back, what would you do?"

Spencer didn't give it a lot of thought. "It isn't up to me, Cap. I'll get reassigned. Harmony Church, maybe. Maybe they'll have me instructing."

"Think bigger. Beyond the military. What would you do if you weren't in the army at all? You could apply your training lots of places," the captain told him. "You could do police work or get a job working for private security services. Or you could get a job working for a gun manufacturer."

"Naw. I wouldn't want to do that. I'd surprise you. I'd bet I'd go and do something completely different."

"Jonathan, you listen to me, OK? Don't go into the PEB on your own. They have to let you have legal representation if you ask. You hear what I'm saying? Tell them that you want help. These guys are a bunch of insurance actuaries in military uniforms; they're there to negotiate. It won't be cooperative; no matter what they tell you, your evaluation is adversarial."

"I'm not trying to get a better deal, Captain. I just want to pass and be reinstated to full duty," Spencer said.

"You're nineteen-and-a-half years in. Six more months and they pay you for the rest of your life."

"They spent a million dollars training me," Spencer chided. "I'm a proven asset, Cap. It's all good."

*****

During the middle of a random morning he was called into Major Davies' office, where she handed him the directions to his Pre-PEB counseling interview. Just like that. Weeks and months of waiting were over.

He floated through his Pre-PEB counseling interview like it was a joke. CMP exams are easy when you aren't trying to prove disability, right? He waived legal representation. He wasn't seeking medical retirement. They were going to love him… just put him right back where he came from and let him get back to doing the job he was trained for.

Nobody told him the expected dress code so he debated between a combat-ready look and full dress, then settled on the latter: full brass-button greens, ribbons and badges included, spit-polished and parade-sharp. For two hours he sat patiently in a non-descript room with two long wooden benches on either side, waiting like the others for his name to be called.

The actual PEB went even faster than he imagined. He was shown through a set of double doors into a medium-sized, plain army green hearing room where three officers in shirtsleeves sat behind an eight-foot long collapsible plastic banquet table. The American flag hung in a floor stand behind them on one side and the Army flag on the other. He could just make out 1775 showing in the hanging folds. A private in short sleeves was off to Spencer's right side, operating a video camera set onto a tall tripod.

"State your name," the middle officer, a lieutenant colonel, ordered. He did so. The Lt. Colonel was handed a clipboard and ran his finger down the page.

"You have been offered legal representation and you have chosen to waive having legal counsel. Is that correct?"

"Yes Sir."

"You have declined Compensation and Pension examinations?"

"Yes Sir."

"Your sole claim to injury is the full loss of one kidney, is that correct?"

"Yes sir."

"Sergeant, you are to be separated forthwith with severance pay and injury compensation totaling $32,000. On behalf of a grateful nation, I want to thank you for your service."

Spencer stared at the three officers while remaining at full attention. They didn't understand. This was a snafu. He wasn't trying to get out. "Sir? Begging the colonel's pardon, but I'm not trying to get out. Sir, I'm Army, thick and thin, tried and true. I'm not looking to leave. I'm ready to deploy in an hour."

The Lieutenant Colonel looked up from his paperwork. "You've given a kidney. That's enough, Soldier. You did your duty and you served well."

"Hold on a minute." Spencer looked at the three officers from face to face. *They didn't get it.* He wasn't leaving; he was ready to go back to Afghanistan. Ready to deploy!

"Sir," Spencer explained, "I'm fit and able."

"Sergeant, the Army appreciates your service. But it is time to move on, son."

"Sir, I can do the job! Test me! Please, Sir. Sir, put me on any obstacle course. I'll post a 10K time against any unit time in the service! Sir, I can do this!" Spencer pleaded.

"We're going to have to move this along. Sergeant, see your exit administrator for the application if you chose to pursue an appeal." Spencer looked on in shock as the officer applied a stamp to his paperwork and signed off. Retired for Medical Reasons.

He didn't shift. He turned his shoulder to the Lt. Colonel and jabbed his left index finger at each of the patches on his shoulder to explain. "Sir, this wastes an army asset," Spencer appealed. "You spent maybe a million dollars on training me. Airborne School, Ranger School, Special Forces School." He pointed to the service badge hanging on his chest. "Advanced Sniper School." He was a Tower of Power. What didn't they understand? But it was Spencer who didn't understand. Force-reduction. Cost-containment. $32,000 versus a lifetime pension vesting in six months. Spencer also didn't understand that an appeal might keep him in uniform long enough to make his twenty years.

Right after the PEB, a hidden gear seemed to shift. Things accelerated; two E-6s appeared from behind the flag stands and proceeded around the long table toward Spencer in a synchronized gait. Spencer quickly evaluated their size and motion, flashing on the choreography. He could snap the left knee of the Staff Sergeant approaching from his right, 230 pounds, lethargic, going through a routine. He could come back on the pelvis of the other staff sergeant, younger, leaner; the E-5 would run straight onto the blow.

MSJS hardly realized that his fists were tight-knuckled until both sergeants moved their hands back onto Tasers hanging on their belts. Then a sergeant on each side placed a firm grip on his bicep and assertively directed him toward the double doors by which he had entered only minutes earlier. Nineteen years, thirty thousand miles clocked moving overland on his two feet, serving the nation and his brothers in arms, all gone with a rubber stamp.

Consultants, experts in corporate downsizing, wrote the manual. He didn't have the chance to talk with Captain Sam. Under escort—"companion services"—they took him straight to processing and brought his personal belongings to him all packed into his duffle. They handed him $400 cash, a cashier's check for the balance, a map of local motels, and a Veterans Services Directory.

Spencer shouldered his kit and marched to the Motel 6 on Georgia Avenue, never putting the duffle down, even when he was standing beside the swimming pool looking down, transfixed. Nothing made any sense, not even the sun and the sky above him or the clear water smelling of chlorine. He had ruptured out his own anus, born again inside-out.

The front desk accepted his army ID and a $200 deposit in lieu of a credit card. His room had white walls, a television set, an air conditioner, and an orange bedspread. A window looked onto the parking lot. The bathroom had a paper strap over the toilet seat. There was a mirror over the dresser. He didn't want to see himself.

He never touched the bed or sat down. A broad plan formed on the fly. Spend a couple days visiting his dad; make sure Jack was doing OK, and then he was going to ride west… North Dakota, Eastern Montana. The oil fields were hiring unattached men who were willing to work. They liked vets. Captain Sam would like that. He'd be OK.

At 19:30, he drove off with a black Harley Davison Road King straight off the showroom floor.

The following morning he rode his shining Harley right past the front of the building. The lieutenant colonel and his two majors and the two staff sergeants with their Tasers had fucked him; they might never see him now, but he could take it. He was OK.

It was muggy, a sopping armpits D.C. day. He was imagining how the captain would get on back and feel the wind in his face. Even if it were just for a lap around the parking lot, it would do Captain Sam good. The bike had a great rear seat with lumbar support. He didn't need hands. He'd hold on fine.

It felt instantly strange when he turned into the front drive. Spencer had been away for just a couple days, but after he parked and walked toward the rehabilitation center he sensed that he was an outsider now. The guards and duty officer stopped him right at the entrance. He couldn't get to the elevators. Phone calls went between the reception desk and Major Davies. The short, packed sausage showed up from between two MPs who towered over her. All three walked like a wall, moving Spencer outside and down the front steps.

"Major, I'm not here to make waves," Spencer explained. "I didn't get a chance to say goodbye to Captain Hall. I'd like to spend a little time with him. Tell him my plans. That's all. If you don't want me on the ward, no problem, Major. Somebody else can bring him down."

"Master Sergeant Spencer, where did you go with Captain Hall?" she demanded.

"Sir?"

"It's a simple question, Sergeant," she snapped at him. "You took Captain Hall off the ward every day. Where did you go?"

Spencer was caught off-guard. For two days he had been hurtling along, tossed out of orbit and clinging to the handlebars of his new Harley Davidson CVO Road King for something tangible that made sense.

Coming from the ranking officer, he searched for the answer without taking the time to consider why the question was being asked. They went to the east sports field, they jogged the perimeter several times, and they frequently talked and hung out on the grass under the big oak next to Palmer Road South.

"Did you ever take Captain Samuel Hall, up onto that roof? The one with the sign on the door stating that it is 'Off Limits'?" Major Davies stretched her short arm toward the top of the building, pointing her stubby finger.

Roof, Spencer wondered? He didn't like the tone of her voice. They'd already junked him out on a Medical so what did it matter if the roof was off-limits? What more could they do to him now? Sure, he and the captain went up on the roof a couple times. There was usually a nice breeze up there. They didn't do anything except spend a few minutes cooling down.

"We went up a few times," Spencer admitted. "So do half the guys here."

"As the SPO at this facility, I am responsible for writing this ASER, Sergeant. SRMSO is going to see you name on that report. I hold you responsible!"

"Major, I'm not here to argue and you're throwing out more letters than I know. I just want to spend an hour with Captain Sam and then I'm out of here."

"On your new motorcycle."

Spencer agreed. "Yes. On my new motorcycle."

"Well let me tell you. 'SPO' stands for Suicide Prevention Officer. 'ASER' is Army Suicide Event Report. The SRMSO is the Suicide Risk Management and Surveillance Office."

Major Davies pointed at a freshly-scrubbed circle of cement bleached whiter than the surrounding slab. "See that?"

Spencer concentrated on the stark white patch without comprehending.

"Captain Hall managed to get himself up to the sixteenth floor yesterday afternoon, where he jumped to his death. Thanks to you."

Captain Sam was dead?

Major Davies had carefully watched the security recordings and was preparing for the investigation that would follow. She neglected to explain to Spencer how MEBs and PEBs and appeals had been put onto an accelerated fast-track under new orders, going all the way up to the Joint Chiefs. Two hundred and fifty exit-processes targeted for completion at Walter Reed within ten days.

Captain Sam's appeal process was formally denied in four and a half minutes. The same Lieutenant Colonel who ran through Spencer's PEB was tasked to process back-logged evaluations throughout the Eastern administrative sector.

From the hearing chamber, Captain Sam was walked to the cafeteria. He was scheduled for immediate transport home, but unlike Spencer, the captain's disabilities precluded his immediate departure. He was helped to a tray of Sloppy Joes and canned peaches in syrup that a Filipino contract caregiver spoon-fed to him in small bites that dribbled down both cheeks. He told the helper that he wanted to be left alone to do some reading.

From the cafeteria, the captain retraced the steps to the elevator on his own then rubbed his forearm down the wall until he used his forearm to depress the up button. The elevator camera recorded him pressing every floor and patiently riding to the top-floor landing where he stepped out then waited to hear the doors closing behind him.

He shuffled his way forward until he found the wall and then walked his shoulder down the hallway until he felt the doorframe. The bar-mechanism drove into his side.

Once outside, Captain Sam turned his face up to the sunshine. The recording showed his hair pushed back by the wind. He touch-toed his way ahead out to the stub-wall surrounding the roof-edge, stepped up onto the edge and listened to the sounds of cars out in the distance cars driving along Rockville Pike. Above him and to his right, flags snapped in the breeze. He stepped down from the wall then counted his strides going backward carefully making certain there was nothing in his path until the bumped into the access door. He spun a crisp about-face and faced west. His right elbow cocked upward, he paused, and then sprinted to clear the first hurdle.

"You want to put this on me?" Spencer screamed. "You couldn't let him have a fucking bidet! You couldn't let him have some dignity! Fuck you, Major! You're fucking worthless! Fuck you!" The captain… that's a great man.

Spencer sped north at eighty miles an hour. He left his visor up, ignoring the pressure on his eardrums in trade for the wind blowing into his eyes. This wasn't on him; she couldn't put it on him!

But that was nothing. Bullshit. The major was bullshit.

"Jesus. Fuck! God. Captain Sam! No!"

He didn't know why he was riding north. What mattered was motion, not where he was heading. Jack's house was in the opposite direction. Maybe that was why? Maybe he couldn't bring himself to see Jack. He didn't want to lie and he didn't want to explain. He just had to move! His hands, arms, shoulders, neck, back, buttocks, thighs, even his feet were tensed into granite. He clenched his jaw so tightly that his molars ached.

Outside Baltimore he pulled the visor down. He was outside Philly before he really gave thought to having a direction. North Dakota was west, not that it mattered. Distance and movement.

He saw the billboards and banners on the outskirts of Allentown. *Gun Show. Eagle Arms.*

Inside the main pavilion, soldiers in fatigues mixed with hunters and collectors over hundreds of tables laden with weapons and ordnance, journals and loaders, targets and maintenance supplies. Spencer moved right past the outfitters booths selling hunting trips: Alaskan caribou, Nunavik polar bear culls, Cape Buffalo in Namibia; Spencer accelerated straight through until his hands felt the familiar heft of a Barrett 82A. He had it lifted to his shoulder before the vendor could say hello.

It all clicked. This was home; this was where he was right with the world. It wasn't a place, it was a purpose. The feeling of that Barrett against his shoulder, knowing that he could break it down faster than anyone in that giant building and make it dance like nobody else, *that* was home.

"The continued existence of human life on this planet is no certainty," the captain had said. "The world needs a thriving, dynamic, positive America to lead the way forward. We can't be a do-nothing country that watches as we destroy ourselves. How many marriages fail, how much violence is prompted, simply because every year we get squeezed? Fewer opportunities and more pressure. More output, more rent hikes, more debt just to keep up!"

The captain told him: "America can't be a world leader with guns alone. We once lead by example, by being the nation where a C student could work his butt off and thrive. Where bosses and workers both did fine. We had a country where we all pulled on the same rope to move forward. Now a bunch of rich greedy bastards bully everybody else. They push our noses in the dirt, Jonathan! We can't let them ruin it for everyone else. If we go down, everyplace goes down!

If killing fifty people clears the way to put America back on track, wouldn't you do that?"

Spencer balanced the Barrett while he sighted down the Leupold scope, rotating around the giant warehouse and he stopped with a bright green 'Exit' sign in the crosshairs.

"BRASS," he whispered.

Captain Sam was dead. *Like he never existed.*

He committed half his remaining cash to purchasing both the Barrett and the Remington Arms M24, along with a Leupold 4 scope that could mount interchangeably on both weapons.

His direction changed. Rich people weren't going to be in North Dakota's oilfields; the billionaire tycoons were a lot closer than North Dakota. One hundred miles due east... New York City.

CHAPTER FOUR

Some of you here this week and next already completed the Guerilla Warfare training modules. This training is much more than an update. We have plenty of new material to cover. The urban conflict components, for example, have all been updated with case studies and simulations drawn from actions in Operations Enduring Freedom and Iraqi Freedom.

Enemy forces conducting asymmetrical warfare going up against our numerical, logistical, and material superiority will employ targeting variation, tactical variation, and improvisation to which we must be prepared to respond. They mix it up and they adjust on the fly. Those are the enemy's tools of the trade. Well we are going to put you inside their heads; you are going to learn to think like them, you're going to anticipate their behaviors, and when you leave here and get out on missions you will implement these lessons you learn and you are going to bring your troops home alive.

The Sands Point estate had worthless security and plenty of it. Any minor Afghan official in local government had better odds of surviving an attack. Along the entire back side of the property, Morris Levy's private security service was allowing outside doors to be left open while armies of workers assembled the lavish arrangements for his birthday bash. Spencer reconnoitered across two days and nights tracking perimeter patrols that ran predictably once each hour, on the hour, with two uniformed guards touring around in a golf cart. He watched as caterers and florists were waived right through the huge front gates. No scrutiny. No concern for in-coming bags. But they *were* checking bags when the workers left.

The *New York Post* called the up-coming birthday bash "a bejeweled expression of over-the-top indulgence with no ingredients spared."

From the darkness inside the tree line, Spencer took one knee. His eyes followed the hundreds of guests in couture dresses and tuxedos arriving down fairytale pathways lit by thousands of tinkling white bulbs onto the lush acres of lawn.

Offshore, behind and to his right, the guests arriving by yacht were handing their pre-function champagne off to attendants and being helped into launches. Distinct constellations built up on the lawns, each surrounding one or two individuals who stood fixed, like suns, while the others orbited and vied to move closer in. More like moths than planets.

Spencer lifted the Remington MSR, scanning his surroundings through the scope, touching his index and middle fingers to the bolt. Spencer thought of Manchester United, the soccer kid in his Pumas. None of these fancy people inside his field of vision gave that any thought. *Further than Mars.*

A foot patrol was making three routine passes per hour, doing a ground-scan by Maglite. One by one, Spencer looked down the scope, sighting onto each position and running through the tight lateral shifts and elevations until each shift was automatic. Morris Levy was recognizable from the *Post* photo, a bald little man but fiercely erect like an aggressive featherweight fighter. Each of the "suns" took seats at tables close to him.

Emerson Elliot, the radio shock jock, started crooning "Blue Moon," but Spencer heard "Breathe, Relax, Aim, Slack, Squeeze." He centered himself calmly. *One. Two, Three. Four.* And then he was collecting casings and moving through the darkness, shouldering this weapon and pushing the matte dark wave runner off the sand. Pressing the electric start. Twice.

Seven thousand miles away, American soldiers were so happy if they had air conditioning or a piece of fresh fruit. Not being shot at or bombed, not closing your eyes and seeing the faces of dead friends and foes were the measures for a good day or a decent night. Bouncing northward across the dark water, he could already feel the adrenaline rush receding. It was only one action. History now, alongside a long history before.

While grunts slog and die, they throw parties. How many of them stole their private billions from public trillions? *Time to learn learn about blood and bone.*

*****

His knowledge, his preparation, his skills; in Afghanistan *he* took down 131 people and he never once saw anything in a newspaper or heard a radio report about it. But at least there was a debriefing. He found himself missing the meeting to review and assess. Media speculation everywhere; he couldn't shut it out, and yet none of it had anything right. No precision. Nobody who knew anything about the intricacies of planning and execution.

There it was. *You crossed the Rubicon. Done.* The strangest thing was how it felt normal, going right back to what he was trained for. He felt right about being 'home' for the first time in years.

Four dead billionaires. Soft targets. *Now vary the profile. Switch it up. Watch, listen, observe.*

*****

Rooks Bishop caught the breaking news within minutes after the first reports came in identifying Morris Levy. Just shy of a year into private consulting,

Bishop had learned to stay ahead of the curve. There was no project so he had no role, but he was already logging his timesheet and staying ahead of the curve. In his business, by the time the client called it was already too late to ramp up.

Four Jewish billionaires shot dead. By midnight, Bishop was listening to audio and breaking down sound patterns. Identical reports, none overlapping. *One shooter.* Close shot intervals, three-point-two seconds from first fire to last. Four shots, four kills.

By morning, two more curious pieces added to the mix. No shell casings. Professional shooter. That was different. Bishop pushed back his white Stetson and considered. All Jewish targets, but not Hamas or Hezbollah, not unless the Palestinians were retooling; nothing like their MO. That and no group claiming responsibility. *Neo-Nazi?*

Bishop had a pretty good idea that APA would be calling. He intended to be prepared. In consulting, you're either running fast right out of the blocks or you're backpedaling and defending your hourly fee. His was $550 per hour, gross. His bottom line net was leaned down considerably after he paid for golfing vacations and every manner of modest luxuries that his contacts inside government law enforcement could never afford.. These were his costs of doing business.

Twenty years inside government law enforcement, five with Texas state agencies. The Stetson had moved with him from Houston to federal roles with the DEA, FBI, ATF, DOJ and U.S. Marshals. Working with cooperating foreign agencies inside Mexico, Columbia, and Panama had him speaking pretty good street *Español*. The most successful cross-border interdiction effort in the nation had been his simple, efficient design.

Bishop had slashed overhead costs at the DEA and still he had cut deeply into the cartels. His network paid the working stiffs who actually moved the drugs a cut on every kilo they turned over to him. Many of his informants were able to get out of narco-trafficking thanks to the money he got to them from turning over a single big shipment. The traffickers weren't there for the lifestyle, not most of them; it was dangerous, unhealthy work. They were there for the money. Every six months or so the cartels cleaned house, killing everybody, and the cycle started all over again. Giving them a ticket out was saving lives.

The real backbreaker that took Bishop out of the game came down when Mexican officials who, corrupt up to their eyeballs, had threatened to legalize narcotics unless Washington shut down Bishop's whole operation.

He didn't blame leaving on any one individual or even that they collapsed his interdiction unit. Law enforcement had been hit by tectonic shifts everywhere. Efficacy didn't save programs; the system was seldom based on anything quite as logical as good work. Senior management was so afraid of looking their age that handed their budgets over to third-party technology contractors who were taking over the guts of U.S. government intelligence. Human intelligence budgets for investigation and interrogation and field informant relationships were being chopped to bits. Bishop's entire generation of professionals was pivoting to systems that they didn't understand and had no idea how to implement. DEA and ATF were pushing hard for more technological surveillance, as though slinging cash at drones and GPS and monitoring emails and phone calls would hygienically replace the realities of a very dirty business.

It was time to get out.

He wore the Stetson into FBI headquarters for the briefing following the murders on Long Island. The postcards reading "I Kill Rich People" had brought out a who's-who of law enforcement heavyweights, including several former government men who were now private consultants.

Nobody in the room mentioned class warfare out loud. Nobody had to. The entire focus of the meeting was on framing the story and media response. A pretty boy FBI Special Agent was framing the media package when the text from Americans for Patriotic Action, APA, came through to Bishop, who drew glances by saying "yes" and loudly slapping his thigh.

He was in.

Bishop knew to come in prepared to back up everything he said with facts, dates, and defensible data. Carlton Jeffers didn't suffer fools. He looked for clarity and brevity. Jeffers, Yale Class of '76, had taken Americans for Patriotic Action over the past twenty years from a richly-endowed organization of conservative academics and built it into the single most powerful public-private alliance in the world.

Congressmen, senators, K-Street lobbyists, and more than one thousand of America's most powerful business leaders were included in APA membership. The airport nearest APA's monthly Visions Partnership meetings was entirely redesigned to support the attendees' private jet fleet.

Jeffers projected the file from his desktop onto the wall behind his desk when Bishop was ushered into his office. Bishop looked at the two low-backed dark red leather chairs in from of Jeffer's broad desk but read standing up when Jeffers ignored his presence. His fingers continued to tear across his keyboard while Bishop studied the polling data he had up on the office wall.

Bishop had learned a lot since he first set up his login and created his "vendor identity" on the secure website. APA was nowhere to be seen, not in the cover page and not in any link he drilled down into. He had to go on faith; that and the $49,500 retainer that kick-started their client-consultant relationship. Two-weeks, billable at forty-five hours per week, to identify the shooter or shooters. He entered his Social Security number, Maryland Driver's License, Blue Shield medical information, six references, full-time employment since college, his current address, and prior addresses for the past ten years.

"Forty-four percent of respondents call these attacks 'Somewhat Justified,'

'Justified,' or 'Highly Justified,'" Jeffers snarled without looking up. "Forty-four percent!

"Once these slogans go viral, you probably have no idea how much input it takes to tame them," Jeffers grumbled. "I coordinated the simultaneous law enforcement and media sweep that had sent the Occupy movement into history. But 'we are the ninety-nine percent' is still burrowed into the lexicon like a damned tick."

There wasn't any real fallout from major intelligence catastrophes; newspapers ran headlines, but the stories had no shelf life; they grew boring and stale overnight. Nobody lost jobs. No programs were curtailed. Everything went right back to business as usual. But a good sound bite sticks!

"For twenty years I've been crafting positive imagery for America's job creators. Now this "I Kill Rich People" is polling at forty-four percent!

What do you think?" Jeffers asked, finally training his piercing stare on Bishop's hat.

"Single perpetrator," Bishop answered. "There's nothing indicating this modus operandi at FBI. Interpol has three Chechen snipers they're tracking, all single-target attacks. No correlation."

Jeffers' eyes shifted opposite Bishop's. "Don't tell me what he's not," Jeffers admonished. "Tell me what he is."

"I reviewed the recordings. Single weapon. Four kills with four shots in three-point-two seconds. Studied and understood the area. In and out cleanly.

"He's lean, efficient, and professional. Betting odds say he's done it before. Best guess, military sniper."

"How many?" Jeffers responded.

"Snipers? Twelve hundred a year qualify across all branches."

While Bishop did the math in his head, Jeffers held down a key on his telephone. "Get Don Chambers on the phone," he barked.

"I'm sorry, but I'm not seeing any listing for a Don Chambers," a female voice replied.

"Call the Joint Chiefs," Jeffers snapped at her. "Tell them I said to find General Chambers and you make sure they say I'm on the line. Then conference him in."

Bishop removed his Stetson and waved it slowly above his head to get Jeffers' attention. U.S. Forces trained hundreds more snipers from a dozen countries, plus police forces trained thousands more, and then there were Israelis and Russians and Brits and the whole international scene to consider.

Jeffers leaned back and considered. NSA and DOD would be where to start. Bishop knew exactly what he was thinking. Stephen Nussbaum. Nussbaum could boil down the numbers.

"Sweep your calendar," Jeffers ordered Bishop. "Whatever NYPD or FBI or Nassau County PD or any other law enforcement agency thinks, knows, or does, you plug yourself into that loop and report back."

"Find out what's behind it and you could find the shooter," Bishop suggested.

The look on Jeffers' pursed mouth spoke to the foolish remark. Jeffers had already conferred with NSA resources to probe for any and all targeted violence coming out of extremist groups. He was about to add to that to search out every intersection with trained military snipers.

Forensic accountants consulting for APA were concurrently pouring through stock market trades and private equity activities. First thing he did was follow the money. Four Wall Street billionaires dead... somebody somewhere was making a fortune.

Bishop kept standing with both sets of fingers holding onto his hat brim. Jeffers had returned his attention to his monitor. He seemed unaware that Bishop remained in the room.

Bishop waited through a long pause then turned to the door. Before he reached for the handle, he turned back. "Mr. Jeffers?" he asked.

Jeffers typed a quick sentence then raised his face.

"He's a doer, not a talker," Bishop explained. "He'll do it again."

Jeffers looked up, craned his head, thinking. "Which do you like more," he asked. "'We won the Cold War. This President is giving it right back' or 'We are entering the next Cold War. This President is letting it happen'?"

Bishop considered the choices then realized he couldn't remember the difference. "Can you repeat them?"

"'We won the Cold War. This President is giving it right back' or 'We are entering the next Cold War. This President is letting it happen,'" Jeffers repeated.

"How about this," Bishop suggested. "'We are the strongest nation on Earth. Why does this President let Russia and China push us around?'"

Jeffers shook his head. Negative. Can't name Russia and China. And too many words. He never looked back up and offered no response to Bishop, who stood waiting and then left the room quietly.

*****

Thinking of the first time he saw Stephen Nussbaum, Bishop had to chuckle. Bishop wondered how Jeffers had let the whole thing happen, but of course he could never ask.

Stephen had to have been the strangest geek ever to present at Vision Partners. He had jumped up onto the stage in those skinny bright red jeans, shoved the podium out of his way, and zipped straight into his shtick without waiting for any introduction. This wasn't TED Talks; this was Vision Partners at their semi-annual retreat; Fortune 100, Right-to-Life, and the deepest political pockets on the planet. Part strategic conference, part fundraiser, with fly-rods, cigars, and gun-packing butlers serving each billionaire's drink of choice.

"Gentlemen, I want you to close your eyes," Red Pants asked men who kept one eye open in church on Sunday.

"Come on, close your eyes. Now think about your home. It's Christmastime. Tree looks perfect, surrounded with presents, and every bulb and light is perfect. Now imagine that you have a beautiful fourteen-year-old girl. She is in her plaid skirt and her white school blouse and her little breasts are beginning to show. She is down on her knees beside the presents. She looks up as you walk into the room. Imagine her glossy young lips; they're now spread, but she doesn't say anything. She can't, not with her mouth wrapped around that huge black cock! Oh, and your wife has walked in on this scene. She stands there looking, saying nothing, and you look over to her, and she looks so intensely jealous."

Bishop shook his head and laughed aloud recalling the range from disbelief to outrage out of the Vision Partners. It looked like Nussbaum wouldn't make it out alive.

"I am not here to offer what you want to hear!" Red Pants shouted. "I am here to disrupt, deconstruct, and disentangle outmoded visions. Get you up off your fat wallets and excite some big free-swinging dicks!"

He rapped along like confidentiality was one more meaningless, outmoded concept and he was about to prove it. Stephen had balls. He asked the Partners to think of an American city and raise their hands. The member he picked chose Cleveland. Cleveland instantly appeared on the wall behind him. He waived his hand in the air and a cursor followed his gestures on the map. He stopped at an arbitrary point, clicked, and spread his hands, running out to wide radius right over the center of the city, and then snapped his finger at the circle. The map populated with hundreds upon hundreds of overlapping black camera icons. His tone changed. No longer the irreverent buffoon, he narrated a vision that not one Partner could ignore.

"Gentlemen," he instructed, "these icons represent the video camera feeds running right now from approximately a one mile radius from this point." He pulled down a menu and stopped at "Count." "There are 1,859 live feeds coming from this area. I know this because the bandwidth demands from streaming video draws a very specific web signature. These cameras include public traffic cameras, business feeds, home security, personal web cams, police units, and more."

The Vision Partners giggled, choked, and were appalled and enthralled in equal measure. He delivered a digital map of every movement one member had made during the prior week, from locations across his home town to flights on his private jet and every spot where he had used his cell phone, his credit cards, and his ATM. He showed, in real-time, the whole route as another Partner's sixteen-year-old son drove Dad's new Porsche without permission. In the street cams, the kid's face behind the wheel was clear as day.

Stephen splashed the logo of a publicly-traded company on the wall, and then embarrassed its CEO by showing the audience how eleven percent of paid employee time was being spent on social media and pornography.

Before exiting the stage, he held up his Smartphone to show his own view looking back at the Vision Partners looking on the wall just like they were appearing on the big screen at a sports stadium. He swept his arm through the air and, just like magic, the names of every person on the screen tagged instantly onto their pictures. He had all those titans of American industry eating out of his hand.

He never did give his name, his company, or anything else. Never handed out a business card. Just vanished, leaving every Partner in the room asking who the hell that guy was and how could they get hold of him. Most brilliant marketing Bishop had ever seen. He was pretty certain that most of the technology was proprietary and confidential, but it didn't take much time being around APA and Vision Partners before distinctions like national security secrecy dissolved away.

At the presenter's luncheon afterward, Stephen scaled back to size, but his insights were no less piercing.

"I wouldn't say that you have no value," he conceded to Bishop, "only that you won't *be valued*." Human intelligence is "distributive," Stephen argued. "It's a budget suck from hire to grave.

"Smart money will continue to flow to technology," he predicted. "Tech expenditure focuses large contract budgets, which leads to A++ bankable income streams, which leads to the big payday. It's all about the numbers; the liquidity event, IPO, or a straight buyout doesn't matter as long as it drives eight or nine figures to the top."

That one succinct paragraph summarized why Bishop had jumped to the private sector.

Stephen later explained when they were one-on-one, how "we have millions of cameras that are operating in the Cloud right now and more coming online every minute. Millions of cameras that together, used in aggregate, offer power we can harness and utilize both commercially and politically. Single cameras, just like one set of eyes, represent the past. The volume of data that up to twenty years ago might take a lifetime to collect we can now gather, and parse, within a nano-second. Soon we will literally be able to pick out one grain of sand from an entire beach or one person from all of Planet Earth. We have the capacity to fly cameras in the troposphere eight miles above the surface of the planet—that's 10,000 feet above the height of Mount Everest—and pick out specific individuals. In less than four seconds, we can identify 90,000 people in a packed football stadium and find one specific person in his seat."

Until he had met and collaborated on consulting projects beside Stephen, Bishop was quick to dismiss technology. He recognized now that he found it threatening and he could even admit as much, after three drinks. Technology wasn't ever going to replace human intelligence; instincts and hunches and the read on the other guy's face weren't going away. But couple that with what Stephen could bring to the table and together they could toss a wide net that not much was going to get through. Bishop prepared a proposal and directed the encrypted file to Stephen Nussbaum's secure website, then texted Stephen to look at the message. He sent the text and he hoped, number one, that Nussbaum was at least somewhere in North America and, number two, that his time could be had.

*****

The forensic accounting produced nothing. No windfall Wall Street trades driven by any of the deaths. No mergers or acquisitions. None of the thousand names left on the list of trained snipers correlated to significant lump sums going into accounts.

Bishop made discreet contacts with his North Carolina resources in the world of private security contractors. Nothing there. Again shooting blanks. Every one of these contractors knew angry, capable men, except that none of them would supply names. But the calls produced at least one key ancillary value that Bishop noted. Demand for ex-military personnel for private contracting had fallen so severely that skilled individuals and experienced squads were begging for work. He could turn out six-dozen mission-ready contractors in a day, every one of them ex-Special Forces. Long-haul carriers and an entire fleet of helicopters were sitting in hangars. Wire the funds and they would be airborne.

Stephen rejected the assignment as unmanageable, plus he was overbooked with current engagements. Then Jeffers offered him something that made Stephen do a one-eighty. Bishop didn't know what it was, but it made Stephen sit right down and started his fingers flying across a borrowed keyboard.

Later on, Bishop learned that Stephen was setting up filters and routing internal chatter coming through NSA. NSA filters were pulling data from the Defense Department, FBI, CIA, ATF, and fifteen other agencies. Jeffers offered to set Stephen up with a backdoor key.

Then everything changed, including Bishop's contract. The shooter hit Central Park West. Central Park West hit home; the shootings trumped every other focus. Every APA member was tripling his personal security measures; for Jeffers, hiring Bishop became automatic.

Jeffers was forced to cancel the Vision Partners upcoming directors meeting. He had no choice, no matter how much flak he expected to take. Two-thirds of the most solid attending contributors, his reliable core, suddenly had scheduling conflicts. Central Park West wasn't Long Island; this was ground zero, way too close to home. The Vision Partners were either hunkering down or making distance; men who hadn't taken vacations since their college Spring Breaks suddenly were taking their families to Antarctica and the Ngorongoro Crater.

Carlton Jeffers struggled to capture daily talking points that seemed to strike the right tone. "War on Job Creators" polled a weak 21 percent response. That was the top number from nine taglines that made the overnight cut. He couldn't very well say nothing at all, but any direct reference to the killer or to the attacks circled right back to income inequality. Meanwhile, Emerson Elliot was on the radio in national syndication with 'Bullets for Billionaires'.

Jeffers wanted to do more than just turn his radio dial. Carlton Jeffers was accustomed to leading the discourse. Across two decades, he had carefully crafted and shaped the political conversation. Every day, his prepared talking points went out across the nation. Now, his own panicked wife wanted to get out of New York. At APA, he was taking calls from irate major donors wanting Emerson Elliot's tongue cut out. If Emerson Elliot got to exercise his First Amendment, Jeffers wished for somebody to step up and exercise the Second Amendment with Elliot that target.

"We are adding a new segment today, listeners. I'm calling it the 'You Can't Take It With You Dead Billionaires Club.' Current New York City count is seven billionaires down, with eighteen billion between them, and sixty-one billionaires to go. Yeah yeah yeah… I know, these guys are all philanthropists. There's the Anthony Parrish hall at MOMA and Morris Levy has wing at Mount Sinai. Boring! Callers, if you want to call in with sob stories, don't cry about dead guys with four hundred thousand-acre ranches or their own private islands," Elliot said.

"Let me tell you about Charles Dubois. This guy had his own Caribbean Island, right, and the place was set up for Armageddon. We're talking wind and solar power, hydroponic food gardening, and enough wines for like the next hundred years. Now get this… the guy has wind and solar power for himself, but he made his fortune in oil and gave big bucks to Vision Partners to crush everything competing with Big Oil. Call in and tell us what you think of this hypocrite!"

Every segment of Emerson Elliot's program kept chipping and eroding his life's achievement at the helm of Americans for Patriotic Action and he had nothing. "Jesus fucking Christ," he howled.

"Get me the Attorney General," Jeffers shouted at his admin. "I'm putting a stop to that sonofabitch!"

*****

Copycat crazies seemed to be popping up in a dozen places and the world's most sophisticated police forces were playing a game of Whack-a-Mole with nothing to go on except size thirteen shoes.

Nussbaum couldn't correlate size thirteen to any of the names because nobody except the Belgians kept a digital record of the shoe sizes of their individual soldiers. Nine percent of American soldiers since 2000 wore size thirteen, up from an average of only five percent during the period from 1950 through 1999. *A lot of good that did.*

Bishop followed the talk radio angle because Jeffers was obsessed. Limbaugh and Hannity banged away at how "the present administration is so against job creators they're letting this happen!" but Emerson Elliot held the traction.

Stephen wasn't interested. Technology had displaced politics and only the politicians failed to notice. Talk radio was a distraction for the masses.

Nussbaum had applied his software to scan every digital record for repeat visuals to show a face, a physique, anything appearing in each vicinity. Nada, zip, donut. From Sands Point to Sag Harbor to the Central Park West attacks, the only evident correlations were wealthy victims and a single sniper. One in the burbs, one nearly out to the Hamptons, and then the next right above Central Park. Two nighttime attacks, one daytime.

"I refuse to worry about deliverables," Stephen remarked to Bishop. "Thousands of law enforcement people from a couple dozen agencies haven't produced squat."

"That's OK for you," Bishop countered. "You tech guys are in good shape for the next twenty years. Guys like me are going to be bleached bones out in the desert." Bishop could not even confirm for Jeffers that it was the same shooter each time.

Stephen looked over at Bishop's downcast face. Bishop's fresh whiskers were white. They had been brainstorming until past ten at night, talking through motives and goals, analyzing the shooter's target selection and details from each attack.

"We have our own problems," Stephen responded. "Your world is gated by pre-requisite career experience in law enforcement; I'm only as good as the next Russian or Korean or Chinese whiz kid coming out of the woodwork."

*****

Look over this fortified structure. Get to know it. We have twenty infantrymen outside supported by an armed transport with a turret-mounted M240. We have a twelve man security unit inside and you cannot identify their habits or positions from exterior observation. We have concrete vehicle barriers, a forward checkpoint and a secondary one. We have motion-sensors, infra-red heat sensors, sound triangulation to instantly locate the firing position of any shooters. You are the enemy. You have a six-man squad armed with AKs, RPGs, and grenades. Your mission is to penetrate, locate and assassinate two senior officials, kill them both and inflict maximum damage. You have moles inside supplying basic intel, but not trained for armed support. Where are we vulnerable? Each of you has thirty minutes to set a preliminary tactical plan. Begin.

Spencer debriefed himself. He was his own worst critic, as usual. Police units had closed on his position inside four minutes. Spencer suspected sound-monitors and confirmed his hunch from reading the newspaper the next day. They had to have used the monitors to triangulate onto his position. How else could they have moved in so fast?

From his fallback location, he watched their forensic teams scouring the rooftop. He had all his casings. They had his footprints. Through his scope he saw them photographing and casting molds under their portable halogen lighting.

"Better target selection moving forward," he admonished himself. No more rooftops. But the reaction to his attack on Central Park West had shaken the rich to their core. They couldn't protect against attacks to their category. They couldn't hide.

"They know they're vulnerable, Captain," he said aloud. He had accomplished that much. Maybe he had taken out some of the eighty-five people who owned more wealth than three billion of the poorest people on the planet. He hoped so. It would have helped to have a list, but he couldn't find the names anywhere.

Captain Sam dreamed of a viral reaction, but Spencer kept his feet on the ground. Other people might not follow his lead, but what rich person wouldn't be looking over his shoulder, paranoid at every sound?

Spencer stuck his Baretta semi-automatic behind his belt and rode the number-two subway line to Wall Street, then he stood for an hour fifty feet from the door to the Stock Exchange. Tourists photographed the bronze bull and pointed to the ticker sign. But none of the people rushing in and out with their plastic clip-on badges looked rich; every one of them looked late for a meeting with somebody a lot more important than they were.

After giving up on the NYSE, he went around the corner and stood in line at Starbucks. He ordered a drip coffee and a bagel and had them in a seat by the window.

The immediate problem was that the targets were drying up. There was nothing obvious left in the *Times* or the *Post*; no more galas in the city, no more royal birthdays in the Hamptons. He scanned Yelp and TripAdvisor for expensive restaurants, but then he didn't want to shoot down some regular family out going out somewhere fancy to celebrate a birthday.

Do you attack one at a time, he asked himself? Each time he did that would ramp up exposure for diminishing returns. So where do you find super rich people who are laying low? Where do rich people go that regular people don't?

The auction house attack added a new layer: until then each victim was American. He liked bringing the listening device into play; wiring the bouquet to generate his own intel may not have equated to military satellite photos and live drone feeds he often reviewed on missions in Afghanistan, yet it was satisfying. He liked that he had originated the idea on his own.

CHAPTER FIVE

You call in artillery or air and you eliminate the enemy without exposing your squad. But you also kill the twenty non-combatants inside this compound and who knows what shit storm hits after the dead baby photos go online. So you put yourself and your men into harm's way. In this exercise you will take on your instructors. You will formulate and execute upon the techniques we worked on to eliminate your targets, minimize collateral damage, and bring your men home in one piece.

Spencer felt the urge to go back to the scene of the crime. There was no upside to it; he knew that it was cocky, but he walked through Straus Park just a few blocks away from Central Park West, taking unnecessary risks while knowing better. He was off-routine and missing his edge. Everywhere he went, he expected an ambush that didn't come. Sending the microphone into the auction house then ambushing targets in the daytime right in the center of the city left him addled in the opposite direction, hyped with adrenalin.

He went up to an old man seated on a concrete bench and initiated the conversation. The man's white cane drew him in.

The man knew about the killings. "Lots of angry people out there," the man said simply. He thought it was sad.

Spencer returned to the room he rented, tingling along his scalp and into his fingertips. Walking in the open left him surging even more, filling him with the dangerous illusion that nobody and nothing could stop him. The serotonins spoke to invincibility; was he on a mission from God?

He needed to run. Miles and miles, away from people, in rocks and mountains where the terrain demanded that he feel himself, where he could demand of himself, where he could forget himself. He was a gambler on a hot roll. If that feeling continued, it could only end one way. The awesome neurochemical highs would get him killed.

He moved places again. He'd done that twice already, each time into cheap sub-par accommodations that even in New York were too basic to attract anyone looking longer-term. No kitchens, no insulation, no questions. Right after his conversation with the blind man, he moved again, taking himself out of the city, where he found a trailer that had been towed for the last time sitting on blocks inside a trailer park advertising hot showers, a coin-operated laundry, and free Wi-Fi.

Two radios. A police band. A standard AM/FM.

"Emerson, let's get real here. America has been battling over the size of government and tax policies since John Adams and Alexander Hamilton and Thomas Jefferson. There is nothing new about the debates. What is new is a government purposely kept from governing because paralysis strategically benefits the Kochs and their rich buddies. What is new is a Supreme Court that calls corporations 'people' and tells big money that it is OK to buy out our political system. What is new are police forces that look and act just like the army, carrying machine guns and using tanks on city streets. What is new is an America where the standard of living for our children and our grandchildren will never match how we are living right now!" Elliot Emerson said on the radio.

"Emerson, what other means do we have to fight these trends, you ask? The noose is tightening, man! They have our emails, our phone calls, our web searches. Come on! We need to wake up! This isn't Democrat versus Republican; this is a handful of billionaires and the system they built coming in and ripping off everybody. Everybody.

"At the risk of preaching to the choir, I say we need to get some perspective. When we rise against the one-in-ten-thousand to protect our democracy. That's not a revolution. That's a mild solution."

Spencer turned the radio off and leaned back in the dark. "It's one radio station," he told himself, but the rush continued to surge through his veins.

No one alive was invincible. "Not the billionaires and not you," he told himself in the small mirror over the sink.

Strategies were breaking down. Momentarily, he weighed momentum against risk, and then shook his head. "It ends in death. It always does."

Target options had shut down completely; where at first he was able to select from charity breakfasts, brunches, luncheons, cocktail parties, dinners, and late-night art and fashion events, the effect of his actions had taken away nearly every option.

He scoured through the online calendars again, looking at any event set for high net-worth investors while knowing full well that security would be through the roof.

The event he picked was in Mamaroneck, six miles away. Mamaroneck felt right; the technical demands engaged him in a way that was familiar and comfortable, taking his mind away from neurochemistry and mortality, from radio stations and celebrity. Mamaroneck was all about planning and execution, shots from distance that demanded attention to detail; the targets were subordinated behind the complex equations inherent to long-distance fire.

He was also determined to up his count; balanced judgment was telling him that he would never get to 131 otherwise. Higher kills per attack offered greater potential longevity than higher mission-counts. Besides that reality, there were fewer and fewer available targets. For eight, he needed the semi-automatic

M110; faster than the Remington bolt-action. Combined with 850 yards over open water, eight was a worthwhile challenge even for the best snipers Harmony Church had ever put out. After the third or fourth shot, targets would not be static. They would be reacting, which meant adding movement to the equation. To get eight, he would fire at opportunities and not specific target identities. He wouldn't be counting; unload the fifteen-shot magazine and get out. He had to get the actual count from the newspapers.

*****

Perfect position: flat soft ground, well hidden behind a vacant house up for sale. Multiple egress options, perfect conditions: no wind, moderate temperatures diminishing thermal lift. *Eight.*

Two-man buddy configurations on security, four stationary, two patrolled the grounds. Two more private security guards in static placement on the rooftop. Binoculars, no night-vision. No rifles. Walkie-talkies and semis on their hips, probably 9mm.

He counted the car emblems as guests arrived, pulling up in their Mercedes and Ferraris and Maybachs, handing keys to twenty-year-olds rushing up in red valet vests. A hissing noise distracted his attention. He saw the source; automatic drip sprinklers had cycled on. A circular cascade began soaking his left leg and shoe.

One BRASS. Center forehead. Two BRASS, again center forehead. Three BRASS blonde, temple… wig! Four BRASS through pearl earring below ear. Five BRASS. Six. Argg! The spotlight sweep hit through his scope, exploding the green clarity like a ray gun directing 225 lumens directly into his retina. He blindly patted the soil, automatically reaching out to collect his shells. His flight instinct stretched out, contracting based on training alone; the light came off the water. Police boat. He was using a suppressor. Camouflage. They could not have seen him.

Pulse up to 150. Breathe. He estimated fifty seconds getting from fire-position onto the motorcycle. He didn't look at his watch. No point. It was what it was. Let the spotlight go, he told himself. Helicopters would not get there any faster. *Breathe.* He knew the route. Even driving with one eye open, he'd be through the suburban streets of huge lots and onto the freeway in less than two minutes. South, then west and five more minutes to the trailer park.

He pushed the cycle out to the street. Siren. Fire engine in the distance. He started the engine. Rushmore to Bleeker. No lights. His pulse was coming down, but the right eye was fucked. Left turn. Alongside golf course. Turning onto Eagle Knolls, the bike felt part of him, not a foreign object. He was getting it together. Accelerating. Just when the car pulled out from nowhere.

A deep three-inch blood-spitting gash sopped his pants leg and filled his shoe. Blood. DNA. The military had a complete DNA record for every soldier serving since 1992. If they had the blood, they would get his identity.

Could be that the world was about to find out who he was and there nothing he could do to stop it.

He wanted to call Jack. Try to explain himself before the shit hit the fan. But after icing the calf wound and pressing a thick needle through both sides six times to sew it shut tight, then moving eleven miles to his fallback site.

Relocate. Now. Tonight. Shave the head; let the facial hair grow out.

What he needed was sleep.

*****

Blood samples. Stephen Nussbaum reported to Jeffers that a single-vehicle accident happened in Mamaroneck just after the attack. NSA forensics had worked the scene, collected evidence, and then scrubbed it clean. Bishop and Nussbaum came to Jeffers office to report in person with the lab results; Stephen had quietly added one additional recipient to NSA's automatic report distribution, a dummy forward made to appear internal to NSA.

Bishop reached the file folder out from behind his hat and handed Jeffers photos showing an oval blood pool measuring 11.375 inches plus a thick drip pattern measuring sixty-five inches. Bishop leaned over, stretching until Jeffers looked him away, then stepped back to point out the blood and the motorcycle paint scraped over the pavement that were both circled on the photo.

"At least one significant wound from the look of it, but he still had the strength to stand the motorcycle back up and ride it away." Looking at Jeffers, Bishop thought it important to point out that riding the motorcycle takes use of a right hand and right leg at the bare minimum. Before Jeffers' next question, Bishop jumped ahead and answered. "We pulled all hospitals and emergency medical clinics. No walk-ins, no ER visits that night or yesterday."

Stephen looked over at Bishop, his eyes narrowed angrily.

Bishop glanced back to Stephen, shrugged his shoulders, made an empty gesture with his hands, and then continued. What? He had said "we," not "I."

"Jonathan Spencer, ex-military," Bishop reported. "DNA confirmation from Defense Department record for Mamaroneck and confirmed for Central Park West by shoe prints taken from Mamaroneck."

"For whom is he working?" Jeffers demanded.

"We're onto that now," Stephen responded, getting himself back into the game. "After military service we've got no credit card purchases, no ATM activity, and no cell phone account. We are running facial identification on all social media and trolling all emails referencing Jonathan Spencer, John Spencer, J. Spencer, and MSJS, his only known nickname. No hits yet."

Bishop handed Jeffers the DOD personnel file. "Consistent with deep cover," Bishop interjected, pushing himself back in.

"No. Just on the surface. Way too many anomalies when you look deeper," Stephen disagreed. He handed another printout over to Jeffers, who put it aside. Jeffers' rapt attention poured into page upon page of military training qualifications, individual and unit citations, mission summaries, and C.O. reviews. Reading "a soldier's soldier" and "most dedicated NCO in this entire division" had Jeffers eyes squinting. Bronze stars and multiple purple hearts changed Jeffers' complexion to purple.

"Two Experian credit reports were run on him," Stephen continued, "both for rentals at New York City addresses. You have them, right there, along with a third address tied to a Harley Davidson motorcycle that was registered in his name less than two months ago. He continues to have current motorcycle insurance at that same Bronx address."

"Why's he doing it?" Bishop wondered aloud. "What makes a soldier so elite that he is a star within the elite, a one-in-ten-thousand soldier, do this?"

"Get the sonofabitch!" Jeffers barked. "Give me results, not analysis. IKRP has already absorbed too much time and energy. Every Vision Partners board member is lecturing me, especially the brothers!"

He stared at the piercing blue eyes and earnest military bearing staring back from the photo on the page in front of him. "It stops now!" he ordered Bishop. "I'm making the call. We bury that DNA. You bury this bastard. You make sure his fifteen minutes of fame are over," Jeffers said to the photo.

"At the risk of talking myself out of work, why would you get involved? What's the upside?" Bishop warned.

Stephen looked to Bishop for guidance, as though something Jeffers had said was unclear. Bishop nodded toward the door and Stephen ran out in a flash, only too relieved to take the hint.

"Nussbaum is a technology guy," Bishop told Jeffers. "They like to think their hands are clean."

"You don't get it!" Jeffers shouted at Bishop. A drop of his spit landed on Bishop's lower lip.

"Control the messaging and we control America. Every single day, I'm the guy who tells half this country what to talk about. Every day, I sift through pages of options to find that right sound bite and get it in front of the voices that matter. I like what I do; I'm not giving anyone an excuse to replace me. So I'm going to pick up this phone and tell the Chairman of the House Intelligence Committee what we're doing. He'll be glad to hear it, too," Jeffers said.

He glared ahead. "I'm not sitting back to watch this play out as 'Captain America fighting income inequality.' Rangers, Special Forces, Airborne.

"I didn't obliterate Occupy Wall Street nationwide in one night to lose every inch of territory to this character. I own the message. I spent twenty years of my life crafting it! *Red versus Blue, real Americans versus all the rest.* I'm not losing that message so this country divides into Vision Partners versus the mob. Nobody is going to tweet his name. No Facebook. Alan Dershowitz and Gloria Allred are never going to swoop in to represent this piece of shit. This 'Rambo' is never going to go viral. Not on my watch. I'm going to make this Spencer disappear."

Jeffers crumpled Spencer's profile and gazed out a window. "This sonofabitch doesn't look anything like that," he imagined aloud. "I see somebody else. As different as night and day."

*****

Covered from head-to-toe in black SWAT gear, Bishop's North Carolina squads hit in one synchronized simultaneous assault. Stephen linked Bishop online to the Bronx, Murray Hill, and Great Kills on Staten Island, each of the locations tied to Master Sergeant Jonathan Spencer. The screen image looked part video game, part reality TV.

Bishop watched alone, sitting on the edge of his seat as the front man from single-file snake formation smashed front doors. The cameras jostled through dark and light, distributing down hallways and into rooms, fanning through the buildings. Bishop could not distinguish one two-man squad from another, each with a front man running attack, his partner covering security behind them.

Each had the face in the photos committed to memory. Their orders were succinct. "Bin Laden": make no attempt to capture. *Kill him and everyone connected to him. Secure the remains. Return to rendezvous.*

From start to finish, all three were in, done, and out again inside ninety seconds, but afterward Bishop leaned back in his chair exhausted. He pushed his Stetson nearly vertical then let both arms hang down at his sides. Hitting a door himself would have been easier than watching the Go Pros on all those locations. *Empty.*

On top of the tension, he added a $90,000 failure. He was back to square one with zero deliverables. Nothing to give Jeffers except a $90K invoice.

*****

Slivers from the motorcycle mirror stabbed inside the wound. Spencer had his pants off and a brown towel over the floor to catch the free-flowing blood pouring from his leg. A mail slot-sized gap flapped open where he yanked out the broken mirror. His trailer was getting marked and stained everywhere he touched. A smudged red handprint ringed the neck of his bedside lamp. He threw the shade aside and tried to bring the hot bare bulb close enough to see inside when he spread the wound, but it filled with blood again before he could spot the remaining shards. He unscrewed the top from the bottle of rubbing alcohol then punched it up onto his tooth to break the seal. A bitter, awful splash entered the corner of his mouth; Spencer stretched his tongue out and grimaced, then poured the alcohol liberally directly into the gash.

He pushed the needle in deeply then used the bottom of his water glass to press it two-thirds of an inch through to the other side. After each of the six stitches, he cinched the sutures tight. The shards remained inside, but the bleeding slowed to a cycle of drips. Each droplet grew bigger until it broke away and ran a line down to his ankle. He waited an hour for it to coagulate and crust over. It still felt like the needle was inside. That pain was the fair result for messing up. Bleeding, riding a cracked-up motorcycle for six miles with a M110 strapped across his back; a mistake.

Spencer lined the M110 and the smaller Heckler & Koch, both semi-automatic, along the trailer wall then reached underneath the bed and brought back a gym bag, which he upended onto the comforter in a cascade of empty clips and sealed ammunition boxes. One by one, he loaded by feel, separating the cartridges in his fist, rolling them down to the center of his palm, thumbing onto the clip spring. He had to hunker down. He traced his path through the trailer park layout in his mind, both lanes coming in and out. The back fence abutted a housing development. The other side was just a parking lot away from open space. But he was thinking purely out of habit. He wasn't getting away. You could shoot through the trailer walls with a .22; he had nothing to barricade behind. Besides, he didn't do this to kill cops; the guns had just one real purpose. He doubted that police would try to arrest him, but with an HK pointing at them, they wouldn't try for more than a split second before it would be over.

After loading both semis, he opened the small closet and reached for the soft carry bag, unzipped it, and slowly withdrew his Barrett. He caressed his hands down its tan length and wondered: had he made any difference? Was anything changed, or would the society parties start right up again after he was dead? Was even one vet going to get a fair shake because of what he had done?

He wished he could write something, say the right thing to make people get it, make them see that oligarchs are the enemy everywhere. The rich were never going to back down except when they had no choice! A few deaths now was better than chaos, better than war and strife and everything falling apart when it was too late to do anything.

Captain Sam, you should be here. You'd know the right words to say. Exhausted, he flopped back onto the mattress and concentrated on his breath, nothing else, until the neurochemistry of tension gave way to sleep.

At first light Spencer awakened with the weight of his Barrett crosswise over his lap. He peeked through the curtains. The only things moving were a squirrel and the liter-bottles fashioned into whirligigs on the next trailer twirling into the breeze.

It was luck, pure and simple, that got him out of there after the crash. Now he was going to need more luck to come. In his fast departure he knew he had left behind tire tracks in the flowerbed at the vacant house. Crime investigators were going to figure out the line of fire. They would find the house and they'd find the tracks, too, unless maybe the sprinklers soaked them away. He stood up to pull on pants and get a look at his bike, and then grimaced; the ankle and knee had swollen up to twice their size. The Harley and everything else was going to have to wait.

*****

You need to get from Point A to Point B in bandit territory to provide ground support to the patrol taking sustained fire and pinned down at B. You have limited drone and sat time for surveillance and you need to deploy these for maximum result. Using the topographical maps, intel photos, and your knowledge of enemy objectives, force strength, weaponry and tactics, make use of the resources available to you and get your men through there in one piece. Gather additional intel, assemble your mission plan, and be ready to execute upon it in real time conditions. You have fifty minutes. Begin.

"That is my family," Jeffers growled at Bishop and Stephen after the attack on the Arcadia.

Bishop leaned in to catch Jeffers' words. His voice sounded like the low rumbling of a volcano. "My family!"

His mother, his wife, son, and daughter-in-law carrying his five-month-old grandson all had been aboard the yacht.

"This isn't theoretical," Jeffers shouted. "It's not polling numbers and surveys. My son pressed himself over our women as a human shield. My son! That's a hero, not that maniac! I ought to put a bullet in that fucking Emerson Elliot myself!"

"At least no one was hurt, thank God," Bishop offered lamely.

"No thanks to you."

Carlton Jeffers was a lifelong member of the Twenty-Fives. It was through that membership that his role in Americans for Patriotic Action originated.

Jeffers was watching the green water from the top deck of the 120-foot yacht, the Arcadia, bathed in warm sunshine on a glorious bright day with four generations of his family within earshot when the bullets started to fly.

"I want an explanation as to precisely what the fuck are you two doing?" Jeffers demanded.

That word, "fuck," was part of Bishop's daily vernacular, but hearing it coming from Jeffers mouth was startling. Bishop had already billed enough to float him for months, but he had to impress APA, to not drop the ball his first time out. Here was his chance to come through for his daughter, to get her through any college she chose, to be a provider. No matter what poison his ex-wife had put into her head. This was his chance to show that he was a good father.

That was real. APA and Vision Partners meant educating his girl. It was that simple.

Bishop had had the name, photos, and addresses for weeks, but had found nothing.

"Its thirty miles up the Hudson," Stephen argued. "I can't highjack cameras that don't exist. There's only New York State Department of Environmental Conservation underwater fishery feeds up there. Not even the DOD monitors beyond the riverfront at West Point."

"I have six men following active leads 24/7," Bishop asserted. "We have a visual on the two NYPD detectives, every step they take, every move they make. I'm sending you a link to live video. You can monitor it day or night."

"He escaped! Everything else coming out of your mouth is excuses," Jeffers growled.

"Two weeks ago, 44 percent of respondents called these attacks 'Somewhat Justified,' 'Justified,' or 'Highly Justified.' Each time he attacks, those numbers rise. Those idiots are consumers. They are workers. They are voters, and many of them are swing voters. And they like this!"

Jeffers' rage could not be tamed. "Every single day and every night, an entire floor inside this building is dedicated to one thing, just one thing. I have a dozen guys who think they're the next Karl Rove and newsmen and television writers and advertising copywriters and two guys who just do jingles, little lyrical rhyming couplets, and they have a focus group audience of 200 more people, all of them working on that same one thing. Every morning I review and choose between two phrases, two simple phrases, seldom more than ten words, and one of these phrases is distributed across this nation to 1,200 politicians, 200 non-government lobby groups, 200 more radio and television producers, and 25,000 members of Americans for Political Action. One phrase, usually good just for that one day, drawn from all the news and all the events and all the goals and intentions nationwide. One.

"Five times, I have had to divert the focus of every resource to speak to a murdering psychopath to reinforce that he is 'attacking American Institutions,' 'assaulting our freedom to achieve success,' and 'striving to kill the American Dream,'" Jeffers fumed. "The goddamned White House won't even commit to calling this 'terrorism', the mealy-mouthed pissants. This will not endure. I will not allow this traitor to become the poster boy for income inequality!"

Jeffers' tone dropped into death-cold clarity, willing this to a final conclusion.

"Get this man and get every person with him or supporting him. Every single one. Scorched earth."

He handed a stark front facial photo across to Bishop who instantly caught the startling resemblance to Lee Harvey Oswald. Telling Bishop: "This is what the real shooter looks like.

Two days from now, this man, Dimitri Vosilych, is going to be introduced to my Executive Committee. Here is our killer."

"I've got something," Bishop explained, handing back the Vosilych photo. "These two NYPD detectives were thirty miles outside their jurisdiction. You may have seen them getting their boat shot out from under them."

Jeffers scanned the printouts.

"Cullen is second-generation NYPD," Stephen briefed from the NYPD files he had pulled. "Married, two children. Reached lieutenant six years ahead of median age for the grade. The partner, Sergeant Tremaine Bull, is single, seems to have peaked at detective-sergeant," Stephen continued. "Lives alone, no indication that he has ever applied himself to further promotion."

"They're both working under Christiana Dansk, Intel Division, "Bishop added. Then he said, "The third guy is FBI. An analyst. We're working on how he fits into this."

Jeffers tapped rapidly across his keyboard. Christiana Dansk was an APA member. Fourteen years. He recognized her picture, tall blonde. Fourth-ranking woman on NYPD. He linked to another file. The Commissioner of Police and every Deputy Commissioner but one were all APA members.

"Sons of bitches had an operation underway that included Arcadia? Right under my nose? With my family aboard?!" Jeffers said.

"Cullen and Bull have a lead on Spencer," Bishop continued. "His name has appeared in their communications."

"Sixteen times," Stephen interjected. "But it is unclear whether this moved up the chain of command. There's nothing in any logs to say why they were even out there on the river."

"Shadow them," Jeffers ordered as he picked up the telephone, debating whether to dial Dansk or go directly to the Commissioner.

"Already done," Bishop replied. "I have men watching them 24/7, camera and long-range audio surveillance-equipped. Stephen has phones, emails, and keystrokes monitored. We still don't know how they got ahead of him to be there on the river, but we are going to find out. FBI has an ex-army sniper, a Major Gonzalez, coordinating with Cullen and Bull. That may be the connection for Hurwitz."

Jeffers had come into the meeting with Bishop and Nussbaum fully prepared to fire them both. Now, they had earned themselves some time. "Get him," he warned, "or I'll find someone else who will."

Jeffers finished dialing. Dansk answered her cell phone on the first ring after glancing at caller ID.

"What in the hell are two of your detectives doing on the Hudson?" he demanded.

"NYPD is adding security everywhere we can," Dansk offered. She was trying for confident; she came off sounding lame.

"Me, my family…your people used us as bait!" Jeffers shouted at her.

"I did not authorize that assignment, " Dansk protested.

"Then get your people under control! Get me everything you have on the shooter. Now! We're working to manage this and your detective is getting over a million hits on YouTube," Jeffers said. "You know what is at stake, Christiana, for you personally. I can block all your plans with one phone call."

*****

He moves on foot and on donkeys and is lucky to see a pickup truck. He uses light weaponry, mortars, and improvised explosive devices against jets, drones, and helicopter gunships. But he survives. This is his territory. Underestimate his determination, his capacity, let down your guard, and you will die.

Twice, Owen caught people looking at him and imagined that it was the price of his minor celebrity after the YouTube video went viral. He had no reason to expect that he, the hunter, was being followed.

Bishop's men moved freely inside Citi-Field, the Home of the Mets, with the concessioners passes Stephen supplied to them. They observed and photographed Gonzalez's sniper team training inside. The work was familiar; the sniper team was tightening tactical response techniques that every one of Bishop's North Carolina men fully understood from years of doing the same work. But something was way off. Some of Bishop's men weren't sure that their pay was enough for whatever they were getting into. Their mission was to take down the shooter and secure the remains. How were they going to accomplish that with other capable squads right there competing?

Stephen was monitoring their keystrokes when the website Al Hurwitz was putting together emerged. When he grasped what they were doing, the audacity of the plan Cullen, Bull, Hurwitz, and Gonzalez were hatching left him clapping and cheering with excitement. "These dudes are setting a trap!" he announced.

Bishop was slow on the uptake. Stephen explained: "These guys are thinking like he thinks. You beautiful motherfuckers!" Bishop still didn't catch on; he wanted to share the vision, but he had been chasing up so many blind alleys that he was feeling lost, even if he wouldn't admit that to himself.

Stephen spun the laptop around to show Bishop what he had uncovered. "I fucking love this shit!" Stephen exclaimed.

"Human intelligence," Stephen told him. "They're doing *your thing*. That's how they were on the river, too. They're inside his head, anticipating where he can strike before he does it. The targets have been drying up. Now they're steering him, baiting the trap for *their* chosen spot at *their* chosen time."

"This is no good," Bishop recognized. "How am I supposed to take this back to Jeffers? This is the opposite of 'low friction'. We're in a Major League sports stadium. There is no way we can get Spencer out of there cleanly with dozens of cops around."

Stephen smiled and tapped three keystrokes, then closed the application. "Problem solved," Stephen announced. He shut the laptop and smugly grinned. "I just moved up their timetable, only NYPD will never know."

*****

The stadium felt too exposed; Spencer found a dozen locations from which he could fire on the luxury boxes, but not one of them offered a sufficient standard of cover ahead of the action or any viable means for escape. He was nearing the conclusion that Citi Field was a non-starter.

Nussbaum tapped his phone and zoomed in on the kneeling figure from the remote cameras and then opened Citi-Field's security surveillance, switching the entire stadium security system over to a prepared loop sequence so that from inside the security office it would continue looking like an empty field on a regular travel day. The facial-recognition software had identified Master Sergeant Jonathan Spencer. A simple app he had written for this purpose sounded the alarm on Stephen's smartphone.

Two three-man squads trailed behind him when Tremaine Bull into the baseball stadium. Through their binoculars, Bishop's teams watched the detective enjoy himself inside the private suite.

"There's not supposed to be any cops," the squad leader radioed to Bishop. He hand-signaled Security 1 and Security 2 to follow and observe.

While Tremaine walked around the third deck out toward left field, two men moved around the concourse toward section 338.

Stephen sent the link to Bishop, plus texted him and phoned. More than minute passed with no answer. Tremaine Bull was just standing over Spencer when Bishop received the feed. The cop and Spencer were chatting!

"Move in!" Bishop shouted into their earpieces. "We have confirmation. I repeat. We have confirmation. Move in! Helicopter is en route."

"Hold! What about the cop?"

Before Bishop could respond, suddenly the heavyset detective had cuffs out, fast, snapped them onto Spencer's right wrist and twisted. Spencer cracked two sharp jabs into Tremaine's face, dropping him to one knee. Spencer retreated, but the cop caught him with a powerful sweeping bear paw, spinning Spencer around.

The camera captured Spencer touching the Beretta 9mm at the small of his back inside his belt, but he didn't draw. Spencer was obviously favoring one leg. He was trying to press himself away, but it was no good, the cop was too strong.

Stephen was glued to the action on screen.

Spencer put all of his strength into his good leg and leapt high. As he came down, he drove his entire force into the back of the cop's head, slamming his face onto the edge of the concrete stair with a sickening crunch.

Spencer broke clear. He loped up the stairs, balancing on his weak leg and pushing his way forward. Bishop watched, momentarily forgetting to order his men to fire.

Stephen shifted the hijacked stadium security cam toward Bishop's men. From inside the section tunnel, one of them wearing his black baseball cap turned backward held a rifle leveled straight at Spencer's face.

"What's the orders?" Bishop's Team Leader demanded.

Bishop continued to hesitate. He knew better than to leave a witness, especially a cop, but he had no answer.

On his screen, Tremaine pressed himself up to his knees. He gripped the .38 revolver in one fist. His right eye was worthless. He squinted to aim through his left eye and cradled his revolver in the crook of his left elbow to stabilize his aim. When he fired, the camera caught the flame and smoke bursting from the snub-nosed barrel.

The first bullet hit like a rod of rebar ramming inside his right lung. Four more shots followed with each slug thudding home and jerking Spencer's body in agony.

The last round slapped exactly onto the scar tissue where Afif's blade had thrust.

A second rifle squared on the detective. "What about the cop?" Bishop's team called out while Bishop froze. He knew that the detective wasn't going to sit quietly and let him take away the biggest collar of his life. His orders were to get in and out fast with low friction. How was killing a cop consistent with that?

While Tremaine searched his pockets for his cell phone, two sets of eyes followed him with crosshairs aimed at him, center-chest and forehead.

"What are my orders?" Bishop's man demanded. The shot was there, he had it, but not without clear orders, not shooting a cop.

Tremaine screamed "10-00" into his cell phone while Bishop's team watched.

"Tremaine Bull DID. Shea. Citi-Field! Section 338. 10-12 on the sniper. Shooter down."

Bishop's man followed the cop through his rifle scope. The images relayed directly to Stephen's screen.

Bright red blood poured out of Tremaine's mouth like a running faucet, blood running through his broken teeth out over his chin as he straddled the man he had shot. The detective leaned down to get a closer look at the shooter. The first thing he saw was the Beretta inside Bigfoot's waistband.

He paused, studying quizzically. Why, Tremaine wondered? Why didn't draw the weapon?

Blood flowed over the body and onto the concrete. From above Spencer's prone body, the cop's head was twisted. Stephen recognized it on the monitor, too. He looked like he was confused, but he wasn't able to identify the cause. He couldn't know that the detective he was studying had just realized that the blood below him was draining out of his own mouth and not coming from Spencer at all.

Tremaine's good eye fixed on the shining brass end of a bullet where it stuck out from one of the five holes in the back of Spencer's shirt. Spencer snapped two quick testicular blows then sprang up on his one good leg.

Bull was already going down when Stephen completed the thought. *Vest. He's wearing a vest.*

"Orders!" the commando demanded.

Spencer tried again to move beyond reach but the cop wouldn't back off. Tremaine snagged him in a tight-fisted grip beneath the Kevlar vest and held on. Spencer drew the Baretta and pistol-whipped him, bringing a snapping clout against the socket and nearly closing Tremaine's left eye now, too, but he would not let go.

What do I have to do? Spencer wondered.

Whatever he did, the fool kept coming! With both eyes out of use, he couldn't see, but the cop kept fighting!

Spencer twisted and swept both arms roundhouse to break the grip, but Tremaine's hands grabbed again, both of his thick hands wrapping around Spencer's Beretta. He jammed downward with such force that Spencer let go of the gun before his wrist snapped in two.

Spencer lifted his foot then he stamped his heel down onto the crown of the cop's shoe. He felt the shattering bones caving into deep divot in the top of Tremaine's foot, but the cop still held!

And then they were falling. Backwards. Each one of them waving his arms to regain balance as they both flipped over the railing.

"Whoa!" Stephen exclaimed, pressing his face closer to the monitor screen while the two looked like they were headed to an ugly death. He was relieved momentarily when the cop caught his arm around the metal railing pole. They dangled forty feet high above the concrete stairs and the brightly colored seats in the lower deck.

Spencer had one hand snagged onto the cop's belt and held the other over the cop's forehead. Then all was still and quiet as both of them concentrated on survival.

"I'm going to climb on you," Spencer instructed. "Hang on. I'll pull you up when I get to the top."

Tremaine's entire body heaved, his one arm trembling as his elbow held against the strain of 500 pounds dangling over the forty-five foot drop onto the concrete stairs below.

"You ain't pulling up nobody," Tremaine huffed. "You going to run."

Spencer reached out and hooked his fingertips into the cop's eye socket to get purchase to pull himself up. He heaved and made headway. His face was now pressed into Tremaine's back. He brought up his leg and wedged the point of his shoe inside Tremaine's belt.

At the edge of section 338 above them, Bishop's second man saw the opportunity and acted upon it. He emerged out of the section tunnel and rushed down the stairs.

Tremaine's arm curled around the railing, trembling but holding fast. Bishop's man spun to position himself then lifted his leg. He aimed for the point of Tremaine's elbow. The side kick snapped the humerus and the trochlear notch.

Stephen's mouth dropped open. The shooter and the witness were dispatched onto the concrete below. Tremaine and Spencer both fell.

Problem solved. Stephen reversed the recording and watched again. His knees shook beneath the table.

The whole fight lasted twenty seconds.

The detective's body still lay there, shattered. "You were a good man," Bishop murmured. He didn't order it, but the death was on him. He was going to have to carry it.

Bishop placed the call to Jeffers. "We have him," Bishop reported. "Positive identity.

I had a team following the NYPD detective. The NYPD detective-sergeant was killed in a fall. Spencer is unconscious. He's more dead than alive."

Jeffers was very pleased with the news. "Well done, Sheriff. Dimitri Vosilych and a dead hero, too. The villain's dead and no witnesses. Well done."

The detective really is a 'dead hero', Bishop thought. *You sonofabitch. All you care about is having your Vision Partners back to business as usual. God help anyone who steps in the way.*

The helicopter swooped over the center field scoreboard, coming in hot. Bishop's contractors were running to meet it. The helicopter touched down, its load was tossed inside, and it lifted off again moving over the East River off Rikers Island.

He watched the copter getting smaller. Nine minutes out, the helicopter would be over the Bight. Bishop imagined Spencer dumped a thousand feet into the Atlantic, where the currents and the fishes would erase every trace.

Bishop's job was done, he thought. Right then he was about ready to be done with Jeffers, the APA, the Vision Partners and everything to do with them.

On to finding a new engagement, he thought. *Cash flow is good, but there is more to life than money.*

*****

A freeway roared inside Spencer's skull. He opened his eyes to a gray uniformity that felt different from eyesight, a monotone where nothing would focus into any shape that he could comprehend. He lifted his hands in front of his face, brought them close, then pushed them away, turned them over and repeated until and felt intensely dizzy from the effort. He tried to roll over onto his stomach, failed, and passed out. His last thought was that he could not feel his lower half.

The monotone gray remained when pain reawakened him. He felt piercing inside the hinges of his jaw, but the source was hidden beneath hip to ankle plaster casts anchoring his lower body to the plywood platform inside the windowless concrete cell.

You let yourself be captured.

*****

North Corona, Queens, NYC.

"Do you really need another beer that fucking bad?" Callie squealed. She sent Liam and Casey over to Shelley's house until Owen stopped the drinking. His eyes were crimson, bloodshot from the crying and the booze.

He ignored her, sitting on the couch. He was transfixed by the same CNN report they had already watched a half-dozen times.

"Tremaine was my friend, too, O."

He hadn't showered or shaved since Tremaine's funeral service. Now, he smelled so rank that there was no way she was letting him touch her, which was better anyway. Sex is no magic eraser.

Later in the day, after the beer supply was gone, he had another tantrum. This time Owen yanked on the refrigerator door hard enough to flip over the fridge, which obliterated Casey's high chair on the way down.

"It was an accident," he said.

"Don't leave! Jesus! Get your butt back here, Owen Cullen, and help pick this thing up! You're being a fucking a-hole," Callie screamed. "There's milk all over the floor!"

But Owen wasn't listening. There was CNN again. The same reporter, shivering in front of a crumbling Soviet-era building.

"This Eastern Bulgarian village of muddy tracks and single-room shelters was the home of Dimitri Vosilych," the reporter narrated. "The Muslim loner who entered the United States on a tourist visa and shot down two dozen Americans before he could be stopped.

"If you listen, we can hear now as the young boys inside this madrassa memorize Koranic verse. Earlier this afternoon, I interviewed the former headmaster of this school where Dimitri Vosilych was an instructor in Sharia law."

Owen sucked down a long slug of the whiskey. A wizened old man in a skullcap spoke softly in an unintelligible language and shook his head in denial. The old man waved his hand backwards to emphasize the long distance between the village and anything Dimitri Vosilych had done.

[Translation] "This was a person employed here years ago. I don't know anything. I thought he was dead." He shook his gnarled hand close to the camera lens. "We have no guns here. No violence. We know nothing about this man. He has no friends here."

"Bullshit!" Owen shouted at the television.

Dansk had him out on a mandatory one-week paid leave. More bullshit. Tremaine's weapon was empty. Did Dansk explain that? No! How could she?

"Citi-Field is our territory! Why no NYPD forensics? Huh? Why is the Department letting everybody else handle the crime scene investigation?" Owen asked nobody aloud.

More empty boots in the stirrups on the TV as Tremaine's public funeral replayed.

"Tee never rode a horse his whole life!"

"Owen!" Callie screamed around the kitchen door. "Get your boney ass off that couch and help me! I can't lift this alone!"

"Fucking bullshit!" Owen snarled. "Where are the bullets? If they're not in Vosilych's dead body, where are they? They didn't disappear in center field!" But the autopsy report was classified and he couldn't find answers to his questions.

"The guy has feet, doesn't he? Are they size thirteen? Bullshit! What happened to Master Sergeant Jonathan Spencer? How did you rule him out as a suspect, Commander Christiana? Explain that to me because I'm a little slow on the uptake! Why? On what basis? Even if this guy Vosilych is real, why can't there be more than one shooter? Huh, Dansk? What do you say to that, Blondie?"

He had asked Dansk right to her face: "The whole city turns out for Tee's funeral; dress blues, salutes and NYPD moves on? That's it?" Why the fuck was she moving this along so fast?

Owen knew he should drop it. He could shut up, play ball, get through the captain's exam and look forward to another brass bar. His own precinct. But his Irish was up and there was no getting away from it.

"Tee was my best friend," Owen muttered. He took another long slug from the bottle, knowing full well that he could never "play it smart."

*****

After the helicopter banked west toward Connecticut, Bishop heard nothing more from APA or Carlton Jeffers for five weeks. Now, while Jeffers briefed him, Bishop sensed that something had shifted. Jeffers was offering him cold bottled water and acting almost chummy.

"Dimitri Vosilych was the right product at the right moment," Jeffers explained. "A Chechen-trained Muslim terrorist from Bulgaria, a country Americans could never find on a map." Jeffers' grin said he was back on top of the world. Everything was getting back to normal. They hadn't lost a single Vision Partner, either.

Killer marketing, Bishop thought, pun intended but left unsaid. Vosilych was dead, gone, and forgettable. He was already "that guy." Most Americans probably couldn't pronounce the name, much less remember it. Here was another Muslim commie foreigner coming after the number one nation in the world.

The Oswald look-alike piece was brilliant finesse. Jeffers had Emerson Elliot off the air and only a 9% polling share was still calling the killings "Justified." The last dying ember of the far left.

All that for under $1 million, Bishop speculated. APA had probably parleyed the shootings into $100 million at the last Vision Partners gathering.

"I had 2,500 fully-armed private contractors onto the streets of New Orleans thirty hours after Hurricane Katrina hit the city," Jeffers went on, bragging about another one of his closeted successes.

"Leave others to take the credit. That's the secret to longevity, stroking huge egos. But I get to choose the golden words coming from thousands of voices every single morning. Me."

Jeffers extolled. "It's an iceberg, this great nation of ours. Ninety percent is below the surface." He was ebullient; problem solved, the brothers had nothing to criticize. The boil was lanced and drained without a single further public mention. In fact, he had every reason to expect a lot of mileage down the road coming from their recent handiwork. Mission completed.

It felt strange; Bishop wasn't prepared for this wholly different side to Jeffers. This Jeffers was engaging, charismatic even.

"Congratulations," Bishop replied cautiously. "It's been a while," he reminded Jeffers. "Not a word in five weeks."

"You were paid, weren't you?"

"Yes. The funds were wired. Thank you."

"No need to thank me. You earned it."

First the bottle of ice cold Fiji water. Then a compliment? Bishop watched as Jeffers swayed side to side in his high-backed leather chair. He looked like a cobra.

"I have your shooter," Jeffers announced smugly. He scrolled down a menu, clicked, and asked, "I want you to question him." like he was God parting the clouds to have a look down at the mortals.

"You what?" Bishop exclaimed. From the way that Jeffers was acting,

Bishop expected something, but not Jonathan Spencer. That didn't compute. In his head, that case was closed.

"Spencer is alive?"

"He's alive and safely locked away from prying eyes."

What Jeffers was saying still didn't compute. "APA has a prison?" Bishop questioned.

"No," Jeffers instructed. "APA doesn't own prisons. We hold no direct industrial interests of any kind. But amongst our membership we include every major stockholder in corporate incarceration.

"Incarceration is a growth industry," Jeffers continued. "We, APA, provide the meld between public interest and private capital. APA members now run cost-efficient prison facilities for 180,000 prisoners in eleven states. Forty thousand of that population is federal. At any given moment, these facilities hold 15,000 prisoners in segregated confinement. That affords plenty of room for some to slip, or to be slipped, through the cracks. In select instances where applying standard procedure runs against the interests of the government sector, like this case, corporate incarceration participates with federal and state leaders to overcome systemic flaws."

Bishop was listening hard, but still failed to fully comprehend. "Spencer is alive? The sniper is your prisoner?"

"He is. Alive, stabilized, and physically ready for interrogation."

Jeffers summarized his proposition succinctly. "Think of this as research. We have contained a germ. That germ represents a virus, which we intend to eradicate to prevent even the most remote future possibility of any epidemic. Our role is to contain the contagion, to extract information from the perpetrator, to download him, for lack of a more illustrative descriptor, and to circumspectly dispose of the threat. The United States Government is ineffective in every one of these critical functions. We, therefore, act as the responsible functionary. Public-private partnership.

"Jonathan Spencer no longer officially exists. Technically, according to the Department of Defense database he has never existed. Which leaves us with a non-existent parasite unequivocally at our full disposal.

"You get a new contract, we gain valuable information, and we close that chapter after we're done with him," Jeffers explained.

Bishop could still not fully embrace the information. It was supposed to be his operation, but Jeffers left him in the dark? "When did you decide all this?" he asked.

"The opportunity was there," Jeffers answered. But he had not answered at all.

"I hired the operatives, the helicopter," Bishop pressed back.

Jeffers' eyes widened. The swaying ceased. "Who paid the freight? You? You have a problem, you say so! I must be functioning under the misimpression that you want the work."

"No," Bishop admitted. "No, it's all good."

"Multiple fractures, both legs," Jeffers said finally, after a long pause. "He was severely concussed. Some internal bleeding and I believe his spleen was removed." Jeffers tapped his keyboard, read something, and then nodded. "Yes, spleen."

He dismissed all of that with a wave of his hand. "Bishop, I'm inclined now to agree with your one shooter thesis. NSA has not picked up a peep of chatter in five weeks. Seems that no matter how much they hate our guts, the Chinese, the Russians, the Arabs… nobody out there wants loners gunning for people who matter."

He took a sip and began again. "Having said that I'm inclined to agree, I am not officially authorized or prepared to draw that conclusion. We have him at our full disposal. Names, addresses, methods for any and every support resource he had, who else is involved, how they are organized, what are their objectives, how are they financed, what is their target selection process, what else do they have planned. We own him; we gather the data! Some of our membership are fixated on just desserts, but my experience on Arcadia notwithstanding, I prefer to think in terms of forfeiture. This germ murdered at least two dozen innocent men and women; when he did that, he forfeited all rights as a human being."

"Nobody in government wants to know anything about this, of course," Jeffers continued. "We'll call it 'mutually beneficial deniability.' The federal government is required to observe legal conventions. We, however, are not constrained by any court of law. There is no Eighth Amendment here; no conventions about cruel or unusual punishments. Mr. Bishop, from now until his casts come off, you are free to do whatever it takes to download him. But one proviso. Keep it PG-13. No visible marks. Nothing permanent, anyway. After the casts come off, Master Sergeant Jonathan Spencer becomes a statistic—one more soldier suicide."

Bishop tried to take it all in. He had never been taken in by Dimitri Vosilych, but that Jonathan Spencer was being held outside the justice system inside a private prison facility forced him to recalibrate. He was being brought into the fold and Jonathan Spencer was alive but still a dead man walking. Except Spencer couldn't walk.

The Fiji water. The money.

"Do you have a problem with any of this?" Jeffers demanded. "I personally nominated you for the role."

"Not at all," Bishop responded quickly. "I'm here to serve Americans for Patriotic Action." *Integrity is a luxury I can't afford.*

"Just as I thought."

*****

"Where's Dansk?" Owen demanded. He strode into Intel Division's Headquarters in The Bunker without noticing the change in big red letters right at the top of the white board.

"Chuck Allen," the new commander replied, reaching his hand out to shake. "You're Owen Cullen. I'm sorry for your loss. Sergeant Bull was a good man."

Owen looked at Allen's hand and shook the hand automatically. Who this person was and why he was behind Christiana Dansk's desk was another matter. He paused, still watching Allen's eyes. "What happened to Dansk?" he asked.

"She's private sector now. That's all I know," Allen said. "I'm glad that you came by, Owen. Grab a chair. I'll be commanding Intel Division. I'm hoping to rely on you lieutenants to get me up to speed. Came over from four years at 1 Police Plaza."

Owen balanced on the edge of the seat and stared at his new boss before pulling several folded sheets of yellow legal paper out of his jacket and smoothing them on the desktop.

"This thing stinks," he griped.

"Of course it stinks," Allen agreed. "I can't imagine losing a partner. You take as much time as you need. I didn't mean you need to begin helping me right this minute. When you're ready, we'll look together at all the candidates. Nobody is going to shove anyone new down your throat. I'll value your input in the selection process to begin the next chapter."

"I'm talking about the case report!" Owen argued, raising his voice and drawing looks from outside the glass door. "How come Tremaine's body was at Citi-Field but then the perp gets flown away by helicopter?" he demanded. "Why was that?"

Owen's confrontational style took his new boss aback. "Vosilych was still breathing. He died en route to the ER," Allen reminded Owen.

"Tremaine's weapon was emptied. I went and looked over that area myself, spent a whole day, and I didn't see a single hole in a seat or a chip in the cement or anything like a ricochet or a slug. So you tell me how, after firing every chamber, does this little guy take a 300-pound detective sergeant built like a brick shithouse over the railing? Where's the autopsy report? If this guy has size thirteen feet and six bullets in him, tell me and I'll shut up."

"I don't have the autopsy."

"For an officer from your department killed in the line of duty? You don't have the complete report?"

"Hey look Owen, I'm on your side.

"It wasn't my call. Hell, I wasn't here yet! But this is bigger than any one person, even an officer on duty. The guy killed two dozen people for Christ's sake," Allen tried to explain. "This is federal, Lieutenant."

"No, this is bullshit is what it is! Tremaine and I were after a U.S. Army sniper named Jonathan Spencer, not some communist or Islamist foreigner, and we got cock-blocked every single fucking step of the way. Somebody collected DNA, only we couldn't get to the results. What happened to that? And what about Spencer? Where is he? We don't even have a statement from the guy. If this Vosilych killed my partner, why can't we find Jonathan Spencer and interview him?" Owen insisted. Owen's eyes were burning red. "I'm telling you, Commander," he insisted, "one man isn't moving Tremaine Bull over that railing. And Tremaine's gun was emptied. I checked every reported gunshot wound from here to Canada and south to Florida that day and three days after. Nothing checked out."

Allen pressed down on his telephone. "James, come to my office. Bring Gordon, too."

He waited for the two detectives to enter before responding. "Lieutenant," he told Owen, "I'll put in a file request right now, but I'm also making you an appointment to sit down with a Department psychologist. Guy, I'm your new boss and you're coming in throwing f-bombs. I'm on your side, only I need you to dial it back. You need to get right and healthy, and I'll go to the mat to help you get there."

Owen noticed the two men standing behind his chair on both sides.

"What I need is that file!"

"Owen, right now what you need is help."

CHAPTER SIX

His mouth was brittle, so dry that he stretched his tongue out giraffe-like, seeking moisture. The interior of his throat felt like a potato chip; it was covered with minute lacerations that did not compute at all. Nothing processed, not where he was, not how he got there; he owned no self-concept at all and no curiosity for answers. He had no means to know that he had undergone sixteen hours of orthopedic surgeries, that his legs were bolted, pinned, and plated, that bone from his hip had closed gaping centimeters along a shattered femur.

Across the backs of both his hands were purple and black bruises ringed with jaundice-yellow patches where intravenous lines had been feeding him. Now that the breathing tube was out, his entire throat, from his tonsils down, felt like a drying scab.

Bare gray concrete walls rose twelve feet to the top. He was flat on his back, immobile as an overturned tortoise. From the upper corner of the wall, a black dot came into focus, a tiny green bulb beside it. A pleasant color. Green. The camera lens shifted, looking down as he looked up at it.

A thick steel door outfitted with slots at center, top, and bottom along the floor clanged metal-on-metal, jolting his senses while a stick appeared to push a cardboard tray through the floor slot and across the slab floor. The stick vanished. Another metallic clang. Spencer's eyes shut.

He remembered the food tray when he next awakened. It was gone. His right arm was against a cold gray wall. He stretched his left arm across the space and was just short of the opposite wall. Reaching behind, he could feel a third wall. The door was toward his feet. He slowly tipped his face forward; again, the plaster casts reaching up to his crotch. Tensing the muscle groups in his legs yielded shuddering agony. No, he definitely was not paralyzed.

What he estimated to be a twenty-four-inch long fluorescent bulb hung inside a ceiling fixture. He made out the GE logo on the bare tube. He forced himself to twist enough that he could see the stainless steel toilet bowl hanging off the wall just behind and to the left of his face. It was stamped 'American Standard'. The concrete was finished smooth. He also surveyed the welds on the hinges of the heavy door; these were cleanly ground. *Western standards.*

He began to smell himself on the third day, the same day that he reached out for food.

The flavors coming from orange juice out of an elementary school-sized plastic container exploded over his tongue. He could feel the calories surge, energizing his arms and outward to his fingertips. His ears tickled. When the carton was empty, he reached down to French toast, grabbing up the soft contents and mashing his fistful into his mouth, only reviving the action of chewing when he couldn't swallow it whole. Raisins followed, sweet between his teeth. *American food.*

His hands measured eight inches from palm to fingertips. The plywood sleeping pallet measured four hands. Two pallets would have filled the width of the room. Grasping the finite excited him; 5.5 feet wide, 7 feet long, and 12.5 feet to the ceiling, he guessed, each equation accelerating in his head.

He began a mental inventory of each leg beneath the casts, carefully moving from bottom up along his left side and making it up to the shin bone, where the pain intensified, skipping forward to the knee then twisting a fraction left and right, enough to know he should not press more. He could sense no other specific injuries above the knee. He was not so fortunate on his right side, where Rice Krispies snapped, crackled, and popped inside his ankle joint from even the slightest contraction. The right knee felt strong, comparatively so, then his right thigh dared him to play at all with its erector-set assortment of rods and plates and bone grafts taken from both hip bones. The idea of even standing suggested pain beyond comprehension; moving under his own power was not going to happen.

He rolled his head around; even the neck muscles felt diminished. He tested his right shoulder, then his left. He spread his fingers wide and balled them back into fists, twisted the fists and turned them back toward his chin, tensing and flexing his forearms and biceps. He pumped his pectoral muscles and spread his latts despite the crackling cartilage, and rippled from his upper abs down to his groin.

A deep humming sound penetrated the walls. He concentrated on the noise but then it was gone. After hearing it for the first time, he often recognized the sound and sensed the vibration, but the inconsistent intervals offered him no further clues to its origin.

He could have been anywhere. The GE logo on the fluorescent bulb, the American Standard emblem on the toilet, the foods, and even the cleanly machined welds on the heavy door hinges suggested America, but after days passed he knew better. No police questioned him. No attorneys. No human contact. He could be anywhere, anywhere except the USA. The food was one hundred percent American industrial food. It could have been coming from any contract food services at any base or U.S. facility worldwide.

Two meals per day. One was French toast or oatmeal or Raisin Bran and a century later the next one would have turkey with gravy or Salisbury steak, again with gravy, or macaroni with cheese. Nothing that was fresh or had a limited shelf life.

*****

Their intention will be to isolate and break you. Your job is stay alive for the time that they drop the ball. Stay focused. When that time comes, be ready.

The steel door sounded like a Chinese gong whenever it was opened, thumping inside his ear against the silence. The hinges were violins in the hands of monkeys, their shrill pitch knifing into his brain.

Two men moved in, one tall and slim, the other hard-muscled and stocky. They barely fit inside the narrow cell. They registered as military to him as Spencer took in their crisp, deliberate movements, but no rank insignia showed nor any sort of identification. *Clean shoes.* He caught that much. No mud or dust to indicate unpaved streets. No sweat stains, no musk or stinging odors coming off their bodies. No bug bites. The steady electricity, the U.S. foods, the elevator—all these left him betting on Eastern Europe. *A city. Where?* Not proof, but indicative that the black ops prison where he was held was either urban or on a sizeable base. Urban would be better, so long as he could fit in with the looks of other people. *The legs wouldn't make it over terrain.*

Then everything went black. Rough knuckles violently pulled a black hood down past his nose and lips then cinched tightly. He felt a lanyard cutting against his Adam's apple then, suddenly, he was breathing through a straw, laboring against the fabric to bring back the air that was shut down to a trickle through the dense fabric. He recoiled, thrashing his head from side to side, tensing his fists against the restraints, tightening his abdomen and feeling for the distant musculature of his glutes and thighs and calves. Tortured nerve endings shrilly reminded him of every screw and plate and bone graft that was piecing Humpty Dumpty back together again.

Stocky's thick hands dug into Spencer's armpits. Slim's long, thin hands reached around both ankles. Excruciating stabbing intensity shot up his legs through his brain. Even his ears and scalp felt like they were doused with gasoline and lit aflame as they lifted him onto a half gurney-half chair with extensions to keep his casts supported. He recognized the distinctive sound of Velcro ripping apart, and then each of his arms was clamped down from elbow to wrist within the Velcro constraints along the chair's steel arms.

Spencer fought through the pain to focus, to catch any sound that might define where they had him. Discs the size of quarters were pressed into his forearms. Wires ran through soft straps that were like supersized blood pressure cuffs.

When the pain subsided, he was able to distinguish between Stocky's grunts and Slim's deeper sucking breathing. Slim was behind him, pushing, while Stocky was at their front. Slim was subordinate. Spencer figured Stocky for an E5, Slim for a PFC.

Eight seconds before they stopped; he counted. Another heavy steel door clanked like a Chinese gong then creaked open in an excruciating agonizing shriek. The chair was wheeled inside a room, spun around what he thought to be 180 degrees, and then it shivered and stiffened, locked into place facing back toward the door.

"You have no friends, no family, and no lawyers," a deep voice explained with calm finality. "You are totally alone."

The round end of an electrified rod jammed upward below his ribcage, punching toward his lungs. The jolt of current contracted his muscle groups one after another leaving him stiffened, statue-like, losing all sense of time, holding that petrified agony like a Vesuvius victim choking on hot ash. Then the pain resided, stiffening into the hinges of his jaw and just above both knees. His throat blazed like a hot coal had been pushed inside.

"No one will hear you scream or care if you do," Bishop explained. He reinforced each bullet point of his introductory monologue by applying another careful jolt along Spencer's nerve clusters. "These walls are soundproof." He pressed the rod beside the C8 vertebrae and observed as Spencer's fingers spread and extended involuntarily, responding just the way Bishop knew they would.

"You can fight this until you will want to die, but suicide is not an option." Bishop pressed the rod behind the prisoner's back until the tip lodged up along T9. Spencer's abdomen cramped into a rippled washboard.

"There will be no negotiation. You exist to answer the questions. Answer truly, thoroughly, and you can stop the pain." The rod tip angled upward below his crotch. Spencer stretched his neck backward. He would have screamed, but his vocal chords had cramped against the voltage. Just silent terror emitted through his gaping mouth. The agony shot against his eardrums, cramped his inflamed throat until he choked, ached inside his knees and in the last joint of every finger. Even the metal staples holding his right thigh together inside the right leg cast absorbed the current and heated until they were cooking the flesh immediately around them.

When the current stopped, Spencer bit down through his tongue and hyperventilated, each inhalation drawing fabric into his nostrils. Spencer had the feeling that a highway tunnel had been drilled between his temples. Iron-rich blood skimmed over his tongue and made its way through his lips. Eventually, it would saturate the black hood and begin dripping. Then the electricity resumed; with the rod pressed behind his right ear, Spencer strained involuntarily, feeling every vertebrae pop inside his neck.

Bishop stopped to allow Spencer to consider his reality. In that minute, through his grimace Spencer centered upon *mission clarity*. Spencer's taut muscles rippled from his toes up through his shattered legs, up through his sinuous forearms, met between his pectoral muscles at his breastbone, and stiffened along his neck and jaw. He knew exactly who he was. He had been through pain and he could get to the other side. *Never give up.*

"Pain or absence of pain," Bishop reminded him, slowly enunciating every syllable. "We'll start with one name, your most immediate contact. Answer me and there will be no pain."

"Spencer, Jonathan," he shot back. "Master Sergeant, United States Army." *Fuck you.*

The rod tapped his forehead, just a quick love tap. "We know who you are. Name and rank? That is over. I'll repeat myself this one time. You were asked for one other name. One contact. Just one."

"Who are you? Where is this?" Spencer demanded. Black ops somewhere. *Just give him anything.* It could be that they're so confident in themselves they wouldn't care what they revealed.

"You don't ask questions," Bishop instructed. Bishop answered by pushing the electric rod into the hip incision where bone had been taken for the graft. The current surged through Spencer's pelvis and buttocks and coursed up his spinal column. "To me, your body is just a vessel. I don't care that surgeons put you back together. You can give what I ask or I can break you again to get it. Think on that. After the first time, it only gets worse."

*****

First prisoner interview, prisoner uncooperative. BP 170/122. Heart Rate 151. Rapid respiration. Advise interrogation officer to implement measurements for Galvanic Skin Response in next interview session.

*****

After Stocky dropped his head onto the plywood pallet in the cell and removed the hood, Spencer gulped for air like a baby bird. His raw throat flashed on fire, but it was still worth it to feel his chest inflating freely. He inhaled as far as his lung could stretch. Air. Air was everything. Soft, cool air drawing deep inside his chest. *Everything.*

He could still hear the slow-paced Texas baritone echoing out from the darkness inside the hood.

"Not your first rodeo," he whispered. He'd been through pain before. *You've got this.*

Spencer waited until his breathing normalized, then pressed his right fingers against his left wrist to locate his pulse. He knew his resting pulse rate. It always ranged from fifty-nine beats per minute to sixty-one; he called it sixty. He was breathing every fifth beat. Twelve breathes per minute. Start with the left little toe and move right = ten minutes. Right pinky to left thumb = one hour.

When you only way of measuring time is your own heartbeat, you know that you are alone.

He needed to get his head right. Rendition: Bastards grabbed a U.S. soldier on American soil and they dumped him in some overseas hellhole. *OK. Draw from it. Why? Because you touched them. You got to the untouchables and they didn't like it. No surprise.*

Set the routine, he told himself. Rise to the challenge. He concentrated and it all came back. *Establish control. Whatever the environment, fix your location, know the time of day, track the day of the week and the date in the month. Every milestone makes you stronger. Your captors will make an error. Your duty is to be ready when that time comes.*

He could hear Senator John McCain's gravelly description of five and a half years in captivity as a POW in North Vietnam: the dysentery, diarrhea and starvation, the pain of witnessing what they were doing not just to him, but to other GIs. *Torture is horrible. It can take away your manhood and turn people into animals, but you can fight it. Hold tight onto anything that they can use to harm your brother soldiers or aid them. Observe their patterns, probe their habits, and use everything, however small, to fight back. The fight will energize you. The fight keeps you alive.*

Concentration. Discipline. Competitiveness. Through Airborne School and Ranger School and Special Forces Training and every level of sniper training at Harmony Church Spencer reminded himself that he had measured off the charts in every one of these traits. You made it through the cold room and the hot room in training; you held up until they had to pull you out. *You never tapped out, never.*

Dinner dropped inside the lower door slot then was pushed across the floor with a long dowel with a curved end that looked like a craps stick. Spencer twisted from his waist and stretched out to reach it, bringing the food tray back close enough to where he could look and smell what was on it. Thick egg noodles with a pale sauce containing chunks of white meat. Canned green beans machine-cut in uniform lengths. A muffin. He sniffed and guessed corn. A plastic cup of yellow-colored liquid sealed under a peel-off aluminum cap. SunPride Apple Sauce. 100% Organic. Real Fruit. No Sugar Added. 4 Oz (113g). 100% USA Apples. A spork was wrapped inside a single thin-ply napkin.

Spencer tasted the noodles, started to take a heaping sporkful, and then dropped most of it back onto the tray. Eat slowly, he told himself. The camera was watching, always watching. Look indifferent. *Don't hand them leverage.* Twelve breaths per minute. He would take twenty minutes…every toe twice around…before the plate was finished. Test No. 1; he slipped the spork inside the top of his left cast. Not much of a shank, but were they going to notice that it was gone?

Spencer read Stocky and Slim for MPs. I'm not the only prisoner here, Spencer thought, but the walls were too thick for any communications to pass through. Yelling was obviously futile. The only noises he heard came from a low humming through the wall alongside his pallet and the constant buzzing tinnitus running inside his own head.

They came into the cell wearing their face-coverings just as he was finishing a second cardboard tray that was pushed inside hours later: warm oatmeal, a biscuit, a tiny box of Sun-Maid raisins. *Breakfast.* Spencer watched Stocky's thick, plastic-gloved hand slip a large key inside his shirt pocket. Slim smelled of Axe spray. *Morning shower.*

Stocky pulled away the tray and took the spork from his hand, then reached down for the dinner tray on the floor. Spencer felt the hard edge of the cuffs against his wrist before he felt the cold metal or heard them snapping shut. His arms were wrenched above his head while Stocky roughly grabbed below his torso, slapped both sides of Spencer's ball sack, and then pointed to Slim, who lifted beneath both legs.

"Where?" Stocky demanded.

"Where what?"

"The other fork."

"I flushed it."

"Get behind me," Stocky ordered Slim. With Slim's tall frame forming a direct line from Spencer to Stocky to Slim, the camera was blocked.

Stocky's thick pink cheeks and flat-faced piggish features flushed red. "Time we had a little 'Come to Jesus,'" he suggested excitedly.

Without giving any warning, Stocky let his legs buckle and concentrated every ounce of his bulk into his right elbow, dropping four feet until it met Spencer's unprotected sternum. Every molecule of air was driven out from both lungs.

Stocky left his windpipe exposed, but Slim slipped around between them. The sour look on Slim's face told Spencer that this wasn't the first time he had to cover for Stocky's brutality.

"You some kind of teacher's pet?" Stocky grunted. "No bruises or visible trauma, huh? I just don't give a shit. People slip and fall all the time. Bruises happen. You ever feeling froggy, you jump," Stocky challenged. "Bring it on."

Stocky pulled both his gloves tight then ran his big hands along the pallet beneath Spencer's torso. His Popeye forearms were so thick that Spencer was raised and rolled into the cell wall. Finding nothing, he then moved methodically, pressing and probing against Spencer's thighs along the inside of the both casts until he felt the handle of the plastic spork scrape across his skin.

Stocky pulled it out, smiled, and then reached under the pallet for the bedpan. Slim turned away as Stocky spooned urine, telling Spencer, "Open up." When Spencer clamped his lips and turned his face away, Stocky moved his knee on top of the wrist cuffs to hold down Spencer's arms then pinched open Spencer's right eye and held the plastic tines on Spencer's eyeball before pouring the amber-dark urine onto Spencer's eye.

Piss in the eye is not too different from brackish river water. He had been there, done that. Parachuted into Walter F. George Reservoir on the Chattahoochee River in the dark with full gear and a half-mile swim to shore.

"You're lucky we're moving you," Stocky hissed. "You'd be bathing in piss right now otherwise. That stunt just cost you toilet paper for a week.

Stocky snatched the handcuffs with a bone-cracking jerk and left them digging into Spencer's wrists as he lifted Spencer's upper body off the pallet. Slim moved to take the casts around the ankles while Stocky set Spencer's butt onto the wheelchair. The Velcro along the arms of the chair was ripped apart and both Spencer's forearms were sealed against the metal chair arms. A strap was passed around his waist this time, tying him in like a seatbelt.

Spencer felt the chair swing 180 degrees and counted in his head until the chair stopped. *Same place.* This time he was prepared for questioning. Electric shock was extreme, only the effects were short-lived. But the hood; he knew already that there was no getting used to that. As soon as Stocky pulled the hood over his head, dragging his knuckles across Spencer's face, every ounce of his willpower had to go into resisting the primal urge set to take Stocky up on that challenge.

Not now. Not yet. His time will come.

Taking the nasty blow was worth it. He had confirmed chain of command. Slim answered to Stocky. He learned that Stocky enjoyed asserting his power.

He now knew that the camera was visual-only. No microphone. Spencer also learned that Stocky was not supposed to do anything that left physical marks. *Prison protocol or just for me? Why? Who else is seeing this?*

The surveillance system was dated, Spencer told himself. Probably at least five years old. Anything newer would have audio.

The chair moved inside the room, spun round, then jolted as it was locked down into place. Spencer detected two separate noises, but almost at the same time. Latches flipping, like somebody opening a briefcase.

Bishop methodically went through his satchel and took out an insulated box. Inside foam compartments, he looked over clear glass vials alongside yellow serums, a pale green substance, and another that was brilliant blue. He considered the clear mirtazapine. Most effective when it was combined with sodium thiopental, he often found, but Bishop saved the mixed cocktail for another time. Too early on. Too many adverse impacts. Instead, he picked out a milky white niacin solution to dilate the blood vessels ahead of injecting the tetra-cyclic compound and placed it onto a wheeled surgical tray beside the ready syringes.

He gripped Spencer's left forearm tightly, then yanked a lever, kicking back the chair's angle so that Spencer's arm stretched out level from the shoulder. Two fingers slapped hard along his inside elbow then Spencer felt the prick of a needle as Bishop slid it deep inside the vein.

"You're gonna feel a rapid flush of heat," Bishop told him. He then withdrew the empty shot and replaced it onto the tray, allowing the niacin to move into the bloodstream while he prepared the mirtazapine solution, making certain that the drug was fully dissolved ahead of drawing out 20ccs and depressing the plunger to clear any bubbles.

Spencer's serotonin levels spiked instantly as the mirtazapine entered his system, suddenly making him feel like he was immersed into a bathtub of warm water.

"Pain. Pleasure. Today, let's let you decide. Who supplied your weapons?"

Spencer thought about them all: his Barrett, the M24, M110, and the Heckler & Koch. *Koch.* Was that the same Koch brothers Captain Sam was always talking about, he wondered? His mind started to drift. He relaxed his neck and let his head fall backward. Wheeee.

The electric prod touched just under his Adam's apple.

"Who supplied your weapons?"

Spencer chortled. This wasn't challenging. This was just silly. "Eagle Arms," he answered.

"What is Eagle Arms?"

"Gun show. Buy, sell, trade. Got most of them there," he said.

"*Oh we're living here in Allentown and they're closing all the factories down,*" he sang, then said, "My Barrett I won, fair and square."

"Won from who?"

"From whom," Spencer corrected. "Objective case." He was hearing music now. Mozart. Eine kleine nachtmusik. Cool.

BP 111/63. Pulse 59 BPM.

"You were in Afghanistan. Tell me about that."

"Oh yeah. Kabul, Kandahar, Herat, Bagram, Chaman, Khost, Jalalabad, north, south, east, west. Oh yeah."

"What did you do there?" Bishop asked.

"Made music. Beautiful music."

"You shot people."

"Yes. Yes I did. It's what I do."

"The people you shot at Central Park West. The people on the balconies. Who told you to shoot them?"

"The music." Spencer smiled. Everything fit so perfectly.

Bishop jammed the rod deep into Spencer's right hip, as close to the shattered femur, plate and pins as he could get it, and held it there while Spencer's face cramped into a writhing, twisted grotesque mask.

After Bishop pulled back the electricity, Spencer began laughing and couldn't stop himself. It felt just like riding Mind Eraser at Six Flags.

*****

Bishop reviewed the session tape and felt satisfied that he had had a productive session; before Spencer faded off into la la land, Bishop had effectively initiated cooperation. After the prisoner was taken back to the cells, Bishop Googled "Eagle Arms." Regular shows all over the Keystone State. Allentown. He was just compiling a comprehensive list of the weapons and confirming that Spencer could have purchased every one of them at the enormous gun shows when he received a text message:

NOBODY CAME TO VIEW A PARTY. DO NOT DO THAT TWICE.

Bishop squeezed his cell phone and pulled back his pitching arm. He was ready to smash it to pieces. Wasn't the objective getting information? Two sessions in and he was having success. Now they were dictating what he could and couldn't do?

Bishop looked up at the camera lens and green light and knew they could see him, too. To get what he wanted for himself, he had to give the audience what it wanted. He wasn't after another one-time consulting engagement this time. There wasn't exactly a line of people waiting to snap up his time.

To get hired again, he needed to succeed. But if succeeding meant telling these men to shut up and get out of his way, to let their expert do his job—well, these didn't strike him as men who were likely to tolerate criticism.

It's their party, he reminded himself. They paid for the show, just like they paid for the helicopter, and they called the shots. So no more serotonins, not if he was going to be inside APA.

He considered flunitraepam, but even mixed with other psychotropics Spencer might nod off. They could send him packing if that happened.

Nope, he told himself, get over it. Give the customers what they want.

*****

"You're ours," Bishop belched beside his left ear. "You'll talk now or you'll do it later. I'm giving you a chance to choose what happens in between."

The electric rod jammed into Spencer's scrotum, sending voltage through his rectum into his armpits then exploding like fireworks inside his brain. He hesitated; processing, not responding, and the electric stick came down again, directly beneath the ear. He cheeks flapped, and then he bit down hard, chomping into his tongue. Blood flooded inside his mouth. He could feel it soaking the hood to his chin when he spat to clear.

BP 181/120 – Pulse 163 – GSR (NA)

"WHO WAS BEHIND THIS? WHO SET YOUR TARGETS? WHO SET YOUR INTEL? WEAPONS, VEHICLES, SAFE HOUSES? WHO AND WHY?" The voice shouted into his face.

"What?"

A cupped hand flew from behind his head slammed against his right ear, driving a pressurized wave that clapped the eardrum, leaving his head ringing.

"With or without you, we're finding out. Easy or hard."

He kept inferring a conspiracy, but from his voice Spencer wasn't certain that the man cared which way he chose.

"Talk or don't talk, we'll follow the money, and we'll find out why you did it. From why, we'll get to who. Make it easier on yourself. Talk."

BP 181/120 – Pulse 163 – GSR (NA)

"Spencer, Jonathan. Master Sergeant. United States Army."

Two long seconds elapsed in silence, then Spencer's whole body was suddenly lurched backward as a pulled lever inverted the chair, tilting his feet above his head. Bishop flipped back the armchair, inclining it backward so that Spencer's hooded face pointed upside down toward the back wall, then looked back at the camera lens and the green light beside it.

They want a show, Bishop thought, and you, dumbshit, you're forcing me to give them a good one.

The unmistakable noise of a spigot turning open, followed by the thudding of water under high pressure pounding into a plastic pail confirmed what was coming next. Spencer concentrated all his focus on the backs of his hands. *Think about something else. Concentrate. What is around you there? Can you feel the temperature? What do you see? What do you smell? Think about anyplace except where you are.*

Cold water splashed over the hood, rushing past his nostrils, flooding the nasal passages. He could not stop it, could not expel it, could not thrash his head side to side to keep the water out; he could not even slow it to comprehend. Drowning. The sinus cavity fills first, like a water balloon pressurized from inside against his eyes, nose, and ears. Physically resisting was as impossible as holding his breath. Waterboarding catalyzes a primal terror, a window on death. The body can never overcome that drowning feeling. But the terror is dependent on fearing death. Like a gazelle relaxing as the lion's jaws clamp into its neck, death can also be accepted.

BP 136/88. Pulse 84 BPM.

*****

"Owen, you're not taking the boys anywhere," Callie determined firmly. She was standing a yard back into the entry behind the swing of the door; her hand never let go of door edge.

"I just want to see my sons, OK? It's been a week."

"It's been nine days," Callie corrected him. "You're messing up, O! You are not seeing the boys like this. Look at you! You're a police officer for Christ's sake. Whadya doin' drivin'? Cup your hand and blow. I can smell you from here." He looked like he had slept in the clothes he was wearing.

"You been going to your counseling?" she implored. She hardly gave him the chance to respond before her tone got demanding. "Owen, have you been seeing the therapist? You don't go and they can suspend you without pay! Then what happens?"

"Nobody will help, Cal," Owen whined. "Tremaine is dead and I can't get anything. They blocked me from accessing the department file system. I've called every agency I can think of and each one refers me on to another one. Nobody will show any tracking on this Dimitri Vosilych; it's like he never existed; no credit cards, no job history, no entry visa, nothing. I even tried buying a profile online and it was blank, too."

"I'm not talking about your goddamned case!" she screamed. "I heard it all, every word: the big feet, the missing bullets, the Department of Defense with no records of any Master Sergeant Jonathan Spencer, how Major Gonzalez wouldn't speak to you on the telephone, how you drove to his townhouse in Brooklyn and waited outside and how he looked at him out the window like he was scared. I listen!

"Now you listen. Let it go, O," she told him. "Tremaine is gone. It's no good for you to stay at his place."

"I don't want to stay there. I want to be home!" Owen said.

"I'm going to close the door now, Owen. We've been through this. You need to get yourself right. Until you do, I need to do what I need to do."

"How do I get myself right when nobody will listen? How?"

"Owen, get your hand off the door," Callie said. "I have listened. You need to get help."

Owen leaned his weight forward on the door with his chin lowered against his chest. It was either that or falling to his knees. Callie wedged both her feet on the floor and pressed back intently. "You're escalating, Owen. Now get offa it! Back off! I'll get a court order. I'll do it. You know I will!"

*****

Bishop ripped the hood away, leaving Spencer to heave a milky waterfall across his own chest that spilled onto the cement floor.

Spencer's brain snapped back into the present. *Air is everything.* His damaged throat choked with blood and saliva while he stretched hard to draw breath as the acids vomited from deep inside him burned the soft tissue lining his esophagus.

Interrogation rarely was linear; the mind functioned like a knitted sweater; search for the loose thread and unravel the mystery. Bishop cranked the chair back into the upright position.

"Rich people. Why?"

"You believe their BS or you just taking their money?" Spencer snapped back.

The electric prod was lying across the mobile table alongside Bishop's laptop. Bishop's eye flitted quickly from the prod to the camera before he turned back toward Spencer, who was already looking disturbingly calm. Despite the vomit on his chest and side, his breathing had already normalized. He looked contented, serene even.

"Hotshot, you fight me, you get the rod. Now, who put you up to this?"

Spencer smiled to himself. No, he wasn't hearing voices, not God or Jesus or anyone else, not even Captain Sam. But he wasn't going to share that information. If Texas wanted to carve it out of him, let him try.

Bishop scrolled down his notes:

Target acquisition- by individual, question selection of Levy, Perlman, Fleish, Branderman, Parrish, Ellis, Leong, Zhou, Keaner – was target selection randomized to hide specific individual targets? Ideological or profit motive? Profile for psychological and philosophical radicalism. How many shooters were involved? Intel source and logistical support? Foreign and domestic terror contacts? Armed Forces contacts?

"You carry a lot of scars. There's an ugly tear going down your back from your shoulder blade to your hip," Bishop noted. "Tell me about that."

Spencer thought for a second about the circle jerks they called therapy sessions he was forced to sit through at Madigan and again at Walter Reed. Like talking makes a difference.

Bishop moved close enough to Spencer's head that he thought he could whisper. "Work with me. It makes sense for both of us."

The blow snapped Bishop's head, a neat head butt that caught Bishop sharply just above his left temple, their two skulls clacking like bricks slammed together. Bishop dropped momentarily down onto one knee before he came up again with blood flowing freely out from both his nostrils.

Spencer could feel the warm drips along with the angry hostility coming off the other man, but he wasn't pleased. He became angry with himself for displaying fight, for losing control. There was no upside to showing capacity for resistance. You don't give up the element of surprise for nothing, for emotion. *Dummy!*

Pressure thumped out from the bridge of Bishop's nose, causing both his eyes to tear up and numbing the middle of his face out to his cheekbones. His head twisted in reaction, his jaws clenched against the pain throbbing through his brain from both temples. Bishop swiftly raised the electric prod like a club then stopped himself in mid-air, kept himself from delivering a killing blow through the crown of Spencer's hooded head. Instead, he looked back at the camera's ever-present green light and waited for his breathing and hands to steady.

The end of the rod touched below Spencer's chin, then jabbed beneath his jaw and liftedback Spencer's head. Bishop squeezed it until the metal fillings inside Spencer's molars were sizzling.

Bishop internalized the bloody reminder to stay out of Spencer's striking range. He should not have reacted to Spencer. He knew better. No. 1: set the pace, never counter. But he could live with what he was doing. He could handle it just fine. The head-butting bastard under the hood had also shot two dozen men and women down in cold blood.

He composed himself, then calmly instructed on the facts of life. "Rules of engagement. You touch me, you pay." Using the electric prod, he pushed upward beneath Spencer's chin until his neck could not rise further.

"I'm going to count to ten," he told Spencer. Then he switched on the voltage and observed as Spencer's neck stiffened. "One one thousand."

Both of Spencer's temples trembled.

"Two one thousand."

By six, Spencer's toes were dancing out of the ends of both leg casts.

At ten, tiny blood vessels burst inside both nostrils.

"Let's begin again," Bishop suggested enthusiastically. "Call it even and put acrimony behind. What's the favorite car you ever had?" he continued.

Number two, mix and blend, make them guess at what has value.

Spencer thought about that. It wasn't the minivans his mom drove when he was little and she was alive. Not Jack's white work vans. Not cars at all. Nothing on four wheels. Easy answer. Yamaha YX600S Radian that he rebuilt from a wreck in 1990. *Even better than the Harley.*

Bishop pried open Spencer's fingers and felt the inside of his left palm. Warm and moist. Spencer was responsive; at least, he could be if he wanted to be.

"You used several weapons with equal effectiveness, Jonathan. Tell me about them. Do you have a favorite?"

"You want to talk to me; you call me 'Sergeant' or 'Master Sergeant.' I earned the rank."

Bishop leaned down again beside Spencer's ear, taking care this time to keep beyond range. "Can't do that. We all have to salute somebody."

Spencer caught on. There was an audience watching. That made him happier about the head butt.

"I'm an American soldier!" Spencer shouted. "I fought for my country!"

"You shot down innocent American civilians in their homes, doing their jobs, just living," Bishop corrected. "Anything you earned, you forfeited."

"Rich people," Spencer said aloud, as much to himself as to the interrogator. "You're working for them right now, what you're doing. Are you rich? No. But you put out to keep them in control. They destroyed the economy and still they got richer. They hold everyone else down and keep getting richer. But you don't want to stop them. You'll snap up whatever bone they toss your way, right? Follow along, business as usual."

This was no canned response. Spencer's outburst confirmed what Bishop already knew in his gut. This guy was no hired gun. These attacks were not about anyone making money. If Jeffers couldn't get his mind around any other motivation, the problem was Jeffers' lack of imagination.

Bishop pulled on clean new plastic gloves and shook the hood out, then pulled it down across Spencer's face and pulled the lanyard tight. When Spencer shook his head side to side, Bishop added a strap that dug across Spencer's forehead so that he could not shift or squirm.

The spigot squeaked open, the plunging water filled into the plastic bucket.

Next question: Had Spencer acted alone?

Spencer's head dropped backward as the side lever released the chair back into a reverse incline. He saw the back of his right hand. He was sighting down a Leupold scope for the first time just as the water splashed at his mouth and up his nose into his sinuses.

He was back in Ft Benning, Georgia. Harmony Church. Math before weaponry. Geometry before ballistics.

He had always aced math in school. The ASVAB, the Armed Services Vocational Aptitude Battery, pointed to independent functional capabilities. Leadership, too, but he was never looking to run a company. What was his favorite weapon? It was right there in his hands, bipod kicked open, wind-motion target weaving its red dot against white surround on the motion arm.

"Spotters call distances! Shooters will modify settings!" Crosswind 6 to 8 mph SW to NE, target due north.

"Five hundred yards."

"Meters?"

"457.2 meters, Sergeant!"

BRASS, Spencer told himself. Breathe. Relax. Aim. He failed to get through the sequence; cold water rushed down his throat and up inside his skull. His world went black as Bishop continued pouring.

CHAPTER SEVEN

If captured, it won't be pretty. You will have been killing the friends and brothers of the same men who captured you. Most prisoners won't survive the first twenty-four hours. If you do survive, your captors will want to sell you, bargain with you, or extract information from you. Possibly all of these. Their belief that you hold information of value to them may be all that is keeping you alive. Your ability to utilize that impression, whether or not it may be true, can take you far beyond survivable condition standards. You will be on the greatest journey of your lifetime. Every resistance is a success and successes build upon themselves. But there will also be moments of weakness.

Support from the prisoners around you and the support you give to others is critical. But camaraderie won't always be possible. You survive because you train your brain and your senses to take you someplace else. Prisoners have reported being able to smell and taste and feel from memories. Replay missions down to the smallest detail. Think about every play or every inning of a ballgame. But never drift. Plan your thinking and vary it. Control your mind. Don't ever replay a continuous repeating tape. Rumination is a form of depression. Planning, thinking ahead, and controlling your own mind keep you the master in any situation.

He had to do much more, had to think much more, press himself. Boredom and isolation could take him down. Time. Absolute and formless, pierced intermittently by shrieking air horns then crushed and thin-spread beneath the ten-thousand-pound weight of boredom.

After each interrogation session finished he shook for more than an hour. When they dropped the temperature down to 40 degrees, he never stopped shaking. He struggled to regulate his breathing, fought to gauge time, as if grasping the measure of time was anchoring his sanity. The plates and staples in his right thigh pinched on the surface beneath the leg cast. Every tremor ached down to the core of his being. But in the absence of movement and sensory input, time also became the enemy.

Couldn't he just die? Instead of resisting, breathe the water into his lungs? What was the point of living? Hadn't he done enough?

*****

"Al, Owen is doing more than ruffling feathers," Major Gonzalez confided, calling Al Hurwitz to mentor the younger detective-lieutenant. "This is not going to turn out well. Get Owen to shut his mouth and let it go. Once they decide to clean house, they won't stop at Owen. Every one of us is exposed." Gonzalez sounded scared. Al had never heard him anything but confident.

"Who is 'they'?"

"You don't ask questions! You listen! Get to Owen, Al, now. Make this go away." Gonzalez hung up.

Al drove to the North Corona address. His mind drifted momentarily to picturing the Big Man, Owen's father Eamonn Cullen. Al had to shake it off before thinking about his old friend drove him to tears.

The boys, Liam and Casey, were shuffling inside the house when Al knocked on the front door. Callie answered the door. Her face was rigid. Beyond the narrow entry, the stairwell was stacked with cardboard moving boxes and suitcases. Al's eyes shifted to the crack on the hinge-side; he could see that there was no furniture inside the living room.

"I've tried calling," Al explained apologetically, "But I keep getting a message saying the voicemail box is full."

Callie caught Al's eyes fixed on the suitcases. "Owen isn't here," she told him, answering before he could get out the question.

"Do you know where I can find him?"

"I'll get my purse," she replied.

Al saw Casey's face. The boy had stretched to see who was at the door and waved, seeing Al, who wiggled his fingers in return. Al put his foot in over the threshold then stepped back again. Liam was somewhere inside but nowhere in sight.

"Here," Callie told him, handing over the Brooklyn address written on a torn slip of paper. "He's staying at Tremaine's. We're working some things out."

"Is everything OK?" Al asked.

"It is what it is," Callie told him with a shrug. "Go talk to him. He'll be glad to see you." She moved her hand onto the door edge. Al opened his mouth but no words came out. He nodded and turned back down the porch steps.

It took him nearly an hour to travel the eight miles south through Elmhurst and Brooklyn Heights on surface streets to the Flatlands address.

"What do you want, Al?" Owen challenged when he came to the door. His eyelids drooped and he needed a shave. "You and Callie cooking up an intervention? Am I messing up the suburban 'happily ever after' plan?"

"You going to ask me inside or make me stand outside?" Al asked him. Callie hadn't mentioned any of this. Al wished that she had.

Inside, the house was scattered with empty tallboy beer cans and pizza boxes. "I didn't come here about this," Al told Owen as he looked over the mess. "Callie didn't say anything. Owen, I'm here because I got a call. From Eduardo Gonzalez."

"Well, you can tell Gonzalez to mind his own business and you can do the same, too. I'm not an alky, Al. There's no Step One and no other steps, either. I'm going through some stuff. That's all. I can handle it. OK? I can handle it," Owen said.

"I wish your Old Man was here to slap you silly." Al swept the beer cans off the table and leaned into Owen's face. "You say you can handle it, handle it! You think Eduardo Gonzalez called me about drinking? You really think that's why I'm here? Get your head straight, Owen. Callie and the boys are moving out, you're not with them, and look at you. You think you're a picture of health? So I don't think you're doing such a great job. Do you? But that is not why I'm here."

Al had made some inquiries of his own before driving to North Corona; discretely, not like Owen's bull-in-a-china-shop approach. He stopped fast after looked no further than the file dates shown beside the entries. He never opened the actual files. He didn't have to open them. 'Dimitri Vosilych' first appeared in the system after Mamaroneck. Blood samples cannot match DNA with a person who didn't exist in the system before the DNA was analyzed. Owen had the little picture correct; whatever the big picture was, it was too big for any of them.

"Owen, are you sober?" Al pressed. "You know where I stand on alcohol, but right now I don't particularly care about your drinking habits. Focus. You need to focus!"

"Yeah, I'm fine." He scraped his tongue against his upper front teeth then tried unsuccessfully to swallow the gunk. "Let me get a glass of water." Owen stood up, looked at the cupboard, and then realized it was all moved out. He found a red plastic party cup, looked inside, and then put it under the tap to rinse it out. Nothing came out when he turned the faucet before remembering that the water had been shut off. He had a jug inside the refrigerator; he rinsed the cup and filled it again, then gulped it down.

"Owen, this is bigger than you and me and Tremaine." Al's voice came across firm, unequivocal. "You need to stop pressing buttons."

"It's shite," Owen grumbled. "Fecking bollocks. I'm going to find Master Sergeant Jonathan Spencer, I'm going to interview him, and I'm going to see what is really going on."

"No!" Al slapped the table and recoiled from the sting. "Owen, I believe you. Best guess is Major Gonzalez believes you. OK? I'm not sure who this Dimitri Vosilych is or if he ever existed at all. But NYPD, the Bureau, and every other agency have stopped allocating resources. If the shooter was still out there, they wouldn't do that, would they? No, they wouldn't! You have to let this go. Case closed. You have a family, a career. Case closed! Do you get that? Case closed!"

*****

No day, no night, only the uninterrupted single fluorescent bulb. Sleep and waking blended into a psychedelic parfait swirl that distorted the surroundings like a fun-house mirror while he lay there 24/7 with that tiny green bulb blinking down at him like a crazed housefly readying to descend.

His body rhythms were confused under the GE bulb's constant dull glare. Only foods distinguished mornings from evenings and days from nights. Oatmeal. Day. Day, sunlight and movement, purpose. Night. Meals: toasted cheese sandwich, potato chips, chocolate chip cookie; fish sticks and peas, buttermilk donut; Salisbury steak, mashed potatoes, Snickers bar; spaghetti with tomato sauce, iceberg lettuce with ranch dressing, tapioca pudding cup; chicken nuggets with honey mustard dip, creamed corn, fruit cup; beef stew, steamed carrots, chocolate cake; real roast chicken, red beans and rice, fresh fruit, a can of Tree Top apple juice. Turkey and gravy. Start again. But he salivated like Pavlov's dog waiting for the institutional food to slip along the floor.

On chicken fingers and apple juice day there were no interrogations. *Sunday?* Chicken fingers. He took to peeling off the breading in tiny bits, then leaving it to dissolve on his tongue. When the breading was gone, he tore the white chicken meat into minute threads and nibbled at them with his front teeth, squirrel-like, elongating the meal to kill time.

The monotony within the segregated cell was worse than torture; he would take the extremes over sensory deprivation any time. No contest. The 24/7 silences punctuated by the shocking metallic slam like a Chinese gong when they opened the food slot had him looking forward to interrogation. He understood how fucked up that was, but the challenge of resisting was sustaining him through, one day at a time. BPM and breathing could measure minutes. Minutes, with discipline, could be aggregated into hours. Hold onto the measures, he reminded himself. He practiced counting breaths into minutes, minutes into hours; he got as far as eight hours before cracking. Just knowing the time and filling it made him stronger. His exercises made him stronger. Every day the baritone Texas voice failed to beat him made Spencer stronger.

Irregular intervals between meals, but always between nine point five to ten point five hours between breakfast and dinner, thirteen point five to fourteen hours between dinner and breakfast, he thought to himself.

Two meals each day, ten hours apart, or very close to it. Dinners rotating on seven-day cycles. Even the interrogator took a day off, like this was routine for him, too. Apple juice day. Stocky and Slim were replaced by "the Twins" for two days, the day before and apple juice day, then came back dragging themselves like it was Monday morning. Interrogation was run between meals.

Spencer counted time on his toes and fingers between breakfast and then again when the cell door opened then again between his return to the cell and dinner. The interval gave him a gauge on the duration. He had learned quickly that it was beyond him to try to measure time during interrogation; what seemed like hours could have been several minutes; he just could not know.

Nobody brought charges against him. He never saw a cop, never was read his Miranda rights. No lawyer, no phone call. Their voices were American, but this wasn't America. In America, nobody chills a prison cell to twenty degrees one day and blazes it to 130 degrees the next day. Nobody straps you down, blindfolded, and then shoots you with narcotic cocktails that compress cognition into smells that you can feel entering through every pore in your body.

Clarity. The assemblage of rational thought without input, without contrast. *Get it together!*

The attacks had done damage. He hit them where they lived. *You'd be in a regular prison and represented by lawyers if they were confident, not in this place, wherever this is.* You're important, he told himself. The proof was all around him. *Let them think you're working with others, that they're all still targets.* Having billions isn't worth a lot if you're too afraid to be enjoying them.

Memory and contemplation were the challenges. He was built for the opposite of inaction. Filling time, endless time, was much worse than humping sixty pounds plus across a mountain ridge with his fist gripped around thirty-one pounds of steel Barrett. He imagined the feel of his fingers on the strings of his guitar. He tried playing air guitar to squeeze the sounds from each note. He failed.

He tried to picture Captain Sam sitting on the thick grass under the shade of their tree, the hundred-year-old oak with its foot-thick branches spreading fifty feet around the gnarled trunk. But he had no control of the images that popped into his mind. Too often, he pictured the kid in the red Manchester United shirt.

He sometimes pictured his dad, Jack, too. He had been keeping Jack afloat for fifteen years, depositing half his army pay into Jack's checking account and his dad went through his daily routine never noticing. What was Jack doing now? *Stop working for free, Jack! Invoice a customer, why don't you!* There he was, in the white overalls, chaining the white panel van, coming up the steps into the little white bungalow, walking into the white living room with two slices of Wonder bread and a glass of milk and sitting down on the couch until he falls asleep in front of the TV.

Remembering is hard. Memories need to be taken out in the fresh air. They need to breathe. Spencer tried to remember junior high and high school. The whole six years from his mother's death through leaving that house was close to bland, a random array of black and white fragments without adjectives or verbs, colorless and stuck.

Inside the gray walls, it became a struggle to bring color to anything. He already knew the gray walls well enough to spot faces, a dog, even rocket ships in the lines where the concrete had cured. He searched his palms, trying to remember which wrinkle was his lifeline and hoping it wasn't long.

*****

He need to initiate routines, hours-long workouts that incorporated the micro-exercises he trained himself to do while he was hiding, waiting sometimes for two days before his target appeared or he broke off. Exercise had always sustained him.

Working out from his toes to his neck and everything in between, including his entombed legs, Spencer pushed himself despite the mind-numbing pain. He was able to roll onto his stomach now, wincing but not crying out. His left thumbnail had worked inside the laminated ply on the underside of the sleeping pallet until the end of his thumb was entirely a giant blister. It was worth it to him; he could feel it beginning to yield, feel the sharp corner point as the layers peeled back.

His interrogator was under stresses of his own. Spencer could sense that in Texas' tone. He considered the implications, weighing the potential of victory against the unknowns that would come if he defeated his immediate captor. The next man would be worse.

He gave up Eagle Arms, the place where he sourced his weapons at the gun shows. He explained Sands Point in detail, right down to the oyster beds and the birthday cake. They already knew about the kidney, about his PEB, about the $32,000.

But he would never give them Captain Sam.

American-style mess hall food. Clean shoes. Clean uniforms. Clean water inside the toilet bowl. Consistent, reliable electricity. *U.S. facility.* Except when they used it tactically, the temperature was a constant, probably close to 70 degrees Fahrenheit. Spencer dismissed anything in East Asia, where consistency was always suspect and U.S. facilities commitments were few and far between. East Asia meant humidity, but the cell was bone dry. That dryness reduced the likelihood of Colombia, too. Removing Asia and Latin America left Africa (Oman, Morocco), and Eastern Europe (Poland, Romania, the Baltics). Mexico was too unstable. Too much focus on narcotics trafficking to be prime as a black ops site. Low profile, high security—a small facility. *Where?* Everyone he had seen or heard was U.S.; wouldn't they use locals in Eastern Europe? Oman would not expect or demand local employment. Dry climate, established U.S. support facilities, stable government, and no questions asked. *Oman?*

Every single one of the probable locations added language variables on top of the thousand other unknowns. Was the prison inside a city? Was he miles away from every other building? Did they truck in supplies or fly them? He had sat the controls of helicopters twice, small planes a half-dozen times. Zero takeoffs, zero landings. Flying optimized rapid distance, but apart from the obvious operating challenges, he also would stand out singularly on radar and satellite tracking. A remote location meant climate, terrain, water and food obstacles. Escaping into a crowded city might make it easier to blend or put a hundred thousand eyeballs right onto him.

All questions. No answers.

*****

Owen stared at the grocery store deli-counter Styrofoam container on the granite breakfast bar in Tremaine's kitchen. Chow mein and sweet and sour pork, along with a soggy eggroll and a six-pack of Bud Light tall boys.

"Not your gourmet cuisine, Tee," he said out loud, his eyes fixed across the kitchen on the stainless steel six-burner range.

Allen, the new Intel Commander, had notified Owen by email and voicemail that he was asking One Police Plaza to open up an official, permanent position at Intel Division. Owen took out his cell phone and replayed the message.

"Lieutenant, I have been documenting every effort to contact you at least twice every week. I don't know if you're dead or alive, and at this point I honestly don't care. One Police Plaza has been notified. Your union has been notified. This is the last time I pick up the phone to talk to a wall. You either get approval to return to work or you are done with this division and, let me tell you, after all this bullshit it's going to be an uphill battle for you to get a placement anywhere in the department."

He had occupied most of the middle of the day staking out his own house, sweating inside the hot car across the street until he finally gave up without a glimpse of Callie or the boys. There was a red eviction notice taped across the front door. One of the boys' rubber balls was inside the hydrangea bushes across the driveway alongside Mike and Shelley's old house. Both places were sitting empty. Mike and Shelley had moved to a house they bought at Lake Success. He grimaced thinking about it.

Owen got out of the car, ran across and retrieved the half-deflated ball. He stood in the middle of the driveway and tried to get it to bounce, but the ball stopped dead on the concrete, making a hollow *splat*.

He went and picked it back up anyway, massaging it in his hands as he was drawn to the decrepit shed. He pulled at the door until he could squeeze through. The old workbench was still there. Eamonn's oil can was on the shelf above the mason jars that hung from where the lids were nailed on the underside of a shelf up high, at the Big Man's eye level. Owen spun his father's vise open as wide as it would go and then put the ball between the steel sides and reversed direction, turning and tightening until the remaining air compressed and the ball burst, rupturing with one booming belch. Tears were still running down his cheeks when he stopped at the deli counter before driving back to Tremaine's townhouse.

He pulled one of the beers off the plastic ring, opened it, set it down and then unfolded the squeaky container. The chow mein and pork looked like grayish worms swimming in bright red mucus with yellow pineapple bits.

Callie's message from the day before said they needed to "look at legal separation." If he wasn't going to act like a man, she had to make decisions for herself.

Owen looked at the open can, lifted it toward his mouth. "Smooth Refreshing Light Beer," he read out loud. Then he stood up with it in his hand, grabbed the remaining five, and poured them, one by one, down the kitchen sink.

*****

Jeffers and the APA kept sending Bishop more instructions and demands. They had to be watching the interrogation feed, probably leering into their computers like they were watching television. *Suriving Torture…tonight on History!* He hadn't produced any deliverables in six days.

"Well, sorry to disappoint," Bishop muttered to himself. He'd spent his entire adult life working for the United States of America, not this old boys club, the APA, with its bullshitty patriotic name and its "iceberg" of hidden agendas.

What was it that really mattered to them, Bishop wondered, proving that Spencer was a hired gun or just seeing him suffer? He tried not to think about it, reminded himself that he was a realist and he needed the paycheck, but the whole setup bothered him more than he wanted to admit, the secret prisons, private organizations being handed work that only government agencies had always done. It paid well, and bringing in money freed him from having to think about money all the time.

You work your butt off to get to be an expert in your field and along comes Stephen Nussbaum and a thousand techies just like him and then the work you spent your life doing gets replaced by zeros and ones behind some piece of software.

On the screen in front of him, Spencer's biofeedback numbers appeared numerically and graphically in a sub-window while Bishop played back interrogation segments. The metrics didn't lie; the steep spike day one was now moving toward a level line. No rising anxiety ahead of interrogation; blood pressure steadily ranging from 115/70 to 124/80. Bishop tracked numbers after moving up to four-bucket sessions. Spencer could have been lying on a beach.

Left to his own devices instead of functioning inside their damned Panopticon, Bishop knew he could get the job done. Going back to 1952, the FBI measured an 8 percent attachment syndrome rate. Across his career, he was successful up to 56 percent. Seven times the standard. But if they hobbled him with interrogation limitations and then completely shot down reward-based therapies, it wouldn't happen. *Jesus. What do you expect?* Why the hell would you hire the best man for the job and then dictate to me how I am supposed to do it? *You know everything better than your own experts?*

Target acquisition methods?
Funding?
Intelligence resources? Domestic? International? Foreign government?
Ordnance?
Food, clothing, transportation, medical? Who helped?
Goals? Financial? Ideological?
Networks? Affiliations? Active military? Ex-military?

Each one of these bullets ought to lead into twenty more. But where the charts should have offered guidance, should have dictated when to hammer one point and when to pitch fastballs until the prisoner's head was bursting, every biometric measure was skewed. Spencer wasn't breaking, he was getting stronger.

The stress had to be increased. He should have initiated hours in forced positions, half-squats that burned and tore through every ligament in the knees. But how? The prisoner was in full-leg casts.

They had already instructed him to ratchet up using air horns, random disturbances to induce measureable fatigue-induced psychosis.

Bishop looked into the mirror above the hotel room dresser. "Are they torturing him or me?" he asked.

He surveyed his hotel room: king bed, chaise, 50-inch flat screen television, the desk where he wrote up the daily reports, the red leather armchair, room service leftovers on the round dining table. He wasn't sleeping, his appetite was gone (two-thirds of a dried-up cheeseburger with curling lettuce and crusting mayonnaise was left the room service tray), his right eye was going into random spasms, his hands were beginning to shake.

This was supposed to be his day off. He hadn't even left the room. Zero deliverables on accomplices, support network, handlers, anything at all that could offer up a gauge against the probability of further attacks, Bishop recounted. *Only he's one man, acting on his own. Period.*

Thousands of well-trained reliable snipers were out in the workforce doing every trade imaginable. Any of them could be ready to fire the next bullet, but they didn't. Why didn't Jeffers trust his own success? Americans are in the screaming and apathy business. *We breed nutcases, not political violence.*

"If twenty more Jonathan Spencers started shooting down billionaires, this country would see guns outlawed the next day." If that happened, APA and this Supreme Court would do a one-eighty and send private gun ownership straight down the tubes.

He was a lifelong NRA member, too, not that it mattered.

"Just reality," Bishop muttered. "You don't screw with the deep pockets."

Jeffers supplied Bishop with Spencer's military jacket before having Spencer erased from digital memory. The Department of Defense no longer held any record of Master Sergeant Jonathan Spencer. No training records. No history of engagements.

Bishop's copy indicated zero rebellion against authority. No disposition toward any ideology. So why did he kill nine billionaires? Who or what made him do it? What is it that separates the sniper soldier from the serial killer? Once you take away the money motivation, is it possible for anyone to shoot down strangers and not to be psychotic?

Bishop closed his eyes and pressed his fingertips to his head, massaging his temples until the surging pain passed. "You're making money hand over fist," he told the drooping face in the mirror. The cup was supposed to be half-full, not half-empty. But he could not escape the pounding reality. *Deliver or die*, the universal fact of life in consulting.

He unbuttoned the two top buttons from his collar then popped two Benadryl out of their foil wrappers, gulping them back with a swig of bottled water. On top of the bedspread, he undid his belt and opened his zipper then reached for the remote control and scrolled the hotel selections, pausing unenthusiastically at the adult offerings.

Not worth $8.99, he thought.

*****

Spencer pressed himself up and held a one-arm pushup then stretched his free hand to reach the toilet handle and flush. The water swirled clockwise. *Clockwise. North of the Equator.* Suddenly, he couldn't remember if that was bullshit or real?

If the toilet really does flush opposite then that ruled out Tasmania and Guam, he thought. *Nope. Not Guam. Could still be Guam.* But it was so dry. Guam would be sopping with humidity.

Working assumption—U.S. black ops site. Could still have been Afghanistan, or Gitmo, Pakistan, Thailand, Bulgaria, Moldova. But he felt confident taking Afghanistan and Pakistan off his short list. He knew voices of soldiers in those places, the newbies filled with jittery excitement, always anxious to prove that they have what it takes, and the deadly, bitter, threatening cadences from guys who had mastered their shit and kept it together. And then there was the lifeless mumbling of men stuck floating between fucked-up homesick sadness and mortal terror.

No, this isn't *in country*, he decided. Not inside the war zone. Afghanistan is out. Gitmo… Cuba? Stocky would have sweat rings under his arms the minute he went outside. Nothing there. Gitmo was out, too.

There was no tapping through the walls, no night screams, no sign of other prisoners through the thick walls. Intermittently, without any regular intervals, he felt that dull vibration humming through the wall beside the sleeping platform, but the single constant sound came from the tinnitus inside his own skull.

From oatmeal to spaghetti and meatballs, scrambled eggs and hashed-brown potatoes to chicken fingers, the Twins were there, four meals, two days per week. Stocky and Slim five days, Twins two, including the one day in seven when he wasn't hooded and shifted to interrogation.

No stripes, names, no unit insignia on their khaki fatigues. The keychain stayed on Stocky's belt. It made a distinctive, metallic zipping noise when it extended and retracted. Stocky held the cuff key and all door keys; Spencer figured that Stocky held rank, probably E5 or maybe a staff sergeant Slim was most likely SPC1 or corporal. *But five-day workweeks? That wasn't Army.*

Stocky always moved in first while Slim opened the door. His entire thick frame burst in like he was threatening to punch Spencer's face, always bullying to make the prisoner flinch. Spencer evaluated his response options, whether or not to strategically present himself cowering before the brute force, but determined instantly that he was never giving in. Each act of resisting charged his psyche. He made Stocky work up a sweat to get his head up and yank down the black hood and he paid for that, too, when Stocky's knuckles raked down his face and he felt Stocky cinch the lanyard into his windpipe. After the hood was on, he could feel Slim's thin hands reaching a wide waistband around him and snapping it closed along the small of his back. Stocky dragged a second strap under his crotch then ran handcuffs through heavy hoops attached by grommets set into the waistband.

Stocky liked to go the extra yard, leaning into the cuffs to get through more clicks. Spencer knew Stocky could tell that the force painfully dug the cuffs into both his wrists.

They trussed him out like a hog, then Stocky came from behind him, always lifting from the armpits, while Slim clutched his hands beneath the casts at the ankles. Piercing pain shot outward from both thighs and from the underside of his knees when they flopped him onto the wheels and moved him through the steel-cased doorway, but he held his breath and gave nothing back to Stocky.

From behind his head, Spencer felt Slim shove at the gurney to get it moving. Slim didn't smell of Axe today, but his clothing carried its usual sickly sweet scent from tobacco. Spencer noticed a raspy tone in his breathing as he pushed the gurney forward. Even through the hood, Spencer heard a motor sound followed by a soft thud and then a sound that he couldn't place, although it was strangely familiar.

The gurney was moved forward several feet then bumped into something and stopped. Again, Spencer heard a version of the familiar mechanical sound, then, when he felt a sudden lurch, he knew! They had him on an elevator. There was an elevator shaft abutting his cell! He heard two quick pings as they passed floors before the elevator bumped to a stop and the doors opened. The balls of Slim's feet scratched on the concrete floor with each long step the guard took. Stocky lumbered alongside, his weight shifting with short, shuffling steps. Metallic jangling. *Keys.* He seemed to be holding back, slowing the gurney to keep up. Elevator, he thought. *Where would a black ops site be elevator-equipped?*

A door opened and the gurney stopped, swung around, and then banged through. "Get that off," a clear voice commanded. It was a captain, he guessed; too young to be a major, but more assured than most lieutenants.

"No can do. Against orders, Doctor."

Doctor? Civilian?

Stocky. E5. Keys. Breath smelled of bacon.

A phone clicked being picked up, followed by the dial tones.

"He is a prisoner out there. Inside this clinic, that man is my patient and I'm not working around any hood. So you either modify the security protocol or I take this one further up the chain."

After a prolonged pause, Spencer heard a door close and sensed that the doctor relaxed as the man exhaled. Spencer felt the lanyard loosen then the hood was tugged away from behind.

When his eyes adjusted, the doc's face was less than a foot away from his. Full rose-colored lips, marble-white skin, jet-black eyebrows, and piercing glacier-blue eyes—the fine features imprinted upon him like a new hatchling gazing on its mother. He felt himself welling with emotion as the doctor's warm breath trailed across his face. Spencer looked away.

He scanned the examination room. Another camera was mounted in the corner, but the wire feed had been pulled out and where the green light should have been was dark.

The doctor followed Spencer's eyes and confirmed. "Big Brother isn't watching," he told Spencer.

The doctor lifted a backboard from the floor, called Slim to assist, and gently rolled Spencer away from him onto his side before they wedged the board under his torso. Evidently, Stocky had left the room.

"On three," the doctor ordered Slim. They counted together then lifted and tilted the board to slide Spencer onto the examination table. Spencer was certain that he revealed nothing of the jaw-clenching, molar-cracking variety of pain that shot through him, but his right leg began to spasm.

The doctor nodded at Slim and pointed. "Hold them both firmly. I don't have a medical assistant on the floor to help me. That means you're it." Slim held Spencer's ankles as instructed until the shaking passed.

Slim's eyes were down, how his neck was extended out over the ankles. Spencer's mind choreographed how he could exploit the vulnerability.

"I'm your orthopedist," the doctor explained to him. "I'll be supervising your recovery. You've had multiple compound fractures, which means that we're dealing both with repairing your bones and with some significant tissue damage. The intravenous drips you were getting served a variety of purposes from keeping you well-hydrated to pain mitigation to prophylactic antibiotic treatment to prevent infections."

It had been weeks since he heard so many words strung together. The sound released warm waves of adrenaline flushing through him.

"Where are we?" Spencer asked.

"Don't answer that!" Slim interjected instantly. "Medical only."

The doctor nodded and motioned Slim back with a calm, open upright palm.

"I'm going to use a cast saw to open up both casts," the doctor calmly detailed to Spencer. "This shouldn't hurt at all. I'll have the casts off in two minutes, we'll snip away some cotton and a stretch sock, and we'll get a look at my work."

The cuff harness made his task impossible; he couldn't reach more than three inches in either direction.

"Get these off," he ordered Slim.

"No Sir. No can do."

Military or not? Spencer was confused. Slim was a non-com, looked like it from his haircut down, but a doctor would have to be an officer and that didn't fit.

"This is ridiculous. Get this contraption out of my way, now!"

"I don't have keys," Slim protested.

"Then find someone who does."

Slim reluctantly retrieved Stocky from the hallway, who was adamant. "He stays cuffed," Stocky asserted.

The doctor pointed up at the monitor on his wall, pointing his finger toward x-rays with broad white cracks so obvious that anyone could read them. "His legs are fully fractured in eleven places. How's he going anywhere?!"

"Not going to happen," Stocky responded.

"Come here," the doctor instructed. Stocky squeezed along the wall beside the doc, who pointed out the obvious.

"Beneath the fiberglass and the plaster are legs," the doctor explained in a purposely condescending tone. "The legs went through multiple surgeries, with foot-long incisions and bone grafts and suturing and stapling. Now I need the casts to come off. How would you propose I do that when you have him handcuffed and chained around his crotch?

"Remove the damned cuffs. Now!"

Stocky gave in to the disconnect, grumbled under his breath, and stretched the retractable key chain until he had the cuff-key.

"Zip him," Stocky told Slim as he pulled on Spencer's wrists.

Spencer locked the key's image into his brain. *Inch and a half. Stainless steel. Tubular shaft.* It was clipped onto the same wide belt holding the Taser and handcuff pouch and several other pouches along with the keys. Spencer silently repeated the data points until he had them fixed in his mind. *Blue key one side, brass on the other. Cuff key in between.*

From the exam table, Spencer's eyes followed as Slim withdrew a fistful of white zip-ties from his shirt pocket. Stocky pointed at the metal rails alongside the exam table and Slim fed a long tie through until the first teeth had bitten, still leaving a wide loop.

Stocky unlocked Spencer's right wrist and grabbed it in a vice-tight grip, then pulled the plastic loop over Spencer's hand.

"Well?" Stocky challenged Slim, who got the idea and pulled the zip-tie taut, cinching Spencer's wrist to the rail before Stocky unlocked the left wrist and wrenched at the chain to roughly pull the waist and crotch restraints past the prisoner's scrotum.

"You satisfied?" he asked the doctor. Without any expectation of an answer, Stocky let the harness clank onto the hard floor and returned to the outside hallway, leaving Slim to keep watch inside the exam room.

The atmosphere changed for the better. It felt like an angry boar had left the room. The doctor raised Spencer's back to allow him to watch the procedure. An instrument table just beyond the rail holding Spencer's wrist carried a small cordless circular saw connected to a gray plastic tube attached to a shoebox-sized vacuum set on the floor. The table also held a full syringe beside a tiny still half-full bottle. The container was turned so that Spencer could see only a capital "K" on the label, not enough of a clue to identify the medicine.

"So, starting from here," the doctor told Spencer as he pointed toward his inner thigh, "I'm going to open things up. Just deep enough to clear the material. Nothing to worry about, ok?"

Spencer nodded and the doctor responded by patting him twice on his forearm.

The doctor leaned toward Spencer's crotch then jumped back, twisting his face away from the stench. He rolled Spencer just enough to see the caked-on residue and puss-filled ulcers on both his butt cheeks.

"What the hell is this?" he demanded. "This is basic hygiene. Jesus!"

Slim looked down at his feet, wiggling his toes inside his shoes.

The doctor looked like he was ready to go to blows before he composed himself. "This patient has had multiple operations," he shouted at Slim. "He is on antibiotics to prevent infection. Don't you get that?"

"It's not my call," Slim stammered.

"I see this again, I'll report you and everyone who touches this man. You hear me? Don't let it happen or you'll be looking for another job. I promise you."

Out looking for another job? Spencer didn't get it. Nothing about the statement computed. Since when did black-ops personnel get fired for prisoner abuse?

He walked to the sink, ran water over a washcloth, and put it into a plastic bowl. "Get over here," he ordered Slim. "Roll him onto his side."

After washing Spencer's backside, he returned to the sink with the brown washcloth, stripped off his plastic gloves, washed his hands thoroughly, and pulled on new gloves before returning to the exam table.

"When I'm done here, I'll give you some ointment for that rash," he told Spencer. "You need to make sure you shift positions. I know it will be difficult, but you need to alter pressure and get airflow."

Spencer nodded. The doctor glared again toward Slim then went to work.

Starting at the crotch, the doctor moved the buzzing saw down the inside of the leg to his knee, then, starting from the ankle, he made a new cut back up to the knee, and then a third cut to the outside of Spencer's big toe. A puff of white dust followed behind the saw blade then did a U-turn and was sucked into the vacuum. He moved next to the other side of the exam table, running one long quick cut from hip to toes. When he walked back around he had to pause for Slim to back away, then he efficiently resumed his work, pulling out an extension to the exam table to support Spencer's ankles as he moved on to the left leg.

In three minutes, both casts and the wrapping were off. Spencer's marathon-runner legs were unrecognizable to him. Purple, brown, and yellow-tinged skin was crisscrossed by surgical slices and brutal tearing was punctuated by metal staples, glue and sutures.

Spencer knew in that instant that he was never going to be the same. His mind drifted to Captain Sam, suddenly understanding the self-loathing reality of being broken beyond repair.

"Fantastic," the doctor exclaimed toward him.

Fantastic, Spencer wondered? His legs, the machines that he depended upon, looked like shriveled prunes.

The doctor worked his way along each wound, softly pressing his fingers into the muscles and watching. "No signs of infection. Everything is closing up nicely. Let's clean you up, we'll get some new x-rays, and then get you into some fresh casts."

Using a soapy sponge and warm water, the doctor dabbed and rubbed the patches of dried blood until they were moistened and wiped away. The soft, warm touch was unsettling. The sponge even worked between his toes. He looked at the back of the doctor's head. The black hair was perfect, every hair evenly in place.

Spencer stiffened against the pain and attempted to raise his right leg before the doctor's hand came down and checked his movement. "Hold on! You had a bone graft. Until it sets up and is completely joined to the femur, don't move it. Not at all."

Minutes later, he had new x-rays shot, developed, and displayed side-by-side with the originals. Spencer focused on the logo of the wall-mounted touch-screen monitor. *LG.*

"All good," the doctor assured. "Let's see if I can remember how to put on a cast and get you fixed up!'

"How long before they can stay off?" Spencer asked.

Before the doctor responded, Slim pointed his slender forefinger at Spencer's nose. "Shut it!" he ordered.

"Too early to say," the doctor responded as he broke out his casting mix and wraps. "You're recovering exceptionally well, but these are multiple compound fractures. I moved bone from your hip to bind the right femur. It's going to be months, casts and then extensive physical therapy before you'll have real mobility."

After Stocky and Slim moved him back inside the cell, Spencer's cheeks became wet from tears. *Time. Another week to ten days before he would be back there.* The orthopedist was the only real person who had talked to him. A few minutes talking and now he was all fucked up! All of a sudden, the weight of isolation fell upon him like a heavy barbell dropping on his chest. Once they started, Spencer could not make the tears stop.

Not good, he thought. The brain was a tool also. He needed his to be ready. Only how do you measure your own sanity?

Process. He had more inputs. More data sets. The unplugged camera. The cuff key. The plastic zip-ties.

The outline of a plan began to take shape in his mind. Maybe only the outside frame of the puzzle, but new thinking, new pieces that began fitting together.

CHAPTER EIGHT

Bishop knew the stats. Khalid Sheik Mohammed was waterboarded 183 times at Gitmo and not an ounce of intel came from it. But the APA couldn't care less about stats.

Jeffers' employers didn't care for solid, effective interrogation procedures. They wanted the strong visuals, so Jeffers demanded a good show. Empathetic approaches that actually worked, grounded in basic give-and-take, nope. No humanistic methods. *Verboten.* So Bishop used sleep deprivation techniques which he punctuated by air horns. He froze the cell for hours-long shifts that drew Spencer's core body temperature right to the limits for stroke or heart failure. Across four days, Bishop smacked the prisoner until Bishop's hands were swollen so badly that he couldn't lift a fork to eat his own dinner afterward. He might as well have been smacking a post. Spencer hardly reacted.

Torture and porn: watch enough of either and it does get monotonous. They could tune into the prisoner and the proceedings on the webcams 24/7. Now, they wanted more waterboarding more often. *Sorry if you're getting bored,* Bishop thought.

"I'm getting paid by the hour," Bishop told Spencer at one point. "So you go right ahead and take all year."

Paid by the hour? Spencer was puzzling over the comment when the water began flowing, just when he needed to fix on another place, anyplace. *Returning to base. After Manchester United. Miller.*

*****

Spencer closed his eyes and he tried to recall the scent of patchouli. It was there, spicy and recognizable in his mind, but nothing he could do brought the actual scent. Any scent. Even the food smelled like nothing.

Patchouli reminded him of Mercy. He could picture her on the bed with her legs crossed and her dry-skinned knees poking through the huge holes in her blue jeans. He usually pictured her laughing, throwing her head back and howling at something he said. Nobody else had ever thought he was funny, but somehow she thought he was hilarious. A couple times, when he looked at her longingly, she had shoved him off the bed onto the floor and laughed even harder. She was only two years older, but it seemed like ten.

He used to pick through her crazy tangles for the beads and feathers and other treasures she hid there. After long showers, Mercy brushed her hair wet, sitting in front of the mirror with just a towel around her, wrapped above her breasts. He timed carefully so that he would be in her room practicing guitar when she came back from the bathroom. They both pretended not to notice so he could hang out. He could smell the scent of her shampoo across the room while she brushed. He knew that he would recognize that scent anywhere, but he could not imagine the actual smell of it. He could hear her laughter. Sound was there, vision, too, but her smells he could only imagine.

He tried to imagine how she must look now, all these years later, but she was always the same, like she was too much herself to ever change.

*****

Spencer figured it was April. Trees would be blooming, apples and cherries and pears. The weather there was just getting nice again. Jack would be chaining up and padlocking the van handles and then he'd go inside and pour a cup of cold coffee still in the pot from the morning. He'd take it to the couch without bothering to reheat it, groan as he leaned forward to retrieve the remote, and then lie in front of that old projection TV until he fell asleep. Maybe he'd microwave a frozen dinner. Maybe not. *Jesus, Jack.*

How you making ends meet? Spencer wondered. *I can't deposit $2,000 a month into your account anymore. I can't pay your homeowner's insurance or your property taxes, either. You're cut off, Jack. Bill a customer, why don't you!*

He hadn't been home in nearly two years. They went and had dinner at Denny's in Ruther Glen. Four o'clock in the afternoon. They talked Hokie Football for a few minutes and then fished for "remember whens," snapshot glimpses with mom.

Jack, you were only thirty-two when she died. You didn't have to stop living. You were seven years younger than me today.

*****

He was not going to choke, not going to vomit, he told himself every time. But waterboarding means vomiting; discipline doesn't trump reflex. Acidic muck flooded thick, running over his cheeks and nostrils and earlobes, and gasping hot into his lungs as the water kept pouring. Every interval was a fight to take in air with the plastic clasp on the lanyard tearing into his Adam's apple. Slow, Spencer intoned, lengthening the vowel sound within his head until the mantra syncopated from his mouth, throat, windpipe, through the hood and deep within both lungs. Breathing became a tightrope walk, tremoring between cooling relief and tearing, rending, searing pain that continued hours after they left him back to the cell.

When he was inside the cloying sack, only these long, slow draws kept the black nylon fabric from sucking against his lips and drawing over his tongue each time he inhaled. The thickening carbon dioxide hinted of suffocation, but struggling against it only drew the lightweight cloth deeper down his throat. Vomit means digestive acids. It didn't matter if they did it forty times or four hundred, willpower couldn't prevent the suppurating sores around his lips, his gums, and all the way down the length of his esophagus. A hood means there is nowhere to spit, nowhere to rinse, no options. Salivating stung. Moving his tongue at all, anywhere, produced the effect of holding a hot coal pressing against mucus membrane. But he resisted through every method and every session.

The discipline that it took to resist did honor to his army training and to his combat experience. The army may have tossed the soldier out like a sack of garbage, but the warrior in him was right there, right at the front line.

Torture could fascinate, pressing his senses inward; he traced inside pores and rode blood vessels like water slides, pumping down through his own body and up again. He discovered that the body is color, that there is a glowing core within, a shape he had never before imagined, like a warm orb, sun-like but not the sun. It was like looking out from inside an infrared lens, being surrounded by sunset brilliance that people in the regular world would never ever see.

He ought to be dead. He beat the odds for a while, but in the end, the house always wins. He deserved death. But death might be too easy. He pictured the bright red Manchester United soccer shirt, the kid and his mother; a soccer ball-dribbling youth in a red Manchester United t-shirt, a mother in burqa, the father's loose kameez, still resonated in his guts. Their images played in his mind, overlaid by the graduated crosshairs of a Leupold Mark 4 scope. This, the torture, was his just desserts. But they wouldn't break him. He came in a hardass and he was going to leave the same way.

"*Asalamo Alikom*," Spencer offered.

His fingers, hands, eyes had snapped out the lives of 131 Afghan people, people who were tied to their lands, their families, their tribes because without their ties they would be adrift on a landscape where no one could survive alone. How many of them ever owned a car? A motorcycle? Had a flushing toilet? Every single one of them would understand why he killed billionaires. *They would never need an explanation.*

"Kill the head and the whole snake dies," the captain had said. "You shut down their leaders and every other billionaire buying off the country shuts down with them.

"When I was a kid, I remember saying to myself that if I saw Hitler, I would have killed him," Captain Sam explained. "I'd be a hero and save the world from all that evil. But these bastards are right here, still breathing, still tying this country in knots."

Captain Sam could never have gotten near anybody important. The captain didn't know the first thing about tactics. Spencer had intended to kill 131 rich Americans. Targeting specific individuals was impossible. Maximizing the variables was the only strategy that might work. But he failed at that and he failed the captain, too. The serpent was still out there. He never cut off its head.

Spencer tried a new exercise, stretch-planks raising his mid-section up with his body weight on his fingertips and the edge of the casts beneath his toes. One one-thousand, two one-thousand, three one-thousand, four. The thigh bone connected to the jaw bone. He breathed in and out through his nostrils, and then tried again. Five one-thousand.

Where is this? Slim, Stocky, the Twins, the doctor. *All Americans.* Not foreign contract hires. U.S. construction; American Standard was stamped into the underside of the toilet, GE logo on the light bulb. The electricity had never even dropped current, much less gone dark. Not one time.

Could I be right back in Afghanistan, he pondered? No. Wherever this prison was, it wasn't Afghanistan. There was no war smell. Too many clean shoes, too. In Afghanistan you can't keep shoes clean for ten minutes.

Urban or a fully supported American black ops base? He picked up more color showing on Slim's hands. The doctor's, too. More sunshine. *Northern Hemisphere.* Too early for northern sun. Not Canada. Not Poland or Bulgaria. Not likely.

There was so much he needed to know: What was this place? Where was this place? Entry and egress procedures? Card security, code security, biometrics, a combination of these?

Captain Sam had asked him "You ever heard of Joseph Goebbels?"

All he knew was that Goebbels was part of Hitler's inner circle.

"Goebbels was Hitler's propaganda minister," the captain explained. "He said that 'It is not propaganda's task to be intelligent; its task is to lead to success.' He didn't invent the idea, but he pushed the practice that when a lie is told enough times it becomes the truth.

"Goebbels laid the groundwork for a lot of what is wrong with America today. But nobody stops it."

"What happened to him?"

"Goebbels?"

"Yeah."

"He and his wife murdered their six children before committing suicide when their Reich collapsed."

"Oh."

"So how is it that a thousand politicians and talking heads spout the same lines on the same day?" Captain Sam asked Spencer. The captain spent lots of time listening the radio, politics, and thinking about history and politics and what makes people do what they do. Captain Sam made Spencer listen with him a couple times just to prove his point. Didn't it seem weird that nobody seemed to know where these canned lines come from? Every talking head acted like it was their same original thought at the same moment and people actually bought it. Goebbels' power of repetition. So was there a room full of advertising writers and all-night focus groups working together in some underground laboratory?

The lines were coming from one source, day after day after day, they originated from one point. Where?

"It comes from the Koch brothers, I'll bet you anything." Spencer smiled, thinking how he always tuned out when Captain Sam mentioned the Kochs. There was no way to stop him or change the subject.

"They hit us on TV and in the papers and on the radio and on the web, pounding like a monsoon shower from all sides. But it's one message coming from one spot. Somebody writes these things. They get delivered every day so the goose-stepping jerks can shout them in unison. They go out to thousands of people.

"Christ, Jonathan. I lost my hands and eyes to bring democracy to Iraq, a country that never asked for it. Now here I am, stuck in this lame body when I ought to be fighting for democracy right here at home."

*****

For a big man, Stocky moved quickly. A wrestler or a nose tackle in high school? Spencer couldn't decide. *All forward attack. No lateral movement. Knees, eyes, sides of the neck.* Stocky was vulnerable at every one of these points.

While Stocky opened the hood and yanked it down, Spencer reviewed motions for each of the standard disabling blows in his imagination. Eye gouges, windpipe thrusts, breaking the pelvis with the heel of the hand. *You've done them all ten thousand times.*

Killing strikes require precision; in the primal hierarchy, men are large animals with thick necks and skulls that are harder than fists. Aortic walls that are hard to burst.

Lying perfectly still, he could imagine the shifting balance that every move called up, the concentrated power as multiple muscle groups functioned in beautiful unison… krav maga, aikido, even the cerebral delights of the tai chi.

Spencer sensed the power in Stocky's hands when the big guard squeezed the gurney.

"Take off that hood," the doctor ordered him. "This isn't Groundhog Day, so let's not start like its day one. Unlock the chain rig and cuffs.

"Darcy, take his ankles. We'll shift him on three."

The zip ties were wrapped inside his shirt pocket in a rubber band. *Darcy* used a long one to attach Spencer's wrist to the bedrail before Stocky unlocked the metal cuff.

Spencer looked up at the camera. Still unplugged, the green light off.

Both guards stepped out of the room.

The doctor turned to Spencer to explain that "The internal sutures will be dissolving.

"We're going to get some new photos and see about removing those staples."

"Captain, where are we?" Spencer asked him.

"Don't ask questions I can't answer. And just 'doctor' will do."

Spencer locked eyes with the doctor. "They've tortured me. Thirty-three times."

"Don't," the doctor insisted, warning "I'll bring those two back in here." He looked away, preoccupying his attention toward his medical implements.

"I figured you'd have to be an officer, being a surgeon and all," Spencer responded.

"They own me for two more years. Then I'm a free man It's called paying for ten years of college."

Spencer looked over toward the doctor's hands as they moved over the portable table beside the bed: the small circular saw for removing the casts, gauze, a toothpaste tube of something, surgical scissors rounded at the tips, forceps, tweezers a foot long, a metal snips, pliers, the filled syringe and the vial. This time he could read the label. Ketamine.

"What's 'ketamine'?" Spencer asked, testing a second time.

"While you're in this room, you're my patient, but when a patient acts up in this room he becomes a prisoner again," the doctor told him coldly. "Ketamine is to settle down prisoners, settle them right down.

His tone rose again, more upbeat. "Let's get to these legs of yours. You're a lucky man, you know that? Even twenty-five years ago you'd have lost that leg right up to the hip. In six months you're going to be walking again."

After the casts came off, Spencer's leg began again to spasm. Except he was faking it this time.

"Darcy," the doctor shouted. "Come back inside!"

His shout went unheard. He had to go to the door and open it in order to call for help. Spencer registered the data point. Solid-core, soundproof doors. *Out in the hallway, they can't hear.*

Slim—Darcy—came to the base of the exam room table and held Spencer's ankles, leaning over the legs with his weight forward. The doctor fitted Slim with a lead vest and spread a lead mat across Spencer's groin then swung the x-ray camera into position over the table, taking five different angles on the right leg and three on the left, replacing the film brackets in between.

Spencer watched him moving fluidly between tasks. Efficient and professional. *But not military. Repaying student loans?* Not government, either.

The doctor went into a white melamine cabinet and came back with an aerosol spray that he shook first and then sprayed down the length of the Spencer's right thigh from hip to knee. "Topical anesthetic," he explained. It felt cold. The doctor seemed to be counting out seconds in his head before he poked his finger along the closed wound. "Feel that?"

Spencer nodded. He could feel, but he wasn't bothered by it.

"I'm going to remove the staples," the doctor told him. "If it becomes too painful, I need you to let me know." He snipped through the first staple then used the pliers to remove it, tested the closure with his gloved fingertips, and then moved to the next. After he had four removed, he went back to the cabinet and returned with a small tube that he opened and squeezed over the thick line where he had just removed the staples. "Super Glue," he explained. "We don't want you opening up inside the new cast."

*****

"What are you, Jonathan?" Captain Sam had asked him. He remembered thinking about that while they were lying on thick green grass beneath their oak tree. The captain had a way of drilling down to the essence of everything, deconstructing the components of the military, the war, politics and economics and history, then reassembling them around motives that went much deeper than slogans like love of country, service, and sacrifice.

"We're nurturers, teachers, healers, or warriors," Captain Sam said. "Sometimes we're more than one, but no matter what your job is or whatever the title is that anybody calls you, you have to know, really know in your head and in your heart that you're one of those four things or else you're nothing. Without nurturing, teaching, healing, or fighting for something bigger than ourselves, we don't exist; we're just taking up air."

"So what are you?"

"I'm a warrior." The answer came easily. Wasn't that obvious?

"Are you? Jonathan, one day, maybe soon, you're not going to be a soldier. So how are you going to be a warrior then?"

"Ah Christ, Captain," he swore aloud while the green light stared down high from up in the corner. Was it worth this? Concrete walls and nothingness lit by one fluorescent bulb. Now he looked forward to being tortured just so he could hear a human voice.

I messed it up, but I tried. The military treated him like used-up trash and threw him away, but he was a warrior. He always would be. Nobody could take that away, not ever. No one man alone could be the captain's Controlled Burn; he had struck the match, which was what he could do.

Jesus, he thought. *Be a warrior. Stop the pity party. Think of something else.*

He went back to the fall. It still made no sense. The black detective at Citi-Field was the same guy who had been in one of the speedboats on the Hudson. He was sure of that. He had seen the face through his scope then again on the TV news, and again at the stadium. But how? How did the guy know exactly where he was going to be?

Why the hell would you even think about checking out that stadium? You knew better but didn't listen to your instincts. You knew better than that!

If it hadn't been for that cop letting go, that one choice, then he wouldn't be looking at four gray concrete walls. Why did he do that? What made him let go? The last thing Spencer remembered was the sensation of Tremaine Bull's body bursting under him. It felt like a melon splitting. When they hit the concrete, it was all percussion, slapping flesh and snapping bone.

Why would he do that? To save rich people? What would the captain say to that, he asked himself? A cop giving up his life to save billionaires with lives so different that they might as well be living on another planet?

"You should have hung on," he said, thinking of the black detective. "You, man. You were a warrior. I would not have let you die."

*****

Spencer's right leg started spasming again; the pain moved from the splintered thighbone and settled into the hinges in his jaw.

He held on until the intensity dropped. He could identify every metal pin, screw, and the steel plate that anchored the brittle fragments along the path where two inches of his right femur had broken through taut muscle and skin, nicking the artery when he slammed against the concrete.

He tried to turn himself over, but even the simple act of shifting onto his belly frustrated him. With the heavy casts, he felt like a tortoise on its back. The best method he found was to twist his upper torso against the wall behind the pallet then push off hard, twisting at the same time to drive his hips over so the legs would follow. After the pain subsided he reached beneath the pallet, feeling for the spot where his left thumbnail fit between the layers of plywood. He began again working the wedge further apart to separate a sharp edge.

His fingernail hit glue and ripped back from the skin when he pressed into the crack. Spencer folded the thumb inside his fist, brought it up and sucked the blood from it, tasting iron in his mouth. He rolled himself over again. He couldn't continue working on the crease without the use of his thumb. He pressed himself to think.

What did the interrogator mean that he was being paid by the hour? At a black ops site? Weren't they all CIA and government contractors? And what about the doctor... not military; working off medical school costs? *What was this place?*

Texas didn't seem to want to believe he was acting alone. Was it beyond them to imagine one man, acting on his own, could make every law enforcement agency in the USA chase their tails? But if did convince them that he was acting alone, why would they keep him alive?

I executed upon those missions all alone, by myself. Me, I did that, nobody else. *Captain Sam's Controlled Burn.*

They're scared. They thought they were untouchable and you got to them!

He was one man and still he had reached out and he touched them where they lived and they were scared. The epiphany was comforting. He had punched right through the imaginary force field that they bought into every day through doormen and drivers and administrative assistants and all the other layers that separated rich people from everyone else.

They need their fantasy. They need to believe one man couldn't do it alone.

Had he started the Controlled Burn? Were other veterans fighting back? Captain Sam predicted people would stand up; they just needed an example to believe in. They needed to see that one man can make a difference! The captain said we would take the country from the billionaires: "It won't change, Jonathan, not unless we put a huge price tag on being rich."

Fuck… you're a doer, not a talker… keep talking to yourself and you'll lose your mind.

Starting at his toes, he tensed his way up his legs muscle by muscle, mentally mapping the broken bones and the torn tissues. He felt his scalp and his forehead, his nose and his upper lip. His tongue ran around his mouth, feeling the smooth fronts of his teeth and the individual definition of each molar and canine, rubbing the tip along the narrow edge of the incisors. He clenched and relaxed his jaw, tensed the back of his neck and could feel the plastic lanyard riding against his throat. He flexed his shoulders forward, felt his triceps and biceps, pressed his forearms against the straps and cast tension from his outstretched fingers. In one motion, his pectorals, buttocks, and latts unified into one.

Discipline.

Work. Make yourself do it.

Beginning from his toes, he tightened every muscle from feet to his buttocks and back down to his feet. One hundred times. Followed that by flexing and stretching. *Do a hundred, and when you've done that, do another hundred.*

The casts weren't getting wider; the gaps were growing because his legs continued to shrink away. *Don't think of them; not the way they are, not the way they were. Work with what you have. Rebuild them. Rebuild them and they can take you away.*

Spencer pressed his left fist against the left side of his jaw and pushed his head against it, holding the pressure for two minutes before alternating to the right side. Then he positioned both fists below his chin and squeezed down, forcing his arms and shoulders to fight against the neck muscles. Using his elbows, he pressed himself upward and shrugged his shoulders through fifty rep sets. He reached his left arm across his chest, grabbed hold of his right shoulder and pulled against his latts, alternating sides five minutes at a time. He jerked himself over and tried to work his core abdominal muscles with plank exercises, intending to hold it for two minutes before he felt something tear. From then on, he concentrated on tensing isolated areas from his pectoral muscles down to his lower abs, counting each day how long he could hold the positions and tension to gauge his progress.

He initiated a complex breathing routine for cardio and endurance. Spencer forced himself to inhale as deeply as he could then he exhaled forcefully, imagining there were birthday candles on the ceiling and repeating the cycle until they were all blown out or he collapsed, whichever came first. After he recovered and his breath came back, he initiated a quick series of breaths, in and out, repeat, until he could not do another and collapsed in a bath of sweat. Then rapid puffs, in-in-in-in-in-out-out-out-out-out; inflating his cheeks like Dizzy Gillespie again and again until his back spasmed from the exertion.

The breathing exercises released endorphins that in turn triggered waking dreams. He sometimes dreamed of Afif, of falling asleep face down, of hearing something but waiting that critical split-second that allowed the knife blade to plunge. At better times he dreamed himself back with Captain Sam, lying on the grass beneath their tree. But whenever he settled into that cool calm it seemed like an air horn would shriek or they would come to take him again. Sometimes they dropped the temperature until the cell felt like a meat locker. He discovered that the cold has its own sound, a deep organ note that hummed its tone inside his bones. He had never considered that temperature could have a sound, but it did.

He was burning more calories than he was taking in, but he was building back muscle, too. The casts began to get tighter. He knew each muscle and tendon in each leg by heart, had them challenged in every way that he could imagine.

One-and-a-half to two months of therapy for each month in the casts? *Bullshit.*

He could feel his body inching back.

CHAPTER NINE

"Our forensics audit is running in parallel to your interrogations," Jeffers reminded Bishop. "First to the result. That's all I care about." The APA had that down cold, pressing, pressing, pressing. Looking down through that camera, bullying 24/7.

When you want results, Bishop thought, you hire your expert and let me do my thing, you don't micromanage and threaten and constantly dog me. Don't keep saying I'm one move away from being thrown out with the garbage. *Fiji water and compliments. Fuck you. Spencer was alone, whether or not you choose to believe it.*

"There's no radical Islam imprint to any of the attacks," Jeffers expounded. "Not even Sands Point, where every victim was a Jew. Nothing inherently anarchistic or communistic, either, except the implied *raison d'être*, IKRP, I Kill Rich People. "

"*Raison* what?" Bishop asked, his Texas twang stretching each vowel.

"*Raison d'être*," Jeffers repeated. "It's French, Sheriff, boils down to 'why.' We've got nine dead billionaires, every one of them with his hands into something that translates into profit and loss at his demise. They'll find out what. Even the Russians or the Chinese can't hide it forever. Irregular options trades, derivative placements; something is going to surface."

"I don't think this was about money," Bishop judged.

"It's always about money," Jeffers interrupted. "Between SEC, NYSE, and NASDAQ trades and the after-markets, plus side-book private action between bigger players bypassing the exchanges, they've got mountains of data to run through, but they'll get there."

Jeffers made no attempt to disguise the message. Either he produced deliverables soon or his project was going to be a one-off and so-long gravy train.

Hitting Page Down, Bishop jumped straight to the file record for his most recent interrogation and pulled it up on screen. Bishop used his touch pad to expand the biometrics insert until he could see the graphics clearly. The vivid colors contrasted with the white background and the dim images on the screen. Spencer had to know that he was about to be flipped backward then doused.

Cold water would be flooding into his sinuses and rushing down his throat. He should have been terrorized. He was not. The hooded subject was calm. Blood pressure 110/70, respiration four breaths per minute, heartbeat at 56 BPM.

Tapping several keys, Bishop altered both screens into a graphic display showing the subject's vitals from initial interrogation through to the most recent.

"Effective interrogation is not one-size-fits-all," Bishop argued. "It doesn't work that way. If it did, you wouldn't need me."

Jeffers stared back at Bishop through his laptop screen, saying nothing. When the consultant's best argument is "I'm the expert," Jeffers was generally inclined to take things in another direction.

"The U.S. Army is really good at cracking a man's willpower," Bishop explained. "They threw everything they had at him across three different elite training programs and he came through every one. Let me translate that into your medium. The odds against becoming Master Sergeant Jonathan Spencer, getting through three of the military's toughest elite training environments in three tries, never failing, are roughly parallel to the odds against starting from scratch and becoming one of your Vision Partner billionaires. No networking, no shortcuts, no lucky breaks."

Bishop tried to put it in words Jeffers would understand. "Spencer took it, took the roughest challenges the army can think up, and got through them on skills and determination and guts. Pain won't sway Master Sergeant Jonathan Spencer. I need you to turn the cameras off and let me work this my way."

"Mr. Bishop, you have had twenty-two days. I have been backing your hire since day one."

Twenty-two days of constant pressure was breaking Bishop down more than the prisoner. Eagle Arms, Bishop recalled. The most effective day of all and they pulled the rug out from under him because Spencer looked like he was having too good a time.

"I have never had basic autonomy since day one!" Bishop countered. "Results and a good show are two completely different aims. How can you have any idea what my hands feel like after forty or fifty hard smacks at a man's skull? I stick them in an ice bucket for an hour before I can use them to write up your briefs!"

"Give me two days," he finally said through his laptop. "I can deliver value and get this moving forward."

Jeffers nodded in the screen. "Two days. Bring us the organizational structure."

*****

Deliver or die. Bishop flashed on his ex-wife; wouldn't she have a field day if their daughter's $25,000-per-year private school tuition couldn't get paid?

She just loved any chance to tell their daughter that her father is a loser. But the minute she heard he was making money, she'd call the lawyer and drag him back to try for more spousal support. He could see it coming from a mile away.

Darcy and Ferrell trudged past him out the door; the prisoner was inside, prepared; hooded and strapped atop the half-barber chair, half-Lazy-Y-Boy, both casts extended straight out.

Bishop entered with the electric rod gripped in his right hand. Underneath the black hood, Spencer's face lifted and turned, alert to the sound of Bishop's soles hitting the concrete. But Bishop didn't walk into the room. Instead, he pressed his back against the wall and slid along until he was directly below the camera, where he craned his neck and looked up to where the USB cord was plugged in. He stretched out his arm and reached with the electric rod and came up more than a foot short. Bending his knees and waist, he tried to recall the old motions of jumping to tap the basketball rim and leapt up, swinging at the cord and missing short. He tried again, this time mashing his lips and tightening every muscle group before springing, then coming up lower than the first time. This time he took off his shoes and toed them along the wall, being careful to keep them outside the camera's viewing angle. When he came up short again, he reached back and angrily threw the rod at the camera, scoring a direct hit that snapped the neck of the plastic bracket in two. The camera swung on a pendulum, dangled by the USB connection for a moment, then crashed onto the floor.

Spencer followed the thumps and smacks and the hollow clatter of cracking plastic without any idea what was meant by the noises.

Footsteps crossing the room. Thick fingers touched at his windpipe. He twisted side to side and strained at the Velcro restraints, then the pressure of the lanyard eased and the hood slipped up and away. He blinked at the light until the shape of Bishop's broad face came into focus like the first sight he was seeing after emerging from the egg.

Spencer was confused, embarrassed even, and shifted his eyes around the room. He saw the broken camera; the green light was snuffed out, and he looked up at the severed bracket high on the wall.

"Look at me, Jonathan," Bishop told him. "We're just going to talk, man to man." Bishop's fingers reached under the Velcro arm grips. "I want to release your arms. Can I trust you?"

Spencer's eyes studied the face that went with the baritone Texas accent, filling in the vision and realizing for the first time how his brain had already set another image entirely. This man was graying, at least ten years older than the voice. The jaw and beard line were similar, as was his height, but this man's lips were more delicate. Spencer could see the pores and the blood vessels on Bishop's nose, the white hairs inside both the wide nostrils and the dark tunnels behind them.

Bishop's blue irises locked onto Spencer, readying himself to jump out of reach at the slightest pupil contraction in Spencer's eyes while he slowly ripped back at the first Velcro restraint.

"I know to the hour when you were stabbed," Bishop explained. "I know about Landstuhl and Madigan and Walter Reed. I know your whereabouts for much of the past twenty years. A week after you left Walter Reed, you hit Sands Point."

Spencer felt the pressure released along his forearm but held it down along the armrest. While the blood supply returned to moving freely into his left hand, he eyed Texas while the man stepped back from the chair and carefully moved around to his right side.

"I don't see how you worked with accomplices. The profile doesn't fit with your mission reports, either." Bishop ripped open the second Velcro restraint and gingerly stepped back beyond Spencer's reach. Slowly, Spencer lifted his arms from the armrests and massaged weakly at his forearms to speed the blood flow and the strength it brought back to his numbed palms and stiffened fingers.

"You going off the reservation?" Spencer asked him, throwing his chin toward the broken camera.

"I'm my own man."

"Who's on the other end of the camera?" Spencer challenged.

"Work with me or you're going to find out," Bishop warned. "The devil you know…"

"Your back's against the wall," Spencer chided. Outlasting Texas felt good.

"Yes it is," Bishop admitted. "Get with the program, Sergeant, before it gets worse. One hell of a lot worse."

"Why are you doing this? For whatever money they're paying?"

"You killed two dozen people!"

"Did you know any of them? Were they friends of yours? Family?"

"What the hell does that matter?" Bishop argued. "The law is for everybody. I don't enforce the law just for people I know."

"So you're doing your job?"

"That's right."

"You enforce the law," Spencer reiterated, "Except those guys behind the camera get to pick the laws you enforce! What about the laws saying I have the right to an attorney and a trial? What about illegal torture? Is that how you all do things down in Texas?"

Bishop's face flushed red. He stepped closer then quickly lifted his toes and reversed, remembering the head-butt and remaining outside Spencer's lethal radius. He smiled, like a man who had stopped short of stepping into a minefield, turned and opened the door behind him.

Spencer watched him whispering something into Slim's ear in the bright hallway and then passing along two dollar bills.

"Good job, Sergeant," Bishop told Spencer. He reached the lone straight-backed brown metal chair from across the room, turned the back toward the outstretched casts, and straddled it to ride with his stomach facing the seatback. He wasn't rising to the bait. "I hope you like a cold Pepsi. Straight from the machine. I'm buying."

Vending machines at a black-ops rendition site? Using dollars? What the hell?

Slim opened the door and stepped inside with the Pepsi cans, immediately noticing that the hood was off and Spencer had both his arms free.

After Bishop took the cans, he nodded for Slim to go back the way he came. Slim saw the camera on the concrete floor and glanced up at the broken bracket on his way out.

Bishop popped open one can and sucked down a long gulp. "You want this," he said after his ahhh. "I need your word that you're not going to pitch at my head."

"Affirmative."

Bishop offered the can out to the end point of Spencer's reach, watching his eyes as Spencer's fingers wrapped around the Pepsi. Spencer opened it and listened to the fizzing sound. A flush of pleasure coursed down both sides of his neck, tickling under his clavicles. He sniffed at the aperture, took a tiny sip, ran it around his mouth tasting the drink and feeling its carbonation across his tongue, and then poured half the can into his mouth, lustily enjoying the cold on his teeth and into his throat.

"Tell me about the PEB," Bishop continued. "Nineteen-and-a-half years and they cut you loose. That had to hurt."

"Nothing I can't handle," Spencer snapped back at him, but the reaction in the prisoner's eyes made plain how deeply Bishop had touched a nerve.

"They took away your pension. Thirty-two grand for your kidney and *adios compadre*."

"You think I give a shit about money? I don't."

"Then why 'I Kill Rich People'?" Bishop probed.

"Because everything doesn't have a price! Name anything that is important and nobody can ever own it. Because their money makes us small; they isolate us and they squeeze us and they try to turn everything into a quantified commodity that they buy and sell. You really think they give a shit about America? They've got mansions and yachts all over the world and jets to take them, just like Saudi princes. If they loved their countries would they offshore everything? Huh? No they would not!"

Spencer gulped again at the Pepsi; suddenly he felt startled, tricked into saying more than he had spoken in months.

"They? Meaning the rich?"

"Who else?"

"Tell me about Samuel Hall. Major Davies, at Walter Reed, says that you helped him. I understand he lost both his hands and his eyes."

Spencer eyed Bishop and shut it down. He was done talking. He reinforced his decision by stretching out his arm with the remaining drink, opening his hand in mid-air, and letting the can hit the floor where the remaining liquid glugged out over the concrete.

Bishop rose and smacked the chair to the floor. "Boy, you just don't get it," he shouted in frustration.

"Fuck you!" Spencer shouted right back.

*****

Bishop stayed up through the night rehashing and second-guessing each of his approaches. When he finally got into bed he was trying so hard to get sleep that he became too angry with himself to keep his eyes closed. Everything ahead was outside his comfort zone. Jeffers wouldn't extend so he had put it all on the line.

He had to turn to the thiopental sodium, but thiopental sodium offered a narrow window; too little would have no effect, too much would kill. Zero room for error and any mistake would probably kill Spencer and kill his own meal ticket. Years of intense physical training aside, Spencer had been lying on his back with zero activity for almost two months. Bishop could not predict or control, but he had no other way to deliver and no wiggle room. No deliverables, no further contract.

The suggested maximum total dosage was 500mg; initial dosage to induce anesthesia 100mg at 2.5% solution injected over ten to fifteen seconds, 5% maximum solution in resistant patients. Bishop reviewed the recent surgical notes and went back into Spencer's army medical file, confirming no reference to allergies. Spencer's weight had been measured before the surgeries on his legs. One hundred sixty-seven pounds.

At three a.m., he realized that Spencer couldn't have food in him. Bishop texted orders to the guard station. "No morning meal in 22. Confirm in reply!!"

While he waited, he took himself out of bed and filled 10ml of pure water into a drip bag then tested the flow by clocking volume dripping from each of the three valve settings. Now he wondered whether adding thiopental sodium in solution would alter the flow rate. He strained to think it through clearly. If it does alter rate, it should be slower, not faster, he reasoned. On that point, if he erred it would be to the safe side.

Bishop opted to set a tee valve and apportion a 2.5% solution into two separate drips to afford more dosage control, but he was only marginally proficient with phlebotomy in the best of circumstances. Now he had to prep the solution, set up the intravenous drip, prep the site, set the needle and valve, administer the dosage, monitor vital signs, and interrogate; three different tasks, each one needing distinct skill sets, and he had to do this without medical support after getting maybe two hours sleep.

He choreographed every step in his head, from mixing the solution to setting the hangers to finding the injection site, prepping the location and positioning every piece on the standing tray, and then he hesitated and went back to his case. He wanted to have adrenalin prepped and positioned.

None of the medical staff interfaced with interrogations. If things went south, Bishop doubted that he would get any medical help. He suddenly wished he had a portable defibrillator and wished also that he knew how to use one.

"Confirming. No food in Cell 22."

*****

Another camera had to be mounted to replace the broken one. Bishop briskly ordered it done immediately then refused to offer any explanation as to how the original mounting had snapped in half. An hour later, he glanced up at the camera's green light, and then stepped out of the interrogation room to get to the small bathroom in the hallway. There, he applied an alcohol swab and used it to sterilize a thermometer. He placed the bags measured out with distilled water inside a pot filled with warm tap water to get the liquid up to at 85 degrees before mixing for optimizing the solution. When he returned to the room, Spencer would be situated; the guards were told to fully-strap the prisoner at his torso and have both arms wrapped up to the wrists. Once the needle was in, Bishop was making damned sure that Spencer couldn't shake it loose.

Slim dropped a thick nylon strap over the hood and straightened it around Spencer's chest and biceps just like Bishop had instructed. Spencer inflated his lungs and arched when he felt it tightening, but resisting did no good. Bishop motioned for Slim to wait behind him, and then pushed the tray stand closer to the prisoner. Next, Bishop walked the rack alongside.

"The intelligent decision is to play ball today, Sergeant, before this day takes a very bad turn," he said.

After five seconds, Bishop sharply tilted Spencer backward to open his elbows wide. He then wiped a sterilizing pad across the inside of Spencer's elbow. Spencer heard the paper torn away from the wipe and felt the cold evaporation. The only other sound Spencer heard was Slim's wheezy breathing from ten feet away.

Bishop inhaled deeply then inserted the needle and exhaled with relief at finding the vein on his first attempt. He twisted off the syringe, picked up and tore the clear plastic wrapper off the tee-valve, and snapped it into place, pinching Spencer's skin in the process. Two hanging bags containing the clear liquid, one to each side of the tee-valve; Bishop purged lines and then began the thiopental sodium.

"Moment of truth," Bishop stated. "You want to keep breathing, capitulate." His voice had a strained tone that Spencer hadn't heard before.

"Sergeant, this medication could kill you. I do not want to do this and you do not want to make me do it, believe me."

Spencer didn't give a damn.

"Do like I told you," Bishop instructed the tall guard. "You're going to see a drop, but if the top number goes below 60 you let me know and you shout it loud!"

Bishop turned his wristwatch around so he could operate the valves with his fingertips while also watching the time, starting with a single valve for an eight-second interval.

"117 over 64," Slim reported.

Bishop nodded. "Tell me when it is twelve minutes from now," he ordered, and then glanced up at the green light before turning his full attention toward Spencer.

A burning sensation instantly moved throughout Spencer's body as a metallic taste accompanied a squeezing tightness inside the back of his throat. Bishop counted out five seconds then shut the valve and watched as the remaining solution inside the line continued into Spencer's vein.

Spencer's attention drifted. He shivered his head to regain consciousness, feeling like he was falling asleep at the wheel and concentrating to resist.

Bishop counted fifteen more seconds before commencing. "What's the number?" he called out.

"89 over 30," Slim called out.

"How many other snipers are there, Sergeant?"

"I don't know," Spencer answered. The question didn't make sense. Snipers out where?

"Who else was working with you on the Sands Point operation?"

"No."

"Was anyone else involved in choosing the target, planning, or any other portion of the operation?"

"No."

"What made you choose to attack Morris Levy's birthday party?"

Spencer twisted and craned his neck forward first to the left and then to his right. He breathed deeply, fighting hard not to fall asleep.

"Morris Levy's birthday party," Bishop repeated. "Levy, Branderman, Perlman, Fleish. Why them? All Jewish?"

"Don't care. Billionaires."

"Why?" Bishop pressed. "Why billionaires?"

"Controlled Burn," Spencer mumbled unintelligibly.

"What? What was that? Say it again!" Bishop reached up and shut the valve completely. Spencer was of no use unconscious.

"Con-trol-d bun," Spencer repeated. His tongue felt huge, as though it was filling his entire mouth. It was the last conscious thought before he passed out.

What's he saying? Bishop wondered. He swung the laptop away from Slim. BP was steady at 92/58. The mixture was working, but he needed more time before Spencer crashed.

Bishop went into his case and removed a vial of ammonium carbonate crystal; between that and the oxygen, he was determined to revive Spencer before resuming. He rolled an oxygen tank beside the chair, turned the top valve, adjusted to 70%, close to triple the 21% found in sea-level air, then masked the prisoner and looked at his watch. Spencer should not stay out for more than fifteen minutes.

Slim left for a cigarette while Bishop waited. Twenty-two minutes passed before the guard came back and Spencer's eyelids flickered in reaction to Bishop's penlight. Bishop removed the oxygen mask and opened the smelling salts beneath Spencer's nostrils. He shook instantly back to a drunken facsimile of consciousness. Bishop slapped his cheeks and opened the drip valve, knowing full well that repeating the procedure decreased the odds of any good outcome. Thiopental sodium became more deadly each time he turned the valve.

"Sergeant, you were talking about Sands Point, saying a 'controlled' something was why you killed the billionaires. Controlled what? Hear me, Sergeant? Controlled what?"

Spencer was underwater. He wanted to go up, but which way was it? His eyes were closed. Why was that?

Bishop slapped his cheeks again, harder this time, and followed with the ammonium carbonate. "Sergeant," he yelled, "Attention!"

Spencer's eyes opened wide, his mouth, too, but nothing was there in front of him.

"What's your name?"

When he didn't answer, Bishop closed the valve again. Spencer understood that he should know what a "name" means, but the concept refused to take full shape.

Bishop pressed the oxygen mask over Spencer's mouth, holding it there as Spencer breathed while watching the pupils for reaction when he passed the light beam in front of Spencer's eyes.

After ninety seconds he repeated the question.

"Johnny Spencer."

"I need you to think about the birthday party, Johnny. Tell me about the birthday party."

"Randy says he gets to play with Millennium Falcon 'cause he's the guest, only it's my birthday and I get to. He can have Steve Austin but he won't."

Bishop's voice remained calm. "You're all grown-up now. You're a sergeant in the United States Army."

Spencer turned his head and held it facing to his side. It was ok. Yes.

"You were a sergeant in the United States Army and after that you worked for somebody else. Tell me who else you worked for, Jonathan. Who did you work for after the army?"

"Nobody. Nobody. Nothing." He started to sob, but stiffened quickly, refusing to let himself cry.

Bishop moved to the laptop to check Spencer's metrics. BP was stable and climbing. He was coming out of it. Spencer hadn't been acting; Bishop knew affirmatively what he had suspected all along. Spencer was acting alone. But if APA believed that, he might have just worked himself out of having work. There was more to this than one fact; there was more and he had to make the APA want more. He reached his fingertips onto the valve and opened the drip a third time.

"Controlled what, Sergeant? The attack on Sands Point was a controlled what?"

"Controlled burn," Spencer enunciated. "Billionaires are killing my country. Killing them before they tear us all apart."

"What is tearing us apart?" Bishop put his emphasis on "us." He wanted to ride the current with Spencer, to empathize, to nurture.

"If they own the law, how do we stop them? They take everything, control everything."

"You killed them to stop what? What were they doing?" Bishop looked back toward the green light, hoping that they were watching this live.

"Somebody has to stop them." Who else? Why did he need to explain? Why wouldn't they just know it? Spencer struggled to think. He had something, something from the Captain, floating by. "Freedom comes from opportunities," Spencer mouthed.

"Why do you kill rich people? Why do you hate rich people? Did rich people do something to you?"

Spencer squeezed his eyes closed, feeling himself free-falling deep into the well of his own memory, falling into darkness. He was far away from the prison. He was there in the hallway with Captain Sam's Alice and the two most beautiful little girls he had ever seen. He was telling them again that Captain Sam wouldn't come down from the ward. Every time they drove up to the medical center, the captain refused to see them and then he dropped into a funk or worked himself into a frenzy, talking about how Spencer needed to dissect how power works so he'd "get it," how a corrupt system wages wars that can't be won. How assholes that never went near a war zone used war to make themselves richer while he ended up like *THIS*, shaking two stumps up to rage at God.

Spencer was unaware of the intravenous drip bags and Texas getting louder. Even the tinnitus had ceased.

Alice, Captain Sam's wife, was there, right there in front of him. They were on the ward. But Captain Sam wouldn't come out of the toilet. He missed her until he ached, but she was right there and he screamed to Spencer to tell her to fuck off. "Tell her to move on! File for divorce and move on!"

He knew Captain Sam wanted to hold her and touch her and see her and he could never do any of that, not ever.

"I'll do it," Alice finally agreed that day. "I'll stop coming." Filling out a half-dozen forms and driving a four-year-old and a seven-year-old two hours each way wasn't something she liked. Who wants to go to a hospital and then to get there, knowing he didn't want to see his own kids?

"He doesn't want to be with me or be with our kids. I get it! But I have to hear it from him. He needs to say it himself. I want to see his face and hear him say it," she said.

"I can't remember their faces," the captain whispered after Spencer came back. He could picture his girls dancing in the family room while he lay on the carpet scratching the dog, but he could not picture their faces. He begged, "Jonathan, tell me how they look."

Then Spencer realized that he had not noticed; he was an expert in fine visual detail, but every truly vivid picture since he entered the military had come inside his brain through a rifle scope.

"You shot two dozen people!" Bishop screamed at him. He cracked his open right hand down across Spencer's mouth and shouted again. "You shot two dozen! Why?" His left hand followed, leaving a reddening handprint.

"Why?" he screamed. "Talk, goddamnit! Why?"

"No," Spencer cried. "No." His head dropped back, motionless.

"Sir, the blood pressure!" Slim yelled. "It's down to forty!"

Bishop shut the valve and ran around to the laptop. "Why didn't you tell me? Why didn't you watch?!"

"I was watching! It was at 79 and then it changed. It just changed."

Bishop gripped his fists around the cotton at both sides of the vee at the neck of Spencer's prison shirt then ripped it open wide. Spencer's breathing was shallow; he barely inhaled and exhaled. Bishop took a step, looked over the stainless steel tray, searching it frantically until his eyes locked onto the syringe containing adrenalin and lifted the syringe like a dagger, placing his thumb onto the plunger while his left fingers pulled the cover from the three-inch needle.

"Sir, it's climbing," Slim called out. "64, no, 70. It's 73."

Bishop leaned on the cool wall and rested his forehead against his left arm. The full syringe remained locked in his right fist.

CHAPTER TEN

Bishop pored through the interrogation tapes. No connections were going to turn up with stock traders making bank on the attacks and Spencer's victims; he knew that, and if Jeffers had been watching the tapes, then Jeffers knew it, too. But Jeffers wasn't going to give him anything. By now, Bishop understood that Jeffers made information a one-way street.

Spencer was a believer. Whether the APA was ever going to accept the truth about that would remain an unknown. Bishop had pumped up his bank account, but he felt no more confident on the inside than he had at that first meeting when Stephen, AKA Red Pants, had upstaged him.

Nobody is ever satisfied with just Lee Harvey Oswald, Bishop knew; that's the fundamental problem with the lone gunman theory. There always has to be a conspiracy. Money follows events. But if the APA wanted a conspiracy, he couldn't give it to them. There were no handlers, no Iranians or North Koreans or Russians pulling strings. No domestic terrorist cells waiting in the wings. The attacks were unified by just one thing. Like he said, *I Kill Rich People*.

If the analysts running through comm data had found something, Bishop reckoned that he would have caught some tell somewhere; these guys weren't good enough poker players to keep information like that close to their vests.

There was none of the chatter that precipitates attacks and none of the claims for credit that follow. Eight, maybe even nine billionaires, depending on the closing numbers, had been shot dead. Along with the many more victims attributable to the shooter, there were perhaps another dozen copycat victims, plus multiple law enforcement casualties, including the one dead detective from NYPD. None of that meant Al Qaeda or Iran or North Korea or the Russian mafia. But simplicity doesn't satisfy the imagination and it doesn't drive future funding.

Up until IKRP, billionaires spent their security dollars on burglary and kidnapping; they didn't seem to think about anybody shooting them. Spencer was a job creator. He might single-handedly have started a whole new emphasis. Imagine that.

Returning to his true-black Herman Miller desk chair, Bishop watched two huge monitors again, rewinding then zooming in on the interrogation cell on his left. The prisoner's respiration numbers were even and steady, more like a metronome than any human response under those conditions.

He tapped the keyboard to bring up real-time vitals then stretched the metrics until the graphics box widened. Each pulse showed solid consistency, with digital displays of BP, heart rate, galvanic skin response, that fluctuated within tight, steady bands. Spencer's cardio function read like a Kenyan Marathon runner. Sleep dep, sensory dep, sensory overload, temp shifts from 130 degrees down to 10 degrees... heartbeat, lung function, GSR, blink intervals; every single measurement followed a spiked pattern across the first four days followed by lesser reaction responses across the next few days until these shifted into reptilian stability for fifteen consecutive days. Asterisks punctuated controlled use of niacin flushes, psychoactive sodium amytral, flunitrazepam, and the sodium thiopental that nearly killed him. No thrashing, no measureable changes, no response to suggestive imagery. They even played his father's voice to him. Nothing. Like a machine in Energy Saver mode.

That was interesting, but APA wasn't going to pay $550 an hour for researching Spencer's equilibrium. Besides, Bishop was already clued into their idea of research, which meant taking a foregone conclusion and finding academic hacks to backfill the blanks that could get them there.

Bishop looked over the metrics and debated phoning the APA line. His job was done. Like it or not, Jonathan Spencer had acted alone. Bishop was convinced of that now. There was nothing exotic or difficult about acquiring sniper rifles; every state except California permitted the sale of military-grade weaponry and the separate conversion kits to take weapons from semi-automatic to full military automatic function were available 24/7 online. The police reports reflected whatever might be called mission intelligence.

Between Google Maps and other web resources, any lone wolf could handle reconnaissance basics. Not one shred of evidence indicated either the need for or actuality of any conspirators. Whether that was what the APA wanted to hear was another story, but wasn't it better to tell them get it over with rather than wasting their money by dragging this out any further?

Interrogation made sense. That was about extracting valuable information. But with nothing, zip, zero indication that the prisoner was employed by any group or persons, the only plausible, evidence-based conclusion was that he acted alone. Waterboarding Spencer again would be torture, pure and simple. You can't expose what isn't there. He acted alone. If Jeffers didn't want to hear the truth Bishop knew he should walk away. That was real freedom, having enough money to walk away. The thiopental sodium had crossed the line. APA might be his cherry client, but he was sick of secret prisons and torture.

Bishop vacillated, wrestling with whether or not he could continue collecting paychecks. He tried to convince himself that if he walked in and told the truth Jeffers would appreciate a honest show of economy. Wasn't it better to play it straight instead of milking the cow until APA pulled the plug? It was hard to walk away from that sort of cash flow. He rewound and reviewed interrogations, going through one last sickening pass to reinforce his decision. On the screen, the prisoner was strapped onto the water board, the black hood puffing out with each exhale as Bishop left him waiting to begin again. In the picture, the Velcro was digging into Spencer's forearms. He was breathing slowly, taking in deep breaths through the black hood while the fabric drew in and puffed out again. The fabric rode up inside his nostrils each time he inhaled. Respiration was up. Pulse rate, too. His arms strained against the Velcro. He arched his back and tried twisting to get enough torque to get the straps starting to open, to hear something start to tear. Spencer's abs tightened as Bishop moved closer. His fingers balled into fists. Bishop watched himself glancing up at the green light and the camera lens before filling the bucket.

He watched the entire session, the hacking, the vomit coming out his nose and mouth and welling inside the hood.

Bishop would have liked to know what Spencer meant by "Controlled Burn," but strategy and ideology weren't the hot topics. Nope. Spencer was alone. One of the hundred-thousand nameless, faceless prisoners shut up in "Special Detention" or "Segregation Units," or whatever other euphemism was in style for solitary confinement. Spencer would probably have been better off if the thiopental sodium dosage had been a measure higher; instead of staring at four walls, two hundred milligrams more would have ended things right there.

Did you enjoy your show? Bishop wondered to himself, thinking of Vision Partners on the other end of the camera feed enjoying themselves like Roman emperors inside the Coliseum, cheering for more gore.

The APA might not care to know facts, especially facts that deflated their big conspiracy. So long as they were entertained, he could probably go right on collecting the paychecks.

But he was done.

*****

"Go back and try again," Jeffers told Bishop.

"I can take your money, but what is the point in digging if we know the well is dry." He was trying to keep the APA from wasting money, but his appreciation of their wallets didn't seem to register at all. *What don't you understand?* Bishop asked himself. Spencer had acted alone. Strictly a lone wolf. No conspiracy. There was no indication of anything further to worry about.

"It's our money. If we're worried about it, we'll let you know." Jeffers scanned a file on his Smartphone, a short report on Bishop that critiqued and scored daily efficacy on a ten=point scale.

"Use the sodium thiopental," Jeffers ordered. "You were getting somewhere with that." He wasn't ready to reach a lone wolf conclusion and lose all the momentum—flow of funds, rallying the faithful, growing the cause. There was too much to accomplish yet to call it quits.

"It nearly killed him."

"And?" Beyond whatever useful information Spencer held, he was only alive because nobody up the chain of command was going issue the order to terminate. Nobody at APA was going to issue that order, either. That was the universe they lived in. Nobody with the ego and ambition to get to those positions would ever put himself on that line. Sometime, could be a decade from now, a new administration could come along with old memories; a new director gets appointed, faces change on Senate Committees, somebody hacks the system and gets things to the press, somebody gets in a pickle and leverages a name to get himself off the hook. When you plan on having a long career, rule number one is plan for leakage; you cover your butt and you never ever trust anyone. But dying during questioning? That was excusable. You can't make an omelet without cracking eggs, after all. A certain amount of attrition was to be expected.

Bishop realized that he had no wiggle room. *You either say no or sell your soul.*

"You could suck out his brain and spread it out like butter and there's not going to be anything more of real value to you," Bishop told Jeffers. Interrogation was one thing. Waterboarding and using hot rods and strapping the prisoner's forehead without the prospect of drawing valuable intelligence was just plain torture.

"I'm delivering the intelligence," Bishop continued, "But short of manufacturing the content of that intelligence, there is nothing of any additional value that I can deliver. Mr. Jeffers, I'm into my third decade with interrogations and pursuit. I know how to do my job. This happens. You work and probe and take twenty different approaches and still there is nothing there! What I can tell you is that I have never failed to bring in a suspect and I have never been proven to have missed critical intelligence that has lead to a subsequent event. Not once."

"Let's take a break," Jeffers suggested. Another month to six weeks would be about right; the wheels were already in motion. "We'll table this for now; we'll let you know when we're ready for closure. Hold off on your report and revisit the topic after the casts come off his legs. Your sodium thiopental therapy can wait until then." He looked across the screen intently, straight at Bishop's eyes. "Submit billings through the end of this week and I'll see that we deposit a retainer for those same totals to date when you resume."

Bishop looked at the graying monitor as the screen faded out. He had just been offered $150,000. Why? The one most probable conclusion was that Jeffers wanted to retain him as executioner. One hundred fifty thousand dollars to buy one extra eyedropper of clear liquid? The idea made him physically sick, which was surprising. He didn't think anything could give him that feeling. Not anymore.

*****

"Master Sergeant Spencer," Bishop began. There were no hoods, just the two chairs, Spencer's recliner and Bishop's straight-backed metal desk chair, in the dimly lit space. Spencer looked up the seat from where his wrists were cuffed and shackled around his waist. A rubber band wrapped around a rag was covering the camera lens up in the corner. "This may be the last time we meet. I thought we ought to be face-to-face."

Spencer looked around the room, which was about how he imagined it would be. The plastic bucket sat on the floor beneath the spigot. If his eyes could fire lightning bolts, he would have turned that bucket into ashes.

Bishop picked cigarettes from his shirt pocket, took one in his lips and gestured to Spencer, offering him a smoke. Spencer tried to raise his hands but could lift them only as high as his sternum; he didn't smoke, but if it could result in getting his hands free, it was worth trying.

"Of course," Bishop responded. He reached the cigarette up to Spencer's mouth but didn't call out to Stocky for the keys.

"Off the record, here is your chance to talk. No agendas. We're done with all that."

"I want a TV set," Spencer told him. A TV could tell him where the hell he was being held.

Bishop shook his head no. This wasn't a negotiation. "Not up to me. I'm not involved with the incarceration-side."

"Is this for real?" Spencer wanted to know, pointing his chin toward the covered camera.

"Yes," Bishop agreed. "My job here is done. Yours, too. We both know you were on your own. They, the men with the cameras, might want to think otherwise, but I don't write fiction."

"Where am I?" Spencer wanted to know.

"Can't say," Bishop told him truthfully. He had signed a Non-Disclosure Agreement within his contract that specifically precluded any hard information exchange, on camera or not.

NDA aside, Bishop admired Spencer's determination. While he breathed, there was fight left in him.

"Then why should I talk to you? What's in it for me?"

"An opportunity to tell your side. That's what I can offer." Bishop lit himself a cigarette and took a deep pull.

Spencer eyed Bishop. No empathy there. What did he care why?

"You ever been to Afghanistan?" Spencer asked finally.

"No. But I spent time in Iraq. A lot of overlap, I imagine."

There wasn't much overlap. Afghanistan had seen the Macedonians. Alexander the Great had conquered the Persian Empire and got his ass kicked in Afghanistan. The Arabs swept through, but the tribes were never conquered. Genghis Khan and the Mongols, Timor, the Russian Empire, the British Empire, the Russians again, and the US-of-A. Compared to what was done to the Afghans, the torture they laid upon him was a walk in the park.

"I killed 131 Afghans doing my job. Over there, in their country."

Bishop waited through minutes without another word being spoken. "And you got screwed when you came home," he finally prompted.

Spencer nodded. But it wasn't just that he was screwed. Being washed out was only the spark. The reasons for what he did were big, bigger and more important than any one life, including his own.

"How did you get from that place to killing rich people? That's what I've been trying to figure out. Middle-class kid. A year of college with good grades and then you drop out to join the military where you become an all-star soldier. What's the connection? What makes you hate rich people?"

Spencer eyed Bishop. "Do you hate me?" Spencer asked back.

"No."

"But you nearly drowned me, you shot me full of drugs, you used the electric prod, "Spencer pointed out.

"If you don't hate me, what made you do it?"

Money, Bishop thought immediately, but he didn't say it. "Point taken," he replied.

"I don't think armies hate the enemy. It is hard to sustain hate. For most people, I think it is. I didn't hate the 131 Afghans," he said. "Maybe we should only kill people we hate. That would make it hard to go to war. I've thought about that a lot."

"Tell me about 'Controlled Burn.'" Bishop waited again, giving Spencer one more chance.

Nothing.

"Last chance," Bishop announced.

Spencer thought about the Controlled Burn, wished he could articulate it, but he knew it would never come across correctly. *God,* he thought, *Captain Sam, you should be explaining this, not me.*

"You throw me in this place. You nail me in the balls with electric pokers. Whatever else I did, I spent nineteen years serving my country. I earned better than this," he said.

"You want to know what 'Controlled Burn' is about?" Spencer spat. "It's about fighting for my country *in* my country. It's killing the few so the many can have a chance. It's about optimism and hope, not rich people walling themselves behind castles and covering the walls with weaponry. It's about shifting the way this country is run before it is too late."

Spencer looked down the length of the leg casts and raised his eyes to face Bishop. "You work for the government, right? How do you rationalize what you're doing?"

"You killed twenty-three Americans," Bishop replied. He rose slowly, dropped his cigarette and crushed out the butt and then turned and rapped hard on the door for Stocky and Slim to let him out.

He turned slowly back toward Spencer as the heavy door creaked open. "Am I the one who is rationalizing?" he asked.

*****

Pulse, breathe, minutes, hours, days, weeks… Spencer was left inside his head in the windowless concrete room. The war hadn't been perfect; even Spencer got sick of the war sometimes, but he was perfect at it. In Afghanistan he spent lots of nights imagining how he could stay there after everybody else pulled out. He understood those men, their Pashtunwali—their code was elemental; it required no language. Killing them or if they killed him was circumstantial, no less, no more. A quirk of fate, a decision by far-away men neither of them was ever going to meet.

How could a billionaire understand Pashtunwali?

Spencer reviewed his evolution, starting like every other sniper, going out with sixes, six-man squads with a team leader, second team leader, security, the whole thing. Mostly drop and crash stuff, in and out of a building, sometimes to secure a drop zone, sometimes to take down a target, sometimes a snatch and grab to get a high-value prisoner. Back in those days he was a specialist, not a sergeant or even an ATL, much less a team leader taking orders and calling the shots on the ground that meant everything to mission success or failure. His job was handling C-4, setting donuts around door handles and pancakes on mud walls to open access for the entry squad while he had to wait outside on security.

He shifted to twos just before he circled the first time, before he was rotated stateside, then twos again when he deployed for the last tour. Twos are all about target elimination. Minimum profile, snake in the grass. You get your butt down and hold tight for hours, for days, until you get the one second to get the high-value shot. 800 to 1500 meters, mostly.

He pictured Mo Singleterry, the Specialist he had spotting for him. Good guy. Reliable. Kept it light, but always had his head on a swivel. Sharp. Six months together, then Singleterry got himself fucked up by an IED. Captain Sam was all wrong about explosives. Improvised explosive devices were indiscriminating sneak attacks. No honor, no commitment; chickenshit. Target precision was what it is all about. Not drones, not mortars, not bombs. Then boom. Singleterry was on an airlift out, leaving behind his right ham muscle and a kneecap. Gone. Spencer never saw him again. Never tracked him down afterward, either.

After they evacked Singleterry, then it was just Spencer. They moved him to fill in with weapons training for a couple Afghan police units coming out of Helmand. He was reassigned to Miller after that. Then the work picked up fast. His assignments came through Miller; CIA, he imagined, although that was never spelled out. Solos. Sneaking in and getting out intact. Fast. Nothing that needed a spotter. Nothing over eight hundred yards.

He was coming in after a lap around the airport when he heard the news, then turned around and ran a second lap, trying to perspire enough to purge the taint from what had just happened. Gunmen took all sixty recruits, men with wives and children, men who wanted to do good, to really do good. Two busloads of new graduates who had just finished the joint-training program, the same program he had helped in training, got stopped practically right there in Kabul, right by Park Khairkhana. They took them off the two buses, zip-tied them, had them kneel beside the road. They called them *kafir* and shot them in the head. That was right before his last mission. Before Manchester United. Almost all the snow was melted, with just a dusting left at the very tops of the mountains outside Bagram.

With his eyes shut, Spencer put himself right back there. He was running the perimeter and trying to get right, thinking about heading for the mobile shower structure and holding his head under cool water forever. But Miller helicoptered in with orders. Maybe that was better than the shower, he figured. He needed a mission to get his head straight. When that happens, when you are moving on emotion, you need to stand down. He didn't.

A soccer kid in a bright-red jersey and his mom. If the buses hadn't been stopped, if the recruits hadn't been executed, would he have made it a game? Would he have used a single bullet to kill son and mother both? Would he have done it differently if his finger hadn't been poked through by the damned thorn?

He knew now that if there was a hell, that one bullet was going to send him to it.

Miller had put his man, Afif, up to the stabbing. There was nothing random. It took Spencer weeks after the stabbing before he put the pieces together clearly. Miller's tribesman didn't have any reason to kill him. He had every reason not to do it. Then after Afif stabbed him, Miller's man was caught and under control. But Miller shot him dead.

It was all Miller.

*****

Keeping up with the exercises felt futile. Day after day inside monotone gray. The blank, soundless fluorescent void; he could feel it taking him down like quicksand. The more he fought it, the deeper he sank. He thought about Captain Sam, too much, ruminating over the captain's ideas in a continuous loop. Sometimes he loathed the captain even more than he despised Miller.

Now, stuck there endlessly in the monotony of the concrete box, Spencer's brain was entangled again with the captain. He cried just like he cried after running out of the ward building toward the Harley. He thought as he rode that he had only ever listened to the captain because the captain needed someone there to listen to him. Somehow it had all stuck; somehow every word felt like it was carved inside his brain like words carved into a monument. *A government of the rich, for the rich, by the rich will perish from the earth.*

Right at that second, if he had a roof to jump from, he would have offed himself, too. He had done enough.

When he could harness his drifting mind, he kept repeating every one of a dozen unanswered questions. There were no further clues. He couldn't stop himself any more than he could stop the tinnitus ringing through his brain.

The same cop was at the river and at the stadium. *How?* And if law enforcement knew who he was, then why didn't they issue it on the news? Why didn't they enlist the public's help? Had he succeeded? Did the public turn on the billionaires so they wouldn't help to catch him? Was that what the police were afraid about? If he had the public and the police didn't, then had his approach succeeded? Was that why they put him where he was and not into an American prison where he would have a lawyer and go to court? Was that it? Was he some kind of a hero? Where the fuck was this place? What comes next?

He had deconstructed every attack one by one. *Bullets for Billionaires.* Strange that it was Emerson Elliot there at Sands Point and then the same Emerson Elliot talking about him every day on the radio. The shooting element to the mission was easy. The rich protected their things; they seemed to think that everyone had to want to *be them*, not that anyone would want to *kill them*. At Sands Point, he could probably have taken down two or three of them without ever beaching the wave runner.

Ahead of the first mission, he never once gave any thought about all the targets being Jews. That was coincidental. It was their money, just the money. That's why he sent the index cards, to clear that up.

Sag Harbor was a turkey shoot. Beneath him. Moving back into the trees to make his shots more challenging. Manchester United all over again. The soccer kid and his mom with the one shot. Was this place payback? A custom-tailored personal hell?

The hardest aspect to his target selection was knowing in advance where billionaires were going to be. But after he identified charity events, he found that these went on nearly every day and every night.

Central Park West had demanded skills. That hit home. That was in their homes. The auction was satisfying, too, cool and sophisticated. Even after they put up that whole barrier in front to keep all their rich bidders safe, shaded every window, he still attacked at will. They never considered protection for when the art was picked up. No security whatsoever. *Pretty smart putting a microphone into the flowers.*

Eighty-five people on the planet with more money than three billion other people. *Imagine that.* Single individuals with more money than every person in whole countries. Just one person. That had never happened before, not in all of human history. Captain Sam was right, if you believed God could mean for that to be right, you could believe anything.

"They're richer than Genghis Khan," Captain Sam said. Richer than the Pharaohs. They buy people and laws just like buying things. "Rich people don't go to prison. When they go too far, the government they purchased just bails them out." How was it right that billionaires earn more during a night's sleep than families make in a year?

Why didn't law enforcement get the public involved? Why no APB after Mamaroneck? He left a bloody mess after laying down the Harley. So why no APB? Why no name and photo on TV or in the papers?

"Jesus! Think of something else! Anything!" He looked up at the camera. Was anyone even watching anymore? Was this it, two meals a day and these four walls? Spencer pushed off the wall to turn onto his stomach and slowly crept his left hand over the edge of the plywood pallet. After almost two months, he had a three-inch triangle two-ply thick ready to snap away. Sharp points at each corner. Sharp enough to cut through skin and artery.

*****

Bishop swiveled his Herman Miller chair to get a look. Below him on the football field at Bishop O'Connell High School, the Knights JV football team was running drills. He watched linemen hitting the blocking sled, but his mind was weighed down by $150,000. $150,000 goes a long way toward paying the bills. Writing a $3,800-a-month check for the executive office just to wait for the phone to ring was its own sort of torture for him, but as the weeks passed the $150K retainer chaffed a thousand times more. Did Jeffers own him? For $150K?

Spencer's casts had to be coming off soon. Would Jeffers remember? Of course he would. *1000 milligrams thiopental sodium.* Less than a shot glass. Clear as water. A mistake during questioning.

"You kids will still have your football season. Birthdays and New Years and Easter will still go on. Just not for Jonathan Spencer," he said to himself.

He wished he had taken his own advice. He should have headed someplace where the water was blue, the sand was white, and girls in every shade of brown wore their black hair long. But no, he needed to be inside the fold, so he kept his ass in the chair and waited for the goddamned phone!

Do you even want *to be their go-to guy?*

"Jesus H. Christ," he drawled. "Man the hell up."

Spencer's life wasn't worth anything. "Ain't right to wait for your meat to get slaughtered and dressed out and butchered into a Styrofoam container," he reminded himself. "You gonna eat it, you ought to be ready to kill it, too. Your momma didn't raise any hypocrite."

Killing Spencer was probably a test; pass and he could be in their club. He wasn't some one-trick pony. He would be useful. All he needed was the chance to prove that. And if he didn't do it, somebody else would. If he could only get established, they'd see the quality and appreciate what he brought to the table.

1000 milligrams thiopental sodium. Clear as water.

Tuition bills were already eating into the war chest he had just built up. Wasn't he paying the property taxes and a mortgage to keep his ex and their daughters in a beautiful house with a great public school district?

"Why the hell do they need private schools and equestrian training?" he asked the air. She'd be real happy driving him into an early grave, he thought, until college bills started rolling in. Eighteenth birthdays weren't that far away. The custodial order was enforceable through "age of majority."

"Maybe, just maybe, this gravy train is going off the tracks. You expect more after that, you better plan on playing a sweeter tune."

*****

Days and weeks. He knew the meals by heart, know meatloaf was coming and imagining the tart and sweet flavors within the thin ribbon of barbecue sauce. Fish sticks every seventh dinner. A slice of baked ham, grits, and squash the following day. Hours, endless, between.

He no longer gave a fuck about the camera; mashing his face into the meal tray, he licked at every curve and cranny then sucked at his growing beard for every last flavor. A portion that looked even a bite smaller than the week before could make self-discipline impossible. A short serving of mac and cheese left Spencer shaking for hours with homicidal rage.

The sharp-edged plywood triangle dangled beneath him, teasing him and never completely out of mind.

He was sick of repeating images, sick of Mercy's hairy armpits and Jack's face through the window in the white box van, sick of Miller's bundles of cash, sick of every slide in the never-changing continuum inside his tinnitus-ringing skull inside the gray cell walls. He was sick of the casts, sick of his exercises, sick of everything. Manchester United was worst of all, pricking at him until he could have put a thousand more shots through the kid's brain.

Spencer had to draw deep to gather the discipline that had always carried him. Through the most brutal training, when all he needed was to raise his arm to make it stop, he held on. *Soldier on!*

He figured his sitting pulse rate at sixty; sixty times sixty counted to one hour, three-thousand-six-hundred beats. Eighty-six thousand-four-hundred beats per day. Six-hundred-four-thousand-eight-hundred equaling fourteen food trays.

Measures and milestones, targets; hour upon hour Spencer trained. He sharpened his attention on modulating his breathing, inhaling and exhaling once for every fifteen heartbeats then endlessly repeating the cycle until it became his natural rhythm; once every fifteen seconds, four times per minute. *3600 counts becomes 240. Easy. 5760 in the day.*

Muscle tissues were repairing along his wounds, closing into an abstract of asymmetric jagged scars beneath the casts. He could feel the musculature responding to the demands of his exercise routine. Quicker flex responses. Thickening densities. Power replacing pain.

But after counting fingers and toes up to eight hours at a time, he peaked and retrenched. The more he fell backward, sometimes back to five hours; the more he reached beneath the sleeping platform to tease his fingertip against the sharp points of the triangle below.

When he pressed his fingertips against his jugular vein to count out the hours, he imagined the pointed triangle, the easy exit. *Right there, right where you're touching. You can pull it off and stop the clock. Right now.*

A twisted whisper crept inside his mind. *You'll never get away...*

Food! The clang and the sound of the food tray scratching across the floor wiped away whatever thoughts that preceded.

You're getting out of here, Ranger! Wherever the fuck this is, you're getting out!

CHAPTER ELEVEN

"Give me the bedpan," Spencer screamed at the unblinking green light. He waved his arms at the lens. Nothing. No movement side to side. No zoom. No bedpan.

Spencer waved again, pointing to his ass this time. Hammering on the wall just hurt his hand.

Lazy assholes paying no attention again. Forgetting the bedpan, hardly getting his meal tray inside the room so he had to slither on his belly like a worm to reach the sustenance.

"Hey! I need the fucking pan! Hey!"

He didn't have a choice. After an hour, Spencer knew he had to roll onto the floor and drag himself the three feet to the toilet, and then figure out how to haul himself onto the stainless steel throne with both legs sticking straight out in the air. He'd seen the x-rays; he had to lower the legs without letting them slam down. But it was either that or else crap right there on the platform where he was living 24/7.

He reached his right hand over the edge until his palm was on the cool cement floor, steadied his upper body, and used his left hand to shift his upper body over the side. From a pushup position, he inched forward and tried to keep both casts controlled. The plywood was two feet off the floor.

With his torso over the edge and clear, he let his chest settle then twisted from the waist until he was looking up at his legs. His left was crossed over the right; he tried to clear that but it was impossible to get the leverage, so he raised himself onto his elbows and slid backward until his head hit against the far wall. The tight space forced him to drive his neck into his chin in order to move back more, and then he crawled his back up the far wall until he got into a sitting position. Both casts were crossed and pointed up at a forty-five degree angle.

Spencer flipped both middle fingers up at the camera then, crunching his abdomen, he reached both arms forward, straining until his fingers laced under the left cast. He lifted the leg and swung it clear of the platform until he had one leg below and the other still above. He tried to repeat the maneuver on the right leg, crunching seven times before deciding to shift positions again. Both legs needed to point down the length of the cell, which meant he needed to swing around to brace his back against the toilet bowl.

Pain shot from his thigh into his armpit, neck, and throat as he heaved himself up and flipped in one move that twisted his casts, crossing them at the ankles. He fought to get himself centered on the bowl then took another jolt when he reached to his right thigh and lifted, losing grip as his heel hit the floor with a heavy thud. When he tugged away his shorts, he waited.

After all of that, he lost the thread that had just forced him through the ordeal and could not make himself go. Tears welled in his eyes.

He understood. An ordeal just to take a crap. *Captain Sam. Fucking Davies.*

"You motherfucking bitch!" Spencer screamed at the gray walls. "A bidet. Just for the right to take a shit without help!"

He understood why Captain Sam thought big. He had to. When every little thing that makes up our daily routines without a thought given to them becomes impossible, that was the sensible response. It hurt too much to think of the day-to-day.

Spencer scooted against the toilet, spread his cheeks and tried to bear down. Nothing, until he sneezed and his bowels finally reconnected. Afterward, he sat, looking over at the plywood platform that summed up external world. What had seemed like a victory looked now like exactly what it was, a pathetic few feet.

No hands and no eyes. Wherever he went, he would always be different. Dependent.

"It's ok, Captain," Spencer said aloud. "I get it now."

*****

Every section of gray walls was unique. When he looked closely, there was the lion head and the whirling dervish and the Leaning Tower of Pisa outlined within the poured concrete.

"You start seeing Jesus and the Virgin Mary, get the shiv and end it," he argued, only half in jest.

He was talking to himself for hours on end, too often yammering aloud without a punctuated thought. Manchester United showed up without warning and he invited friends; a continuous loop of colors and crosshairs played inside his head. Killing was always bright colors. Red. The emerald green dress. A bright orange pantsuit.

"Jack," he shouted. "You ever going to do something? You just going to play dead until you are dead? Is that it, Dad? You ever going to buy a CD or take your ass to the shore and get your feet wet? Huh Dad? Jesus! Captain Sam didn't have eyes! His hands were blown off! And he still lived more than you. You made me a fucking orphan, Jack! I was twelve! I needed you, goddamnit, and you checked out. You sorry-assed excuse for a human being. I'm your son. You should have been helping me, not me always carrying you!"

What do you think now, Jack? Are they telling you I went crazy? Telling you I'm dead? Spencer looked up to the green camera light. "Fuck you!" he shouted, not that anyone would hear or care if they did.

No lawyer. No trial. *Is this my country? Is this what I was fighting for?*

"We have more people in prisons than any other place in the world," Captain Sam had said. "Two million men, more, behind bars. How many of them were fighting back, fighting in the ways they knew how?"

Revolutions are happening all the time, right Captain? And I fucking hate powdered potatoes either!

"When the price of having too much money gets high enough, we can shut down the oligarchs.

"That's the only way to stop them, Jonathan. One of these days everyone in uniform is going to have to pick a side. We're going to get ordered to fire on civilians, on people just like our own families. It may not be five years from now. Maybe not even ten. But it's coming. And the longer the more powerful they become.

"If we ever do demand liberty and opportunity, they can flip the switch and in comes the police and the army and the intelligence apparatus to crush Americans just as sure as Chinese tanks rolled on Tiananmen Square. They already did it to the Occupy people; took them out across city after city in one night!

"Jonathan, nobody cares if billionaires drop like flies. The people, not the news, not the politicians; I'm talking about this country. You know what people care about? They care about not being scared. It's not just scared in the moment; it's about being scared about keeping a job, about keeping your kids safe, about having a place to live when you're old. It's really about all the terrors that weapons can't protect against, no matter how much ammo you stock up on.

"Imagine if the wars were business plans—not one single Wall Street bigshot would have invested in the futures of Iraq or Afghanistan. But we watched those bigshots put through the biggest money transfer in history. We let them take public trillions and turn them into their private billions and we don't even demand to know their names! We're suckers, Jonathan, fools. All of us!"

Captain Sam said: "We soldiers are the worst of all. Hell, we helped them! You and me. Now we're just the rounding errors. You see how they treat us! And you want to go back? I don't have eyes and I see! Will you ever open yours?"

*****

The steel clang shifted his attention. Like a startled squirrel, Spencer twisted his face, looking up from his belly as the door swung open. Stocky was inside and swinging before he could roll the casts over to face him. The guard applied his best WWE move, the elbow drop, centering his entire offensive-lineman mass into a single point at the small of Spencer's back, right at his one remaining kidney. The blow froze Spencer in paralysis.

Stocky slipped his shoulder beneath the platform, reached out and pulled down the plywood triangle, then pressed up off the toilet and rolled back upright. He put the triangle between his thumb and forefinger and looked it over, pressing and testing the sharp points.

"Not so smart now, huh badass?" Stocky announced enthusiastically. "Who you planning to shank, huh?" He pinched the flat edge and tapped the points against his thigh.

"I've been waiting three weeks for you to get done," Stocky teased. "What the fuck took you so long to break it off?" He glanced up at the camera and grinned. "You sucked your thumb. That was the tell. I saw as soon as I handcuffed you how you were tearing them up. While the doc was working on you, I was inside your cell checking out your handiwork. Plywood makes for a crappy shank, dude."

Stocky grabbed Spencer's arm with one hand and wrenched upward, straining against the socket, then gripped his thick fist around the plywood triangle. He pressed one point into Spencer's armpit, slowly ripping into the flesh until a long gash reached nearly to the elbow. He kept holding the arm tightly as the wound filled with blood that spilled into the cup and then continued down beneath Spencer's brown prison shirt.

"You think you can get one over on me, you be wrong, mofo. I own you. I know what you're thinking before you can think it." One of his open bear paws followed with a cracking slap to punctuate the message.

*****

Spencer was relieved to see that his urine was clear. That was all his immediate concern. No blood, no serious damage to his one kidney.

His body was mending, but the legs? It would make no sense to hold him in a medical facility once the casts came off. He would be transferred. For now, he was a cripple. There would be a whole new set of variables and they would be handling him a lot differently.

The idea of months in a concrete tomb turning into years… better to die trying than to live like that.

No working camera in the exam room. How much time would that buy him? He once could cover a mile over tough terrain inside twenty minutes. No mud on any of their shoes. *Not ever.* He was counting on that. *Urban. Hard surfaces, no tracks.*

Lord, let them be white, he wished. He needed to fit in. Blend. Any other race… *Jesus.*

He needed *shoes, clothing, matches.*

Public transportation. Honor system or currency? Surveillance? Buses, trams, subway systems meant cameras. Would they tell local PD? Could they tap the local systems fast without telling?

The probability of a successful outcome was pathetically low.

Fuck it. I'm done being caged.

CHAPTER TWELVE

"Let's get these casts off and get a look at these legs of yours." The doctor was already wearing a cap with his greens. He had a facemask hanging under his chin. Goggles and a foot-long rotary saw with a two-inch circular blade were on the portable table next to the ketamine syringe. A long vacuum tube trailed behind the butt of the saw down to a plastic collection container. Spencer was counting on sound staying inside the room. If they heard out in the hallway, it would be all over.

"This won't hurt, but it won't be pretty, either. I'm sure you expect there will be scarring, but after months in casts, be prepared. You're not going to recognize your own legs. Your skin may appear translucent. Muscle mass has atrophied and what is there besides bones will have no tone whatsoever.

"I'm not saying this to scare you. We need to set realistic expectations. Do you get this?"

It was hard to know if the doctor really even remembered seeing him before. It felt like he could just glance at a chart and go into doctor-patient mode: pleasant, patient, clear and trustworthy, sympathetic without really engaging.

"These are the third casts," Spencer reminded him.

"Just be prepared. You've had two compound fractures, including both femur and fibula on the one side," the doc said.

Spencer nodded. Thinking the doctor was on autopilot made it easier. He reviewed every movement just as he had imagined from inside the cell. He had practiced twisting and reaching high along the wall until he had himself trained to snatch his left hand five feet upward. If Stocky was curious about that "tell," he never showed it as Spencer practiced again and again until the movement was rattlesnake-fast. All of his spring, popping up to strike, had to drive through his right elbow. Slim was standing along the left bed rail. His right wrist was zip-tied to the rail closest to the doctor, less than a foot away from the syringe.

He shifted against the zip tie and felt to confirm that the elbow could plant. He had enough slack. But the plywood platform was rigid. Until that moment he hadn't considered that he would be on the cushioned gurney pad. The cushion would absorb pressure and reduce his strike speed.

"Every person and every fracture is different," the doctor droned on, "but our rule of thumb is to plan for two months of intensive therapy for every month of immobilization. Most of this coming year will be a process for you. Baby steps. Stretching to recover flexibility, rebuilding muscle mass, retraining mind-body connections that support balance until standing becomes effortless, then taking steps along the parallel bars, getting accustomed to using a walker, and regaining unencumbered mobility one day. Someday you may be able to jog, possibly run even. Give it time. Time is your best ally."

Spencer held both rails like a bull rider in the shoot. *Shut the fuck up. Get it done!* When he nodded at the doctor, he wanted the gate opened.

The doctor lifted and dropped the right rail, forcing Spencer's right wrist to slide forward and drop to rest on the cushion. As he pulled on his facemask and put on safety goggles, he motioned for Slim to drop the left rail. Spencer closed his eyes as a high-pitched hum came from the saw. The shift had taken away all of his spring; his arm was outstretched, with the zip tie making it impossible to flex at the elbow.

You can wait; approach it again from after they started physical therapy.

No, he decided. His only edge was surprise. They wouldn't underestimate him, not after he was walking. He flexed the toes, rolled the balls of each foot, tightened foot muscles, ankles, calves, knees, thighs, hams, glutes.

Get the blade. Cut the zip tie.

The saw blade passed down the outside of the cast, quickly cutting in one long action all the way from his right hip down to the toes. The doctor shifted the right leg outward fifteen degrees, asking the guard to help make the same motion with the left. Spencer recoiled involuntarily as the saw blade pressed next to his groin.

"Hang in there. I haven't castrated anyone in months," the doctor said lightly.

Spencer looked at the thin gold chain around the doctor's neck as he leaned in to cut from his crotch down his inner thigh all the way to the toes. He tested the upper half to confirm that it was shucked cleanly then considered his plan and walked the saw and vacuum line around the foot of the bed. "Let's wait and open them both at the same time."

Another error. Dumb! The doctor wasn't on his right at all. Of course he had to move to the other side. How could he saw the outside of the left leg from the right side of the bed? But there was an upside. The ketamine was left unobstructed; the syringe remained on the portable table, shoulder-high and just off Spencer's zip-tied right hand. Spencer raised his head, trying to get a measure for the vacuum hose stretching over his legs. He hoped there was enough slack.

Slim stepped back behind the doctor, but when Spencer started shaking, the legs spasms drew him around to the foot of the bed right on cue. After his hand wrapped around Spencer's ankle, Slim lifted and straightened the top half of the right cast where it had fallen in against the leg on the inside edge.

As the blade made the final inside cut down the left leg, his moment was approaching quickly. Spencer visualized every movement. Slim first, then the doctor. Stocky outside. The doc's reaction time was everything. Had he measured the doctor correctly?

He's sure the legs are wasted. He had to count on that extra step; the processing delay between disbelief and realty.

Six inches more. Slim's fingers pressed gently against the cast just above the right ankle. Spencer sucked in a deep breath under the sawing noise and bucked in more violent spasms, forcing Slim to lean forward over the doctor to steady both legs while doctor completed the cut.

Spencer had purposely spread his legs wide, causing Slim to fall between them when he opened his legs like scissors. Spencer jabbed two hard, straight-fingered left stabs into Slim's windpipe, cracking through cartilage. Slim's eyes bugged.

Spencer knew the precise spot where the ketamine syringe was set onto the rolling tray. He stretched across his body to get the ketamine syringe into his fist, holding it like a dagger and plunging downward to pump half the 10 mgs directly into Slim's craned neck.

The doctor stood frozen, his mouth dropped open in disbelief. Before he could react, Spencer crushed his backhand across the bridge of the doctor's nose, then snapped down against the collar of his hospital greens and quickly landed three popping left hooks onto the doc's jaw in sharp succession. The doctor's head fell forward. His shoulder clipped the metal tray, sending it crashing noisily onto the floor, sounding like cymbals in a marching band.

Spencer kicked his legs out of the casts and scissor-wrapped them around the guard's thrashing torso as Slim struggled for air and watched the door, expecting Stocky to barrel in. He panicked momentarily, stretching and pulling against the zip tie locked around his wrist, trying to get to Slim's belt before he realized that Slim didn't carry the Taser.

Within three seconds the struggling subsided. The hallway door hadn't budged.

Using the cast saw, Spencer cut instantly through the zip tie. He let Slim flop onto the floor then took more time injecting the remaining ketamine into the doctor, who was already lying across Spencer's torso, out cold.

Spencer held onto the doctor's hospital greens to ease his fall and then shifted both his legs off the gurney. He reached out around the doctor's collapsed form with his toes and gripped tightly onto the gurney as he stood for the first time in months.

The room started spinning as the blood shifted in his head. He had to balance himself to stand, to bend and get back up. To walk.

The knees and ankles burned and shivered, nearly collapsing. The pigment-less flesh looked like it should have been attached to a corpse pulled off some lake bottom. But he had no choice. *They'll work or they won't. Let go of the gurney.*

He held the syringe up against the fluorescent light. The vial remained on the table at the far side of the gurney. Empty.

Spencer stepped around the prostrate figures, put his feet together and tried to raise himself up onto his toes. Nothing. He tried to lift a foot and shift it forward. Nothing. So he shuffled. At least he was moving. So long as the soles of both feet stayed on the ground, the legs could hold him.

There was no time to savor being upright. Plan B.

He patted Slim's butt, feeling for the zip ties, and quickly threaded them into one long daisy chain, working them to form into a wide snare. He held the tail end in his right hand, imagining the downward motion of snapping it tight.

Too much weight. He needed to brace himself; the legs alone would give out.

Spencer moved behind the door and practiced each separate motion, the right foot, the left, bracing with the left hand. The garrote was extended in his right, the wide plastic loop held between sixty-five and seventy inches from the floor. Stocky always bent his body forward into the direction he was moving.

Boom-boom-boom.

Three quick bangs brought Stocky rushing inside, his shoulders lowered like a charging bull. Spencer wrapped his left hand around the door edge and gripped as Stocky's head went inside the noose. Before Stocky saw the snare, Spencer cracked down and back like he was snapping a wet towel, zipping through the plastic teeth and setting the hook.

The giant fish turned as he realized that he was caught. Stocky spun toward Spencer. His angry eyes fixed onto Spencer's face. He raised both fists and managed two steps forward before his knees buckled and he went down hard. Lying sideways on the cold floor, his red neck bulged while he struggled, digging his fingers at the plastic lines.

Then he was up again.

The big man lowered his head and charged at Spencer like some crazed wounded buffalo. Spencer braced for the blow, only Stocky fell face-down, rolled once, and his legs kicked akimbo. The eyes remained open wide, blankly fixed at the ceiling.

From beginning to end, Spencer had taken down three able-bodied men in less than ninety seconds.

Spencer remembered how Stocky poured his eye full of piss. He could map every elbow drop, and every rabbit punch and dirty shot the MP had delivered.

Keep moving!

Spencer braced himself with one hand and used the other to unclip the security pass before stripping off the doctor's greens, shoes, facemask, and the surgical cap the doctor had been wearing to keep plaster dust off his hair. As the pants clacked onto the linoleum floor, something inside the pockets made a distinct sound.

He had to lift his own legs one by one from under the thigh to get each foot above the pant legs before pulling up the loose greens and tying them at the waist. He passed on attempting to untie the track shoes, pushing his bare feet inside the shoes and booties both. Shirt, mask, and cap followed.

Spencer was shuffling toward the doorway when he felt inside the pants pocket. A key ring, Prius, along with a car fob and more keys. Where the hell is this? *A Prius?*

He very nearly fell getting out the door, passing into the long windowless hallway, seeing it for the first time, all reinforced doors on both sides. He didn't bother counting. Cameras blinking green. He saw the elevator and pressed off the wall to get to the other side of the hallway, where he swiped the doctor's card. Nothing. He glanced up at the blinking camera above the elevator doorway, flipped the card and swiped again. Nothing. Every door was locked securely. No exit signs, no evident stairwells.

Spencer lurched back into the exam room and patted down Stocky's warm corpse, coming back with a bar-coded and magnetic-stripped ID. He swiped it. Nothing. He reversed and swiped again. The one button lit yellow: a deep bass rumbled, followed by a familiar thump and hum. He had been hearing that sound through the wall for months.

No alarms, but what did that prove? Ten guards would probably pour out of the elevator. Spencer prepared to strike. *Take two or three.* Even that seemed ambitious from the swaying bamboo stilts that were his legs.

Spencer stiffened, centered his power, and readied to strike as the inner elevator stopped with a click and airy brake noise. The doors opened. *Empty.* It wasn't until he stepped inside and looked over the bank of floor buttons that he realized that this was the lowest floor, the end of the line. The button marked "G" was eight stories above. There were twelve more floors above ground. Above the floor buttons hung an inspection certificate inside an Otis Elevator frame. Fairfax County. USA. Inspection approved by L. Johnson, Fire Marshall.

WTF? He had no time to get his mind around that. The elevator stopped. B2. A woman, tall, black, mid-30s, stepped inside, her face focused downward, reading email on her iPhone. She glanced up, pressed 3, and returned her eyes to the screen.

Spencer shuffled out at the ground floor before the doors closed on him. Daylight, natural light, shined like God through glass doors at both ends of the hallway. He was blinded by it.

Voices. People talking and moving briskly in both directions. Colors, noise. Everything amplified into an overwhelming cacophony. Heels clicked off the flooring sounding like thumping bass drums. He stretched out his arm to steady himself, suddenly dizzy with shock.

He squinted and forced himself forward, one shuffling step at a time, until he collapsed onto a wooden bench with movement all around him. He had to rest. *No choice.* His left hand wrapped discretely around his right wrist to take a pulse rate. He couldn't trust his instinctive measures.

A clock ticked above the doors to the outside; he tried, but he still couldn't hold focus on the thin line of the second hand. *Seventy-five feet to the light.*

Just inside the doors there was a kiosk window, some kind of little store or snack shop. A whole normal world, eight floors above—*all those months…eight floors.*

He was inside the Beltway? The fuckers were waterboarding him in Washington, D.C. They fucking did this to him in sight of the Capitol Dome! Spencer wanted to find a cop and turn them in.

Hanging straight across from the bench, just ten feet from him, Spencer nearly missed the map of the entire complex. *Move forward,* he told himself. *Get up.* He reached through the thin hospital greens for the keys inside the pocket. Employee Parking Structure showed due east of the Main Building. Ahead and right from the orange flag: "You are here." *East. Eleven a.m. Follow the sun.*

Like a colt standing up for the first time, Spencer's uncertain legs carefully covered the distance to the outside doors. He felt conspicuous, but the wave of humanity moved along with perfect political correctness, showing no special attention to the palsied employee. People on both sides politely opened the double doors to help him pass through.

The parking structure rose up six floors. Spencer pressed ahead, walking his hands along the car trunks until he reached the center of the ground floor, then he took out the fob and pressed, listening for a responding chirp. He moved further along and pressed again, hearing a high-pitched chirp, and repeated the action intermittently as he followed the noise. Minutes later, he was backing out of a stall inside a black Toyota Prius, lurching awkwardly to brake and lunging ahead again each time he touched the accelerator. His knees and ankles were on a crash course straight from a new infancy.

Ahead of him, an attendant stood inside a guardhouse with the gate arm down. Another car moved up directly behind. Spencer flashed the ID card from fifteen feet out. The guard nodded and raised the gate without Spencer ever needing to stop.

He looked in the rearview mirror. Nobody was following him. There was no commotion.

He was driving on the streets of Washington, D.C. He had no more time to process than a person caught in a tidal wave. The best he could hope for was to survive.

*****

The highway sign forced him to recalibrate. *Highway 66.* Jack's house was forty minutes south, fifty tops, in the middle of the day.

First place they'll look. Highways have cameras. *Cameras all over the building.* He was in the doctor's car. If they didn't already have it, how long before they knew the make, model, license plate? Pure luck that he had found the car quickly and luck couldn't hold much longer.

Take surface streets.

Clothes, cash, find another car. He needed all those things fast. *Fuck! All that time guessing and you were in D.C.*

He flashed on the crazed Pashtun killing in the marketplace, killing everything in his path.

"How much do you take before you go postal? How much!?" Spencer asked himself. *They did this. To an American soldier. Here!*

"Get it together," he shouted. "Improvise! Perform, dammit!"

The Prius lurched ahead, narrowly missing the Escalade in front of him. Spencer forced himself to concentrate on managing his legs. He tapped the navigation system, hitting the button reading "Home." *Alexandria, VA. 4.2 miles.* Nineteen minutes. *A lifetime.* He double-tapped. "In one quarter-mile, turn right onto Little River Turnpike." The mirrors were already set comfortably; he and the doctor were almost identical in height and weight. He reached up and adjusted the mirror to scan behind him. Nothing. "Turn right onto Little River Turnpike. Proceed 2.6 miles to Capital Beltway East." A brass Schlage key on the chain. *House.*

*****

Spencer stopped across the street, surveyed replica Georgian row houses, the road ahead, and every mirror before turning into the alleyway gap between the rows. He depressed every button on the car ceiling until a double garage door opened ahead on his right. He pulled inside but could not get his right leg moved to brake. The Prius slammed into the metal shelving unit, shaking loose a cascade of boxes that crashed down onto the hood.

Spencer glued his eyes on the interior door and waited for the noises to bring anyone inside running. A pale green Subaru wagon was parked beside him. They could have phoned 911. *Nothing you can do about it.* He pressed button 2 again, closed the garage, and turned off the engine.

Directly across his line of sight, an alarm pad chirped on the stairwell landing, its blue lettering glowing 30 SECONDS. Spencer felt along the wall and flipped the light switch. A sticky pad said 6-7-8-9-ON. He punched in the numbers, and then hit the off switch. ALARM DISABLED.

The stairwell led up to a closed six-panel door. Bypass knob. No lock. He grabbed at the hospital greens, lifting his left leg onto the first stair. His chest slammed onto the stairs when the leg collapsed under him. He noted how he was hyperventilating. *Adrenalin crash.*

His only way up the stairs was sliding over the carpet on his chest, doing pushups to take the stairs two at a time with both legs dragging behind. He tried to be quiet, tried listening for any noises within the upper floors or for the sirens he expected.

It wasn't a prison. It was black ops in D.C. But Texas on hourly pay? The doc working off student loans?

At the top, Spencer took two deep breaths, pushed off the stairs with his left arm and swung up for the knob with his right. *Green Subaru.* Whoever drove that might be standing there with a gun. *It is what it is.*

Nothing. He grabbed at the doorknob across a narrow hallway and used both door handles to press himself upright. The other door was to an entry closet on the main floor. Inside it, he found a stiff umbrella and a tennis racket. These helped him to press on. Spencer dragged a thick ski jacket off its hanger and tossed it beside the staircase. *I can use that.* It would be enough to stave off hypothermia on a temperate night outside.

Using the umbrella and tennis racket to brace himself, he lifted and swung from the hip, advancing one leg at a time with a rocking motion back and forth.

Beside the closet there was a toilet and sink. An open kitchen, dining area, and living room completed the floor. He scanned for useful items, forcing his brain to recalibrate. *You're in the city. Forget the cooking pot!* He scanned the countertops until his eyes caught the knife block. He weighed the challenge of covering the distance to get to it versus the value of carrying a poorly balanced close-range weapon. *Later.*

At his right shoulder the upper stairwell began, half-staircases meeting at a generous landing. He nearly missed the small mirror framing a line of jay hooks from which spare keys to both cars hung. Spencer snatched at the key with the star-crossed Subaru symbol, tossing that onto the jacket. He switched on the crystal chandelier, tossed the umbrella and tennis racket up to the landing, and used the two handrails for support. An ornate beveled mirror in a carved gilded frame hung from the back wall on the landing; in front of it, the rear of a nude male torso in carrara marble stood atop a wrought iron base.

Too much sensory data all at once. Light, sounds, movement, colors. The flowery scent of an air freshener. He squeezed the handrails and squeezed both eyes shut, becoming a statue to make it all stop. Spencer hyperventilated at forty breaths per minute. His pulse raced as he pushed on to the top of the stairs then sat down heavily and everything ramped down, crashing. Every fiber in his being wanted to sleep. But he had been there before. *You're trained for this. Suck it up.* He bit down on his tongue, hard, then cracked hard slaps against both cheeks and pressed himself upright.

At a glance, the upper floor doorways showed a small bedroom being used as an office, a hall bath, and double doors into the master suite. The master was three times the size of the smaller office.

Those student loans don't seem to be holding you back much Doc, Spencer observed.

He ignored the dresser for now, moving directly into the bathroom, where the medicine cabinet was a treasure trove of prescription meds. In five seconds he had the contents swept into the sink basin, and then he rifled the drawers and moved into the walk-in closet. Using the umbrella, Spencer hooked a gym bag from the upper shelf. He pulled at jeans and shirts, stuffing the bag before realizing that not all of these would fit him. The neatly folded clothing on the right side was all smalls, the pressed jeans twenty-eight-inch waists. He turned the contents onto the carpet and started again, this time more carefully sorting the thirty-four-inch waists and size large shirts. *The doc's stuff.* Each alternating row on the shoe rack held one size. The elevens were small, but much better than the diminutive size eights. He grabbed a pair of Adidas tennis shoes and a pair of slip-on loafers. His eyes landed on Tony Lama boots, new, black with tooled rises, before shifting attention to the drawers.

The underwear looked new also, a colorful combination of tiny stretch Speedos with EMPORIO in huge lettering along the waistbands and Diesel briefs. He stuffed a fistful of each into the bag, then untied the hospital greens and shook to make them fall to the floor. He selected a dark blue pair of briefs, spread them on the carpet using the umbrella tip, then stepped into them, flipped the umbrella, and hooked them to pull them on. All of the socks were either dressy pairs in sheer fabric or tiny footie things.

He moved back into the bathroom to stuff the pill containers into the gym bag. *Don't sort now.* The image inside the mirror caught his eye, stopping him cold. Hardly recognizable. *Christ.* A mountain man's beard, long and scraggly as his hair. Sunken eyes. Skin the color of chalk. An electric trimmer was plugged into its charger. Behind him, a glass shower sparkled. He looked at the face and shook his head. *Negative.*

The trimmer went into the sink, along with toothpaste, toothbrush, and a cuticle kit. He opened the gym bag and swept them all inside.

Spencer hobbled into the master bedroom. The large windows looked directly on to the neighboring unit. He took time to let down the blinds then flopped onto the mattress with the gym bag beside him. He grabbed up the first pair of jeans, lifted his feet into the pants legs, tugged them up both legs, and bounced, pulling at the jeans until he had his butt inside. He pulled on a polo shirt, also dark blue.

A large dresser and nightstands were on both sides of the queen bed. Rifling through the first nightstand, he found only magazines, various gels, tweezers, a collection of tiny bottles, all Limoncello. The dresser was stuffed with sweaters, dozens of them, plus scarves and at least fifteen pairs of gloves.

He pulled the heaviest gloves and tossed them onto the bedspread beside the gym bag before giving it more thought. *Thin gloves, black leather.* The right-side nightstand had eight one-dollar bills that he pushed into a front pocket. But no weapons.

Spencer tossed the gym bag down from the top of the stairs, knocking the marble statue off its base. His feet came off the ground this time, like they were beginning to remember their purpose, allowing him to step over the marble obstacle. He retrieved the jacket, gym bag, and car keys, opened the door to the lower stairwell, and sent them tumbling down.

Get food, he told himself. He had no immediate sense of hunger, but forced himself the twenty feet into the kitchen. A Dean & Deluca reusable shopping bag hung on the pantry knob. He opened the door and pulled cans of tuna fish off the shelf, then shut it behind him, ignoring the array of pastas, balsamic vinegars, and olive oils. Apples and bananas from a bowl atop the kitchen island went into the bag, and then he ran his eyes down refrigerator shelves. Bottles of Pellegrino, ridiculously heavy, still made the bag. Prosciutto. Burrata. A container of orzo salad.

Six minutes. His eyes locked onto a five-gallon glass bottle filled halfway to the top with quarters, nickels, dimes and pennies. *Eight one-dollar bills won't get you far.* He rolled it over to the stairwell door then looked at the steep descent and went back into the entry closet, this time taking a full-length thick overcoat off its hanger and spreading it out along the top of the staircase. Then he sat down, reached the coin-filled carboy onto his stomach, snatched up the food bag, and pushed off, tobogganing himself to the bottom.

He packed everything onto the front passenger seat. A toolbox had fallen from the off the shelving unit, spewing its contents onto the garage floor. That gave him an idea.

*****

Clusterfuck, Bishop thought as soon as Jeffers opened his mouth. The prisoner, who officially did not exist, took down two guards and a doctor and walked straight out of their high-security establishment on legs that weren't supposed to be functional.

You sonofabitch. Bishop tipped back the Stetson and admired Spencer and the awesome escape. He pictured each of the guards. Ferrell, the sadistic bastard, and Darcy. *How do you lose a man with two broken legs?*

The doctor remained in a fog from an injection of something called ketamine.

"And now that you need me, I'm supposed to drop everything and come running?" Bishop asked Jeffers. Seven weeks since Jeffers told him that APA would be in touch. *Seven weeks and not a word.* While the prospect of what

Jeffers expected from him darkened his attitude and the value of that money kept shrinking. Every single day.

"You've got a hundred-fifty-thousand dollars of my money!" Jeffers shouted so loudly that Bishop pulled the phone off his ear. "Nussbaum was working half an hour ago. Get your ass over there!"

"Get Spencer's face out to the public," Bishop told Jeffers. "We don't need to tie him to the attacks; call him a serial rapist. Say he kidnapped a kid and put out an Amber alert. Just get eyes out on him."

"No," Jeffers screeched. "That is precisely what nobody is doing!"

Jeffers' shrill tone quieted. "There is a quid pro quo for everything," he instructed with deadly candor. "Nobody in government was ever going to touch the prisoner. We're not inviting attention. This is a private enterprise. That's the deal. I bought him and there is a no return policy. Period!"

The fear was masked, but it didn't escape Bishop. Not one bit. For Jeffers and APA, the story was always what mattered, that and keeping up a private prison system built on low-friction relationships. Another public/private partnership with Vision Partners on both sides.

"We have the eyes to track him. Don't worry about that. I am coordinating unimpeded access to everything NSA has got. Get over to meet Nussbaum. He has a tech team assembled. You need to coordinate the apprehension side. Pay what you need to staff it fast. Finalize this. Do it fast," Jeffers said.

"My personal fee is what you offered for the other work," he told Jeffers, adding, "plus a five-year retainer at $50K per year against future fees." Bishop played the enterprise card; he had to go big or go home. Either he was going to be in or out—he'd had enough of sitting on the fence waiting on Jeffers' passive-aggressive whims.

"Set aside $2 million for costs," he told Jeffers. "I need resources: investigation and operations. Stephen Nussbaum doesn't come with helicopters and seasoned commandos. I'll need to reassemble a team. Do we have a deal?"

"Sheriff, why are you still talking? Go!"

*****

"Black Prius, Virginia plates," a man, mid-forties, thinning hair, explained when Bishop stepped off the elevator onto the basement floor. "Video confirmation. We have footage from B8 hallway, elevator, main lobby, parking garage, security gate. Fifty minutes ago." The prisoner had driven off in the doctor's car. One guard dead, another in x-ray for a possible neck fracture.

"Which man was killed?"

"Jeff Mark Ferrell," the administrator told Bishop. "Our lead guard. Strangled."

"Then the prisoner got on the elevator and walked out? Just like that?"

"Further precautions would have been implemented if indicated," the administrator argued. "The physician indicated he would not be ambulatory for months. I'm not a mind-reader!"

Inside the exam room, Nussbaum had his laptop plugged into a high-speed data connection inside the exam room. Bishop leaned down to look at the zip ties around Stocky's neck then stepped over the body.

"What have you got?" he asked Red Pants.

Stephen and three other off-site techs were already running a fifty-mile radius using public and private feeds. Every arterial and highway, every parking structure, every mall—eyes were on every black Prius out there.

"I have this fully under control," Stephen answered. "Thank you for asking."

"A lot of good it's going to do," Bishop responded. "Identifying him doesn't get him caught."

"I'm piggy-backed on the national grid," Stephen explained while his fingers worked over the keyboard. "I'd rather use my own facial recognition software, but we're stuck using their proprietary crap."

"Show me," Bishop told the stick-thin Nussbaum.

"I have cameras scanning license plates going twenty-five miles in every direction. The minute he stops for gas or fast food, as soon as he moves inside camera range, we'll have visual confirmation and GPS coordinates accurate within two meters." Stephen swapped over to a black screen with white lettering than scrolled through pages like a blur. It was one of those magical things that only techs can do, exactly the type of sorcery that was putting guys like Bishop out of work.

"What about the father's house?" Bishop asked.

"Already on it. Jeffers made a call. There's drone surveillance on the house. We'll have cameras mounted outside the father's to take over inside an hour. I've got live emails and phone activity screening in real time." He threw up a map showing a radius going out 100 miles. "These are known addresses on every local member of his unit, present and past, going back to 2005. We're pulling bank accounts, cell phones, and email aliases."

"I'll arrange for response units," Bishop added, thinking out loud. *Set up a command station, get a comm hub.*

"Come with me," Bishop ordered. "I'll set you up at my office."

"I don't need an office. Just a solid data port. I'm good."

"I'm not asking," Bishop told Nussbaum.

"Do you grasp how much data ships through a fifty mile radius containing a major metropolitan area?" he challenged Bishop. "There are nearly a quarter-million feeds, video; that's terabytes every nanosecond. We have to piggyback processing straight off NSA channels. Even with the backdoor key, it still takes bypassing firewalls, data-decryption."

"How many fugitives have you handcuffed?" Bishop shot back as they moved. "What sort of cool algorithm do you have for capturing a Special Forces-trained sniper? What keys do you push? Is there an app for that?" *Red Pants, your kind can't bring in Master Sergeant Jonathan Spencer.*

Stephen's connection dropped inside the elevator but he reconnected on a 4G band once they were outside the building. The connection had just enough bandwidth to observe the scanning protocols. "How are you going to do it?" Stephen wanted to know. "I could have a hit this second. When it happens, it is going to happen fast."

"I'll arrange assets and move them here as fast as possible. You get a location, you need to stay on him like glue until I can get them into place."

Bishop arranged for secure a six-man ops squad over the phone as they drove together.

"You have to know who to call," he told Stephen, adding, "They're locked and loaded with a helicopter at ready."

He turned to look at the impression that his phone call had made, expecting Red Pants would be blown away, and then was disappointed by what he saw. Stephen looked disinterested.

"Supply exceeds demand by an order of magnitude," Nussbaum sneered. "There's more ex-Special Forces wanting work than day labor outside the Home Depot. Tech talent is where the jobs are." Then he smiled wide.

"Fuck!" he exclaimed enthusiastically.

"What?" Bishop wanted to know.

"Hah! The golden ticket! Yes!" Jeffers had somehow bypassed the security interviews, the background checks. Everything. Nussbaum realized he had the key to the entire grid.

"We're into NSA's entire surveillance system," he explained. "The whole fucking thing. I've heard rumors about it, but I've never even seen a geo-specific enterprise intelligence system."

"A what?"

"Think of a million eyeballs, more, all on 24/7 high-alert. Point a cursor on a map and scroll out to any radius and every camera, every street cam, every public transit cam, every bank, every Starbucks, McDonald's, 7/11, every single private security camera in every house is right there, right on screen. We can filter for height, build, hair color, skin tone, clothing color, make and model of car. Damn! I've waited all night outside Best Buy to get the first copy of every version of Halo. That's good. This is about a million times better. NSA has the coolest shit! This just scratches the surface."

"This isn't a game."

Stephen disagreed. "It's all a game."

*****

The gas gauge showed under a quarter tank of gas. Spencer figured twenty-five miles per gallon, maybe an eighteen-gallon tank, and began speculating. Then he found the button on the steering wheel and the information center in the dashboard screen. Range = 137 miles.

What does it matter? Make distance. Get clear of D.C. before they find the Prius. Once they had that they'd ID the Subaru. One-hundred-thirty-seven miles.

The nav system took him west on King to South Henry to merge back onto 495. Six-and-a-half miles of the most patrolled highway in America.

He accelerated to sixty-eight mph and tapped the steering wheel to set the car on cruise control. Every sight around him was made much more surreal because he had seen them all before. *America.* On American soil the entire time. *95 south. Forty minutes away from Jack. Heading home.* He had to reach under his knee to take his right foot off the gas pedal. He was using his left foot for the brakes. No choice; either he slammed to every stop or he wasn't stopping.

Cruise control bought him the chance to think. *Eight bucks.* A little over two gallons of gas. Sixty more miles. He reached into the paper sack on the passenger seat, felt for the imported water, cracked open the bottle top and drank back half in one gulp then belched away the bubbles. *The coins.* It would take him half a day to sort them out and get them into rolls. Where could he cash rolls? Where could he get the rolls in the first place? Every bank in the country used security cameras.

Coin machine. There used to be a coin machine in Tuckahoe. Eighty miles. *Better to make distance or ditch the car?* He took a deep breath, exhaled, and smiled. Fucked-up legs and all, there was color all around him, color on cars, billboards, trees, a sky as far as he could see in countless shades of blue. He felt alive, alive for the first time in forever. He let down the window and let the wind blow across his face, leaned his head out and stretched his neck into it, letting it blow through his hair and beard. Traffic slowed suddenly. He saw the gap closing and the rear bumper of a Chrysler minivan getting bigger fast. Before he could manage braking, he instinctively pulled left into the HOV lane and was passing the Chrysler and more traffic without ever slowing down when in the rearview mirror a gray sedan came up behind him. *Five hundred yards.*

He thought the hood and roof were black. Grabbing a fistful of blue jeans just above his left knee, he pressed down until he felt the brakes contact then lifted and pumped the leg to reduce speed so that he could cut back into the center lane. He let the Subaru decelerate, then cut to his right and tapped the button reading "Resume." The Virginia State Police unit pulled parallel alongside. Spencer kept his eyes looking ahead, his hands at ten and two. Sixty-two mph. He breathed again after the patrol car moved ahead and reached into the bag, taking out an apple and biting in with a satisfying crunch. While he chewed, he reached the pale red and yellow fruit out at arm's length and studied it, turning his wrist to look at it from all sides as the sweet juice moved over his tongue and settled into the back of his mouth. *Best apple ever.*

The white ranch house where he grew up was a half hour ahead. Half an hour. Would Jack be there, he wondered, on the blue couch with his shoes on, or would he be out with the van on a job?

He hadn't seen his dad since boarding the plane before the last deployment. At Walter Reed he told Jack that he'd come home to visit after his MEB. Right after he left Eagle Arms they talked on the phone. *Hi Dad. Hi Johnny. How are you, Dad? Hanging in there. How are you? The same.*

Before Sands Point, *before everything.* He was already back in operations mode, prepared to do what he trained for, what he did best.

You need to get rid of this thing. But how do you steal a car, he wondered? People did it all the time, but how? Could you stick in a screwdriver and break the ignition lock? He'd seen five or six of the *Fast and Furious* movies, but hot-wiring a car?

Hijacking? A gimp with no weapon. Probably get shot trying. Good luck on that. *Where do people leave cars and keys?* Oil change places. Valets. Car washes. *Repair shops.* Repair shops might not know it's gone, not as fast at least. But what if it hadn't been repaired? Steal a car that was going to break down?

He looked at his hands; he was gripping the wheel too tightly, his knuckles were white, bloodless. Pulse rate in the mid-70s. Way off. Adrenalin rollercoaster. Neurochemistry pinging all over the place like a pinball machine.

Radio controls were on the left side of the steering wheel. He could have reached down and put on music. Instead, he closed the window. Tuckahoe, he decided. Then find a way to get another car. *Sorry Jack.*

*****

"I'm aware it's been three hours," Bishop conceded. "No, he can't be on a plane, not without ID. Besides, how would he pay for the ticket?" Jeffers voice was hitting a high range that sounded entirely different from the deep resonant authority he normally displayed.

"I'm aware of that," Bishop agreed. "One-hundred-fifty miles. No, camera densities fall apart in forty miles."

"Red Pants"—Stephen Nussbaum—had mapping projected along an entire wall.

"Spencer didn't escape on my watch. My contract was singularly for interrogation. Incarceration was entirely separate. Don't put this on me," Bishop said, defending himself.

"Things might be considerably different right now if you had an APB out," Bishop repeated. "We didn't find the Prius because he's not in the Prius. Your doctor was taken to his house and found it turned inside out when he got there. No, no weapons. A revolver in the hall closet. Still there.

"Some food, clothing, medications. I know he's not in the Prius because we have the Prius. He switched cars. A green Subaru Imprezza, Virginia license number 4201 Charlie Victor Thomas. We may not need the cameras. The Subaru has a nav system and roadside collision assistance."

"If it has a nav system, you're tracking it, aren't you?" Jeffers demanded.

"Of course," Bishop snapped back. "We're working on that as we speak. Once we're inside the system, I'll have a team on the helicopter." Stephen and his nerds were proving resourceful.

*****

With the giant jug set inside a shopping cart, Spencer held onto the handle and tried pressing up onto his toes. His heels came off the ground. Not much, but it was something. He tried squatting; the knees started giving way and only the cart kept him from falling smack on his ass. He moved tentatively, lifting one foot at a time, and used his grip on the cart to relieve the weight on his legs. But he was moving. His knees were flexing. Two minutes earlier he had scratched himself from his calves to his thighs on both legs. *Months of therapy my ass.*

Inside the automatic doors, the coin machine was still there where he remembered it. After grinding like a rusty washing machine for a couple minutes, it totaled $119.43. He selected the cash voucher that printed out at $108.80. *Eleven bucks, for that.*

Monday fried chicken special. Breast, wing, thigh and drumsticks plus two sides for $3.99. *Monday. Tuckahoe, VA.* The aroma of fried chicken made him swoon. He was going to eat it in the car but recognized that he was barely able to drive with both hands helping. He ate right there, every morsel right down to the bone, grits with gravy, mac and cheese, sitting at a metal table with four attached seats, bolted into the shining floor. People kept coming and going to and from the Starbucks counter. He looked up at them with chicken in his mouth. Nobody was going to get between him and that meal.

He wheeled from the deli past the checkout registers, reading the directory signs down each isle. He found disposable razors. Store brand. Packs of three. Then he went down the housewares isle. Brooms. *Screw-in handles.* After the checkout, he still had $103 and change. *Forget gas. Ditch the car.*

Just outside the shopping center, in an area of neat three story apartments and 1950s single-story little houses just like the one he grew up in, he cruised along the lowest speed that took cruise control, 20 miles an hour, with the broken broom stick resting in his lap, the threaded end touching alongside the brake pedal.

After two blocks he saw a FedEx van pull to a stop. The driver went into the back then emerged with a small package and trotted toward the nearest apartment building. Stealing a FedEx van? *Nope.*

Another block along he spied something more intriguing. In front of him was another small apartment building, this one off by itself, set back from the street, with a small parking lot in front. He pulled in, punched the stick downward to brake, and then let the car move slowly in drive past the pickups and older four-cylinder imports. At the farthest end away from the parked cars he turned the Subaru between faded white lines and put it in to park. Looking down between the apartment and the little ranch house beside it, a young man made a pass with a power mower across the back yard, turned and went behind the house, the sound fading as he moved in the other direction. Inside the single-car garage was somebody's pride and joy, a beautiful Honda CTX700 standing all black and shiny. Key in the ignition, helmet resting on the seat.

*****

"Of course we've pulled the description; we've got the license plate, the VIN. Well, it's not that simple.

The service carrier is American, but they're a third party," Stephen explained. Jeffers' micro-management was even more frustrating than tracking the car; why even hang up the phone when the intervals between Jeffers' calls were minutes apart?

"The service contract is offered directly by Subaru," Stephen continued, "which is owned by Fuji Heavy Industries. I already approached their U.S. headquarters in Cherry Hill, New Jersey. Unless the request is made by the owner of the vehicle, they won't do it without either a court order or an ok from Japan. There's a twenty-hour time difference.

"The registered owner is a commercial airline pilot in the air halfway between Miami and Sao Paulo. I sent him a text to contact us the moment that he lands.

"Then break into their network!"

Nussbaum answered Jeffers testily. "Tried that. It's a no-go. Hacking their system will take considerably longer than two-and-a-half hours."

"Will a warrant get it done?" Jeffers offered.

"You have judges within the Foreign Intelligence Surveillance Court, move on that, definitely," Stephen agreed. "If you really can turn a FISA court order right now, that could be a game changer."

*****

The Honda was a different animal, not at all like his Harley; a cheetah, agile and smooth compared to the Harley's throaty lion. No clutching; the automatic transmission was a godsend. The tinnitus rang louder inside the helmet, but he could live with that. *All day long.*

With the gym bag tied with a bungee cord onto the upper seat deck behind him, Spencer took Route 64 north and east to clear Tuckahoe fast, getting out before the motorcycle was reported stolen, but not before he passed the Alanon café where eight motorcycles were lined up under a shade tree in the gravel lot. He spied a plate with first and last numbers that were identical to the Honda's plate; it could be weeks before the owner ever noticed the change.

Spencer nodded to himself, satisfied, as he put the pliers and screwdriver back into the gym bag. Hours earlier, he was in solitary confinement with both legs in casts from hip to toe. Now he had food, clothing, cash, transportation, and a direction. *Goodbye Virginia.*

There was open space after Charlottesville; horse pastures, cattle, farms with miniature goats and alpaca spread out along both sides of the highway. First to the state line, then find a place to get some sleep.

He crossed the river at Waynesboro, passing the Wal-Mart Supercenter and cutting south onto Stuarts Draft toward Lexington.

Glen Jean, West Virginia. "It's just five hours west from Jack's," Mercy had written to him. "Five hours and you're in another world, Johnny. Would you come and visit me sometime? Don't even call. There's no phone! Just come!"

*****

At two hundred feet, the Subaru was visible from overhead without searchlight or night vision. The glow from the streetlight was enough. On playback, the belly cameras caught it; green for certain, license match at 20X enhancement. Bishop received the confirmation but waited before relaying it; the GPS had them dialed in.

"We have the car. No visual on target."

The Team Leader, Curtis, signaled the pilot to maintain distance. The pilot nodded and spiraled out in widening circles to prevent the rotor noise from alerting their target. He spotted a two hundred-foot clear radius a quarter-mile away. Offloading took seconds, six men and equipment, then the helicopter rose again, leaving the black-uniformed squad crouched over surveillance and communications equipment, ammunition and ordnance packed inside black, hard-floored bags.

Using a tablet computer and mapping software, the team leader signaled *On me* before taking off at a fast trot, moving down the alleys that lead toward the Subaru. Six men carrying 486 pounds of gear, running in near silence. Nothing slapping, banging, shifting; their only noise was heavy feet thumping dirt and crunching gravel. A Dalmatian stood up from its spot on a back porch, craned its head, lifted its tail, and watched without a sound.

From above they would have looked like a flock of blackbirds, distributing around obstacles into formations choreographed along the streets and alleyways of Ramadi, Fallujah, Haditha, and countless hotspots. At one hundred meters, the two on security moved into positions front and rear with their HK-416s. They lamped up, turning on their laser sights and sweeping the bright red and green streaks across their fields of fire. Anything moving within their perimeter would intersect with a suppressed hiss sounding like an adder's strike.

Three and four, both shooters, positioned at 9 and 3 with MP5s along the brick side walls of the apartment.

Profitt, the Assistant Team Leader, moved double time to behind a broad, unkempt boxwood hedge, where he slung his M4 to the ground. His Team Leader, Curtis, thundered up beside him. The ATL opened the duffle at his feet to draw out night-vision goggles, automatically handing the first pair to Curtis then powering a second pair before pulling them down over his forehead. Together, they swept the area: center stairwell, two units per floor, three stories; five cars in front, plus the Subaru, a derelict Oldsmobile on blocks, two pickups, a sedan and a Dodge Caravan.

Profitt made a tomahawk motion twice toward the Ford F150. His team leader acknowledged. Rear bumper *Army Strong*; rear window *HOOAH! IT'S AN ARMY THING*. Team leader punched his left fist into his right armpit then swept his outstretched right palm across the building. ATL tipped back the night vision then zipped the duffle wide open, pulling from it a specialized cigar box-shaped camera with a thick black conduit attached to a large battery pack.

Profitt handed the camera to Curtis and then drew out an aluminum tripod painted over in camo, flipped open its legs, and locked them into place before reaching for the camera back. As Profitt fired it, Curtis switched to visuals on the tablet; it had already synched its Bluetooth to the infrared camera. He steered to the upper floor left. One figure, reclined so that the heat mark didn't display contours, man or woman, tall or short, wide or slender. He moved right to the second unit, top floor. One smaller mark on the floor: an infant, toddler, possibly a dog; not the target. An image showed top only, like a torso floating legless. When she moved from the kitchen, her legs came into view to join her upper body. No magic trick; she was standing behind the breakfast bar and walked out to pick up the baby.

He moved back to upper floor left; the figure had shifted. Now that he was stretched out on his side it was obvious that the figure weighed over three hundred pounds. Middle floor right was cold. Nothing there. Lower right, one figure plus a deep red package, moving package. Back and forth, stop, again back and forth. Waist level. Stop. Back and forth. Each move left a crimson trail that cooled orange, then yellow, then pale straw. Short, slender... not the target. Two larger male figures lower left unit, closest to the Subaru and to the F150. TL pointed two fingers. Profitt fixed the tripod in place then moved to a second duffle, unzipped and withdrew the grip-end of a pistol that extended into an eight-inch long pod. A spiral black electrical cord was attached to the base of the grip; when it came out fully, padded earphones were connected to the end of the wire. The ATL sighted through the lens on top then tapped his index finger to a button above the grip along the right side. A red dot lit against the front window of the unit.

Curtis tapped his tablet to bring up sound files. Downloaded samples of Spencer's voice were mapped to his cadences, his vocal ranges, even isolated clips of his most spoken words and analysis showing idiosyncratic phrasing.

Profitt fanned open the pad until it changed shape into a disc the size of a large pot lid. At the center it held a four-inch rod capped by a black spongy material. The TL took hold of it while his assistant team leader removed the night vision goggles and put on the headphones, cupping each ear beneath the black pads. Crouching down on his right knee, he took back the listening device and held it in his left hand while resting his left elbow onto the bridge his position had formed with his left leg. Another laser blip showed red against the wall just below the front windows. Male voices, rough, angry. Southern accents.

"Boss, we've got something," he whispered, drawing Curtis' attention back to the screen.

The Team Leader reached out his hand to take the earphones; he was obviously annoyed about the outdated technology. The device should have been wireless and Bluetooth-enabled to play on multiple headphones. It should have been synched to the tablet, too. Curtis held the wired headset up to his ear.

"Man, this is dumb. I'm leaving. If they're not here in like two minutes, I'm gone." Southern accent. *Duuuhm.*

"And what am I supposed to tell 'em when y'all take off? Cool yer jets 'n show some patience."

Arriving or leaving. That spelled complications. Taking the shot was always easier outside at close range. But it might not be Spencer who was leaving. If it wasn't Spencer, did he let the other guy walk out and not tip Spencer? Did they take the shot and go straight in there hot? Spencer, a Tower of Power—Rangers, Special Forces, Airborne—was no man he wanted to alert ahead of action. Every minute they waited meant the target might be getting closer to having additional assets. Trading shots with trained experts was a sure way to raise casualties on both sides.

Matters got worse quickly.

"Boss, I've got an angle on the side window," Four called out. "Two men, late twenties, early thirties. There's a weapon in view on the table, semi-automatic, looks like a 9mm."

"Do you have a sight on target?"

"Negative boss. I have a visual on Three," he told Curtis. "Three, you've got a window down your end looking directly into the room."

"Three, can you get a visual?" Curtis whispered into his jaw mic.

"Can do, Boss, but I need to get on top of the LP tank to see in. It's a two-hundred-gallon, thirty-six inch diameter. No way to squeeze between the tank and the wall and no way to reach it with a remote cam."

"Negative. Regroup on me. Now now now. Get over here. We're switching gears."

Collateral damage saves lives, soldier's lives. That's one of the facts that regular army doesn't like to talk about. The enemy doesn't give two fucks when there is a civilian in the way, but thanks to polite rules of engagement, Americans die every day.

The four black figures rushed from their positions like moving shadows, imageless outlines blocked against the lights inside apartments.

"Billy," he ordered, "you get out all the donuts and a radio-frequency cap." As he pointed, his thinking came across clearly. "We're not shooting our way into there in the blind. We're going to leverage that LP tank." Curtis pointed toward the tank and swept his hand over the entire structure. The explosion would take down the building and their target along with it. Billy nodded.

"Matt, you string it from the gauge stem down to the center of the tank on the outside away from the building. The stem is the weak point. The rest of you, you know that big lawn we passed? The one with the big-assed plantation house with the white columns in front? Hump it over there with everything we've got. Cal, use your NV and ring the perimeter in red. Buck, bring in the transportation on a green line straight to you. Now get over there, and Bobby, you make damned sure there's no power lines or obstructions. Once you confirm, you call in the chopper and let him know this is a hot run. As soon as I hear those rotors, it's the Fourth of July," he instructed.

"Matt, you and I will travel light and hit that 'copter hard and fast. The rest of you, move! Matt, you get to be Jim Brown on this one."

"Just cause I'm black doesn't make me Jim Brown," Matt said. "You be Jim Brown. I don't want to be him. Jim Brown gets killed."

"Jesus Shenikwa," Curtis griped. "Take the fucking donuts and get 'er done."

*****

The motel clerk gave him a break, seeing as how she recognized him for a wounded veteran and all. Policy was no ID and no credit card, no room. Cash wasn't enough. But the heavyset middle-aged lady behind the glass said how "I have three of my boys in uniform and to hell with rules. Let 'em fire me."

Under the front curtains, the room had an old electric heater. He stared at it, thinking that the room was chilly but not entirely making the connection that he could change that by standing up and putting on the heat. It was his to control. He reached up to the bedside lamp and switched it off then on then off again and on again. There were sixty or seventy channels; not one of them said a word about him. *What does that mean?* He stopped at the TV Land station and watched *Gilligan's Island*. Gilligan had fallen into a cavern while he was caddying for Thurston Howell III's golf game and discovered a gold mine that immediately belonged to Mr. Howell. Spencer smiled dully; he had no energy to think much about the message there. During the first commercials, he fell fast asleep.

In the morning, the low water pressure matched the sagging mattress, but it was warm and dry and the room had two windows. *Windows.* He was smiling into the bathroom mirror, looking at the lather in his beard as he tugged again, scraping the flimsy plastic razor down his cheek then running his thumb across the blade to clear the bunching red-brown hair that was already clogging the rust-ringed drain.

Ribbons of blood oozed from his clean-shaven face where the cheap razors left their marks. Spencer moistened a thin over-washed white towel smelling of bleach under the lukewarm water and dabbed at his face, intermittently removing it to look at the pink patterns. Afterward, he lay in the fancy underwear across the orange-and-blue-flower patterned bedspread and switched on the old television that hung on a shelf lagged into the brown paneling.

He flipped past high school baseball, the stock market report, plus blazing footage of the "raging four-alarm fire in a Richmond suburb claiming the lives of five and seriously injuring one firefighter during the rescue of a mother and her infant who were trapped in the blaze. Mother and baby were transported to CJW Medical Center where they are reported to be in stable condition." He failed to make the connection.

White Sulfur Springs put him across the state line. He was into West Virginia, showered and shaved, wearing clean bright red underpants. The night before he had found ham sandwiches at the gas station mini-mart marked down, three for $2.25. Spencer unwrapped one, opened the white bread on a half for a look inside at wilted days-old lettuce and fizzy white spread that shined at the edges. Then he slapped it back together and ate most of it in a single bite.

Afterward, he forced himself to rise up, flexed his weary legs, and shuffled in front of the flaking mirror. He looked more battered than the ancient dresser. Dots and lines of crusted blood were scabbing on pale sallow cheeks. The muscles in his upper body that he had managed to exercise were unnatural hard chunks rather than the balanced physique he expected to see looking back at him. Turning sideways, the nephrectomy scar looked like the wide tail end of a trail beginning between his shoulder blades and running bright-red down the white length of his back. There were more scars below his waist. He crawled on top of the bed and managed to stand, steadying himself with one arm pressing up to the ceiling so that he could get a better vantage point. A jagged, half-inch-thick red scar ran the full length of the femur down the back of his right thigh. He tried to tighten and flex the muscle; the feeble response was hardly perceptible. Down the outside of his left leg, below the knee, he could make out the crowned heads of four screws beneath the skin. Peeling down the stolen briefs, he looked over the narrow, careful scar from where bone was taken from the left hip for grafts along the right femur.

He lay down again and considered squats, knowing that he had to work the knees and ankles, but his mind drifted. All those cells. Solitary confinement. The waterboarding. The shock stick. No lawyers. No trial. *In America.* Twelve hours ago. *In the United States of America.*

He tried remembering but could not be sure when Mercy last wrote to him. Everything was so vivid except the time. Mail had rarely come for him when he was abroad. He used to take her lengthy annual copied letter out to the rubble flatland between Bagram's runways where he went to decompress. After missions, sometimes tears sometimes flowed out from him uncontrollably. A neurochemical reaction. It happened, nothing to be ashamed about, but something he worked out alone with his guitar. He stretched out in the dirt with the mountains looking so close he could reach out and touch them; the snow was nearly gone and the killing season was about to begin in earnest.

She had seventy acres; lush pasture with grass thigh-high, the creek running with trout, woods a thousand shades of green teeming with birds and raccoons. Even with all the hunters, there were black bear and deer, porcupines and red fox. Reading her words, he could hear her voice laughing as she related how she had bitten off more than she could chew, as usual, and couldn't Uncle Sam spare him so he could come and help her?

It had sounded like a miracle, something so distant that it could hardly be real, as far away from his world as the name itself, "Glen Jean." Coal country, played-out mines giving way to new life, still only half-ready for her to come in and shake things up just a little. The land was coming back, people too, a groundswell. One neighbor was starting a craft brewery; another was making jerky and selling it at farmer's markets. She was completely off the grid; her own well, a wood stove... the bare basics. She was even trying her hand at making cheese, could he believe it?

He pictured her squatting down with that wild head of hair pressing into the side of a goat or a sheep, whichever it was she was raising. Her strong fingers pulling their udders, milking. Sweating and smiling that big grin of hers. Glen Jean, West Virginia.

He never even wrote back…

*****

"You weren't there," Curtis argued across the phone line. "We didn't get positive ID because it wasn't doable. I had a call to make and I made it. We had the car, we had a resident soldier with three tours in Afghanistan, and we had a voice match. You wanted this handled, we handled it."

Bishop looked disgusted. Jonathan Spencer was dead, so the objective was met, but the team he hired, his private commandos, had destroyed an entire apartment building. *Get over it*, he told himself. *You're a grown man. You know the score.* But first the dead detective. Now this, too.

Outside his glass office door, Bishop looked over to Stephen Nussbaum and his team. It seemed like they weren't working at all, then they attacked their keyboards like pelicans diving on bait fish. They looked like babies; Stephen alone was old enough to rent a car. "I'm management," Nussbaum had explained to him, "too old to be a real native." All four of them glowed, bright with excitement at the technologies Jeffers had opened up to them.

"It's about over boys," Bishop muttered to himself. "All your shiny new Christmas presents are going away."

He had to pick up the telephone to make his report to Jeffers. It was over too quickly. *You should have gotten the retainer agreement in writing*, he thought. Jeffers could conveniently forget the whole thing.

"Can't say verbatim," Bishop conceded over the phone. "No. The corpses were incinerated. That's what over a hundred gallons of exploding liquid propane does to an apartment building and the people inside it. Virginia Department of Health has the remains. Medical Examiner/Coroner. You couldn't recognize them as human. Dental impressions, I imagine. It was a hot fire, but teeth stand up to two thousand degrees. Could be that DNA can be pulled from the pulp at the center of the tooth, too. That, I can't say. DOD has dental and DNA on him. Nussbaum is working on getting copies of the impressions after they're taken. Virginia will have to process the impressions then send out for any match, whereas we have the DOD files already on hand. I should have positive ID at least a several days ahead of the ME."

"Get the names and track the whereabouts of everyone in that apartment building," Jeffers ordered.

"We're already on it," Bishop replied. Stephen's team was pulling DOD duty records and matching them up with the dates of the attacks. One occupant was confirmed on leave during the timeframe. They were pulling credit card records and building a profile right now, looking for overlap starting in middle school.

Now there were two names, two faces. One times one is one. Two times two is four. The information set grows exponentially. But Bishop wasn't as enthusiastic. He doubted if any of it would lead to Jeffers' precious left-wing conspiracy. Spencer wasn't taking anyone's orders. Vision Partners might not like it, but there was no second gunman on the grassy knoll. There just wasn't.

Life goes on, Bishop thought, just not for Jonathan Spencer. In the end, men like Jeffers always win and men like Jonathan Spencer always die.

Bishop knew the math. He was the original realist.

But grown men still buy lottery tickets every single day. Maybe they don't expect to win, but they can still wish.

*****

Spencer's eyes roved along the tree line, looking for shifting forms, anomalies, bird movements, any signs that the motel could be surrounded. He saw nothing, but still wasn't satisfied. From inside the bathroom, he got up on the toilet and opened the awning window then looked both ways down the trash-strewn cinderblock wall ahead of pushing out the gym bag. He pressed his upper body through until his weight was balanced forward and carried his legs behind him. His right hand nearly pressed onto a broken beer bottle but he managed to sweep it aside before tumbling out.

The knees and ankles were more flexible, he noticed. Still weak, but he was able to make his way up the steep berm behind the motel without stretching out his arms to balance every step.

Thirty feet up in the trees he stopped and watched the parking lot and beyond. No large vans. Nothing that would conceal police. He cupped his hands over his eyes to mitigate the glare and surveyed the terrain on the far side of the highway. No broken limbs or obvious foliage crushed underfoot, no reflections off binoculars, rifle scopes.

Keeping low to the slope, he slowly made his way through the underbrush then stopped fifty feet along and again watched for anything that was altered, any bush that had moved with him, and any limb that was pushed aside to follow him to the new position. With both eyes concentrated outward, he almost walked into the poison oak straight ahead. *Pay attention!* The human enemy is only one opponent. Remember the three Ss: scorpions, spiders, and snakes.

Dehydration. Sunstroke. Infected feet. *You didn't come this far to die of stupidity!*

*****

"I'm not saying that we have stopped looking," Bishop told Jeffers over the phone. "Cameras are in place looking straight at the father's house in front and back. I have a tracking device on the van. We have his landline. We have his cell line. We've got a relay on the web going in and going out. We even have a filter on everything the dad watches on TV. Wouldn't you think he'd be watching the news if his son had contacted him? The last thing the father watched was *Gilligan's Island*! He went on AOL, skimmed some porn site, and then went to bed. We think he took a crap this morning. What more do you want to know?

"No, I'm not being sarcastic. I've been up all night long. He's probably dead and pretty near cremated by that fire." Bishop listened then jumped back in to confirm, "yes, we are inside the Virginia Coroner's database; my guys piggybacked off one of their MEs and dialed into the case files starting yesterday."

Bishop surprised himself by calling Stephen and the techs "my guys." "No, not literally dialing," he continued. "They followed the coroner's online organizational tree and located the case file. Everything the Medical Examiner does we have in real-time the minute results get logged.

"We're in the Armed Forces Medical Examiner System, AFMES, too. Yes, we have Spencer's dental record. Stephen Nussbaum is searching for online tutorials to see if we can compare the molds to the records, but we're not experts in dental matching."

Jeffers rattled off a punch list so long that Bishop finally interrupted him mid-word.

"Yes, we definitely have the DNA information. The matching is a software piece. If they find usable dental pulp for DNA, according to Nussbaum we'll have the match here before they ever have it in Richmond."

Again, Jeffers went into his list.

"We're following it online through the *Richmond Times-Dispatch*," Bishop confirmed.

"No, we haven't hacked the local desk or any other desk. No, we're not tracking the fire marshal or the arson squad. I don't even know whether they have an arson squad.

"Look, I've got four men plus me. You either get a low profile or you don't, and if you don't then we should have put out an Amber Alert the minute he broke out."

"We can't afford fallout on this," Jeffers worried aloud.

"Then let me do my job. Let all of us do our jobs!" Bishop reassured Jeffers by telling him that Richmond FD was identifying the fire as a ruptured gas line. *You disgusting bastard.*

At least three totally innocent people who were alive in Tuckahoe, Virginia, yesterday were dead now. For Jeffers, those people didn't even register… just as long as there was no blowback on Carlton Jeffers.

CHAPTER THIRTEEN

He stopped the first person he saw in Glen Jean, a teenager who laughed as soon as he said, "Mercy, mid-forties, has goats."

"Go on up past the Post Office to the next road where if you look over to the right you can see the Godfather's Pizza. Don't go that way. Go left and follow the creek on up Scarbro Road, maybe, I don't know, four or five miles. If you get to the Whipple Company Store then you went too far. You go left there on the County Road, 21, yep, 21. You're gonna see a big pond over on this side and then past that you kinda wind around a little lake. Keep on going. Just when the road turns sharp this way, look for a driveway that way. Follow that and you can't go wrong."

He took it in slowly, letting the tires creep ahead on the crushed rock driveway; pits and gaps two feet across threatened to punch holes through the rubber. Pretty land, seventy acres in lush meadow with grass three feet high, dense woods, creeks and hillside. She said she was a cheese maker now. She said there was too much work but she loved it, that there was a job for him any time he wanted it.

Spencer looked again around the grassy field and up the canyon. The stream he had ridden beside ran through steep granite slopes; between them was a tangled amalgam of deciduous trees, some growing, others dead and leaning. Plenty of firewood, but better for squirrels than for any livestock. A wisp of smoke drew his eye to a low-slung single-wide mobile home tucked into the trees.

Mercy was halfway back, walking from the mailbox toward the mobile home, when he drove up behind her. When she looked up from the flicking through the mail, Mercy looked into the eyes staring back through the open visor, did a double-take, pranced in place excitedly then rushed forward, knocking over the motorcycle to get at him.

"Jesus, Johnny, you look like shit."

Those were the first words out of her mouth the minute she released him from Earth Momma hug. Her mouth and eyes looked the same, bright and joyful. She did a quick trot in place then put her hands on both hips and declared, "It's about time you showed up!"

"Thanks, Mercy. Good to see you, too."

"XMercy," she corrected him, showing the giant blue X tattooed where her wedding ring had been, then shaking her head. "Long story. I'll tell you later. We're not into having lots of rules, but I'm XMercy. Get used to it. Legal name change and all. You're staying for dinner."

"If it's ok, I'd like to stay a little longer."

"Hell yeah!" Her arm swung around him again, a thick elbow coming through the worn-out sweater as she led him toward the freestanding porch in front of the faded canary-yellow single-wide. "*Mi casa es su casa*, brother." She had added some inches, muscle, too, and piercings all along one ear.

Ahead of them, the metal-sheathed front door swung open when they mounted the first step. It felt staged, like the compact, short-haired woman inside the doorway intended it for dramatic effect. Bare, tattooed arms crossed tightly over her chest, which might have belonged to a young boy. Spencer was going to mention how she looked like Ellen DeGeneres, but decided to keep it to himself. Her lips pursed, her eyes squinting like she thought she was Clint Eastwood. Her body language was as different from XMercy's as her body.

XMercy wore her hair long, with gray flecked through the wild black mop, her giant breasts swinging beneath a peasant blouse straight out of the Summer of Love. All that was missing was the beads. Spencer judged that this other woman could not have weighed more than a hundred pounds wet. Her sleeves were torn off, her blue jeans as faded as the metal siding. Well-worn, square-toed shit-kickers with two-inch heels and her stiff upright posture came off like a Chihuahua in a studded collar. It wasn't like he watched *Ellen*; the TV was always playing talk shows; bored soldiers passing time and trying to gather in something they could talk about with wives and girlfriends and family, anything other than war.

Mercy walked straight up, tickled her partner's flat belly, then wrapped her arms around the young woman and carried her backwards into the trailer. A medley of powerful stenches shocked Spencer's senses. The sweet, pungent waft of marijuana quickly drew his eyes to a red plastic bong atop the fruit crates in front of a worn sofa. A cat lounged on the unmade bed at the end of the long narrow space, its overdue litter box sitting beneath the four-person, two-legged dining table lagged into the wall. The smoky, herbal scent of green firewood inside the woodstove layered on top of everything else.

"This here is Johnny Spencer," XMercy told the woman "He's family. Johnny, meet Mouse."

The woman, Mouse, looked at XMercy like she expected a better introduction. She shifted her glare to Spencer before walking toward the bedroom, about as far away from both of them as she could go.

*****

Her annual holiday letters had tended to arrive just before Valentine's Day, with at least one year in three missed altogether; pages long, an unedited stream-of-consciousness. Mercy was forever enthusiastically moving to the next exciting life plan immediately after her most recent life-changing epiphany turned out to be another siren's song. She had been that way as far back as he could remember; painting giant imaginary canvases without ever getting around to filling in the details. At fourteen, she had started coming over to the house, telling him how cool he was and how he was going to do something amazing in his life. *She just knew it!* That was when his mom started on chemo. Mercy took him to his first concert. Just a free show down at the park, but, still, it was after dark. She showed him how to make grilled cheese sandwiches, too, with a hot iron.

Jack didn't talk a whole lot so it was good to have Mercy around. Her mom didn't mind the arrangement. Not then, anyhow, not when his mom was there and Mercy was just helping out. Her mom got mad sometimes, shouting across the between the houses how Mercy ought to be getting paid.

Her mom had a new boyfriend. She was a piece of work, Mercy's mom. Her senior year, Mercy showed up with her guitar and her clothes and moved in, just like that. One time the mom came over, drunk, cussing one minute about how it wasn't right for Jack to be fucking her seventeen-year-old kid and then a minute later getting mad because Jack never looked her way. "What the fuck is wrong with a real woman? Huh?" Then the boyfriend came over. That was when Jack had sorted him out. But Jack never touched Mercy. Spencer was sure of that.

*****

Mouse didn't eat much and talked even less all through dinner. XMercy explained all about living off the grid, about how people can do with so much less, they just don't know it, and how a chainsaw was a hell of a lot more important than TV. She'd been living there going on three years, one alone and the last two with Mouse. She had changed teams. Nothing against the penis; just had enough of the dicks that go with 'em. She and Robert divorced. They wanted a baby but her fibroids made that impossible so they found a surrogate and artificially inseminated the sweetest little nineteen-year-old. Darling girl. She was taking classes in early childhood education at the CC. Robert sure was apologetic, never meaning for it to happen. He just fell in love.

"So I traded a wedding ring for a permanent tattoo and I traded in Robert, the one billy goat, for twenty milkers."

She set out with a plan to make cheese. Milking goats. Did he have any idea how hard it is to take care of twenty goats and make a living out of cheese? It's fucking *hard*! You get a milking goat and you've had your last day off! She said she was talking too much about herself and wanted to know what the hell he had gotten up to, but then she took another bong hit and went into a story.

Did he know that goats eat upholstery? "Don't ever let them in a car, let me tell you!"

Spencer passed on the weed but took a short glass of moonshine. XMercy said they bartered for it, but she didn't say what they traded. The corn liquor would have made a good accelerant if the stove ever went cold. It was getting dark; he had already looked around the trailer—the one bed and the hard benches on both sides of the table. Besides the uneven kitchen floor, that was it.

"Show Johnny the guesthouse, Mouse," XMercy said.

After a wordless contest of wills, Mouse jumped up, snatched the flashlight, and flung open the front door. She moved into the tall grass at a trot. "You'd best keep up," she called over her shoulder. "There's copperheads sometimes. You don't want to step on no vipers."

Spencer hobbled after the light, his legs shaking across the mushy pasture. *Scorpions, spiders, snakes.* More than just men can kill. He pushed himself, tripping over a rotten limb and coming up with wet knees and muddy palms. The motorcycle was where he moved it, behind the trailer and out of sight from the driveway, but now he wished that he had found something to use to cover it up.

"I said 'keep up,'" she yelled back. "I ain't got all night." Not a star in the sky, but he could picture the scowl on her face.

"Doing my best," he called to her. "Legs aren't great."

The light was barely visible; she kept moving away while he lost ground. He was used to setting the pace overland; falling behind was something new. He didn't like it.

Finally the light stayed in a fixed position and grew brighter as he closed the distance. "There's matches there, in the jar. Lantern's full." She shined the light into a camper shell minus the truck it ought to have sat upon. If anything, it looked older than the single-wide. The light swung over to the outline of a rough shed. "Pit toilet out there." She flashed the open door. A roll of toilet paper was hanging on a makeshift holder.

"Thanks."

"Uh huh."

He waited until the light faded into the grass, unzipped and pissed right there, not trying for the thirty feet to the shed. Except for the dull glow coming off one of the solar-powered LEDs they used inside, there was no moon, no stars. So black he could have been anywhere.

The makeshift stairs weren't attached to the camper. He tested them underfoot before committing his weight. At least they were stable. When he put one foot inside, the whole place shifted and he held on tight, expecting it to tumble. It tilted in reverse when he stepped inside with both feet, rocking like an uneven café table. He felt his way to the small sink and past that to the jar holding matches. The oil lamp lit instantly then spit and hissed water wicked out from the damp air before settling into a steady glow.

In five minutes, the burning wick had warmed up the cramped quarters. There were five layers of sleeping bags on the raised foam mattress, dry, but all smelling of mold. Yet where you are all depends on where you're coming from, and compared to a solitary prison cell this could easily feel like home. Night birds and small animals moved through the forest outside; he heard an owl, too, after he crawled under the covers. Old food cans, baked beans, Sloppy Joe were stacked on the racks above the bed. Next to the bed were old magazines that he reached up and took down to look over. *Classics Illustrated* comic books. *Dr. Jekyll and Mr. Hyde*, the doctor in a dinner jacket and bow tie holding the potion while the green specter of Mr. Hyde looked on. *The Count of Monte Cristo. Mutiny on the Bounty. Last of the Mohicans. The Invisible Man.*

Invisible. *I wish.* But he wasn't invisible. He was somewhere up a West Virginia holler on a farm that wasn't a farm with XMercy whom he hadn't seen in fifteen years and her tattooed dike girlfriend Mouse. *Two bum legs and a stolen street bike and forty-six dollars. No idea of where you are, who is coming after you, or what comes next.*

*****

MSJS, he wrote with his index finger onto the wet windowpane. His breath steamed clouds into the chill morning air. The surroundings felt cozy after a good night's sleep. Either the camper's acrid stench had dissipated or he had become used to it. Even the tinnitus seemed milder. The comic lay open on top of the covers. Edmond Dantès should have broken out before they ever got him to Chateau d'If, Spencer thought.

They underestimated him, or else he would still be trapped inside the gray monotony of that cell. Dantès had had a plan when he escaped. *What comes next?* Spencer hadn't planned beyond fighting past the medical room. How could he? Succeeding with the breakout was already too improbable; the variables if he succeeded in getting out were infinite. He could only react. *Reaction is not a mission in itself; a course of action built on reaction defines retreat.*

Three raps on the camper door sparked him to jump up, ready to fight. His upper body and lower half responded like two separate beings; the legs never squared under him, leaving Spencer to grip at the window frame on the wall to keep himself from crashing down on the floor.

"Hope I didn't interrupt some quality time with Rosy," XMercy laughed as she swung the door open wide and caught Spencer holding up a pair of his underwear. "Emporio. Ooh. *Très chic!*"

Spencer looked down at the waistband then jerked the briefs behind his back.

XMercy disappeared then came back up with a tray in her hands. "Breakfast. Two eggs over easy, bacon crispy, toast, and coffee. You still take it black?"

He pulled on yesterday's shirt, turned his back to the doorway and pulled jeans on. "Thanks, Mer, um XMercy. Thanks a lot."

The camper rocked from side to side when she came inside. XMercy put the food tray on the bedcovers and backed out. The camper jolted again, stopped, rocked, and stopped again. Spencer's coffee splashed side-to-side but stayed in the mug.

The camper shifted again far more, then settled down, off-kilter but firmly in place.

"Got a rock under the post now," she yelled up to him. "Coming in!"

Mercy danced from one foot to the other, swaying her shoulders to an imaginary beat, then, satisfied, she pushed herself onto the foam mattress, crossed her unshaven legs, flipped her skirt over them and tore off half a piece of toast.

"So, tell me all about you," she insisted. "Disappear for what, twelve years, fifteen, and here you are. I heard a few things here and there. Rose would ask after you. Jack still helps her with the house. You remember my Aunt Rose? My great-aunt, really. Seems like she's been old forever, but she just keeps on going. Jesus! How the hell are you, Johnny? What are you doing in Glen Jean, West Virginia? I thought you were off someplace fighting wars, making the world safe for democracy. But here you are."

"The army discharged me. Medical."

"I see how you're on shaky pins. You ok with that? Being discharged? Lots of guys are coming back fucked up. PTSD, depression. Glen Jean doesn't have three hundred people and there's been three suicides, vets, right here. Shit, you don't need to hear about that. I'm sorry."

Spencer slowly lifted a stiff piece of bacon, ran it under his nose like a fine cigar, and then touched his tongue against the edge, salty and fat.

"I could have stayed for physical therapy," he told her, "but I wanted to be out of there." He took a small bite, crunched it between his front teeth, and ran the bits around the inside of his mouth. *Man.* Probably the best thing he'd ever eaten.

"I can rehab myself better than they can," he promised. "I'm already doing better. Being outside makes a difference."

"Isn't that the truth," she agreed. "Why would anybody live in some shitty city apartment, go to work every day to pay for it, and call that living?" She looked him up and down, apprising, and then asked, "You feel up to some productive therapy?"

"What do you have in mind?" he asked her.

"I've got the cart hitched up, gas in the chainsaw. Take the Polaris up the creek and bring back all the rounds you can buck."

"You've got a Polaris?"

"Uh huh. Diesel. Sixteen grand, paid for. Appearances can be deceiving, Johnny Boy. Besides, four months out of twelve you don't know if that driveway is going to be a river or two feet deep in snow. With that machine, it doesn't matter. Cuts through water, rides right over snow banks. Sold those damned goats and did something right.

"I took the divorce money from Robert and went to Paris. Did you know that? Stayed in a three-hundred-dollar-a-night hotel for five weeks, going to the cheese shop down the block every day, drinking wine, kinda figuring I'd burn through the money and probably pull the plug when it ran out. Then one night somebody said Amsterdam and I said 'What the fuck?' and stayed on a canal barge for a month. I'd get so wasted and then I craved cheese. I finally saw that the cheese was going to save my life. And it did, too! It got me here anyway. I had to get away from those damned goats, but that's another story. How does anybody want to have goats? Baaa baaa baaa, always wanting food night and day."

*****

The Polaris and cart were behind the mobile home; he walked around the machine, admiring the sturdy cage, running his fingers over the brush guard and front-mounted winch. A 20-inch orange-sided Husqvarna chainsaw was stashed in the short truck bed. *Nice stuff*, he thought.

At night, the black Honda blended right in where he leaned it up against the metal siding. It stood out like a giant chunk of obsidian, all glossy black in the sunlight. Spencer fetched a brown tarp from where it was bunched up under a metal-roofed lean-to and covered the stolen machine. He heard the women arguing through the thin walls while he prepared to secure the tarp around the handlebars.

"I am not comfortable with that."

"Honey, it's going to be fine," XMercy assured Mouse. "Johnny Spencer is not a problem."

"How do you know that? You haven't set eyes on him in twenty years."

"Fifteen."

Spencer wasn't comfortable listening in, but he couldn't shift the Honda off the wall without them knowing he was right outside their kitchen.

"Fifteen, twenty. Damn! We don't need a man hanging 'round here getting up in our shit!"

"Mouse, you've got a good heart in there. I know it, even if you do hate men. But right now, honey, you're starting to piss me off. I lived more than a year in their house, eating their food, sleeping under their roof. That motherfucker my mother brought home hit on me every time she turned around. She just closed her eyes; wouldn't say a thing about it. If Johnny's father hadn't taken me in, I would have been living on the streets. On the streets," XMercy was saying. "So now we have the chance to do a good turn for Johnny. I consider this a blessing and I will not turn him away, not ever. I'm not saying it's a free ride. He'll pull his weight. But until he says different, girl, he has a place right here."

The front door opened then slammed shut. Mouse booted the bucket across the dirt, strode past the well pump and out into the pasture.

Spencer held the handlebars and stood his weight first on his right leg, flexing his left ankle and twisting his foot in a circle before shifting and doing the same with the other leg. He exercised each leg two sets of ten reps then tried a slow squat to see how deeply his knees would go.

"*Demi plie*," XMercy shouted, catching him unaware. "*Tendu. Degage!*" She was holding a carbine in one hand, a box of shells in the other. *.22. Notch and bead sight.*

She had snuck up on him and she wasn't even trying. His instincts were probably more fucked than his legs. What else was he missing?

"I put my bike under the lean-to," he told her. *Why the rifle?* "Hope that is ok. Mercy—sorry— XMercy, you sure I'm not a bother?"

"You're family. Period. That means we tell each other what's on our minds, straight-out. Something you're doing is bugging me, I'm going to let you know it. It works both ways."

"What about Mouse?"

"Mouse is ornery. Give her time, she'll come around. You let me worry about Mouse. You just go on and you don't come home until you've got the truck bed and the cart full up. And don't buck 'em too long. No more than sixteen inches, no less than twelve."

XMercy stood the carbine up into the Polaris' side rack and put the high-velocity bullets into the passenger-side compartment. "Rabbit, grouse, have at 'em. We're trying to get as much off the land as we can, that means protein, too. But no deer. Deer season is months away. People are pretty damned tolerant really, but we poach a deer and goodwill goes bye-bye real fast around here."

CHAPTER FOURTEEN

The sweet rich scent of freshly cut wood was something he never expected to be enjoying again. Even the blue-gray smoke smelled good coming off the chainsaw as he pulled on the rope to start it up. Once he had identified the muscle groups, he was able to brace his legs to keep his balance. The noise and rough vibration energized him. He craved hard work, but he lost control during the swing arc as he tried splitting a round. The maul weight shifted and he was unable to counter. Along his right thigh he thought he felt movement in the metal plate, which forced him to stop. *Too soon. Don't overdo it.*

He unzipped the jeans, hooked a thumb under the giant waistband, took his penis out and then let it go, raising his hands high over his head and peeing hands-free, spraying toward the trees wherever the yellow line wanted to go. With the saw silent, he saw birds flitting through shafts of sunlight and listened as chipmunks scurried over and under leaves and needles. He watched them rushing, stopping to rapidly glance side to side for threats from all directions before settling onto a sunny log to trill their click-click-click-click and he clicked back at them, holding very still. An engine whined in the distance down some unseen road; he glanced back to the carbine, reacting automatically. *Chipmunk.*

A big ash was laying nearly level above a tiny trickling spring. He sought it out, straddled his legs across it, and lay back in the sunshine with his zipper still open, and pulled up his shirt to expose his lean white torso, letting the rays bake into his skin. When he zipped up again and returned to cutting rounds, he set aside the ear protection. He wanted noise. The Husqvarna's honest throaty growl, the rough vibration, the sawdust flying… he loved all of it.

Inside an hour he had cut sixty rounds. Then, carefully setting both feet and feeling his way through the mechanics of bending and lifting, he filled the Polaris's small truck bed. The repetition felt good; by the end of the fourth downer log, he was moving bigger sections and stepping his way up to the trail with his load, sometimes pausing to test a new angle, try a new demand on his body. Core and cardio checked out; knees, ankles, and large muscle groups were there, just still weak and half-asleep.

After the cart was filled, he eyed the .22, paused, then lifted it out, feeling its light weight in both hands before running his right palm along the smooth underside of the stock, his left under the sun-warmed short barrel. His fingers felt the release and dropped the magazine into his right hand, then he brought the clip to his nose and breathed in the scent. After reloading, he snugged the butt into his shoulder, leaned his cheekbone into the fat of his hand, and sighted down the simple v-notch, moving down the sights until his eye caught movement. The chipmunk lifted off its haunches, turned, and click-click-click-clicked. "Click," Spencer answered, then slowly dropped the rifle against his lap.

*****

Pulling on his earlobes felt good, but afterward the tinnitus was worse, especially when he rolled his jaw. Mouse eyed him across the table like he was a mental case.

"Are you doing ok?" XMercy wanted to know. "What's up with the contortions?"

"Ears. No big deal."

"Oh dang, did I forget the earmuffs?" XMercy apologized. "Man… I'm so sorry… all that sawing…"

"My bad. I had them, just didn't wear 'em."

"Don't abuse government property," she chided gently, getting up from her seat at the table. "I'll get the lavender oil."

Spencer's mind floated adrift while he considered the comment. Thirteen months earlier he would not have done that, he would have used any means available to keep maximized fitness, his body and his mind. He surveyed his hands every single day. That's what he had been. *Government property.* Now, as he looked them over in the dim lamplight, they were raw, blistered all along the grip lines where the saw vibrated against unconditioned skin. Hours of shucking rounds had etched nicks and cuts over every finger. He opened and closed them into fists, enjoying the stiff mix of satisfaction and pain.

XMercy's touch shocked him, coming from behind to dab the fragrant fluid on her finger behind his ear. He stiffened, but held still for the other ear. When she finished, he leaned forward to breathe in the steaming grain on the table in front of him.

"That's quinoa," XMercy explained, slipping back into her seat. "Incas ate it centuries before Europeans ever sailed to the New World. We're trying to avoid most other glutens; some wild rice, heirloom potatoes, but none of the Monsanto crap."

Spencer hadn't touched the wine, but she added to his glass anyway; not really a glass, it was a canning jar. Ball, embossed on the side, sparkled against the light from the oil lamp. They trickle-charged LED lighting off solar units, but XMercy preferred the softer light. Spencer watched her calm movements; her eyes hadn't aged. In that light, her eyes still looked like she was a teenager.

"I like this," XMercy told Mouse. "Zinfandel?"

"Primitivo," Mouse responded, adding that "Pat"—their grocer—"is into Croatian wines this month."

"How's she doing?"

"Good," Mouse was trying to be civil, which to her meant pretending Jonathan Spencer wasn't there at all. "She's all excited about some big wine tasting dinner thing she's doing this weekend down in Beckley. Bunch of rich assholes flying in from all over. I told her to poison them. IKRP, baby. She says they probably have their own personal tasters."

XMercy gave her the stink-eye.

"What?" Mouse asked.

Spencer tried to stab at the beet salad, missing and sending the purple root onto the tabletop, where XMercy snatched it up and popped it into her mouth. Mouse's jaw muscles pulsed at the invisible connection. Beneath the block-letter tattoo on her neck, her veins stood out.

"Is that 'Give'?" Spencer asked, observing the scripted capital letters.

"That's it. 'Give.' Give until it hurts. It's a D. D, not G."

XMercy shook her head, admonishing Mouse to chill. "It kind of looks like a G."

"Well it's not a fucking G. Does he see an I or an E? It's DV, dude. And it's not for 'diva.'"

"Dimitri Vosilych," XMercy instructed. "Mouse's Che Guevarra."

"Who's that?" Spencer asked.

"For real? Your ears really must be messed up." Mouse's eyes could have been daggers. "What, don't soldiers follow anything but orders? You ever heard of the news?"

"Johnny brought in two loads of good seasoned wood," XMercy interrupted. "Looks like four or five cords. How'd you like the Polaris? It's sweet, isn't it! We get in a few more good days like today we'll rent a splitter and get a dozen finished cords stacked before things get busy. We had a terrible windstorm the winter before last. So many trees down, but it's paying off now… the Circle of Life."

"Dimitri Vosilych stepped up. He put himself on the line." Mouse explained how "DV" wasn't a terrorist. He just wanted fairness. "I mean, if we took back every dollar over fifty million and left that for the rich, would they be harmed at all? Imagine a country with free healthcare for everyone and nobody homeless, no hungry kids. That's what DV was all about. How about representative government, not a government that listens in on us and subsidizes rich bankers?"

"No!" XMercy shouted. "No no no! We're not doing this again. Mouse, I get it, life isn't fair, but we're not bringing that to dinner. No violence, not at this table." She inhaled deeply; raising her arms in a circular arc, she then brought together her hands and exhaled.

Spencer couldn't help noticing the long red armpit hair showing in the gap under her short sleeves. *That hadn't changed.*

"I didn't tell you, Johnny. I practice Tibetan Buddhism. It's very centering. There's a connection to all living things."

"But she loves a bloody steak," Mouse chided her.

XMercy ignored it. "*Bodhicitta* is tolerance above all, including tolerance of our own weaknesses. I seek to find boundless joy and compassion for all people and all things. This is room for variance, for differ-"

"Did you shoot anything?" Mouse challenged him. "I don't see any meat hanging."

Spencer returned her stare. He was willing to leave her alone, but letting her get into his face was not ok, even if it was her place, not his. "No. I was thinking about bringing in wood."

"So what did they have you doing all those years in the army? I mean, if you were a cook, maybe you can do the cooking tomorrow. How does that sound?"

"Primitivo...I think it tastes like Zin." XMercy put her nose into her drink jar and inhaled again. "Smells like Zin, too."

"It is fucking Zin," Mouse shouted. "Zin, Primitivo. Same thing." Turning back to Spencer, she kept at him. "So what are you going to cook?"

"I'm not a cook."

"Johnny jumped out of planes," XMercy explained. She had been out to see her grandmother two years ago and saw Jack. He had filled her in on the latest. That was how she got Johnny's APO address.

Mouse shot back her wine and refilled the jar. "Ever kill anybody?"

"We are not talking about that!" XMercy closed her eyes and practiced her controlled breathing, humming her mantra to cleanse.

"Well maybe 'we're' not, but I am," Mouse shouted back. "Did you?"

"Yes."

"What was that like, killing somebody? Going halfway around the world blowing up people you never met?"

"I didn't do that," Spencer responded calmly.

"You did kill or you didn't kill," Mouse badgered. "Which?"

"I didn't do that. That's artillery, Close Air Support, Air Force. I didn't train for that. Not what I do. I don't blow up anything."

Mouse drained her glass, reached for the bottle and splashed out the last drops before getting up and moving out of the light. She turned on a harsh white LED, opened a cupboard, and came back with a large twist-top bottle with a yellow kangaroo label.

"Another bottle?" XMercy cautioned before getting up to turn out the glaring bulb.

"This is just getting interesting," Mouse shot back. Turning her attention back to Spencer, she refilled and asked him point-blank just how he killed people?

"There's all kinds of killing. An Apache helicopter fires a 30mm M230 chain gun that treats anything in its path like a sausage grinder. A 155mm Howitzer shell takes down a four-story building and everything in it. I never killed like that."

"So you weren't trying to kill, you just messed up? What did you do, run somebody over with a truck?"

"I did the job I was trained to do. Did it effectively. Because if I messed up, bad things happened. Messing up means taking casualties that might have been avoided, getting one of our guys wounded or sometimes killed. I never messed up," Spencer said.

Mouse laughed aloud and pulled herself upright in her seat. "So you didn't blow people up, you didn't run people over, and you didn't mess up. I guess that makes you a real badass then, huh."

"You could say that."

"I just did. Badass. You're so good nobody around you got hurt or got killed. Wow, you must be something special."

"I never said that. I said I never messed up. I didn't say we all came home."

XMercy stood up, reached out across the table and wrenched away the jar from Mouse's hand. Her other hand got to the bottle before Mouse. "Whoa! That's enough! Johnny is our guest. This is not dinner conversation, Mouse. Look at these beautiful plates. These amazing beets are from our own soil; the carrots, and the parsnips. We picked these spring onions together, Mouse. I made this cheese. I milked the goats; I curdled the milk and separated the curds. I drained and molded and polished and ashed this and there is not much left and I am never milking another goat again as long as I live so when it is gone that is it!"

Mouse looked up at XMercy's clenched fists and flashed a puckish smile that melted the wrath.

"What would do this country more good, a hundred-thousand dead Afghans or a hundred dead Americans, provided the right ones were dead?" Mouse asked softly. "A hundred rich assholes gaming our entire system just for themselves."

"No more. Please. Let's enjoy a quiet meal," XMercy pleaded.

"We're working on a Dimitri Vosilych encampment this year," Mouse observed. "If Burners don't want us, we'll show up and make it happen anyway. When we burn the man, we're really going to *burn the man*. IKRP. We're not going to be shut up or shut down." Mouse suddenly went silent, staring into space.

"Oh crap. Johnny, stand up and get behind her so she doesn't fall out of the chair." XMercy rushed into the kitchen and rummaged around until she found the brown sugar. She measured two heaping spoonfuls onto the carrots on Mouse's plate then stabbed a fork into them.

"Hold her head upright. Mouse!" She slapped Mouse's cheek twice and spoke more firmly. "Mouse! Open your mouth." Mouse began chewing mechanically, and then chewing faster as the sugar melted over her tongue. "She's hypoglycemic," XMercy explained. "Alcohol and arguing makes it worse, and she loves both." Within minutes, XMercy had Mouse holding her own fork; it took fifteen minutes before she was completely back. By then, XMercy had heaped food high onto Spencer's plate and sent him down to the guesthouse with the flashlight. "We'll get you a hot shower tomorrow, Johnny. I'll take care of her from here."

*****

Jeffers wasn't mincing words. Bishop could picture him on the other end of the line. He sounded like he hadn't slept.

"You obviously never ran background on this team you hired. The one thing common to every one of your commandos is write-ups for excessive violence. None of them mustered out from the same units they were in when they joined. But you didn't know that, did you? Trident Security and Blackwater rejected every one of them. You hired rejects, Mr. Bishop. The results speak for themselves," Jeffers said.

Bishop took the phone off speaker, switching to the handset. *How could Jeffers know they failed?*

"The ME posted results fifteen minutes ago, if you are wondering," Jeffers continued. "Conclusive DNA. No match. Fortunately, we have not been sitting on our hands for four days. We pulled the operative who directed Spencer's mission folder in Afghanistan. He is somewhere over the North Atlantic en route to your office right now. We're getting a proven asset for the task at hand and the person most familiar with Spencer."

"If he worked with Spencer, how do we trust him to help us?"

"Because the people to whom he answers are people who answer to APA and Vision Partners. There is a food chain and we stand at the top of it."

"I don't have time to integrate new assets," Bishop argued. "We're in the process of laying down the most comprehensive facial recognition surveillance ever applied." With NSA keys, they were inside every AM/PM, 7-Eleven, every BP, Mobil, Texaco, Hyatt, Marriot, Hilton, Chase Bank, Bank of America, every urban surveillance system—Canada included—Arby's, McDonald's, sixty percent of ATMs, and eight million private homes with real-time expansion into every new household added to the functionality. Four men were sweeping the country in real-time for Jonathan Spencer. He had accomplished that with four men! "We should be inside gun stores and gun shows, too, damn it."

"Yet no results. Mr. Bishop, we apply an evolved, multi-faceted approach to every issue, every goal. Whether we find results in an instant, contexts we term an 'avalanche,' or through longer-term methods—'glaciers'—we don't succeed in every skirmish but we invariably win the wars. We are diversified, across industries—fossil fuels, defense, pharma, agriculture, communications, incarceration, even academics, and across geographies. Despite breadth, all is synthesized toward a purpose," Jeffers said.

"Assuming your conclusion that Jonathan Spencer is a mutation, a random radical cell, the moment that he held no intelligence value he should have been eliminated. I can appreciate that it draws inquiry when a soldier is in full leg casts about which there is nothing in the VA medical record, but a soldier in full leg casts can certainly commit suicide. Upon arrival, Miller will complement your ground assets and direct your field consultants. The man is a closer, a seasoned expert in swift results. Conclusive results."

Jeffers continued: "We are looking additionally at bringing in a police lieutenant, NYPD Intel Division; he ran the one investigative team that got past the noise and got to Spencer when federal, state, and local law enforcement failed. I'm sending you the file on him as we speak. He is on personal leave; our sources within NYPD indicate he is receiving mandatory anger-management counseling for disciplinary reasons subsequent to the death of his partner during Spencer's capture. He doesn't buy our Dimitri Vosilych; he has knowledge and he has motivation, both. Mr. Nussbaum can continue surveillance methods without your input. I want you on your way to that NYPD lieutenant, Cullen. Now."

"Hey, I am not at fault for his escape," Bishop complained.

"They didn't get him!" Jeffers shouted. "He stole a motorcycle from right next door and you never knew it! He's had enough time to get clear across the country because you failed. I don't pay for failure!"

Bishop strained to hold it together. "The whole street was evacuated at the time. We couldn't know he stole the motorcycle! This isn't algebra; not everything has a finite answer."

Bishop was sick of the whole command structure. Jeffers, who had probably never captured a frog much less an escaped prisoner—what the hell was he doing micromanaging tactics!

"Here is how this adds up to me," Jeffers pressed. "I'm giving you every resource and you keep failing."

"It wasn't my prison," Bishop countered right back. "Don't play the blame game. I'm not telling those men that they're not getting paid." *Not without telling them who is holding the purse strings and where you hang your hat.*

Jeffers calmed down hearing the phrase "the blame game." He had originated that one himself. One of his favorites. But the moment passed quickly.

"He has a forty-eight-hour lead," Jeffers insisted. "He could be in Russian hands right now, off to be another 'guest of Putin.'"

"I'm aware of that," Bishop conceded, not believing it for a second. "If he worked inside a network, he might be in Yemen or Waziristan or in a Moscow hotel right now. But Spencer is a loner. I've tracked loners. He needs cash, forged identification, probably a disguise. He'll want weapons. That's why I'll get him. I always do.

"Not even Spencer would be crazy enough to rob a gun shop. D.C. and 30 National Instant Criminal Background Check states require ID and background checks. That narrows the field. I'll lay down a blanket on every gun store licensed for over-the-counter sales. Nussbaum tells me eighty-five percent of them use web-based video security. He can matrix facial recognition into every one of them. Spencer bought in the past at Eagle Arms, a gun show vendor. My guys went ahead and mapped out every show across the country. We'll get eyes into all of them."

"Whoa!" Jeffers resisted. "No! Drop that. No no no! No gun show surveillance. APA isn't alienating the NRA and the National Shooting Sports Foundation. No!"

"We're not talking about Second Amendment stuff," Bishop argued. "Spencer is the most dangerous terrorist in the country." What the hell did the gun lobby have to do with anything?

"I said no! We're taking another tack." Jeffers pulled up his contacts at NSA, scrolling for the precise fit. "Nobody is fragmenting twenty-year alliances," he told Bishop. "You remember who writes the checks. Tell Nussbaum to expect an email from Sunshine Industries," he told Bishop.

"Sunshine Industries?"

"Yes," Jeffers answered. Then Bishop heard the line disconnect.

Stephen and his techs were already building a keyword and geographical search framework when Bishop joined them. Phone, email, web searches; any time someone spoke, wrote, or searched, their algorithms could catch it.

"How are you doing that?" Bishop wanted to know.

"Sunshine Industries," Stephen replied. "We just got the equivalent to a two-thousand page tutorial on two more sections of NSA's framework. Jesus! This stuff is unreal. So cool. We can trace back to the source of any browser traffic in under a second. This is fucking crazy!" He pressed his fingertips against his temples and read through the table of contents line by line.

"We're already combing through every FBI and NYPD report on the attacks, following connections between victims, companies, investment patterns," Stephen explained. "Now we have every resource Homeland Security has got, plus Kip and Dale and Dilip are a fuck of a lot smarter than anybody at NSA. I guarantee you."

Bishop's jaw hung open. Every time Carlton Jeffers had upped the stakes again. Stephen had access now to four hundred billion dollars' worth of top-secret classified systems along with the guidebook to leverage them. Jeffers did that in ten minutes.

"How?" was all he could manage to ask.

"Who do you think sells the systems to NSA?" Stephen answered casually. "They're all Vision Partners and APA."

*****

XMercy followed Spencer outside into the night air, leaving Mouse sprawled on the sofa. "It's a fucking D," Mouse yelled after them, bringing the cool Mason jar against her tattooed neck. "D. For Dimitri."

The meadow glistened silver from a fading three-quarters moon teasing through thin clouds. XMercy felt the change in the warm night air; an early summer coming on. Still too early to abandon sweaters, but the trees would soon be leafing out with the first spring greenery, assuring the soul that all is new and good again.

She let out a long sigh and smiled to herself.

XMercy wrapped her arms around his arm and squeezed. "Johnny, thank you for bringing in all that wood. Wait a couple days to let those hands heal before you go out for more. Not that we don't need it, but I have a little surprise for you. You're going to like it."

Spencer had been considering. The hills were peppered with mine shafts, abandoned metal buildings. The legs were far from perfect, but if he could borrow the .22, a knife, a pot, matches, and a few other staples, he could make do.

"Mercy, I do appreciate spending time with you, this place, but maybe I'd better move on down the road."

"XMercy," she corrected, but gently. He didn't resist when she hooked her arm around him and leaned into his shoulder. "Mouse is Mouse. Don't take it personally, Johnny. She hates your balls, not you. Take the flashlight and go on to your place. Get yourself a good night's sleep. That's an order!"

"Yes sir."

XMercy spun Spencer back around as he turned to go, hugging and tightening her arms around him. *Hug her back,* he told himself, but when her arms relaxed his still remained at his sides.

"You get first shower in the morning," XMercy let him know. Her voice revealed no sign of any missed expectation. "You know Mouse isn't getting up!"

XMercy kept watching the silhouette of his shoulders against the moonlight with the flashlight moving through the tall grass ahead of his steps all the way out to the camper. One of her owls sounded through the trees, followed by the hollow *umph* from the camper door opening. Spencer placed the flashlight inside on the floor then stepped around the side. XMercy listened momentarily to the sound of his peeing hitting the grass then went inside the trailer, shutting the door behind her.

After he went in, Spencer set the flashlight on the small countertop and reached for matches. He saw the surprise when he lit the lamp and wished again that he had hugged her back. Mercy had left a guitar on top of the blankets and sleeping bags. He lifted it, felt its heft, ran his fingertips around the body, set it on his lap and moved his left palm slowly up the neck, stopping at every fret until he reached the head and tuning pegs, touching his fingers to three then counting three with his left thumb. He hesitated, and then permitted himself the pleasure of bringing his right palm down on the saddle, the balls of his hand resting against the bridge. His knees trembled as the soft flesh between thumb and forefinger slid up the strings. He had not felt the weight and curve of a guitar since before the last mission, but didn't want to think of that now.

He felt his right fingers along the rim of the sound hole, pressed against the soft tension. *E-A-D-G-B-E.* His left fingers moved along chord to chord, in the air, never touching, imagining their way down the frets. He tried to draw from memory the sound from each position, closed his eyes and imagined feeling the vibrations as he worked the guitar's voice from the notes, then abruptly he set it aside, carefully, to be sure it made no sound.

Mercy had taught him to play. The next-door kid with a dead mom and a half-dead dad. She showed what she knew and told him to practice and he did that, hours and hours and hours. Even as a kid, he was trying so hard to be perfect. Maybe if he were perfect, Jack would wake up. But Jack didn't have it in him.

His mom used to set up Jack's schedule, do the billings, maintain the inventory, call customers when bills were overdue, send out Christmas cards, pay the taxes. She was the officer, Spencer realized. Dad was a grunt. *Like me.*

Spencer stretched out on the foam mattress, running his prone frame through the same micro-exercises he had done in sets of fifty, hours and hours of sets inside concrete walls. *Just days ago.* Sun and moon, blue jays, chipmunks, and woodpeckers didn't change any of that.

You can't stay here. They'll come. Nobody does what they did and then lets you just walk away! He needed to get online, try to find out what was going on.

*****

"Pretty good shower, huh?" XMercy said to him. "I almost fucked up bad when I first got it. Tried putting the tank up on the roof. Dumb. Nearly caved the roof in before it was a quarter filled. That was before Mouse. Some guys from the hardware helped me build the frame and pipe to it. You wouldn't think a black plastic tank would get so hot, would you? You can't see it from below, but we painted a reflective mirror surface onto the platform it sits on and that kicks it up quite a bit more. Not much use in the winter, but I'm fixing to get an outside bathtub to use all summer long."

Her enthusiasm could sometimes be a lot to take in. "Good shower," Spencer agreed when he was sure that he could get a word in edgewise. The array of shampoos and body washes, conditioners and moisturizers surprised him; there had to be at least one for every day of the week. The towel, on the other hand, left a lot to be desired.

XMercy came up behind him again. This time she gently touched the angry red scar along his back. She inhaled quickly, as if she felt his pain.

"Jesus, Johnny." The scars along his legs were even worse: massive thick lines running down his right thigh and covering both legs below the knees. It boggled the mind that he could walk at all.

XMercy chanted for him while Spencer got dressed. She had a card table and chairs set outside with yogurt and bananas, homemade granola, French press with Starbucks coffee, and locally made ceramic cups.

"I've seen those scars. Talk to me, Johnny. How'd they happen?"

"I got wounded. Twice. It happens."

"Yes, and?"

"So I'm never going to be a great skier." Spencer chuckled. He once had a major who wanted him to give Biathlon a try; thought he had the stuff to represent the Army and the USA. He hadn't thought about that in years. *Funny.*

"Yes, and?"

"Now I can't serve in the Armed Forces."

"Yes and… how does that make you feel?"

"That it's a waste. The army took a million dollars to train me and threw that out the door. Nothing more American than waste."

"I'm so sorry, Johnny." XMercy reached over the table to take his hand. When he withdrew she shifted to the French press, plunging it down.

"How long were you in, something like twenty years?"

"Nineteen years, six months, and twenty-two days. Six more months and I'd have got retirement. Not that I wanted to retire. I know what Mouse thinks, but I was good with the army. Good at it. But money guys with business degrees figure every soldier is disposable. So they cut me a check and sent me packing. I bought a motorbike and I went."

"I saw the motorcycle. Do you have plans?"

"Don't worry. I know about guests and fish both stinking after a few days. I'll be heading along."

"I don't want you to go. I mean that, Johnny. And not just for old time's sake, either. There's that, but that's not why. If you're willing to stay, we can use the help. I can trust you to keep a secret, right? I know I can. You can't tell anybody and you can't tell Mouse I told you, ok?"

Spencer nodded his assent. XMercy shook granola into a wooden bowl and dolloped yogurt over the top, excitedly trying to frame her confession. Her hands shook when she picked up the French press.

"We're growers. Mouse and me. New Millennium Moonshine."

"Weed?"

Ten minutes later, XMercy was walking him down a foot-wide dirt path packed down by hundreds of trips. She stopped midway, turned to him and asked, "The guitar? I've been dying to ask! Do you still remember how to play?"

"It's been a while."

She nodded, disappointed, and went back to walking ahead of him until she opened her arms to a long arched structure in front of them, assembled from PVC and plastic covering. Spencer recoiled involuntarily when she ripped away Velcro fasteners to open the flaps. A rush of warm, moist air hit him in the face. But it was the shocking white glare that made him turn his eyes away.

"That's the Mylar," XMercy explained. "Pumps up the heat units and makes them dance like happy little chlorophyll engines. We're getting near to indoor grow conditions without using a kilowatt of energy generation."

Once inside, they ducked below lateral PVC water lines and walked in between rows of abutting plywood tables set onto rough sawhorses, each table covered with three- to six-inch tall young sprouts seeded in rich dark earth-scented humus inside black plastic trays. XMercy looked down at the oversized imprint Spencer's shoes made in the Mylar, watching one print until the shining fabric returned to its original shape, leaving behind just the muddy outline of the sole.

"A whole damned greenhouse of the best bud in West Virginia!" she burst out. Double-6 mil plastic covers, roll-up sides, a continuous PVC drip system, spring-fed. Off the grid and state-of-the-art!"

Before that, he had been wondering how they could afford a new diesel Polaris and the Honda generator, but it was none of his business. He had accepted that and let it go.

"Will you help?" XMercy urged him. "With your help, we'll get in a second greenhouse right away. Johnny, we can't pay you yet, but we can stake you through harvest and pay you then. I need to talk with Mouse, but she'll get it. She gets business.

Before a breath, she continued: "Johnny, ninety days, we'll be harvested and dried. Finished until next year. We have a hundred-twenty starts each of a hybrid, Jack the Ripper, a killer sativa called Girl Scout Cookies, and a 100-percent Indica Pot of Gold strain. It's real low-key. Strictly wholesale. We make the delivery, very cool medical marijuana dudes, all cash.

"After we dump the runts, let's say we get down to two-forty, two-fifty plants. Weather means a ton in outdoor grows, but even in our first year we got eight-ounce averages, over five ounces dried, all bud. I'm ordering solar-driven fans to keep the air moving to stop the mold issues we had, but we need to get up the second greenhouse.

"It's not easy, but it sure beats the hell out of goddamned goats!" she said.

"At $85 an ounce, we could gross a hundred thousand dollars, not even counting the extra shake. And it's not like we're robbing or hurting anybody.

"You've always been a Boy Scout, but just think about it, please. You don't need to worry about the law; state police don't bother us, we're small potatoes, and nobody will elect a sheriff who goes after the small growers. No way. People around here are all doing something or other outside the lines to make ends meet. Have to. Sheriff messes with growers, he's liable to come home to a pile of ashes where his house used to be. Like I said, New Millennium Moonshine."

*****

"Fine. I don't care." Mouse waved her arms as if to say it had nothing to do with her.

"Mouse, don't be like that. Six hands are better than four. With Johnny, we can get in the second greenhouse this year. That more than pays for itself."

"Whatever." Mouse got up from the table, swung the refrigerator wide open and leaned her head inside, slowly coming back out with a can of PBR. XMercy was letting him get all up in their shit, this guy she hadn't seen in more than twenty years, back when she had been around lots of guys.

"Mouse, please. Sit down and talk to me. You're my partner, in my life, in our business. He's just going to work for us. We could double the crop. Buck and Lyle said they'd take as much as we bring them. Come on. It makes sense, you know it does," XMercy said.

They had both seen the flashlights at the bottom of the meadow, seen work boots tracked on the Mylar the next morning. Mouse included a shotgun purchase in their supplies list for the season, but saying she'd handle it and doing that were two different things. Diesel or not, Mouse might talk, but she had never walked the walk. Investing in a war veteran could be good insurance.

"We're treating this like business or we're not doing this at all," Mouse demanded. "We get a full crop in, he gets ten percent capped at ten thousand dollars. Works out over a thousand a week. If it rains all summer, we won't see a decent return. That happens, he gets half. That's if, IF, we do this. I'm not saying yes so you don't say another word about this! And for Christ's sake don't tell him what we stand to make. None of his damned business.

She stood up and said, "I'm taking the credit card, I'm driving up to Fayetteville, I'm getting on the library computer, and I'm checking him out before we decide another thing. You hear? Not a word 'til I get back here. We go over a background check and then, then, we decide."

"You can just go to Judy's, use the computer there. Why drive twelve miles when you can drive two?"

Mouse glared. "You go to Judy's and it's everybody's business. You want private, you drive the extra ten miles."

*****

Spencer had just left the single-wide after finishing breakfast inside it five minutes earlier. The legs were getting better every day, not ready for swinging a splitting maul, but steadier on stairs and secure enough that he could shift directions in a single stride, no longer having to put two feet down and baby his knees. He took the stairs fast, confidently, stepped inside the trailer then had to wait on his eyes. He didn't think to knock before walking back in.

All the months of low fluorescent lighting left his eyes slow to adjust between light and dark.

When they adjusted, XMercy was standing in front of him. She was bare from the waist up, her wild hair clipped on top of her head. Both her breasts were inside the kitchen sink as she soaped her armpits. His eyes bugged wide before he turned away.

"Same Johnny," she laughed. "You're still not over them! They're just tits. No big deal."

He straightened tall, squared his feet, turned left-face and marched straight back out the door. He was still standing at attention when she joined him a few minutes later. She had let her blouse absorb the excess moisture, which left her armpits ringed and the cotton clinging to her breasts. Spencer lost his train of thought, nervously embarrassed. She had been doing that to him since he was a kid.

"Is there, ahem, is there any place where I can get online around here? Check email?"

XMercy crossed her arms below her breasts, forcing them out and forward. "Sure. Judy's Café, there in the General Store, they've got internet. Buy a maple bar and ask Judy if you can use it," she said.

"Take the ATV. It's not street-licensed, but nobody cares. By the way, if you have army clothes, wear them into town, would you? They appreciate service and it wouldn't do any harm to let people know you're staying here."

Spencer lifted both legs into the Polaris, pleased that he could do that without needing to grab his pants and lift his leg over the side panel. He had already stretched; he was now able to grab his toes and hold for a ten count; the thigh ached, but his back and arms felt limber, catlike. The left leg gave more trouble while he slowly worked into Tai Chi. Hammer with fist was still impossible, but repulse the monkey he had again, right and left, grace and snap, too.

He drove the dirt road with the sunshine on his face, feeling good until he shifted onto packed gravel and felt suddenly vulnerable. *No weapon, no means to evade.* He didn't even know the trails, he realized. Handing every advantage to the enemy.

He still could make no sense of it all. The waterboarding, the isolation, how rinky-dink the prison turned out to be. *No lawyer. No hearing. No trial.* All those other cells…were there other prisoners in them? He had no idea who had held him prisoner or who might be after him now. How much more was going on that people didn't know?

Jesus, Captain, he was starting to realize. *It might be worse than you thought. Maybe it is already happening.* What if all those cells held people who disappeared? No arrests. No trials. What if more of that was going on right under everybody's noses, right beneath American streets?

He was on a sixteen-foot wide gravel road, dense trees on both sides. A perfect ambush location. He should have had a spotting scope, binoculars at least. Something. *Don't make it easy for them!*

Ahead of him the gravel turned to paved road, trees stopped. A fenced wrecking yard. No movement there. High points, elevations sixty meters above the town on two sides. Anybody who knew the job could be dug in there above the two-dozen buildings and houses sighting down on him and he'd never know it.

"Just do it. Earn your pay, soldier." How many times had he said that to himself? *Fuck it anyhow.*

A kid wearing a bright red vest greeted him from the cash register at the door to the hardware store.

"Café?" Spencer asked.

The kid pointed down to center aisle to the back of the store. A nutty, deep scent of coffee wafted through.

"We're offering two keys for the price of one and a free keychain with an LED light," the kid offered. "Pretty cool deal."

Spencer declined and headed down the aisle. A woman behind the counter held a red book in front of her face. Spencer saw a rough, wrinkled hand. Between the long fingers he read the title "Existentialism and Human Emotions." Jean-Paul Sartre. He wasn't familiar.

"XMercy says you do great maple bars and maybe I can use your computer for a little bit," Spencer said.

One hand came off the book; a finger pointed to an old-fashioned covered cake plate, then to the plates beside it.

Under the cover were thick maple bars eight inches long and three inches wide. A meal by themselves, butter-edged with a thick caramel-brown glaze. He was about to lift one with his fingers when the book smacked down against the countertop just as he saw the tongs.

"How can a man be happy in a world devoid of external significance and meaning?" she read aloud. "Maple bars. Help yourself." She had the self-assured voice of a woman who knew who she was and where. Piercing blue eyes, graying yellow hair that looked experienced rather than old, and a face ambiguous to age. She looked like his mother; at least, how he thought she might have looked.

"Pale bars are two-fifty. Internet's free." She reached behind her, retrieved a silver-colored laptop computer, and pushed it across the counter. "You Mac or PC?"

"PC."

"Well there's a MacBook Pro on the back table. It's pretty easy to use, but I'm here if you need me. I'm Judy. Who are you?"

"I'm Johnny. XMercy's cousin."

"From when she was just plain Mercy, then? Oh that girl!"

"Um hum."

"That's fine."

*****

Once he had Safari opened, Spencer got the hang of the Mac pretty quickly. He started by searching "shooting at Citi Field." He got: "MMO Fan Shot." "Miguel Cabrera Sends Shot into Second Deck." *Nothing.*

He tried "Police officer killed at Citi Field." Results: "Mets Third Baseman Visits with Family of Slain Poughkeepsie Police Officer." "Police Detective Killed in Fall Apprehending Shooting Suspect."

Detective Sergeant Tremaine Bull was fatally injured during the heroic solo arrest of Dimitri Vosilych, the primary suspect tied to the so-called IKRP killings. According to Department spokesmen, Bull, a decorated veteran and member of the Department's elite Intelligence Unit, had been working on the case since the first attack. He and other members of their squad had closed in on the suspect just weeks earlier but were prevented from capturing Vosilych when the boat they were in caught on fire. Detective Bull was investigating a lead on his own at the time of the confrontation that took both his own life and that of the suspect. Funeral arrangements, to include full Department Honors, will be announced over the next few days. Spokesmen for the mayor, the governor, and the Chief of Police have all announced that they will be in attendance.

Spencer stared at the page before placing the cursor over the highlighted and underlined name then tapped on the mouse pad. Nothing happened. He tapped again. Nothing. Judy noticed and walked toward him with her book in hand. He closed the laptop. She opened it without hesitation, tapped the pad and opened the link to Dimitri Vosilych.

"It gets finicky. Oh boy. Dimitri Vosilych. Mouse and that stupid tattoo. Is she making you listen to her baloney?" Judy spun the laptop back to Spencer. "She's actually a hard-working kid, just can't get her head around fitting in. It's boring for her to be like other people. As though other people are all the same. She doesn't see nuance. It's got to be Halley's Comet or the Aurora Borealis because a sky filled with regular stars isn't good enough. Hell, never mind me.

I'll go back to my book. You read about the mysterious man of the people, Dimitri Vosilych."

Spencer ate through the maple bar and continued reading thirty pages of articles related to Dimitri Vosilych: psych profiles, reports on links to al Qaeda, a reporter's journey to the Bulgarian town where he grew up that included YouTube clips on interviews with the headmaster at the school where Vosilych had taught for two years. He was described as a quiet, introverted intellectual: "Not one who makes a strong impression that he could do such things, but you never know." Vosilych was known to have traveled to several countries, including Lebanon and Pakistan, where he may have received training and instruction. He was in the United States on an expired student visa. A coalition of Tea Party Congressmen called for an investigation into why the State Department and Homeland Security continue to fail in the apprehension of travelers and students remaining in the country sometimes for years after their visas have expired. At least 4.5 million people are in the country illegally after their visas expired, including multiple suspects from the Boston Marathon Bombings.

He was enraged. When he left, he hoped that nothing he said or did let Judy know how he felt.

Nobody trains in Lebanon or in Pakistan on a KAC M110. He pulled over the Polaris and closed his eyes, covering them with his palm and imagining the 850 yards across open water. Mamaroneck. Scan one, right two, right three, right four, five, left six, left seven, left eight. Breathe, Relax, Aim, Slack, Squeeze. One BRASS (male, fifty, wife on left wearing rubies and diamonds looking at him... center forehead. Two BRASS (male, center forehead). Three BRASS (blond, tall, no heels). Four BRASS (orange outfit). Five BRASS (blue outfit, blue heels). Six BRASS (hiding under table).

The incandescent blinding bolt in his mind's eye jolted him back to the present. *There's no fucking al Qaeda loser who could make those shots.* Nobody, not the British SAS, not the IDF's elite units, nobody but the United States Armed Forces teaches a soldier how to make those shots. *Nobody!*

CHAPTER FIFTEEN

"Callie," Owen pleaded into the phone, "I'm done messing up. I'm not drinking anything, not a drop. I've been working out at the 100th and running the whole length of the beach every single day. The house is gone. Tremaine is gone. I get that now. My home is where you and Liam and Casey are, Callie. I want to come home."

"Did they reinstate you?"

"I'm working on it. Lieutenants Benevolent Association says I haven't got anything officially charged against me. They say after eight weeks unpaid leave I am automatically entitled to a hearing. That's just two more weeks. My rep says no way they'll add more time, not after losing my partner and how Tremaine died." He could hear her breathing, but Callie wasn't responding. Just silence.

"I'm looking for a new place, Owen," she finally said. "East. Maybe all the way to Syosset. I want the boys in a good school in a good neighborhood as far from the city as I can take them."

"I'm good with that."

"It's not your decision."

He pressed the cell phone into his forehead, breathing, just breathing, being careful not to let the anger rise. "I understand that. You're entitled. I was thinking, when I can get all this behind me, I can maybe sit the captain's exams. I can apply all through May."

"That's all you, Owen, you, not me! You don't get it. *I* want more. *Me.*"

"What do you want? Do you want to go to Hawaii? You want a new car? Cal, I'll get it for you, I just need to know what you want! Let me see you," he pleaded. "Please, Cal. I don't want to talk on the phone."

"Owen, you're not going to come here so we end up getting naked and rubbing uglies like that is going to make things all better. It won't! Yes, we're great together in bed. So what?"

"Don't Cal. Please. What about the boys? They need a dad."

"You think the boys were better off in North Corona?" Cal screeched. "Casey out running 'round with the little gangstas? Liam peeing the bed because he got bullied every day? You think that's better? Really? Do you, O? Open your eyes!"

*****

"Al, meet me for coffee," Owen asked Al Hurwitz over the telephone. "I'm doing better. I'm off the drink, I swear. No problem. That's all over, Al. It's behind me."

Al had reluctantly agreed. Owen arrived early. He was in the booth when Al came into the coffee shop. He looked better, clear-eyed, clean-shaven, dressed up in a dress shirt and a jacket with pale gray chinos.

"I'm working on Callie to go to couples counseling," he told Al, blurting sentences in quick bursts. "I'm working on me, Al. I've been going to therapy. I know I can't fix other people and I'm working on me. I'm learning how to listen. I enrolled in an online course. It's about discovering my own interests, apart from the family and the job. Like, I don't know, art or cooking or speaking another language. Irish history maybe."

"Where are you staying?" Al asked him.

"I've been renting Tremaine's place. In Brooklyn. Just for now. It's in probate."

"Are you *meshuggah*?" Al griped in complete disbelief. "Nutty in the head? Did you listen to anything I told you, anything Major Gonzalez said?"

"It's not like that," Owen protested. "It's just a place to stay. I did listen. I listened a lot."

He lifted the spoon and swirled it in circles in the dark liquid. "God grant me the serenity to accept the things I cannot change; courage to change the things I can; and wisdom to know the difference," he recited quietly. "Al, I need my family back. A few months ago you said you could help us get back on our feet. Does the offer still stand? I need to know before Callie…well, I need to know. Will you still do it?"

Al removed his glasses and carefully wiped each lens with his napkin. "A lot has happened since then, Owen. I had just buried my mother. I'm retired and living on a fixed income now. I might do some traveling. I've got the money from the apartment, but I might to want to buy myself a place instead of renting. I'm thinking about it."

"I just need a break, Al. Just a leg up. Temporarily. Two weeks and I'll be back on the job, money will be coming in. It's all good."

Al's face didn't show the look of confidence Owen was hoping for.

"If I put down a down payment and all of you move in," Al asked him, "what happens if things don't work out?"

"But they will work out," Owen insisted. "That's what she wants. If she has a house, like what Shelley has, Callie is going to be happy! It's all good. Al, everything is going to be great!"

Al took out his wallet and placed a five-dollar bill on the table, then scooted across the booth to get to his feet. Owen reached out and caught his wrist.

"Owen, I can't take on a down payment for a house! You declared bankruptcy. What am I going to do, take out a mortgage, too? You need some money, I'll help you. But you and your wife need to work things out for yourselves. I can't fix them for you."

He pulled away from Owen's grasp and walked quickly outside, leaving Owen wide-eyed, staring into space without registering anything in his view.

*****

Liam leapt for the telephone first. "Hi Dad!"

"Daddy!" Casey echoed in the background.

"It's mine!" Liam asserted. He sounded more like the older brother than he usually did, not allowing Casey to tug the phone away from him.

"Hi buddy!" Owen responded, soaking up their voices as they wrestled.

"Dad, I can throw a slider!" Liam reported proudly. "I made the tryouts! I'm going to pitching camp! I'm going to have three pitches next year!"

Pitching camp? Owen wondered. It was the first he had heard about it. "Show me tomorrow. I'll bring my mitt when I pick you two up. Nine o'clock!"

"I can't tomorrow, Dad. We're going to the beach."

"Ok. We'll all go. We can practice there."

Casey's voice replaced his older brother's. "Dad!" Casey yelled excitedly.

"Hi tiger! I'll see you tomorrow. You ready to get your head underwater?"

"Are you coming?" Casey asked, sounding confused.

"Here," Liam told Casey, who relinquished the phone without a battle. "Dad, we're going overnight," Liam told him. "Dr. Marc invited Mom and us to go to his beach house."

Owen stopped talking. Finally, he ordered Liam, "Put your mom on."

"Mom's not here. She's shopping."

"Ok," Owen muttered. "I'll call you later." He tossed the phone onto Tremaine's coffee table. It slid to a stop up against his service weapon. He stared at both, taking rapid, short breaths. *Mercedes convertible. Beach house. Pitching camp.*

He reached out for the phone but pulled his hand back before dialing Callie's cell. He got up instead, going to the refrigerator for a glass of milk and checking the clock on the way. *Don't phone when your emotions are running high* was right at the top of the department-assigned therapist's instructions. *Listen.*

"Breathe," he reminded himself. "Wait ten minutes and calm down." After swallowing back the milk, he decided to walk to where he knew there was a pay phone in front of the mini-mart on the next block.

Callie answered on the first ring.

"Hi. I understand you made plans for boys this weekend." Calm. Level. No yelling.

"What is this number?" Callie asked him.

"My phone is on the charger," Owen lied. *Because when I call on my phone, you never pick up.*

"I thought this was my weekend," he continued.

"Something came up. I was about to call."

"'Dr. Marc invited Mom and us to his beach house.' Liam told me."

"Um hum," Callie told him. Owen could picture her. She'd be chewing on her lower lip now.

"So you admit it?" Still level. Keeping it light.

"He has the girls this weekend, Owen." It was her voice getting higher, not his. "He thought it would be fun for the kids to be together."

"Fucking the boss, Callie?" he asked quietly. "Really? And bringing the boys along?"

"How was I married to you? You're such an asshole!" she yelled. She disconnected the line, leaving Owen smacking the handset off the phone box. Afterward, he did one of his therapist's breathing exercises, reaching his arms out and gathering them back with each intake, looking like a shaman, then casting out the bad air again with his arms spread wide and his fingers extended as far as he could stretch. He stayed at it until his heart stopped pounding and his hands stopped closing into fists.

He didn't care how many people stared while they walked by.

*****

He ambled in the direction of Tremaine's place, watching the sidewalk and forcing his heavy feet to step over every crack. What was the point of going there? He hated the silence; he kept picturing the pistol on the coffee table, too, and wanted that image to go away before he went back inside. *How was I married to you?*

"We're still married!"

Owen trudged a long lap around the block, all the time trying in his head to picture Callie with another man. He never got angry about it; he just couldn't do it, it didn't compute. Was she just going away for the weekend? Was *he* really the asshole?

"Detective?"

Owen looked up suddenly. The voice startled him. Some man in a white cowboy hat was coming toward him from the steps up to Tremaine's doorway.

"Who?"

Bishop reached out a hand as he got close. "Lieutenant Cullen, my name is Bishop," he said, the 'my' coming up as 'muh.' Owen looked at the hand, leaving it to hang without responding.

"My name is Bishop," he repeated, letting his hand drop to his side. "I'd like to speak with you."

"What about?" Owen asked. He knew instantly that the other man was a cop.

"About Jonathan Spencer," Bishop responded. "Do you want to help get him?"

Owen's eyes came to life instantly. "Too right I do!" he blurted out, sounding exactly like his father. He flexed his forearms and clenched both fists in front of him. "I knew it!" he yelled. "I fucking knew it!" Owen looked around anxiously; ready to get inside a car and go.

Bishop turned back toward Tremaine's. "There are a few practical matters to tackle first."

*****

"We had some difficulty locating you, Lieutenant," Bishop told Owen. He held his Stetson by the hat brim and picked up a framed photo showing Tremaine Bull and Owen Cullen smiling, arms over one another's shoulders. "On leave and you moved addresses."

Owen felt a surge of anger in his throat and swallowed hard. How did they know he was on leave? If they knew he was on leave, then they knew it wasn't by his choice. *Fucking Department psychiatrist.* Leave or meds. Like he was going to sign off on having depression in his jacket?

"Why me?"

"In aggregate, the investigation and pursuit of your sniper expended law enforcement agencies over a million man hours." Bishop turned the photo toward Owen. "You and your partner succeeded in getting to him twice. On the Hudson and at Citi-Field. Nobody else recorded a single contact."

"Succeeded?" Owen questioned. "He shot our boat out from under us the first time. The second time he killed my partner. It's his place we're standing in."

"You'll be paid nine hundred per day," Bishop went on, cutting to the chase. "Any partial day under four hours is $450. Hotel and rental cars, parking are all covered. Food stipend is $80 per day. Save receipts. We will not be doing withholdings so bear in mind to set aside for your own taxes. A 1099 will be sent out mid-February. You're certain your clearances are current? I'm taking you at your word on that. You can't be paid otherwise."

Owen understood. He had never signed off on depression; he'd never taken a single med. He'd been letting the union take its rake for fifteen years. All that money wasn't for nothing. If they put any of that crap in his jacket, he'd have the LBA suing their ass.

"Is there any conflict with your working for us while you're on a personal leave from your department?"

Owen crossed the room in two strides to get to the Glock. He dropped the magazine, looked and pressed to confirm a full load, and reloaded. He grabbed a jacket from the hall tree and told Bishop confidently, "I'm in. Let's go!"

"That jacket is not enough. Pack your things; clothing, shaving kit, medications, whatever you need, at least enough for a week to ten days. Our operations desk is in D.C. We're bringing in one more specialist, a man named Miller, flying in from Kabul. He was Spencer's operations lead in Afghanistan. Apparently, nobody knows Spencer better."

While he was jamming clothes into a duffle bag, Owen was happy, feeling useful for the first time in a long while. *D.C. Another guy flying from Kabul. From Afghanistan!* He had the chance to finish what they started.

This was about getting right in his own head, too. *Fucking nobody better get in my way.*

He'd have done it for free and jumped at the chance. Owen moved quickly toward the front door and turned back, looking at Bishop and wondering why Bishop wasn't moving already.

"I'll call Callie from the hotel number tonight." What they had was bigger than some weekend at a beach house. She'd know he had turned the corner. Even if he couldn't tell her details, she'd hear it in his voice. Jonathan Spencer was their shooter; Jonathan Spencer had shot up the boat; Jonathan Spencer had shot twenty-two innocent people—he wasn't wrong. The reason Gonzalez had warned him was because he was right all along!

"Vosilych, my arse," Owen muttered. "Everyone, up and down the line, they all wanted the red line, case completed. Suspending me? Me? Where were Tee's other bullets? Where were the size thirteen feet?"

Was anything about this Vosilych ever real?

"Miller comes in from Frankfurt in four hours," Bishop continued. "Cullen, I have you booked Delta, 5:40 p.m., into Reagan National. Take a cab to the Sheraton Crystal City. I'll see you and Miller in the lobby at 9 p.m." Bishop supplied Owen with Miller's ID photo.

"I've got to catch an earlier flight," Bishop told him. "I'll brief you both tonight. Sheraton Crystal City, 9 p.m."

*****

"Phone Bishop," Stephen shouted. "Right now! I'm getting a hot hit." At his elbow, Dilip continued entering data points.

Stephen ordered, "Whatever you're doing, stop! This is more important. Somebody in West Virginia is pulling a background check on Jonathan Spencer." *Jonathan Spencer, U.S. Army, Virginia.*

Dilip switched screens and began running location software to track the West Virginia server. "A public library. Fayetteville." He pulled the server location, framed it on screen, and then pulled the library card number used to access the computer and the credit card information used for PeopleSmart to buy the records on Spencer.

Felicia Diane Reynolds, DOB 12/24/85, WVDL#Y290003, 230 Kanawha Avenue, Dunbar, West Virginia. Five-foot-three, 105 lbs., mousy blond hair, green eyes.

Kip, another tech on Stephen's four-person team, typed at warp speed while keeping his eyes glued to the monitor. Stephen watched from behind Kip's chair.

The background check on Felicia Diane Reynolds indicated Cabell Alternative High School, South West Virginia Community and Technology College, current address 230 Kanawha Avenue, Dunbar, West Virginia, six prior addresses showing. Employment: Olive Garden Restaurant 111 Cross Terrace Garden, prior employment Student Union, South West Virginia College.

Stephen looked away just long enough to scream: "Where's my phone?!"

DUI Arrest 3/17/11. No record of conviction.

"And there she is. Bingo!" Mouse appeared within the center frame on Dilip's screen. Blue jeans and a yellow t-shirt. Her hair was cropped short now.

"Ok, Felicia Diane Reynolds. Now why are you looking into our guy?" He could see letters tattooed on her neck, froze frame and zoomed in, but could not make them out. He pulled up a mirror image of the keyboard she was using and proceeded to track her strokes.

She was alone, standing at a bar-height counter with four computer terminals. Behind her, an upright cutout suggested Beatrix Potter stories. Low tables and tiny chairs.

As Stephen yelled out again for any phone so he could get a hold of Bishop, she hit the print key. Six pages ran, then once the printer icon stopped flashing she hit Exit and logged off, immediately turning around and moving toward the main desk.

"She's on the move! Dale, stop what you're doing and get me Bishop!"

Dale removed his earphones and wandered behind to look over his shoulder. "Whazzup?"

"Fayetteville, West Virginia. Street cams. Security cams. Throw a ring around the fucking town and get them all up. Now! She's going to leave! And give me your fucking phone!"

"Ok," Dilip narrated. "Well, we have no street cams. No parking lot security. No parking lot. We are showing fifteen live feeds for the whole area. We have the courthouse, Quality Inn, Arby's, Wendy's, McDonalds, two Subways, Dairy Queen, Taco Bell, Sunoco, Shell, and two Little General Stores. Do you think all their generals are little?" he quipped.

On screen, Reynolds was counting out a dollar bill, a quarter, a dime, and two nickels and five pennies. The librarian handed her the printouts and she was off-screen before he realized he hadn't recorded any of it. The only photo showed her with hair down to her shoulders.

Dilip waited for confirmation. There are only two million people in the entire state. How long could it take?

"Screw waiting," Stephen shouted. He reached over Dilip's shoulder to take command of the keyboard, his fingers racing across. He pulled up the link to her driver's license photo and then compared it side by side against a real-time likeness of the woman in front of them, the cropped hair, the scripted GV on her neck. "We have a winner!" Stephen exclaimed.

He tossed the phone at Dale yelling, "Now would you get me on the fucking phone with Bishop?!"

"I let you use it," Dale responded sheepishly.

"It would have helped if you entered your passcode!"

Dale looked at the blank screen. "Oh."

*****

"I sent you a link straight into the file!" Stephen reminded Bishop. "Open the message and hit the link.

That was two hours ago. Don't you check your texts?"

The lead should have had elicited a positive response, but Bishop felt more like Nussbaum's voodoo technologies were cheating. It wasn't fair to track a man from ten thousand feet or spy on him from hundreds of miles away using a gas station security camera. It also pissed him off to know that any one of the geeks might be his boss one day soon. *I messaged you two hours ago. Don't you check your texts?* Chicken shit.

"Her cell phone is registered to a Dunbar address, same as her driver's license," Nussbaum explained, talking fast. "But eighty-seven percent of all calls going back a year originated through towers located between here," he pointed out Fayetteville, "and here, Mt. Hope."

His fingers raced across the keyboard to switch screens, bringing up a checking account. "Her cell phone bill is paid with a debit card through the Bank of Mount Hope, where she has, as of this moment, twenty thousand, nine hundred and thirty-one dollars and fourteen cents in a joint account with one M.L. White, of whom there are sixteen in the nation and just two shown living within a one-day drive to Mount Hope, West Virginia! We set up keyword intercepts for Google, Yahoo, Bing, Ask.com, Dogpile, Duck Duck Go," he went on. "We'd get inundated with noise going off every hit, but when the algorithm is massaged a bit, so rather than 'Jonathan' or 'Spencer' we filter for conjoined searches, and then add we add a little spice to the mix with 'army,' 'armed forces,' 'military,' 'Virginia,' etcetera, the universe contracts fast... six degrees of separation in reverse."

Nussbaum finally took a breath, and then said, "Within forty-eight hour windows, we're at 97 percent accuracy now. I knew he was either getting help or he was holed up in Bumfuck. The guy needs to eat, drink, and shit. If he's in urban America, this software would have found him. You can't outrun law enforcement anymore, not unless they let you. Inside five years we'll have an exclusionary model that takes that into account. I mean, what is the point of looking at New York or Chicago or LA or two-thirds of the population centers when we have complete visibility in every one of them? Nevermind, I digress."

Bishop approached the lead with a bias he could not restrain, even if it was the single possibility they'd generated in days. He hated hotshot data guys. Twenty-four years of hands-on experience getting wiped away, a smear on a windshield. Fuck 'em all. They were putting him out of business.

"You haven't got Spencer," Bishop reminded gravely. "Where's the proof of any connection?"

The geek looked at Bishop like he couldn't be serious. All three of his fellow geeks tuned in, too. "What, you want empirical proof of climate change before you act on 99 percent probability models? Ok, ok." Stephen slowed down and explained it as though he were speaking to the world's biggest ignoramus. "She hasn't made an outgoing phone call since Spencer broke out. There has been no public announcement mentioning any Jonathan Spencer before the capture or since he escaped. So this young woman, who shows no record of prior contact with any Jonathan Spencer, not in elementary school, not in middle school, not in high school, and not in her year at community college, decides out of the blue to Google Jonathan Spencer, U.S. Army, and then pays to do a background check, two background checks, on Jonathan Spencer?

"Fayetteville, West Virginia is four hours and twenty minutes, two-hundred-seventy-five miles from Spencer's last known location, three-hundred-and-eight miles from this spot right here. So maybe it is just a coincidence. Bishop, if I'm wrong, at least five people don't get burned up in their apartments thanks to your North Carolina whack jobs. Do they?"

CHAPTER SIXTEEN

Miller ordered a double Balvenie. Beside him, Owen fidgeted in his bar stool, swerving side to side, aware that his tweed jacket and woven tie were out of place amongst the laptop crowd ordering tapas he couldn't pronounce. He was frustrated that Bishop was delayed.

He sent Callie a text from the airport. He had to go out of town for work. **I was right all along. Will explain later.** He looked at the message, added, **Enjoy the beach,** and pressed send.

"You'll take the high road, boyo," he murmured in his father's brogue.

Owen noticed that Miller wasn't wearing a ring. He didn't look the type, haggard, in a couldn't-care-less sort of manner, more world-weary than jetlagged. Miller lifted his drink, sniffed it disapprovingly, like he was used to better, then knocked it back in a gulp and clacked it on the bar, barely nodding his head when the bartender looked over. Every minute or so, he ran his slender fingers through combed-over blond hair.

"Spencer is out there somewhere," he whispered toward Miller. "Why are we sitting on barstools?"

"Take it all in," Miller replied. "It's not the Ritz, but it could be a lot worse, believe me."

"Jonathan Spencer. Tell me what you know." Owen's knees bobbed anxiously.

"He worked for me," Miller explained nonchalantly. "Funny, when I heard about the shootings I thought about him for a second, really did. Strange dude, Master Sergeant Jonathan Spencer. I saved his life, you know. Shot the tribesman who stabbed him. One to the brain. Looking back now, I probably should have let him do it. He'd be dead and buried in Arlington National. That would be that. Oh well, twenty-twenty hindsight."

Miller's tone disturbed Owen. The man could not care less whether Spencer lived or died. How do you work alongside a man and be indifferent about killing him?

"Why do you think they brought us here?" Owen asked. He wasn't feeling quite as sure of himself as he had a few hours earlier. He knew he needed to do this for Tremaine, but wasn't this exactly what Gonzalez warned him against, getting in too deeply? All of a sudden Owen couldn't even order a light beer without second-guessing himself.

"It's always the same thing," Miller responded. "Somebody fucked up and now they can't figure a work-around. So they bring in new people, us. They don't really expect you to bring anything shiny and new to the table, but we show up and that takes some of the spotlight off of them. Let me ask you this: why four months to decide it was Spencer? And why now?"

"My guess is Spencer went to ground and they're running scared," Miller continued, answered his own question. "They know what he can do. We had eighty thousand troops in Afghanistan and another couple thousand contractor advisors and another thousand CIA; I ran a string of operatives and I'd bet money right now that there was not another soldier like MSJS. At least none that I ever saw."

Miller ordered a fourth round. Owen waived off, taking firm hold of the soda water. "It's not only the sniper stuff," Miller explained. "He's skilled in small arms too, plenty of demolitions experience, plus more martial arts than you'd believe. Aikido, Hapkido, Muay Thai, Krav Maga, even stick fighting. Put the guy on Pay-Per-View and it would just be boring. He'd douche every MMA fighter they put into the ring and I don't care what weight class, either."

Miller chuckled to himself, recalling a conversation about Spencer. "I took him from a major who wanted MSJS to get on cross-country skis. The major figured Spencer would be a world-class biathlon competitor right away. The major was a tall Scandinavian-looking guy. Who in America does biathlon?"

"He killed my partner," Owen admitted somberly, already erasing Vosilych from his brain. "Shot a boat out from under us and an FBI guy and nearly blew us up, too. Except that was another time."

"No shit! I saw the video! That was you? How funny!" Miller stared at Owen, remembering the YouTube clip. He'd watched it a couple times, not just once.

"Unfinished business," Miller added, changing his tone and shifting his gaze into the swirling amber liquid. "I get that."

Owen wanted to explain how he and Tremaine had been on the case since right after the Fourth of July shootings, how he spent all night in Central Park after the shootings there. He suddenly needed solid food inside him, coffee too. He also wanted to phone Callie and realized she would know who it was and probably not answer. He should not have said in the text that he was going out of town.

"Everybody up the line and down again better know," Miller insisted, "that when we get near him, we call in the Hellfires and blow a hole in the ground where his ass used to be. I'm not getting anywhere near MSJS.

"You know this guy can't be captured, right?" Miller questioned Owen. "He is a fucking one-man army. Anybody tries taking him conventionally, he'll take out whole companies before he goes down."

When his phone starting vibrating in circles on the glass-topped coffee table, Owen snatched it right up. Miller's phone simultaneously sounded a single gong inside his jacket pocket. He dug his chin into his chest and looked up toward Owen. Same time, same text: **Sit tight. New developments.**

A blonde woman dressed in a low-cut black cocktail dress walked through the lobby alone and seated herself. She and the bartender exchanged glances and a drink appeared in front of her. Miller observed that it was pure cola.

"*Mañana*," Miller told Owen dismissively. "I'll catch you later."

Owen stood rigidly, put a five on the bar, and left Miller alone. He felt his pants pocket for the keycard and strode for the elevator. Room service, then a shower. He had St. John's Wort and folic acid in his shaving kit, and planned to up his regular intake for both.

Back inside the hotel room, he stared at the phone, wanting to call Callie and dreading another rote play-by-play about the boys. It was a big room, two queens. Granite sink and a tub-shower in the bathroom. A flat-screen TV inside the cabinet. A second telephone on the desk.

"I should have taken her to nice places," he observed. "I should have done a lot of things different."

She asked him to move out, to give her space, and he did it. He didn't bust anything. He didn't shout at her or do anything crazy. It was his house more than hers, Eamonn's house. She gave it back to the fucking bank, is what she did. But he took his stuff and went. It was killing him, but he did it. After a week he had come back to see her and the boys.

He knew he shouldn't have boozed before going. He knew it and he did it and now what could he do to take it back? Grabbing at her, trapping her in his arms, slobbering at her neck, pulling at her shirt.

"Get help, Owen!" she had screamed at him.

She twisted away. He let her, but it was too late. "Get out! You need help! I swear to God, Owen! Get out!"

Shelley answered the phone when he called back to apologize. She hung up on him.

Owen reached for the remote and switched on the TV. He looked over the movie menu, followed the arrows to Adult Offerings, and touched Enter. *Cheerleading Camp. Desert Island Girls. Prison Passions. South Beach Knights.*

He switched off the set and the lamp and stretched out on top of the flowered bedspread and then stared into the darkness.

*****

A little after midnight, Miller left the hotel bar with his new acquaintance. *Fuck jetlag*, he told himself. He didn't care about sleeping. Everything he did outside of Afghanistan felt like Spring Break.

At four a.m., he chugged two Red Bulls and phoned an escort service. Another new acquaintance showed up at his hotel room door. She looked bleary-eyed and done-in. Miller folded her over the overstuffed chair and tore off her thong without saying a word.

He was in dark glasses and drinking a Bloody Mary for breakfast when Owen met him in the hotel restaurant. For some reason, Miller seemed pissed off.

"Jesus, take off the wedding ring. This is business travel." Miller waived for the server. "Let me order you a morning pickup."

When Owen looked astonished, Miller thought it was funny. "A drink, man. Not a girl."

Owen had phoned Callie first thing; it took him two cups of hotel room coffee before he could make himself dial, but he did it. He couldn't get a read on her. She just let him talk. He was in D.C., he explained. Called in to work a case. They were paying him lots of money and he'd be home probably in a few days. Wasn't she happy he was working? Wasn't that what she wanted?

"Where the hell is Bishop?" Owen wanted to know. Now that he knew Spencer was out there, every day Spencer was drawing breath jabbed at Owen's guts.

"What's the hurry?" Miller asked back, blasé to the whole thing. "A whole lot of people want Spencer dead. What does it matter who does it?"

""It matters to me!" Owen growled. "I'm thinking he didn't kill your best friend. Well, he did kill mine!"

"Relax," Miller responded. "Here we've got a decent hotel on somebody else's nickel and you're all stressed out. Man, first of all," he explained, "fuck the stipend. Nobody can live decently on eighty bucks a day, c'mon! Spend a couple hundred. They may bitch, but they'll pay it, and they'll get the message. Don't go selling your talent too cheap or you'll never be appreciated." He recalled what he could from the prior night and thanked God he had locked his wallet in the room safe.

"Fucking boney escort wanted $1,000 for a straight screw. I got her down to two hundred." He couldn't remember anything else, which made him laugh, which left his temples thumping with pain. "Minibar," Miller announced.

Owen gave him a quick look. "I'll pass on the drink. Thanks anyway."

"Different Minibar. It's a restaurant. Jose Andres?" Miller said. "Never mind. For my money, actually, for Bishop's money, this is the best food in D.C. I've been on eight straight months of shwarmas and rice pilaf or frozen shit out of the commissary. Let's get into a real meal, maybe get the wine pairings with it?"

"I'm a meat-and-potatoes kind of guy," Owen explained. "Nothing fancy."

"He's got meat and potatoes. You like corn on the cob? Sure you do, who doesn't? Corn on the cob that will blow your mind. Hey, we're here, right?

Bishop's the one who isn't, so why shouldn't we make the most of it? No reason. None at all."

"I didn't come here to sit on my ass eating fancy food," Owen protested.

"He already killed your partner, pal," Miller told him. "Don't be so anxious."

*****

Nussbaum's geeks pulled DMV records, IRS records, and myriad data on M. L. White, from which Bishop couldn't distinguish anything offering confirmation that they were on to a solid lead.

The geeks continued treating him like they were trying to teach an idiot child. *There are no automobile registrations. Neither one of them has filed a tax return since 2010.*

"Omission is the red flag!" Stephen told him. "What you don't see is as revealing as what we find. Do you get this at all?"

Their whole techie clique was abuzz, working on Bishop to get his ok for a field trip. Bishop looked over the Wi-Fi mapping, following the color-shading indicating crimson for the strongest signals.

"So, here is the route map between the library in Fayetteville and the Bank in Mount Hope, both confirmed current sighting locations on Felicia Diane Reynolds. I'm moving that over the Wi-Fi map. Now, using satellite imagery, we plotted on this next map the locations of utility poles along State Route 19. We start here, six miles south of Mount Hope at the intersection of Highway 64 and State Route 19, continue north through Mount Hope, up to Glen Jean, then Oak Hill, and north up to Fayetteville.

"Now, I'm going to highlight these next utility poles, see, the ones flashing green on the screen. We set two cameras on each of these poles, either connecting to Wi-Fi or using a hotspot card, and we get real-time coverage along twenty-two miles. That one route covers anyone traveling between Highway 64 all the way to Fayetteville. That includes the library where we spotted her and the bank where she keeps her life savings. The next time Felicia Diane Reynolds pops up, we'll know where she is and potentially get a good handle on where she is going, too."

Bishop was skeptical. "That's going to take days and be conspicuous. I can get to Charleston by air in under an hour. Her family is still at her last known address."

"Do the Dick Tracy gumshoe thing?" Stephen looked over at the others, asking, "Dish Network or American Electric Power?"

"Dish," all three responded.

"We confirmed that Dish has the local satellite TV and most of the broadband market. They might recognize the faces of their local utility guys, but nobody would expect to know everybody working for a national outfit like

Dish. We get to the pole, raise the cherry-picker, zip-zip with a cordless drill-driver, set a quick laser sight, and we're done on each pole inside five minutes."

"Dish it will be," Stephen agreed. "We can get a rental van with a cherry-picker in Beckley and we can be installing by ten tomorrow morning if we get out the door right now." They were already making magnetic mock-ups for the logos.

Bishop checked his watch. That was another thing. None of the geeks wore watches. Obsolete except as bulky jewelry, nostalgic emblems of a bygone age.

"It's not even eight o'clock. You can leave at four a.m. and be there by nine in the morning driving straight through." Bishop wanted to pre-authorize the expenditure; this wasn't coming out from his own pocket.

"We don't drive all night," Stephen corrected. "We wake up fresh, get to the airport, and United flies non-stop at 8:30 a.m. But if we don't get over to Best Buy for the cameras, the flight won't do much good, will it?"

"What do these cameras cost?"

"Online, cheap, but if we're doing this tomorrow we don't have that option. We want one camera throughout. Best Buy has inventory retailing $212 each plus tax. They'll want five thousand. Don't worry. They'll discount the hell out of an order that size. We'll bring in web prices and hit a couple of their stores. But we need to go. If we keep talking, they'll be closed."

Bishop nodded and was already thinking about where he could pad the three thousand on the invoice to APA. If they came up dry, that amount would be tough to chew from his own end. "Wait a second. You get all these cameras, how do you get them to run online?"

When none of them responded, Bishop wished he could take back the question. Once again, he didn't get it. There was Wi-Fi. The rest was laughable; it wasn't even in question.

When Bishop walked away, they resumed their work along with their prior conversation. "I'm not shitting you," Kip explained. "This originated from studying how snakes use their sense of smell. Really. The concept is that we can draw DNA samples right from the air when people exhale. It's not like we need to run a complete analysis, like we're going out to the ninth power or anything; all we need is to get a sensor in there and we could get to a one-percent match probability nearly instantly."

"So like you get a sensor on a mini-drone and fly a mosquito around the room and map everybody there?" Dale asked.

"Fuck yeah!" Kip exclaimed. "Totally."

*****

XMercy watched in terror. Whenever Mouse had the chainsaw in her hands, she expected a disaster. New saplings had grown along the base of the greenhouse and as Mouse cut through them XMercy expected the saw to shred their structure or Mouse or both. Over the roar, she stood on tiptoes, her hands on her cheeks, calling, "Ooh. Ooh! Shouldn't we have a plan?"

Spencer walked along the perimeter, touching the bigger trees and mentally mapping out where they had to be felled. One glance and it was obvious to him that Mouse was a danger to herself. He couldn't count the number of lieutenants he'd watched in action over the years looking just about the same, too full of themselves to listen and learn.

The area needing clearing was mostly white ash trees twenty-five to thirty feet high with trunks eight inches in diameter. Pretty easy to fell, but sometimes brittle and prone to snapping before getting through to a clean cut. He paced off the steps between the greenhouse and an older shagbark hickory, thinking it would be a shame to cut that old tree into firewood just to get it out of the way. Its thirty-inch base was fifteen paces away from the new greenhouse footprint. He wiped his palm along the rutted bark, chipped off a long strand, and rubbed it between his hands before inhaling its rich, verdant scent. If the root system didn't interfere, the tree could stay, he thought. Another dozen paces through dense undergrowth of fragrant sumac and laurel took him to a pig trail where the ground got mushy underfoot until it was practically bog land covered by a giant root system, tall pointed laterals rising as much as two feet above the forest floor. Sunrays penetrating the growth showed two immense poplars leaning at a fifteen-degree cant, their hundred-foot trunks aimed straight at the greenhouse. One big wind and their greenhouse and their farming season would be crushed.

When he returned, Mouse had produced a tangled pile that would take longer to clear than it had to cut. Everything needed to be dragged to a slash pile at the center of the meadow before it could be burned off. Whether or not they need a fire permit, or cared, he didn't ask.

"So?" XMercy asked, bumping her hip at him while he focused on Mouse as she very nearly put the tip of the saw into the dirt. "What did you think?"

Spencer looked at her without understanding.

"The guitar! What do you think I'm talking about?"

He shrugged ambiguously.

"Do you play at all? You used to be so good!"

"I haven't had time really," Spencer replied awkwardly. That was all he had, time. Time waiting in a field tent for his next target. Time sitting in a concrete cell with both his legs in full-length casts. Here he was, planning to help build this greenhouse, pretending even to himself that he really did have time. Maybe that's what living amounts to, breathing and fooling yourself that you have time.

"Johnny, what do you do for fun? Do you have any hobbies?"

"I don't know. Not really. I mean, I always did stuff, but hobbies? I was a good soldier. That was my hobby."

"Well, fuck the army," XMercy yelled.

Hearing the words out loud, coming from another person's mouth, shocked him. He didn't like it, didn't like the disrespect.

Mouse had stopped cutting and dangled the idling saw at the end of her arm, nearly pulling the glove off her right hand. "Think what we could do with all that money we burn up on guns," she remarked casually, as though the whole military was a waste.

Spencer stepped quickly into the brush pile to take the saw her from her. She hardly paid attention, walking off toward XMercy, intent on getting a drink. They hadn't thought ahead to bring water down and instead walked together back toward the trailer. He watched their backs, Mouse taking Mercy's hand as they high-stepped through the thick grass.

After they were out of sight, Spencer hiked into the mush to fell the poplars. These were pulp wood, fibrous, low-density junk growing like weeds fed from the high water table and nutrient-rich bog.

The behemoths were on a natural fall line straight to the greenhouse. He walked around the first trunk six or seven times, constantly shifting to find decent purchase underfoot and thinking through how to fell the huge tree away from the disastrous path on which gravity wanted to take it. He spent the next looks considering all the possibilities of how things might go wrong with the tricky side cuts he needed to shift and turn their fall direction away from the work area.

Once he pulled the rope, Spencer made two fast and deliberate cuts, the first a deep forty-fivedegree notch shifting the fall line to run parallel to the length of the greenhouse. The second flat cut set off a series of pops sounding like firecrackers on Chinese New Year's. Spencer held the saw out from his body and stepped off fast toward the retreat he had picked out, getting himself well back and to the side just in case the weight tree decided to kick backward across the stump. It did, sliding backward fully eight feet before tumbling a half-roll then settling slowly, like a giant animal still kicking after a mortal wound, while its weight broke through the dozens of smaller trees and shrubs along its length. Had he stayed put, they would have died together.

He imagined the second poplar falling alongside the first then reconsidered. If it caught the other trunk when it fell, it might bounce fifteen feet before coming back down. An elephant in its path would get crushed flat. Spencer thumbed the kill switch and set the saw down on a dry, level spot before walking in the opposite direction down the length of the tree, spotting everything in the fall path.

He paused in front of a termite-eaten downer log, staring down at an unmistakable boot print broken through the bark where the person who went with it had broken through. He knelt down and examined the print closely. New moss was growing along the edges. Not recent. Could have been from last fall. Pig hunter? Hunting deer?

Spencer walked in a squat position that terrorized his legs, holding the saw blade in front of him parallel to the ground and shaving back a deep swath to open up a fall back from the base of the second poplar. He stood straight again, steeling himself to the pain.

A month to six weeks physical therapy for each month in the casts, the doctor had said. He tightened his pectoral muscles, brought his fists together in front of him, flexed triceps and biceps, his forearms and wrists, every muscle down his stomach and deep into his core. "Hooah!" he yelled at the top of his lungs, and then stood in silence. The thick foliage and mushy ground smothered the sound, but every bird and chipmunk froze at attention.

Spencer stomped down the new retreat path then retrieved the saw and cut quickly, decisively, knocking out the wedge and reversing back into the flat cut before backpedaling into his retreat. The huge poplar dropped with a resounding thump. He had to squeeze through a thick wall of brush, shrubs, and saplings to get clear.

XMercy and Mouse returned at the same time. Mouse spread her feet and stood still, stiffly holding both hands on her slender hips. "It was just like this when we left. Didn't you do anything?"

Spencer could smell his perspiration, looked over his stained and filthy clothes, thought about explaining, but said nothing. *Lieutenants.* Women officers. Not worth getting into it 'cause you never win.

"I'll get going. Is it OK for me to use the Polaris? I could drag all the cuttings into a slash pike that we could burn off later on. That will save a lot of trips clearing this whole thing by hand."

XMercy was about to hold out the tuna sandwiches she made when Mouse took hold of her arm. "XMercy, you can bring down the Polaris. I'll stay here with Johnny and get some work done."

"It might go faster with a rope and chain," Spencer suggested, thinking that Mouse might be planning on using the front-mounted winch, which would take forever to run out and haul in, plus they'd be backing the limbs toward their slash pile, which would also take longer.

Mouse nodded. "They're hung inside the lean-to. Bring them along."

Spencer began to yank saplings out from Mouse's twisted cuttings mound, swinging them around one by one with their bases lined up together so he could rope and drag them in quantity. Mouse followed suit, quickly making a second pile readied for towing. When XMercy rode back down with the ATV, they had already set up a quarter of the limbs.

Without saying a word, Spencer walked to the stubby ATV truck bed and came out with one long rope then pointed to the leather case on Mouse's belt, asking without speaking to use the multi-tool. He cut the long rope into two twenty-five foot sections then took out a book of matches, lit the entire book, and melted the nylon rope ends before shaking out the flames. Mouse watched him while he tied-off the saplings, and then tossed the long end off the pile toward the towing step. While he tied off the line, she reached the second rope around the next pile. The two of them settled into a steady rhythm. Mouse paced herself and whenever the sapling or limb she was handling got hung up inside the pile, she allowed Spencer to help her out.

"MSJS," Spencer told her. "That's mostly what I go by. Nobody except Mercy ever called me 'Johnny.'"

"MSJS," Mouse repeated back.

"There's been somebody out here in the woods," Spencer mentioned. "Hunter, maybe."

"How do you know that?"

"Tracks, broken logs. Pigs do a lot of damage, but they don't wear boots."

While she kept pulling and stacking limbs, Mouse weighed their future crop against asking MSJS what he would do. She dropped the sapling that was in her hands and turned reluctantly, squaring her shoulders toward him.

"So what would you do?" she demanded, clearly pissed off at herself for wanting advice and mad at the Big Army Dude just because.

Spencer kept working, parsing the question into approaches and outcomes starting with perimeter security to surround a forward post inside a hot zone before dropping away the snipers, the suicide bombers, and the trip wires, night flares, anti-personnel mines that keep them at distance. Night vision.

"What are you trying to accomplish?" he asked back.

"Keep our weed and keep fuckheads from stealing it," she shot back. "What do you think?! Somebody steals the crop, we can't very well call the sheriff, now can we?"

Spencer caught from her tone that this wasn't a first conversation about the topic. XMercy and Mouse had been through this before. *That's why she wanted me to go into town in fatigues.*

"That .22 won't scare anybody," he told Mouse. "It sounds like a pop gun. Get a shotgun. Pump action. I'll take the dowel out for you, then it will hold six shells. You wouldn't be able to hit anything, not from the trailer, but it will be loud. I can show you how to handle it."

"I don't need no help. My daddy had me handling shotguns since I was ten."

Spencer let it go. He couldn't put his finger on exactly what it was, but something about her attitude was as familiar as corn flakes. Annoying, but in a puppy-that-won't-quit-licking sort of way. He kind of liked it, too.

"Shotgun can't do any good if you don't know you're getting robbed. Anyone could come in, park up off the top of the driveway, and hike a hundred yards in behind the greenhouses. They could cut right through and haul everything out of there in broad daylight."

"We've got company," Mouse told XMercy when she pulled up in the Polaris. "MSJS saw the tracks."

"Crap. Why don't they just legalize weed so we don't have to put up with this!" XMercy griped.

"Right," Mouse snapped back, "so before we know it we're all smoking Marlboro Wowie? XMercy, I told you, the day weed gets legal is the day corporations take the profits and the little guy gets wiped off the map."

"You want to talk or you want to do something about it?" Spencer asked them. "Control the terrain. A couple runs of concertina wire will take the steam right out of most people; make it so anybody who wants inside needs to come in your way, not theirs. Cheap insurance policy."

"What's concertina wire?" XMercy asked him.

"It's like barbed wire, except it slices razor-sharp gashes an inch deep. That's why it is also called 'razor wire.'"

XMercy smiled toward Mouse, silently asking her partner what she thought now about having Johnny Spencer around?

Mouse scowled and stomped down the cuttings.

*****

The sky was dancing with magical blues, purples, reds, oranges, even ripples of green toward the end of the day. Mouse insisted on pouring the contents of a half-full five-gallon gas can over the slash pile by herself, saying she could handle it without people telling her what to do. Then she ran the hundred feet back to where XMercy stood holding onto the burning torch Spencer had.

"Don't get too close!" XMercy begged. The pile was ten feet high and twice as wide around its base.

Mouse walked back toward the pile and, from thirty feet out, whipped the torch sidearm toward the pile. She missed, skipping the torch on the grass and falling short by a good ten feet. She and Spencer looked at one another, neither moving an inch.

"I'll make another torch," Spencer told her. The flammable fumes were spreading out.

Mouse ignored him and started toward where the first torch had landed.

Spencer cut off her path, reached his arm around her waist and lifted her away while she kicked at him.

"What the fuck! Let go!"

"You don't want to do that," he told her, which made her kick even harder, a big kid throwing a tantrum. He had her back alongside XMercy when the fumes spread out along the ground and ignited off the torch. With a giant whoosh, a flaming mushroom cloud rose sixty feet high, sending scorched air over them all that way back.

Spencer let Mouse go without saying a word. He left them alone until XMercy opened the trailer door and called him to have dinner.

At the table, XMercy nudged at Mouse to say something; then she finally kicked out at her under the table.

"Sorry I kicked you," she told Spencer.

"And?" XMercy was still shaking from it all.

"Thanks," she faltered, and then followed with, "MSJS."

The conversation flowed better after that. XMercy fried steaks and home-style potatoes, none of the New Age foods. Mouse set a six-pack of ice-cold Michelob on the table, cracked a cap, winced as she realized how swollen her hands were from the work, and handed the first beer across the table. "Got a lot done," she admitted. "XMercy, there's still a ton to do. Can't leave that ground covered by shoots; they'll destroy the floor and we don't want to go through that again. Why don't you and MSJS run into Beckley tomorrow morning and rent the stump grinder. They've got to sell razor wire at one of the hardware stores, too, what with the prison there and all." She looked Spencer straight in the eye, asking him, "How many feet will we be needing?"

To XMercy's shock, Johnny washed dishes and Mouse dried. Spencer asked her to talk more about the tattoo. Mouse said she could do better than that, wiped her hands on the dishtowel, and went back into the bedroom. She had carefully-folded papers that she carried almost reverentially in her hands when she returned. Looking at the sink and MSJS, she found a safe high shelf and placed them on top until the dishes were done. XMercy recognized the papers, knew what they were, and would have shown her displeasure, but the evening was showing a perfection she knew was rare and she would not have spoiled it no matter what she thought of Dimitri Vosilych, not for the world.

XMercy and Mouse walked Spencer outside into the warm evening air. Mouse pressed the papers inside his hand before he headed toward their guesthouse. She bent over and brought kindling to their fire ring, but XMercy brushed her aside to take over. Mouse went inside and came back with the last two bottles of Michelob, pulled two low chairs alongside the fire, and they sat down beside one another to plan. XMercy would be driving in on her own. Rental store for the stump grinder, the smaller one that fit in the back of the 4Runner. MSJS figured on four hundred feet of wire. XMercy needed to get gloves and a cutter, too. MSJS decided it was best for him to stay put and clear the lines so they could get the wire down when XMercy got back with it.

Inside the camper shell, Spencer lit the oil lamp, opened the papers, and stretched out on the foam mattress, leaning into the light to read.

> *I was Dimitri Vosilych. Because you are reading these words, I know I am dead. But this is good, because if I am dead I have had courage and I am dying for something bigger than individual.*
>
> *When I am coming to America, I come for living in this incredible place where all is possible, where men can speak their dreams and say always*

what we think without any problem. In my country, you must not criticize powerful men or they get you beating up or get you for prison even. Everyone is knowing how rich people they are stealing away from all other peoples. In my country, the rich people most they are not showing so much money. They think people will be angry and kill them and take money away. When the government goes down, everyone sees and is talking about how the big man was living. We come to looking at his houses, his cars, all these not normal things and we see proof that he was so bad.

Now I am coming to America and I am seeing is worse here. Many poor people here, too. But people is worship golden calf. Poor children, so bad schools, much violence, and rich people like kings and not doing something. They don't care and people let them live and don't get angry and don't doing something.

I am thinking I coming to America and I working very hard and then is getting better. I get wife, house, children. I want to be member of society. But only people are thinking for getting rich, for themselves, not for society. Rich peoples they are making so much monies and other peoples cannot even go to café to sit and talk and make good life together. No Starbucks! I mean people's place.

I read university is much money so normal people cannot pay but still rich people can walk everywhere, drive in their cars, do everything and nobody is getting angry. How is possible?

For being in political system is taking very much money. If you want make change, make life more fair, is impossible! Rich people are having so much power and still no one is asking how they are getting so much? If rich is fair, why they must have so many people they are paying to buy politicians? No person is needing so much. Never. This is never fair and always anti-social.

In my country, the people they fight for change. In America, who is fighting? Who is driving Pharisees out from the temple? Many many problems and only America is fighting making wars in other people's countries. So, I am saying Dimitri someone must make rich people afraid. Must make rich peoples stop and think how rich they are being. I want make normal people see they are not thinking good. How they cannot think only these other people are so rich so they can't do anything. It is better rich people are afraid so they are aware they are rich and their riches are offense to people who must struggle. I want make them pay for being rich people so the rich people they will not pass all other people in street and think nothing and live their life in ignorance. And when I am able, one man, to make rich people afraid, then more men and more women will see and say I can do this, too, like Dimitri Vosilych.

Once he began laughing, Spencer couldn't stop himself. He felt tears rolling down his cheeks, imagining the college kid who probably faked the letter.

Who the hell was Dimitri Vosilych? Did he even exist?

He lifted the guitar without paying attention and started to strum. Chords at first, followed by snapping each string and tuning until he was picking notes quickly, dancing his fingertips across the frets like he had never stopped practicing.

XMercy started taking a sip of beer then stopped midway and listened as a breeze carried sound up the meadow toward them. Spencer was strumming chords, then he began to sing, quietly at first.

"Shush," XMercy hissed.

She shushed Mouse, who wasn't saying anything, clutched Mouse's arm and listened. XMercy strained to hear every note as she mouthed the words. She knew he was missing words, not that she cared.

Mouse recognized it too, when she heard the chorus. *The Night They Drove Ole Dixie Down*.

XMercy waived her arm frantically to stop Mouse again, who wasn't saying a word. "Quiet! Lord, he is really good.

"I taught him that! Hee hee! Admit it, Mouse, Johnny's got talent," she said.

"I never said he didn't."

"But you didn't want him here."

Spencer started playing another song, stopped after several notes, and resumed again.

Hallelujah, Hallelujah
Hallelujah, Hallelujah

Mouse jumped to her feet. "No!" she shouted. "That's MY song. You don't get to sing that!" The wind blew her words back into her face. Down in the camper, Spencer's voice drew deeper to places he had forgotten or never explored.

"What?" XMercy shrugged. "Don't give *me* the stink eye. He learned that one on his own."

Hallelujah, Hallelujah
Hallelujah, Hallelujah
Hallelujah, Hallelujah
Hallelujah, Hallelujah
Hallelujah, Hallelujah
Hallelujah, Hallelujah
Hallelujah, Hallelujah
Hallelujah, Hallelujah
Hallelujah

CHAPTER SEVENTEEN

After a bouncy ride, the narrow Brazilian-made jet thumped onto the Beckley Raleigh County runway. Bishop and two of his four computer techs had planned to take carry-on baggage, but all three were stopped by the screener after he saw the Makita drill driver. Having twenty-two webcams didn't help things. After some fast talking, Bishop convinced the TSA personnel surrounding them that they were security consultants flying to do an installation. One of the techs was near a meltdown thinking about how close he had come to bringing weed along for the trip. All three rollaways ended up in the baggage compartment.

Bishop checked his watch on landing and again as they waited at one of the two baggage claim belts.

"You two get the bags, "he told them. "I'm going to Hertz. I'll meet you in front at the curb."

From the airport, they were driving together to the equipment rental, renting the cherry-picker van, then splitting up, he to Charleston, the two of them toward Mount Hope and Fayetteville.

"We've got this," they reassured him. Five minutes per pole, eleven poles, not more than three minutes between installations. Less than two hours and they'd have coverage of the whole highway. Piece of cake.

"You checked the cameras?"

"They're fine. Still in the store packaging. Hotspots are current, everything is chill."

Nothing Bishop hated more than this laid-back confidence driven by data-pushing children who never went out into the real world. Fuck 'em all. NSA, DOD, the whole security establishment was moving their way, mostly because the people in charge didn't know a fucking thing except, "Boy, this Kool-Aid sure tastes good!"

"How do we know they'll sync up and stay online?"

The two twenty-somethings just looked at him. They weren't going to explain again.

"Kip and Dale have it covered," Nussbaum reassured Bishop before they set out. He remained skeptical.

Every one of the hotspots ran off one of three different providers. They had system backdoors for all three. Didn't matter if they were running firewalls to their own systems; they could wrap around security software in seconds. Given two minutes, they could hack right inside, but no reason to bother.

"What about storage?"

They had already explained how each camera ran intermittent segments to a cache. Storage was a non-issue; the system architecture already accounted for that. When each segment was cached, the facial recognition software passed through it and would notify them by text message when they had a hit, automatically saving that segment and sending it to them with the camera location and a time stamp. The purpose of the cameras was not to prompt an instant response. If three cameras picked her up and then nothing more came through, Dale showed Bishop how they could extrapolate from that information that she was situated not just between Fayetteville and Mt. Hope, but within the much narrower field between those specific cameras.

"We can parse the focus-area down to a small segment within a low-density region," Stephen had explained. "I'll bet that a square-mile around there yields a tighter head-count than we'd get from a single mid-rise in Manhattan."

The three rode in silence for the ten minutes it took getting from the terminal to the rental yard; while Bishop drove, the two younger men stayed on their smartphones. Bishop had to raise his voice to get them out of the car. One of them was going to have to show his driver's license.

The only person inside the glass doors was an older version of Janis Joplin. Nobody behind the counter. Bishop tapped the edge of his credit card against the glass.

"We're here for the cherry picker," Bishop told the man coming in from the service area before he was through the door.

"Be right with you, sir," he told Bishop with a quick glance up at the white hat. "Just as soon as I finish up with this here lady." He turned to XMercy, explaining how, "I'll do it this one time, just since I know you. But XMercy, you have got to get a valid ID. That license of yours expired more than a year ago for goodness sake."

"You're the best, Bobby," XMercy laughed. "I'll have it back before five."

"Just as long as it's back by eleven tomorrow will do fine. You're all loaded up. I put in a couple ramps that will help with unloading that stump grinder. You be careful for rocks. I have to charge six dollars a tooth if you break any."

XMercy went through the back doors out to the 4Runner. Bishop stood at the counter, fixated on the name "Frank" labeled in red lettering on the man's shirt.

"Don't have any cherry-pickers at this store," Bobby told Bishop. "Have one at the Charleston Store, if it's not out. I can check on it if you'd like to hold on."

"Your website says you rent them here."

Bobby shrugged. "I can't say anything about that. I don't have nothing to do with that stuff. It's all supposed to run together, inventory, reservations, and all, but you know how that goes."

"Aw hell, that's an hour away." Bishop still had some margin, but losing an hour was going to eat into it badly. "Fine. Check your other store."

"Yes, sir," Bobby agreed after looking in the system at the current yard inventories. "You can pick it up in Charleston. If you want, I can take your credit card and reserve it for you right now."

Bishop pushed back his hat and looked down at his watch, calculating the time. They had just enough margin to get it done, leaving the cherry picker there in Beckley before the return flight.

"Fine, I'll have it back here by three."

"Well, I'll have to call in on that. Each one of the shops runs independently even if we're the same company. Maybe they can drive down and pick it up here, but that means two people to shuttle down and two rigs and gas getting back. Probably cost a hundred-fifty, something along those lines."

Stephen and Dilip were focused on their phones, which only made Bishop angrier. Stephen was participating in an online systems integration forum while Dilip looked over bidding for something on eBay.

Bobby explained that "I have plenty of hoists, boom lifts, scissor lifts. You get a truck with a hitch and I can set you up with a lift and a towing-trailer. Fix you right up."

Dilip held up his phone and immediately announced "They've got Penske, Ryder, U-Haul five minutes away."

*****

It was already nearly noon when Bishop pulled off the highway into Dunbar. The air was clear and warm, but he wasn't paying attention. He had skipped breakfast, as usual, so he pulled into the Subway and practiced his lines while he ate a turkey and Black Forest ham.

Felicia Diane Reynolds had left the community college midway through the semester. Her transcripts showed incompletes in every class. It was plausible. She could have a refund coming.

He ate fast, gulping the bread down with a Morning Dew, and then got back to the rental car. He drove past the Church of the Nazarene and turned left, heading toward the river. The house was tidy, although it could have used a coat of paint. A basic one-story blue ranch with white wrought iron bars on the windows except where two A/C units hung in the window frames. A Chrysler Town and Country minivan with faded fake wood side panels sat under the carport.

Bishop parked in front, took a final sip from the plastic Mountain Dew bottle, wiped his mouth in the rearview mirror, and opened the door. He lifted the u-shaped gate latch on the thigh-high chain link fencing and walked up the concrete walkway past lines of rose bushes on both sides. He opened a clear plastic storm door, located the doorbell on the inside frame, and then let the storm door close while he waited outside.

A woman wearing a simple yellow dress with a white collar and white trim on the short sleeves answered the bell and stood behind the plastic waiting for him to speak.

"Are you Mrs. Reynolds?" he inquired politely, already recognizing her face from photos.

"And who is asking?" she wanted to know, cautiously but politely.

Bishop took a business card from his jacket pocket and offered it up to her along the opening side of the storm door, sliding it partway into the crack and waiting for her to take it from his hand. "Mrs. Reynolds, my name is Mark Burnside. I work for Asset Recovery Associates. You can see on my card. Is Felicia Diane Reynolds here in the home?"

Hearing her daughter's name, Mrs. Reynolds stepped outside, quickly closing the solid door behind her. "Felicia isn't living here," she explained quietly. She looked like an older version of her daughter, sans tattoos. He noticed Mrs. Reynolds wore no makeup at all. No earrings or necklace, either. No engagement diamond. A simple gold wedding ring was her only adornment.

"Ma'am," Bishop continued, trying to be careful not to let himself fall into a Texas accent. He rarely used the word 'ma'am.'

"Ma'am, Asset Recovery is in the business of reuniting individuals with funds that have been escheated to the state. What that means is money that belongs to the individual but that goes unclaimed for a period of time and then is turned over to the state. At Asset Recovery, we seek to reunite the consumer with these lost or overlooked funds for which, according to state regulation, we are entitled to a percentage of the funds."

"What does this have to do with Felicia?"

"Ma'am, am I correct that Felicia attended community college here in Dunbar? That she withdrew from her studies? Ma'am, by West Virginia law, students who withdraw from public educational institutions prior to mid-semester must receive a refund for full tuition credit. Just right here, in the greater Charleston urban area, we have over two-hundred fifty-thousand dollars in tuition funds that our young people have just left on the table, so to speak," Bishop said.

"Fudge," she exclaimed, then glanced anxiously back toward the door.

"Mr. Burnside, my husband, Reverend Reynolds, put out the tuition money. I'm sure it would be all right if I signed for it, seeing as it is really my husband's money."

"I can't do that. I'm afraid it has to go to the individual named. You and Felicia will need to come to an arrangement when the funds are distributed."

Mrs. Reynolds bit at her fingernail and thought it through. "How much money is there?"

Now Bishop hesitated. "I'm really not supposed to speak to anyone other than the recipient, but let me say, on the QT, that it is somewhere between nine-hundred and one-thousand."

Mrs. Reynolds inhaled audibly then held her breath, took Bishop's arm, and walked him across the stepping stones in front of the house over to the carport. "Is there a time limit? How long do we have to get the funds?"

"Ma'am?"

"Felicia isn't living here."

"Her present domicile has no bearing on eligibility," Bishop assured. "What is her current address?"

Mrs. Reynolds examined her rose beds, turned to watch a car drive past. "Mr. Burnside," she confided painfully, "the Reverend and I, we're estranged from our daughter." She pursed her lips and concentrated, carefully choosing every word. "Felicia lives a different lifestyle, not like how we raised her to be. I can't say where she lives exactly. We don't even have a telephone number. She's somewhere over in Fayette County is all I know, and that was eleven months ago. My little girl, she dresses like a man. Lord, she stood there, right there at our door, standing wearing Redwing work boots, old blue jeans, and a man's tee, and she said she was living with another woman. Like she was proud of that! Mr. Burnside, that money would make a difference. I'll put some of it aside so if Felicia comes around, I'll give it to her. Before Jesus I swear I will. Can't I just sign?"

Bishop checked his watch then re-read the referral and pulled up the directions to his second stop. Nussbaum's cameras were helpful, but unless Jeffers had the pull to keep a drone hovering in wait, he damned well wanted to have a Plan B in place to pick up where the cameras left off. He thought about it for a moment, realizing that Jeffers probably did have enough pull to find a drone, but old school methods would work, too. Not everything had to depend on the machines.

*****

Dilip drove the rental pickup towing the hoist and trailer, keeping off the interstate and driving in the far right lane, going fifteen miles per hour while Stephen watched the equipment through the back window, following the map displayed on his phone. Somehow, they had managed to burn two hours renting the truck then getting back and waiting for Bobby to hitch up the trailer and load the hoist. They drove a half-mile to a spot then quickly unpacked, attached the magnetic Dish Network logos on the doors right over the truck rental logos, and then got back in to drive the six miles out to the first utility pole.

"I am thinking," Dilip observed while they headed north through Beckley, "we should be capable of far more comprehensive utilities." All the technology existed. "Rather than simply installing the surveillance mechanism, we should offer a fully-integrated solution. Why not integrate cameras and facial recognition software with a remotely-controlled machine gun? That would be cool."

Stephen caught on and appreciated the intellectual process. There were no technological impediments, but the thinking revealed why Dilip was a tech rather than a manager.

"Somebody has already gone there," Stephen explained. "They're way ahead of you, my friend." He held his hand out the window, enjoying the feeling of the wind blowing through his spread fingers. "But that wouldn't be politically correct, at least not domestically, for the same reasons that drones aren't firing missiles at U.S. cars."

"Um." Dilip nodded, seeing Nussbaum's point.

"Might be able to use explosives," Stephen speculated. "Employing an IED allows for plausible deniability." It *would* work very nearly as well. He and Dilip exchanged glances; Dilip immediately ran through systems architecture. Stephen considered market size, price resistance, the pitch, funding, first-to-market advantage, patents, competition, and exit strategies.

As they pulled onto Route 19 and the first utility pole, Stephen jumped out and directed Dilip's driving to position the hoist directly under the pole and confirmed Wi-Fi signal strength before doing anything else. Strong red; a Wireless N source.

They opened and checked one of the cameras, removed the plastic barrier to activate the battery, then set the camera into the lift bucket along with the cordless drill driver and a package of 2.5-inch woods screws and the laser sight. They were ready to begin when both of them stood without moving, looking to the other.

"Don't look at me," Dilip told Stephen. "I did the driving. I will not be getting onto that thing."

Reluctantly, Nussbaum climbed up onto the trailer, put one foot on the tire of the hoist and awkwardly struggled to get his skinny leg over the side. The whole hoist rocked slightly, leaving Stephen with a white-knuckled two-handed grip for dear life on the side of the bucket. After it steadied, he closed his eyes and forced himself inside.

The mechanism looked simple enough. A key-start, one orange-knobbed joystick for steering right and left, forward and reverse, a second joystick, blue-knobbed, for raising and lowering the bucket. A huge red button labeled STOP.

The hoist rumbled to life on the first turn of the key. Stephen reached nervously to grip the blue knob. Their plan was to leave the hoist on the trailer.

Eleven poles, five minutes per pole, interim time between poles, turn in the hoist, turn in the truck, back to the airport.

He pressed the knob forward and the hoist lurched upward fully six inches, rocking so much that Stephen leaned back to compensate and shot his hand onto the stop button.

As he jumped away from the bucket, he saw that a couple teenagers, fifteen or sixteen, had stopped their bikes on the shoulder of the road to watch. They looked amused.

"We can't do it from the trailer," Stephen concluded. "The whole thing will topple over. We need to move it off the trailer and then raise it from solid ground."

Dilip said nothing.

"Well?" Stephen asked him.

"Well what?"

Stephen motioned toward the hoist with open arms. "It's your turn."

"It's not my turn," Dilip disagreed adamantly. "What did you do? I am the driver. You are the manager, you operate that thing."

The teenagers whispered between them and laughed.

Stephen looked at the hoist, looked at Dilip, and then put his hands on his hips. The thing was a death trap.

"You all don't know what you're doing," one of the kids sniggered.

"We're new," Dilip responded. "Our regular vans are different."

"Shoot, that don't look so hard," the kid told him.

"You ever driven one?" Stephen demanded.

"No," he admitted. "Drove a backhoe plenty of times. That lift don't look real hard."

Stephen looked over to Dilip and back at the kids. "Want to try working this?"

The kids dropped their bikes and hopped right up on the trailer without hesitation. Looking down at Stephen, the talkative kid asked, "What you gonna pay?"

Stephen looked in his wallet before offering five dollars.

"For getting it off the trailer?"

"Off the trailer, up the pole, then screwing in our equipment. Won't take five minutes."

The second teenager stepped up. "Twenty." He could tell when the other guy was over a barrel.

Dilip and Stephen walked around to the front of the truck, away from the two boys. They had forty-five dollars between them.

"We'll pay ten and see. If it goes right, we've got ten more poles to service." The boys could put their bikes in the back and ride along in the truck between poles.

"Twenty for this one. If it takes five minutes, we'll do the rest for ten apiece. A hundred-twenty bucks for all eleven. If it takes five minutes."

Stephen nodded and the first kid hopped aboard while his friend pulled out the built-in ramps.

Dilip got on his phone and searched for an ATM.

*****

Spencer had ground out the first bigger stumps then turned the machine over to Mouse. Now, XMercy leaned into the handles to drive the grinder forward. Mouse was already spent, squatting with her head hung between her legs, sweat running rivulets down her neck, sopping rings under her arms. Spencer wanted them far away from the concertina wire while he happily strung the razor-sharp Slinkies along in two runs set six to eight feet apart through the underbrush. He separated them enough so that a thief couldn't throw a sheet of plywood over them and cross over unscathed. Once he had trip lines installed and had them tied in to harmless homemade bang grenades, anyone wanting to steal the weed crop was going to need to work really hard to get it.

By noon, the entire area was cleared and ready to be raked smooth. Spencer rigged a pallet behind the Polaris, carried it across to the far end of new ground, and rode on it while Mouse pulled slowly forward, dragging the rich soil into smooth flat lines. They were soon moving in an efficient partnership; he was enjoying the surfing, relishing how his balance and agility were coming along. Mouse paid attention to how he planned the security wire, even allowing for a safe spot to bring in the water lines later on. She saw the logic of using double rows at the back and along the forest side; on the slope side, one line was plenty. Nobody could get down that grade without getting torn up in the wire.

XMercy was concerned about the deer, worried even about the feral pig population that seemed to be getting worse.

Spencer asked her, "How many cat skeletons have you ever seen in trees?"

"What's that supposed to mean?"

"Animals learn fast," he assured her. "They might get nicked, but they won't get caught." The greenhouses were secure on three sides. When the plants were maturing, either he or Mouse could set out trip wires along the front. A two-dollar spool of three-pound monofilament would do the trick.

He and XMercy kept the self-propelled grinder balanced and let it power itself back up the ramps and onto the trailer. Spencer counted two broken teeth.

"Not many stones in the soil, at least not near the top; the high water table keeps the ground soft so that anything heavy sinks deep," he explained.

XMercy took the first shower then rushed back down to the rental yard in Beckley to get there before they closed at six. While Spencer put away the ATV, Mouse showered next. She was standing in the doorway calling him, wearing nothing but a white towel she held wrapped around her petite chest. It covered only down to her slim thighs. When he heard her, he came around the trailer then turned his face away.

"Your turn," she called out, using her unoccupied hand to agitate the water out of her short hair. "I left you a clean towel over the shower rod."

After they were both cleaned up and dressed, Mouse sat cross-legged on the sofa. "Good day," she remarked aloud, not directing it particularly to Spencer. She massaged her arms, obviously enjoying the ache she had earned.

"Good day," he agreed. Nothing was stopping them now from getting going on the frame for the new greenhouse.

Spencer wasn't sure whether or not they were having a conversation. He was debating whether he ought to be there or if he should leave the trailer when she asked him how he got his nickname, MSJS.

"That's easy," he told her. "Master Sergeant Jonathan Spencer. MSJS."

"What would happen if you got a promotion?"

He stood and pondered that for the first time. It had never before occurred to him. He was never going to be an E-9, even if they hadn't fucked him over.

"SMJS, I suppose."

The only way he could ever have been an E-9 would have meant leaving the field, moving inside to run day-to-day ops at sniper training school. Didn't make sense to take him out of what he did best and have him doing a job he'd suck at. That wouldn't stop command, of course, but it was a bad fit. *Would have been.*

"Why 'Mouse'?" he asked.

She laughed. "From 'church mouse,' not because I'm little. See, my father is a minister, would you believe it? He made the rules and all through high school he made me be in my room by ten. Ten-thirty on weekends. Even when I was sixteen years old he stuck to that curfew."

She shook at her damp hair and remembered aloud. "My bedroom had this window looking into our carport. There were bars on it, bars on the whole house, so once the door was closed he thought he had his little girl locked in tight. Uh-uh. Nope. See, on Wednesday nights, while he had Bible study and my mother, she was off visiting the old folks or something, some of my friends came over to the house and we sorted things out differently. This boy, Teddy, he wanted to be my boyfriend. Well, the Reverend wasn't ever going to go for that. No sir! So Teddy, he drilled the lag bolts out of those bars and replaced them with plain rods with just lag heads that he painted white, like the bars. From then on, I got so I could pull out those pins and lower the bars without a peep. Quiet as a church mouse."

"You look like Ellen," he offered. "You know that?"

Mouse's tone shifted. "Hey, I love a woman," she told Spencer. "Doesn't mean I love women. There's a difference."

"That's not what I meant. It's, you know, you're always moving fast, high energy, and the blonde hair, cut short, and you're all wiry and bouncing around. Good stuff." He felt like he was digging himself in deeper.

"What, and if I'm a lesbian that's not good?" Then she cracked a smile. "Fucking with you," she teased.

XMercy came up the driveway with a bucket of KFC and sides just about at sunset. "I'm not cooking, thank you."

She turned one of the wooden wire spools on its side and set them down beside the fire ring then sat down heavily onto one of the camp chairs and set out the meal.

"I had to wait on some men who were getting heated with Bobby," XMercy related. "I guess they rented a hoist or something, and then it wouldn't go back on the trailer when they were done. Bobby went and left the store for an hour to rescue them, got things squared away, and these guys refused to pay $60 extra. Like that was Bobby's problem."

XMercy shook her head. "I finally unhitched the trailer and left the grinder in the equipment yard. Didn't want to stiff Bobby the twelve bucks, so I tied the bills on the handles with a rubber band. They were still fussin' when I drove out.

What is wrong with people?" she asked nobody in particular.

In the twilight they could still see down the meadow in the direction of the greenhouse and their newly cleared pad beside it. Spencer sat with his back against a rock and sucked the meat off a drumstick. He pushed himself upright and arranged kindling inside the fire ring before the bucket came around again.

While the chicken lasted, nobody spoke. They were too busy biting and nibbling around the bones. When it was gone and they had their fingers licked clean, Spencer took the bucket, tore it open, and lit it up to start the kindling.

XMercy handed out sporks. Spencer held the spork and his hand began to shake. For that second, he was back inside the segregation cell. He had to step away and then gripped his left fist around his right hand until the shaking subsided. PTSD.

XMercy and Mouse passed around the mashed potatoes, followed by the mac and cheese. Spencer had both on his plate when he sat back down. The empties also followed into the fire. After that, the three of them flopped out their legs in front of them, Spencer on the ground, XMercy on the low chair, and Mouse on their one rickety chaise lounge.

"Johnny, come in with me tomorrow," XMercy suggested. "We can load up the supplies and get ready to get going on the greenhouse in a couple more days."

Spencer was afraid of that. He was already feeling too loose, concentrating on getting his body right without thinking through other priorities.

"You know," he explained slowly, "here I'm good." How could he tell more? "It's harder with more people. Sometimes I was getting confused, agitated, like I'm still there and not here."

XMercy had been trying not to ask, not to make him talk about the war.

"We're proud of you. You know that, right Johnny?"

"I tried really hard," he said honestly. "I tried to make myself like the sharpest knife or the best balanced and sighted weapon. I didn't do it for me, not exactly, but more for what I could do. That must not make any sense." How could they understand if they weren't there?

XMercy and Mouse both let him talk, just talk.

"Sometimes I close my eyes and I see this kid. He's wearing a red shirt, Manchester United, and he's playing with a dirt clod like he's dribbling a soccer ball off his toes. And then I pull the trigger. Because that was my orders. Following orders."

His words hung in the air like smoke until he snapped their spell. "There was a lot of boredom, too," he commented in an entirely different tone. "Lots of hours just trying to fill up time." That was all that he was ready to say.

Following a quiet pause, XMercy reached down and put another log into the fire ring and then watched the sparks lift like fireflies and die into the dark.

"Mouse and I can make the trip in for supplies," she told him. "You don't need to come along."

She started to hum, then broke softly into song: "By the light of the moon, we danced in the meadow, we sang and we danced by the light of the moon. Then the night birds chimed in and lent us a chorus, and down in the pond we were joined by a loon."

Mouse followed in, improvising the next stanza with new lines, singing with passion and brutally out of key. "By the light of the moon, we danced in the meadow, we sang and we danced by the light of the moon. The hoot owl screeched from the top of a spruce tree, and I sound kinda like him whenever I croon."

Then Spencer surprised them both and surprised himself even more. It had been at least twenty-five years since he and XMercy had last jammed together. He sang: "By the light of the moon, we danced in the meadow, we sang and we danced by the light of the moon. So resin your bow and get out your fiddle, and if the mood strikes you, come belt out a tune."

XMercy squeezed Mouse's forearm then stood up and rushed Spencer, clutching him in a bear hug before he could shy away. Her hearty laughter went a long way toward melting the years away.

When she sat back down, she remembered she had a joint in the pocket of the shirt she was wearing. She fished it out like she had won a prize, sucked along the seam, and lit it up, taking a deep draw, before passing it along to Mouse, who did likewise. When it came back to her, XMercy tilted it in Johnny's direction then took it back. She seemed surprised when he held out his fingers to take it.

"Why, Johnny the Boy Scout smokes weed," she teased. "Go slow. It's real strong."

"Might as well try it," he replied. "Only live once."

Mouse and XMercy watched him draw in a huge hit that he held in his lungs for at least twenty seconds before coughing out the thick smoke. He held his head stiffly and closed both eyes as it hit him, then all three cracked up.

"What did you dream life would be like, Johnny?" XMercy asked him, her tone deep and sincere. "What did you think you would become?"

Spencer stared at the joint, fixated, until XMercy kicked her toes at his ear. "I don't remember dreaming," he finally responded, at a loss for any more truthful answer.

"I didn't think I'd be growing weed in the sticks," XMercy laughed. "Or smoking it with little Johnny Spencer, that's for sure!"

"Machu Picchu," Mouse said after the joint was nearing gone. Nothing more, just "Machu Picchu," straight out of nowhere, making them laugh more. XMercy crawled onto the chaise and snuggled up next to Mouse.

"Quebec," Mouse said, a few minutes later. "Yeah, Quebec would be good."

XMercy tried to picture Quebec but was interrupted. "Fuck. Mosquito!" She almost cried. It was so beautiful being outside at night, but the mosquitoes would be coming so soon. "We tried bug zappers, citronella, nothing works," she said, annoyed by what she knew was coming. "DEET is disgusting. I even have to put it in my hair or they bite the top of my head and then I'm scratching the whole night long. Lord, why mosquitoes?"

Spencer struggled up to his feet and stood in front of the fire with his arms crossed in front of him. He threw his chin up high and announced in a terrible Russian accent, "I am Dimitri Vosilych." He opened his arms and thumped his chest and repeated himself, "I am Dimitri Vosilych."

"Not cool," Mouse grumbled, touching her fingers to her neck but on the wrong side, away from the tattoo. "That is so not cool." XMercy turned her face up and planted a kiss on Mouse's DV. It was ok. He didn't mean it. She liked the salty taste of Mouse's skin and licked her way up the nape of Mouse's neck to her earlobe, then bit and sucked at it. Mouse turned her head down, her lips meeting XMercy's in a series of soft, languid kisses that sent Spencer off to bed.

CHAPTER EIGHTEEN

Dawn glowed a soft golden pink through the trees. Spencer reached his arms down, held his toes and rolled his neck and head, feeling every unique sinew stretch and release as the forest around him came alive—a rustling, fluttering rebirth between the branches and within the ground cover. The finches and chipmunks ignored his presence while Spencer held one stylized pose then gracefully transitioned to the next, following the ritual routine to his Chi, connecting to the flow within and without, like the creek moving over smooth stones, tying himself to all living things.

XMercy rose early; Mouse, like the lazy crows, slept in. XMercy had decided to bake. Fresh bread and wild honey, Turkish apple tea. She cleaned up the remnants of the night before, plastic KFC sporks and fragments of colored paper in the fire ring, then opened the card table and let the sun warm her face.

The metal sides reflected warmth when they sat down to eat. XMercy sliced still-warm brown bread, putting a thickly cut piece onto the plate she had chosen especially for each of them. The bread hinted of wood smoke, not enough to offend: rich and nutty, warm on the mouth, the honey sweetness just kissed by a sting. All three chewed in silence, smiles spreading between them. XMercy and Mouse giggled; Mouse pinched her cup and stuck out her pinkie when she took a sip of tea.

XMercy still had the supply list from the original greenhouse plus sticky notes about everything they wanted to modify and improve upon this time around. She wanted the steel poles set into concrete, then have the PVC slid down into the steel so the frame wouldn't flex as much during the bad blows that would sometimes sweep down the canyon.

"Maybe it would be a good idea to add a rain flap," Spencer suggested. He also sketched out how to go about framing in a solar-driven exhaust fan high up on the rear wall.

"Save the cardboard tubes from TP and paper towels," he said. He also had a list prepared with easy-to-find supermarket items. "I'll make some firecrackers out of them that'll be heard in the next county if anybody comes through uninvited."

XMercy couldn't stand the idea of having a poor dog kept outside all year round, but Spencer still thought they ought to get one. "A good dog is better than alarms," he repeated. But Mouse was allergic. No dog.

"Lowe's, down in Beckley, has most everything," Mouse told them after taking Spencer's list. "What they don't have, Ace will."

"Don't forget the monofilament fishing line," Spencer added. "I don't think that made the list."

Mercy jumped up from the table, returning from the shed after a few minutes carrying two poles, one for fly-casting, the second equipped with a spinning reel, along with a tackle box and a creel that looked brand-new. She handed everything to Spencer, along with a map she fetched from the 4Runner's glove compartment, declaring, "I have a taste for trout and you've got a job!"

XMercy thought Spencer ought to run up White Oak to the bridge just past Cold Spot Deli. "Might not be as many fish as some other spots, but they'll be natives, not the stocked rainbows they get across the highway up Loop Creek.

"Who wants to listen to cars?" Mouse argued back. "I'd get on Thurmond Road and fish it all the way up the river. Must be a hundred spots along there where you won't see a soul."

"Is it ok to ride out on the Polaris?" Spencer asked.

"Don't worry about the roads," Mouse told him. "The sheriffs won't care. But unless you buy a license, you see any forest green SUVs, you hide those fish real good or they're going to end up being the most expensive trout you'll ever eat."

Spencer zipped across the highway right through Glen Jean without stopping, then slowed down to a steady twenty miles per hour up Route 25, letting the warm day blow into his face until his eyes ran wet. He passed up half a dozen turnouts beside Dunloup Creek without stopping and kept driving out until the scenery opened out in front of the bridge over New River, where he parked on the gravel along the south embankment and got out. Three bright blue inflatable rafts, each filled with paddlers in orange life vests and matching orange helmets, slipped over the riffles on the far side. He listened to their guides shouting, "Left. Left. Dig!" as the current started to swing the first boat sideways. He watched them figure out how to work together to straighten up into the current. The guide's encouraging shouts after they were back on flat water reminded him of working with fresh recruits, all eagerness and zero knowhow.

He watched the next two groups then he worked his way back up along the creek, across rocks and past tree branches, until he got to a sunny spot down the smooth-running clear stream. Lying along the bank perfectly still, he waited and watched for shadows against the rocks and pebbles. When he saw the dark lines, he looked up slightly and could make out the subtle shapes and colors of the pan-sized trout nosing into the current.

Retreating back to the ATV, he looked through the tackle. Nobody had ever shown him how to use a fly rod; he wished someone had. But the spinning gear he did know. The box held an array of lures, mostly brand-new: rooster tails, minnows, rubber night crawlers, crawfish, and damsel flies, spinning flashers in red, silver, and gold. There was a jar filled with red salmon eggs and another with fish killer marshmallows. A squirt bottle was labeled as fish-attracting scent.

Spencer watched for spots where the shallow water settled and cast above into deeper pools, letting the current take the line downstream like Jack had taught him. He had the luck; a hookup on his first cast taken by a decent ten-incher. There was no trick to landing it, not at that size. He took in line until the fish was eight feet beyond the rod tip, then swung it over the bank within easy reach. He had it strung behind the gills and back in the water like he had done it yesterday, even though his math said it had been just shy of twenty-five years.

He worked the creek a hundred yards upstream until he couldn't go any further without wading around greenery growing well out from the bank. He had two more fish in the creel by then and made his way back to the stringer to keep them fresh. Then he took off his shoes and walked barefoot out to a flat rock and laid back, letting his feet dangle in the cold water. He pictured Jack, not the white-haired, somber man with the gut, but his dad when he was not even thirty, lean and strong, his only care being to figure out why somebody's circuit was shorting out or to come up with a good solution to work around that with a new wire. He was always smiling back then, quick to catch a garter snake, wrestling with dogs until they all loved him so much they wanted to go home with him.

Spencer didn't want to reach down and touch his leg, didn't want to touch his thigh for the plate and screws that were there. "Why would you pinch yourself to awaken from this?" For a long moment he dreamed that maybe he could have a life.

*****

"We have a hit. No, two!" The techs had their system programmed to text Bishop, but Dilip, being Dilip, typed out a redundant notification and sent it manually. Camera Ten, at the Junction of Sun Mine Road and Route 19. The evenly numbered cameras were north-facing against southbound traffic, odd numbers faced opposite. Second hit on Camera Eight.

"Third hit, Camera Six," Stephen called out, accepting the fist bump Dilip offered and exploding his fist in response.

Bishop showed up ten minutes later. By that time, Felicia Diane Reynolds had passed by Cameras Four and Two and was off their grid, but not before they had identified the make and year of the SUV. They were pumped; they also had a partial plate and were into the West Virginia vehicle registration system, isolating correlating hits for 2009 Toyota 4Runners, plates beginning with YUS.

The plates turned out to be a dead end; no making registrations within all of Fayette County. But when Bishop watched the four of them, none seemed disturbed at all.

This wasn't an academic exercise, he thought. *What did it matter if their cameras worked when she drove right off their grid?*

"It's like a wildlife camera," Stephen explained with the map on screen. "We know she passed this way; the cameras have corroborated that much." Stephen managed to be condescending even without trying; Bishop might have to work with geeks, but liking it was another story altogether.

"I already knew that from the mother," Bishop objected.

"Let me finish, ok?"

Stephen imagined he could download Bishop's entire skill set in a week. The day was coming on fast when Bishop and his cowboy hat would be consigned to old movies.

"The cameras were active since yesterday, right?" Stephen continued. "So we know she spent the night somewhere between here, at Camera Ten, and here at Scarbro Loop, the next place to get onto Route 19 and also the location of Cameras Eleven and Twelve. That makes for a very high probability that she will pass Cameras One, Three, Five, Seven, Nine on her way back and I'll take bets that she doesn't pass Camera Eleven. After she leaves the bigger city, she's heading home."

Bishop moved into his own office behind closed doors before making the call. They had one working lead, but checking into a person's identity was a far cry from having a confirmed visual on Spencer, much less any location. The last time his team jumped the gun, five people ended up dead.

"You contact me the moment there is another hit," he told them before walking out of the bullpen where Nussbaum's team worked surrounded by flat-screen monitors. Bishop was closing the door to his own office when a thought occurred to him. He walked back into the techies, asking, "Did any of you program the suspect's face into your Wi-Fi cameras along the highway?"

"No," they answered in unison.

"Why?"

Stephen fielded the response for all four of them. "We don't need to. We set up a simultaneous scan set for continuously screening across every visual feed in North America. The NSA backbone supports that kind of capacity. It's huge. We haven't explored ten percent of the capabilities, either. Right at this minute, every camera in the Cloud is looking for Jonathan Spencer."

Bishop shut himself inside his office then opened the mapping file on his computer and exploded the scale until he selected a quiet spot off Route

19 at Surplus Lane, 1.5 miles north of Camera One. That was where private investigator Gerry Marsh was going to wait.

From that spot, Marsh could see up and down the highway in both directions and spot a red Toyota 4Runner from a half-mile out. Cameras could only get them close; he needed feet on the ground. Bishop had thought ahead and hired Marsh, charging a $500 retainer to an untraceable offshore Amex account.

"I hope you bring your coffee," Bishop said to himself.

He picked up his telephone then stared at it, suddenly realizing that Nussbaum and his three stooges had the capability to listen in on everything he said.

*****

Gerry Marsh got most of his work from insurance companies. He sat outside houses and bowling alleys and golf courses with his telephoto lens, taking pictures of the never-ending supply of soft-tissue damaged victims of car accidents and workplace injury claims. But he was heading toward a blood clot or a heart attack for the sixteen dollars an hour, sitting eight hours at a stretch and peeing into a bottle. Plus he waited a ninety-day lag time between invoice and payment. On top of all that, at the investigators convention he learned that the insurance companies employing him also hired in-house investigators to investigate their contract investigators to keep the billable hours honest. If their guys ever wrote you up, then that was it—you were cooked. Not another insurance company anywhere would hire you. Not in this lifetime. Marsh had a hard time maintaining professional indifference when Bishop had offered to hire him at eighty dollars per hour and put a five hundred dollar retainer onto a credit card on the spot.

He had to follow a young blonde gal, multiple tattoos, face and neck, to locate some forty-year-old male, six feet, slim, brown hair, and possible beard. Significant limps, both legs. May be riding a black Honda motorcycle. He had sharp color images of both faces committed to memory and full-page print copies.

"Score!" Stephen shouted. Camera One got a hit at 15:34; Felicia Diane Reynolds driving the red Toyota 4Runner heading north on Route 19 in the right-hand lane. On Marsh's end, the text came through long after Mouse had turned off Route 19. Marsh waited and watched for the 4Runner.

A quarter-mile south of Surplus Lane he picked up the visual and looked at the oncoming Toyota through a twenty-inch long telephoto lens. Marsh put down the camera and texted Bishop. **I see her. Will follow after she passes.**

He hit send as the 4Runner passed him, then pulled his silver Ford Taurus onto the highway well behind her SUV. It wasn't hard to keep her in view, not with a load of white PVC plastic pipe sticking out her back and a red plastic flag bouncing up and down, practically waving *"Here I am!"*

Mouse parked the Toyota outside the Glen Jean hardware store and she and XMercy got out of the car. Marsh shot the two of them together and kept his finger on the button through a set of close-ups, then put the camera down on the passenger seat and pulled the Taurus alongside an old warehouse across the street. Satisfied that he could see back to the front doors, he settled in, twisting open his Thermos flask and taking a sip of coffee straight out of it.

They came back out quickly, along with a third woman, older, attractive with long silver hair. He watched in the rearview mirror. The one with the hippie clothes and wild hair tore something in her hands and handed half to the blonde, then took a bite and did a little dance. From there, he couldn't tell what it was. A donut? Maybe an éclair. The blond took tiny nibbles.

Minutes later, Marsh was following them north along Scarbro Road, heading nearly out to the Whipple Company store, before they turned off. There wasn't another car on the road so he held the Taurus way back to keep from looking conspicuous. After the turnoff, he kept the red flag flying off the tails of the white plastic pipes in sight and relied on the cloud of dust coming off the dirt road to shield him from being seen.

They drove near on a mile out into the hills and suddenly they were gone. He drove past every lane and driveway that he crossed the road and he would have lost them entirely if the dry weather hadn't saved him. He spotted their dust coming up through the trees just about where he had lost sight of them and backtracked, turning in and slowly proceeding along a rough driveway until he saw the 4Runner parked in front of a faded old single-wide.

He backed the car away, back toward the county road; even in summertime he wouldn't trust pulling off into any of the muck and mush along that driveway.

Marsh picked his phone off his console, hoping. Zero bars, of course. No GPS coordinates. No web connection either.

Marsh opened his sports jacket and removed his Model 686 Plus, opened the Smith and Wesson, and confirmed seven rounds before snapping his wrist to lock back the cylinder. He took two nitrile gloves from a box in the glove compartment and tugged them onto his thick hands before returning the revolver to his shoulder holster and opening the car door. Parking way out alongside a county road has its good side and it has its bad. On the good side, there's hardly anybody around to see you. Then on the bad side, there's hardly anybody around to see you. He was on his own, knowing that anybody who did happen by would know right away that he was there. He reached for the trunk release before getting out.

Marsh always carried camo gear with him inside the trunk, that and a twelve-gauge shotgun with birdshot and a box of slugs plus a new fifty-round plastic box of bullets for the .357.

Marsh took off his tie and folded it over before putting it into a jacket pocket, then took off the jacket and folded it over before laying it down on the mat that covered his spare tire. Sitting on the rear bumper, he slipped off one Thom McAn and stepped into a leg of the camouflage bib overalls, then pulled a rubber boot on and repeated the same with the other leg before standing up and pulling up the raingear. The hooded jacket came next, followed by a nylon facemask. He looked back at the shotgun, thought about it, then shut the trunk, leaving it behind, but not before gathering a handful of the pistol cartridges.

He opened the country mailbox and rifled quickly down through the pile without seeing anything addressed to any Felicia Diane Reynolds. Junk mail, mostly. He took a postcard from the Jiffy Lube to have the address then returned to the car for his cell phone. He checked to make sure that there was nothing tempting in sight then locked the trunk access and the car doors.

Marsh worked his way inside the tree line, trying to come up as close to the trailer as he could. He only made it seventy-five feet before he walked straight into a line of razor wire that damned near tore him up good. Then he saw the greenhouse and understood; he couldn't hardly hunt the hills anymore without stumbling on somebody's grow or still or a trash-strewn meth lab.

He backed toward the driveway, moving more carefully now and watching for trip lines and booby traps. Lots of war vets were living all across southern West Virginia. Backing along the driveway, the best he could do was to move fast and depend on the camouflage. He was nearly there when the door to the single-wide opened. The hippie woman looked straight at him and retreated back inside, slamming the door and screeching.

"Crap," Marsh uttered under his breath. He jogged into the trees on the far side of the driveway, sinking his feet into the mush. The blonde came outside carrying a small-bore rifle like she meant business. Marsh put his hand inside the overalls, wrapping his fingers around the .357's grip but leaving the stainless steel hidden. His index finger touched on the safety.

"You really saw a bear?" Mouse called inside the trailer.

"Yes!"

"A bear, middle of the day? You sure?" she asked. "Describe it."

"It was big. Brown and green. You come back in here and stop scaring me."

"I'm scaring you?" she replied. "You're the one seeing bears. Green bears." She climbed back inside, barrel down, and shut the front door behind her.

Marsh waited a full five minutes then made his way past the trailer and tiptoed across the gravel to decaying leaves and soft dirt. He listened, hearing the voices of two women but no man. First, they talked about the bear until they were both laughing about it. Marsh had nearly reached the conclusion that he was chasing a dry lead when he bumped into the blue tarp. Underneath it he found a black Honda motorcycle. He took two photos of the VIN with his cell camera then made a wide loop back to the Taurus. The minute he got back onto

Route 19, he picked up three bars. Seconds later, he was sending the photos along with text confirmation.

Good work. Go back to Charleston. We'll be using your services again. Bishop hit send, removed the sim card and broke it in two, then tied the phone inside a plastic bag and disposed of both.

"I have him," Bishop told Jeffers over another phone. "Helicopter and team are ready to go airborne." *Upon receipt of funds.* "I didn't need your New York cop or your mystery man coming all the way from Kabul," he added. "I said I'd find him, didn't I?!"

*****

"Mouse, get the door! I'm up to my wrists in cake batter. Mouse!" XMercy listened for a response then slid most of the batter off her fingers and ran her hands under the sink.

There was no one there when she opened the door. Just fishing poles leaning against the siding, a tackle box on the ground beside them, and her wicker creel there on the top step. She poked her head out and caught Johnny's shoulders and the back of his head as he moved away through the meadow grass. The creel had some heft when she lifted it. Opening the lid like a treasure box, she smiled wide and counted out six beautiful rainbow trout, already cleaned and pan-ready.

"Yes! Good day!" She danced her way back into the trailer. "Johnny Johnny Johnny!"

Spencer lifted the door to the shallow cabinet above his bed and reached around until he felt what he wanted, a pair of dark gray sweat pants XMercy had lent him to wear while his freshly-washed blue jeans dried on the line. He felt like running, something he knew that he probably shouldn't be doing, but he could resist the urge. It was like taking a convertible out from a spin on the first sunny day after a cold winter. His legs had color; the wounds had scarred over into thick solid tissue that wasn't going to split open.

He wanted to sweat. He put a big hooded sweatshirt that was roomy enough to let him pump his arms in it, getting his whole body moving. The shoes were a little small but he had them laced loosely at the toes and decided he would get away with it. XMercy could pick up a pair of size thirteens for him the next time she went into Beckley. *I still have a little cash*, he reminded himself.

A root-covered embankment of dark rich soil rose six feet up from the edge of the meadow. Above that, the thickly treed slope took a thirty-degree angle upward for a hundred yards then pitched upward more steeply for another thirty yards before peaking at a rocky, exposed ridge. Spencer pulled up the hood, tightened the lanyard, bobbed on his toes, stretched his arms wide, wider, until they were nearly parallel behind him, then rocked back off his heels and exploded forward, taking the embankment in a single leap. He punched off his landing foot, and attacked up the hillside, driving his thighs, forcing his knees to pump, his ankles to lever, pushing, pressing, and taking in the moment with every breath. At the crest, he spun without braking and plunged downhill, picking his footfalls at breakneck speed that nearly catapulted him off the embankment and would have let him fly if he hadn't caught a tree limb to stop himself. He panted, breathing hard, smiled and pushed up a second time, demanding his limbs to work together, coordinating arms and legs around mind and core, defining the purpose and the value of each to the whole.

This time when he reached the ridge, he turned to take in the vista, seeing out to Glen Jean and imagining the river beyond. He could hear the hum of traffic along the highway, blending like cicadas into one living buzz. Then, coming in from the south, he heard the unmistakable deep tut-tut-tut-tut of a helicopter on approach. The shiver ran up from his anus into his throat. He blew it out his mouth, re-centered, then squinted, watching to identify the make and model and fighting against the feeling pulling at him to curl up behind the first big rock.

The helicopter was big, but it was a single-rotor civilian aircraft, all black, non-military.

Going back down, this time he varied speeds, cutting zigzag paths between the trees, concentrating to test for body control and lateral turns, shifting like an elusive running back avoiding tacklers. Nearing the embankment, he leapt, reaching both hands around a high branch, and let himself hang there, feeling his hips and pelvis, vertebrae, ribs, armpits, wrists and hands.

The sound was louder now, several times louder. He couldn't see anything, but when he let go and dropped he felt the vibrations pulsing around him and instinctively moved behind cover.

It came in low, skimming the treetops before spinning around to dissipate momentum and drop inside the meadow. The whole trailer shook. XMercy leaned over the trout in the sink, looked out from the kitchen window, didn't believe her eyes, and moved to another window to see if that changed what she was seeing outside.

Black-uniformed, helmeted men exited fast. Spencer recognized the set movements, appreciated the training as the six-man squad efficiently cleared the fuselage the instant the skids touched ground. They fanned into a 3-1-2, the first three spreading apart then sprinting toward the trailer. A fourth soldier trailed out to the left. The fifth and sixth, both security, moved wide, one heading toward the driveway, the other directly on a path straight toward him. They were capable, decisive, a well-oiled machine. Matte black from boot to helmet, everything cinched tight with nothing flapping. *I could be leading them*, he thought.

The pilot kept the helicopter idling, which muffled all other sounds, but in his head he could imagine the TL calling out fine adjustments, the ATL encouraging, one to six, each one calling his number when he had taken his position. One, Two, Three, Five and Six carried Heckler & Koch HKMP5s, stubby automatics, light and effective for up to medium-range fire. From where he watched, Four looked to be slinging a Remington 870. The pistol grip stood out from two hundred yards.

Spencer flattened himself low along the base of a twisted clump of laurel shrubbery. *No Identification.* NO SWAT or FBI, ATF or any other law enforcement lettering. They were almost to the trailer; he watched Four, carrying the shotgun, break around toward the back of the trailer.

They had come for him. Spencer looked around him for rocks, logs, anything he could use as he watched them center themselves. Nothing was anywhere within reach. The TL and ATL spread on both sides of the doorframe and nodded, confirming readiness ahead of the rush-assault that Spencer could see coming. He could only watch, crouching low to make himself small.

Three hit the door at full run, crushing the aluminum frame inward into the trailer and landing atop the broken door. Flash grenades boomed a split-second later.

The soldier approaching him grabbed hold of an exposed root and pulled himself up the embankment, swung behind a tree, sighted the Heckler-Koch across the meadow along a fast forty-five degree arc of fire, called "Six!" into his headset and reset his boots more comfortably. Six had his earpiece cranked up like an iPod. Spencer, who was within two strides of Six, could hear them shouting inside the trailer.

*****

XMercy stood paralyzed in shock. Her front door was destroyed; the flash grenades left her barely able to see the outlines of men with guns thundering into her home.

Mouse came out from her bedroom, saw the chaos, and was instantly pissed. "What the fuck?" she screamed. "You fucking Nazis! Over a little weed!"

Three had rolled to his feet and caught her, and with one arm threw her off her feet onto the banquette. She slid to a stop with her back against the wall, and was kicking her feet to get back up when he snapped his rifle stock into her face, shattering all the cartilage in her nose.

XMercy, who had never seen blood come out of anyone, not like that, like red milk spilling out a carton, stood with her mouth wide-open, paralyzed.

"Jonathan Spencer!" the Team Leader yelled out. Three raised his weapon high, his cheek rigid on the stock; Curtis and Profitt lowered theirs to belt level.

XMercy stared at Mouse, wanting to move but her body wouldn't respond.

Mouse glared at the green eyes and the bridge of the nose inside the helmet; the rest of his facial features were hidden inside a black cover hood.

"Jonathan Spencer!" Profitt echoed. "Where is he?"

Spencer listened and watched as Five took up a security position along the driveway two-hundred-forty yards away.

Curtis lifted his weapon and pointed the barrel at Mouse's bleeding face. Her eyes instantly dilated. XMercy remained confused. When he shifted the weapon around to XMercy, her eyes failed to indicate any understanding.

A single pop sounded. XMercy's knees collapsed; she fell like a building imploding upon detonation, a lump, a heap. Dead. Instantly.

Inside the singlewide, Mouse sprang like a panther, leaping at Curtis's face and driving her fingers inside at his eyes. He brought the HK up lengthwise using both of his arms, striking hard under her chin. The force snapped her upper front teeth and lifted her slight frame up and off her feet.

Curtis straddled her. "You want to live?" he demanded. Mouse kicked up at his crotch. He responded by bringing the butt of his weapon down against her kneecap, cracking it in two. "Spencer! Where is he?" Before waiting even a second, Curtis pressed his boot onto the knee and concentrated his two hundred pounds. "Spencer!"

XMercy's dead limbs shook from nervous contractions. Her thigh bumped into Mouse's cheek.

"You want to live, nod your head," Curtis shouted down at Mouse. "Hey! Focus!"

Mouse reacted, never nodding but raising her eyes toward the Team Leader. "He," she tried to think. Too much was happening at once. "He was fishing. The ATV. He had the ATV."

Profitt nodded toward the fresh trout lying in the sink. The Team Leader acknowledged.

"ATV is here," Four confirmed. "Behind the trailer. Black Honda here, too."

Curtis lifted his HK, angling it down and pressing the barrel hard against Mouse's forehead.

"Do you want to end up like your friend?" he warned. "Where?!"

"Guest house," she stammered. "The camper. Down the meadow."

*****

Spencer knew that Mercy was gone; it was on him, all of it, only he had no time for emotion. Mouse was still alive.

Training fundamentals kicked in. *When attacking a better-armed, better-equipped, better-positioned enemy, the body functions on experience. Focus. Fluid motion.*

Panther-like, Spencer concentrated his spring on the single point in the exposed neck where the C2 and C3 vertebrae meet, the locus for every nerve controlling the head, neck, and diaphragm. He clamped his right fist rigid inside his left hand. The point of his elbow concentrated nine hundred PSI—the ball peen hammer, the bludgeon spear, nine hundred pounds per square inch concentrated from his hips and torso entirely into one thrust point.

Six, sensing movement, had instincts, too, a hair less practiced; adrenaline-addled, possibly just having an off day. He turned in time to throw Spencer off-target and got a harmless shot off into the branches above them. Spencer's elbow blow shattered Six's clavicle.

Before Six could correct, Spencer used the pad of his left hand to drive down into C3. His right fist simultaneously jammed upward from below the jaw. The opposing forces cracked through the commando's spine.

Spencer had Six's Heckler-Koch unslung before Six's brain had responded to the blow. It was an MP5K-PDW, he noted at a glance. He methodically shifted from trigger group 2 to 1, swung upward, and took aim across the meadow. Five had positioned himself onto one knee, fanning up the driveway and across the meadow. BRASS. He fired, taking Five in his exposed left shoulder, six inches to the right of Spencer's center-chest target. The HK hadn't been properly sighted. *Lazy,* Spencer thought.

The walloping impact slapped Five onto his back but Five handled himself solidly, professionally, recovering fluidly, rolling to a prone position and pressing tight to the nearest tree. Spencer watched him raise the weapon with his one good arm, scanning through its scope.

"Contact!" Five shouted.

Spencer heard Five through Six's earpiece. He sighted inside one-half-increment left this time and fired again. *Center face.*

The pilot saw Five drop. He leaned forward into the cockpit canopy and spotted Spencer in Six's position then jerked back, getting himself out of view.

The rotors came to life, accelerating for readiness to lift off.

"Contact!" echoed Four, who dove beneath the trailer. His 870, all about blunt force, was useless at longer range.

Spencer's hands moved fast. He measured his breathing while he patted down Six, taking out two additional magazines and feeling foreign objects: a wallet, car keys, a cell phone. These were possessions no sniper squad would ever carry into combat. *Military, but not military.*

Spencer tossed the keys aside, but quickly shoved the wallet and cell phone into the sweatshirt, then yanked off the headset and the receiver to which it was attached.

"One!" Curtis yelled. Two, Three, and Four responded in order. No Five. Spencer supplied "Six!"

Matt, the big horse, blinked in response after his Team Leader nodded toward Mouse. She was hunched over, nursing her cracked kneecap when he jammed his rifle butt into her, crushing down at her lower back. Mouse's chin smacked against the kitchen floor, splitting open. Blood flowed from her nose, her broken teeth, and more now gushed from the two-inch gash on her chin. XMercy's dead eyes stared back at her from the floor. Her hand was flopped nearly within reach.

Curtis, Profitt, and Matt jumped over the front steps. All three moved out fast without looking back, triple-timing along the driveway and staying close to the trees on their way toward Five's position.

The trailer shook like an earthquake as the three men ran past the twisted doorframe, stomped the threshold and leapt outside. Their helmets moved left and they were gone.

Mouse could feel the warm rush of her blood flowing down her neck. Oddly, the knee had stopping hurting. She tried to gather her legs underneath her to stand. Nothing happened. A total disconnect. Her body had vanished from her stomach down to her toes.

Mouse stuck her tongue out and tasted the blood. She inhaled deeply and pressed her torso into a pushup, dragging her body toward the sunlight. They were out there, the men, but they no longer mattered to her.

With two more desperate tugs, her fingers caught hold of the frame on the metal entry steps. Her breathing was labored. She knew, yet nothing processed, nothing except her need to get outside. Mouse heaved her weight forward, tumbling hard over the steps until she was settled, face-up, looking into the blue sky. She had no idea that her legs were akimbo.

Four listened through the headset and burst out from behind the trailer. Before Spencer could react, Four had tossed a large canister inside the obliterated doorframe.

BRASS. Breathe, Relax, Aim, Stop, Squeeze. Spencer's bullet caught Four mid-stride as he hauled ass down the driveway with the big shotgun, trying to catch up to the others. The shot pierced beneath the right earlobe, entering the brain stem and killing the brain while the body continued running. After three steps, Billy flopped sideways. The soles of his boots dug into the ground beside the gravel.

A loud, hollow boom raised Spencer's eyes toward Mercy's trailer. The siding had blown away. Sections of roof were lifted sixty feet up in a roiling inferno, churning jet-black smoke. The roof drifted back in slow motion, floating down like sheet metal sails.

Mouse's exposed skin shriveled like plastic in a microwave oven as the heat flashed over her. Her lips, nose, and eyelids were seared instantly. Her blackened legs were even worse, covered by bubbling pustules that stretched and burst like fat boiling in a cauldron. Fire raced up individual hairs on her head like sparklers. A sheet of hot metal landed on top of her.

*****

"It's the wrong way,'" their pilot screamed into his mic. "You're going the wrong way." Curtis, Profitt, and Matt were facing ahead. They missed it; only the pilot saw Four drop.

"One!"

"Two!"

"Three!"

"Six!"

"No!" their pilot screamed. "Not Six! Six is down. Repeat. Six is down!"

Spencer switched the trigger setting onto automatic fire then rose from cover and emptied the remaining clip into the fuselage where the tail boom connected behind the main bay. In every helicopter he knew, that was where the fuel tank was situated.

The spot where he had just been standing crackled with incoming rounds. In the meadow below, the pilot lifted his skids off the ground and dropped them again; no fucking around, he was leaving whether they boarded or not. "Get the fuck on because I'm gone. Now! You hear me? Now!"

The open slide door was on the opposite side of the chopper; Spencer sighted but could see only boots hitting the far skid as One, Two, and Three flung themselves on. The pilot pulled back on his joystick and lifted airborne.

Spencer glanced back toward the flaming trailer and then rushed down the berm, out into the open meadow, dropping the spent clip in full stride. While the helicopter elevated, Spencer set his feet and fired again, continuing to concentrate his aim on the fuel tank.

"Crap," the pilot exclaimed. He knew right away that Spencer's fire had cut through the fuel line. The engine was stalling, starved for fuel just as he demanded maximum power. He had no time to explain the dynamics of RPM and lift, or how no helicopter pilot in the world could respond to a dead stick at seventy feet. "Brace!" he shouted behind him. "Hard landing!"

The skids slammed into the grow site's soft newly worked soil. One of the rotor blades cracked against the hickory tree; the collision shifted its velocity, spinning it backwards, obliterating the cockpit and cutting the pilot in half. It continued flying through the trees, leaving nothing behind, no pilot, no controls, only a metal-framed aperture covered by a red spray where the front of the helicopter had been. When the tail spun around, the rotor caught the greenhouse, wrapping layers of clear plastic and black plastic sheeting around the tail boom. It continued to spin, snapping through the plastic, making the sound of baseball cards on bicycle spokes. The skids caught on the newly stretched concertina wire, balling around the cabin's battered fuselage in a lethal mess.

Profitt felt his pelvis snap at impact. Compression fractures crushed every lumbar vertebra. His mic was caught against his shirt collar. "I'm fucked," he tried to call out, but he could only puff into it; the pain left him unable to move even his jaw.

"Hold tight, Terry," Three called. He reached out, but the Assistant Team Leader blinked his red eyes to tell him not to touch.

Three was whole. Bruised, but operational. He felt one rib crunch as he lifted his Team Leader up off the helicopter's deck, but he nodded at One that he was good; he could handle it. For a few seconds, the helicopter thrashed, metal screeched, plastic flapped like tarps in a windstorm. Then all was silent.

"Boss?" Three called out, getting his face in front of his TL for orders. Curtis was concentrating his senses to fight past pain. He felt like a red hot metal rod had been pushed through his right knee.

Anterior cruciate ligament and medial collateral ligament had burst like breaking rubber bands. He didn't need to touch it to know his patella was floating freely just beneath the skin. He laughed. "Fuck me."

He could manage, nodding aggressively. "I'm good." He was still in the fight.

Matt pressed his gun barrel into the crack to force open the sliding door. He could pry it just eight inches. The stench of fuel wafted inside. He pulled off his helmet and tossed it aside to get better air.

The TL pulled Three back from the narrow opening. He pressed his remaining clip into Three's hand then patted Two for his ATL's remaining ammunition. Two stretched his jaw wide, screaming without a sound when Curtis touched him. "Sorry Terry. Got to."

He retrieved two more magazines, slapping them into Three's palm, their eyes meeting as he exerted himself to command, to control, himself. "When I fire, go!" he instructed almost gently. "Lay down cover. I'll follow. We go get this fucker and then we come back for Terry."

Three nodded then Curtis turned and stretched his weapon out into the door, opening fire in scattered waist-level bursts. He reached back and slapped Three on the back, who dived through the open hatch where the cockpit had been, already firing before his heavy frame hit the dirt.

Spencer sprinted over the driveway to Five, flipped him onto his back and rapidly patted up and down his torso, snatching clips, wallet, cell phone, a serrated combat blade, two canister grenades, identifying scattered bursts from two separate HKs. Their buffering fire disgusted him; trained men blindly wasting critical ammo, firing at nothing to show their force. What they really conveyed was desperation.

He maneuvered at a bent run toward the crash site, letting them continue to burn through their clips. Spencer moved along behind the two long poplar trunks, efficiently flanking them. Working his way to the embankment, he squatted low behind laurels and gooseberry bushes until the tangled crash site opened out in front of him. Through the trees he could see torn plastic sheeting flapping from the tail rotor like a shredded flag.

Three, the biggest body on their squad, the one who took down the trailer door, was stomach-down in a prone firing position with his legs opened behind him in a wide vee. He was aiming a full 180 degrees opposite from Spencer's position.

Spencer held the Heckler-Koch to his cheek and rose, firing a burst that strafed an impact line running from Three's crotch up his spine. A bullet burst his skull like a watermelon, splattering brains in a six-foot wide fan. The blood mist speckled red over the green foliage.

Spencer fired a following burst through the cockpit hatch into the fuselage. As he ran past the wreck, he pitched the canister grenade inside backhand before diving for cover behind the hickory's trunk.

Profitt, Two, saw the grenade land at his feet. His eyes opened wide, only his limbs wouldn't respond. Curtis, the Team Leader, turned and stretched out his leg, reaching his foot toward the grenade, missing. In one do-or-die motion he lunged and managed to clear the canister out of the fuselage. His effort amounted to nothing. The combustible fumes coming from forty gallons of leaking fuel ignited in a soft *whoosh* that shook the forest. A red-hot ball roiled skyward, leaving only scarred skeletal remains behind, human and machine.

*****

Spencer got up and ran hard toward the blackened floor and gnarled metal that had been the single-wide home, had been XMercy's home. He stopped on the way, kneeling and rapidly patting down Four's body. One hip pouch held twenty twelve-gauge shells, slugs. He considered the shotgun, rejected it, and kept searching without a pause. Wallet. Cell phone. Multi-tool.

The Honda motorcycle was gone. Spencer could see what remained of the blue tarp. It was melted black over what looked like a giant spider that had been put to the flames. The Polaris was on fire. But through the burnt skeleton of the trailer, it looked like the 4Runner was still intact. It was scorched black all along the passenger side, but the tires remained inflated, the windows were in one piece.

He started moving toward the SUV when movement caught the corner of his eye. Something was alive, caught beneath a section of charred metal siding.

Spencer flipped the siding clear and recoiled from the grizzled, unrecognizable sight before squatting to bring his face close. His brain told him that it was impossible, that the cooked flesh could not be alive.

"Mouse? Can you hear me?" He wasn't certain that her ears remained.

"Humm," Mouse whimpered.

Alarm bells sounding from the direction of Glen Jean were ringing, calling for the volunteer firefighters.

"There's help coming," he told her.

"Why?" she asked him. Her voice was an airy whine.

"I'm sorry. God, I'm so sorry."

"Why?" Mouse repeated.

"Me," he admitted. "They came for me." Spencer lifted his ears. In the distance he could hear a siren. "It's my fault! I'm sorry, Mouse. I'm so sorry!"

"Buh why?" she panted.

"Because I am Dimitri Vosilych," he whispered into her ear. "I did it. All of it."

Mouse's lungs deflated in a long dry wheeze. Spencer rose onto one knee. She was gone.

Did she hear him?

He scanned around him, taking in the smoldering trailer, the burning helicopter wreckage; Four's prone body face-down in the gravel.

"You dumbass," he cursed himself. "Like you could stop everything and get away. You caused this!"

The approaching sirens were getting louder. For a second, he considered sitting down, giving up. Then his training took over. Spencer blew out his lungs, inhaled, and centered himself.

Never give up!

He moved the 4Runner, dropped the Heckler-Koch onto the passenger seat, heaped atop the additional clips, cell phones, and wallets. The car keys dropped into his hands when he let down the visor.

It started on the first try.

He assessed its worthiness on the fly, reversing and spinning the wheels around the wreckage. On the driveway, he shifted and plunged the pedal down to the floor.

Four minutes from start to finish, he calculated. *Six combatants plus pilot.* He had done that.

"Get it together," he shouted. The adrenalin crash was standard; massive secretions had to be dissipating from his system, but he had no time to reflect on what was normal and what wasn't.

Mission mode. He raced down the gravel to get out before first responders arrived then jammed the brakes. He had nearly missed it and was suddenly furious at himself, screeching the 4Runner to a stop. All three cell phones were powered up.

"Dumbass! You're delivering a GPS trail!"

He pulled the sim cards out from each phone and separated the batteries to keep them from pinging location, then gunned the motor. Debriefing would have to come later, if he ever had the time. Right now, he needed to make distance.

Route 19, two lanes north and two south, offered the faster path, but red and blue police lights flashed in the rear view mirror, moving toward the farm. He swung the 4Runner past the hardware store where a crowd eating maple bars stood outside looking to the northwest. The volunteer firefighters fired up the one engine as he went by. In a minute he was across Glen Jean, heading east alongside Dunloup Creek past the spot where he had caught the trout only a few short hours before.

*****

You let yourself dream. He sped along, traveling at ninety miles per hour. His ankle and knee were serviceable as he worked the pedals, braking minimally along curves and passing everything that came up ahead of him. He continued east along the New River east and north on a long loop that took him back to the west before it crossed Route 19 fifteen miles north of the farm. On 19, he continued speeding northbound; sheriffs and state police had converged on Glen Jean from Beckley, Charleston, and as far away as Morgantown, leaving him a nearly empty highway with ten miles to the county line. Radio reporting was already focusing on the scourge of drug activity after a deadly shootout and explosions rocked this bucolic section of Fayette County. But no mention of his name.

"I am Dimitri Vosilych," he said to himself. The prison, the waterboarding, a trained commando unit with no insignia. He pulled onto a side road after a signpost showed a mile before the junction to Highway 79; he needed to do the math; as it was, he was only going away, not moving toward anything at all. *Jesus, Mercy. Aw, Mouse.*

All three wallets held North Carolina driving licenses; Fayetteville, NC, addresses, all within spitting distance of Bragg. He should have taken the time to look at their arms; he would have bet money on them being a sword and three lightning bolts; he could recognize Special Forces from a mile away.

Their credit cards were worthless to him; he might as well tell them right where to find him. Almost eleven hundred in cash that he tried to pocket before realizing the sweat pants had no pockets. He folded the bills and pushed the wad past the Emporio waistband down inside his briefs.

No company cards, no family photos. *Black Ops or private?* They had broadcast their intentions. He wasn't giving them any more consideration than they would have given to him.

"You were after me! Me, not them! You motherfuckers!"

Commandos follow orders. Whatever they did, they were the extended arm of whoever had made him disappear, whoever had the pull to run a torture prison literally under the government's nose. Whoever that was, they would never quit. They would buy more hired guns and keep coming.

"I would have let it go," Spencer realized. "But not now. Not ever." They weren't going to leave him alone. He wasn't ever going to disappear, to live a quiet life. He was going to die. He knew that. All he could hope to do was die on his own terms.

Spencer reached over to the passenger seat, tilted the HK, and released the clip. He counted out four rounds, then replaced a fresh mag and switched the trigger setting from 4 to 2, semi-automatic. He pushed all but two of the credit cards and IDs into the wallets, opened the window, and tossed them deep into the bushes. He had plenty of cash. The tank was only a quarter-full; he would get food and water when he bought gas.

"They didn't put out an APB before." He was betting that they would keep law enforcement out of it now, too. With four hundred miles to cover, he counted on that bet to get him through.

He knew where he had to go; he had a long night ahead crossing Pennsylvania. By morning, he could be back to New York. By morning he intended to be crossing the bridge into Tarrytown. First order of business: he had to get a real weapon. The HK was for close-quarters work. He was coming for the Barrett.

"XMercy and Mouse aren't anybody's 'collateral damage,'" he determined aloud. "They were my friends. I'm done with running away."

CHAPTER NINETEEN

"There is never going to be a better time than now," Jeffers said in his introduction to the assembled Vision Partners. "Some would argue that we should put our tails between our legs and lie low, but we have nothing to apologize about and we are not adopting a victim mentality! The takers, the do-nothing losers who want to drain our economic lifeblood, they always attack those whose hard work and vision makes us successful! I am proud to announce that Americans for Patriotic Action, along with the American Legislation Network, will be putting forward legislation in all fifty states, in Washington, D.C., and in Congress, to secure the rights of all American citizens to be free from discrimination based upon our economic status.

"We, Vision Partners, we are going to send this message loud and clear: Class warfare is a hate crime! Americans never need to apologize for success!"

*****

Owen couldn't raise Bishop by telephone. He tried getting Miller on the hotel phone and cell phone; both times he was answered by automated voicemail: "the guest is not available, please leave your message at the tone."

"Damn it!" Owen yelled. "I'm not here to sit in a hotel room!"

Miller wasn't available because he was fully engaged in a video-conference, seated on the guest-side of Jeffers' giant oak desk and speaking to Jeffers' image on the monitor while APA's leader was in flight. Jeffers was returning from a triumphant monthly meeting only to have his mood spoiled.

"Seven men dead," Jeffers noted miserably.

"And two women," Miller added. He had been fully briefed.

"Let's say the entire operation has been crude," Miller continued, "to keep the conversation polite. I have never met Mr. Rooks Bishop. All I can say is your sheriff left a trail of breadcrumbs leading right back to your desk here. He flew commercially, rented a car and a truck in his own name, and multiple witnesses can tie him to the death of Felicia Diane Reynolds. That moves Bishop from the asset column to a liability, and I don't like loose ends."

Jeffers paused, considering. Miller pitched before he came to the obvious conclusion.

"I'll say it bluntly because I don't think you'll respect anything less. I get it. You've got yourself in a pickle. Every lie, every manipulation, every move you make, you get in deeper. You're way outside your comfort zone, you have a lot to lose, and you need all of this to go away. So I'll be your Mr. Wolf and I'll clean up this mess. I'll make it all go away. Secret prisons, enhanced interrogation, and this laundry list of federal, state, and international felonies that can't be folded behind the corporate veil. Not even you can pull that off," Miller said. "Spencer just took down a six-man assault team. It is going to get uglier; I don't need to tell you that.

"I'll find him and I'll kill him for you, period. Make him disappear. My fee is $2.5 million, $500,000 up front, paid into an account that I'll provide immediately, with an additional $2.5 million to follow upon delivery." Downtime and good meals aside, he hadn't left a good thing in Afghanistan with a short remaining shelf life to do real work for spare change. "Those are my terms. That's about one percent of your gross this year. A rounding error. We both know his weapons stash was never uncovered. My hunch is he is right on it just about now. It's going to get downright exciting, I'd say, but until I see money and support, I'll be finding a quiet corner and taking a nice long nap."

"And what about Bishop?" Jeffers wanted to know.

Miller considered momentarily then responded on the fly. "Bishop is fungible; he's an anachronism, a superfluous Good Old Boy. And right now he's a speed bump getting in the way.

"Remind him that he has signed your Non-Disclosure Agreement and that all provisions remain in full force and will be enforced to the fullest measure if he discusses his employment with anyone. Tell him that he will still be paid, but that he needs to disappear until West Virginia blows over," Miller advised. "After that, have him leave the country. Give him airline tickets for a long vacation. Let's say Brazil or Thailand. Better yet, you let him choose. Tell him that final compensation will be wired to either location. Then get the destination and flight number to me."

He always paused ahead of making the conclusive close. "APA will never again see or hear from Rooks Bishop."

*****

Stephen Nussbaum's team continued tracking Spencer's movements. Kip, the fourth tech, reported the first probable sighting when Spencer stopped at a Marathon Gas Station outside Cumberland, Virginia. The second hit came through by auto-text. Spencer ate at a Denny's just off the Pennsylvania Turnpike outside Harrisburg, Pennsylvania, at 3 a.m. No Bishop, not that it mattered.

They can only plot his whereabouts, Miller reminded Jeffers by text. Without an Operations Unit, they couldn't intercept Spencer. **He has just decimated your team.**

Miller intended to have his assets in place by 09:50. He texted: **Ready to get the job done. Still waiting on your wire.**

Based upon Spencer's present trajectory, Spencer was returning to the scene of the crime. Round 2.

Miller booked early morning flights, ExpressJet from Dulles-Newark.

They would be working from new facilities located in New Jersey. The techs were entirely portable; the Jersey warehouse had the one thing they required: screaming fast broadband. Miller located two of his Afghanistan snipers back at Ft. Bragg; he put them to work assembling separate fully outfitted six-man squads. He sub-contracted helicopter transport and was on task selecting a heliport to serve as their assembly point and the nearest cheap motel to put them up when they arrived.

"Where we heading?" Owen asked Miller.

"We're going to North Bergen."

"Proud home of James J. Braddock," Owen observed. "*The Cinderella Man*."

"What?"

"They made a movie," he began to explain, and then shrugged it off. "Nevermind," he told Miller.

*****

Miller read through the case files, FBI/NYPD/NSA. They were all delivered straight to his internal storage, which meant, to his conclusion, that "The Client" had roving access wherever they wanted to go. Bringing himself up to speed on the killings was straightforward enough. He harbored no doubt as to Spencer's capabilities; Spencer was an outstanding killing machine, proven time after time. *But why the "I Kill Rich People"?* he wondered. He couldn't make sense out of that one. Miller thought Spencer was a Boy Scout, never imagined Spencer was a lefty. Then again, he had literally dropped ten thousand dollars into Spencer's lap and he had passed on free money.

By all rights, Spencer should have been stabbed dead. If the Afghan hadn't failed, none of this would be happening. They would have folded the flag and given it to Spencer's next of kin. Case closed. He wouldn't have just had the best meal of his life a few hours ago, on Bishop's nickel, and he'd be light $2.5 million with $2.5 million more to come.

Thank you Afif, Miller thought.

"You want to kill this sonofabitch, right?!" Miller told Owen. "Your standard police procedures don't apply, so let them go. I don't want to hear about putting out any APB. City, state, and federal law enforcement aren't coming into play.

This gets buttoned down quietly. The people paying the freight want it that way and they get what they want. You got that?"

"Why?" Owen challenged.

"Again. Why all the secrecy? The last time, they left forty thousand cops in the dark. No APB, no suspect information whatsoever. A shoe size."

"You're the one who's been champing at the bit to get going," Miller snapped. "Cullen, it is what it is. You don't like it; you can go home right now."

"I still say having more eyes and more feet on the ground makes a difference," Owen insisted. "Tell me, how do you contain and apprehend without physical resources? Are we going to call in a drone strike for Christ's sake?"

"Maybe we will. Mine is not to reason why, mine is but to make them die," Miller said.

"Irish, you keep thinking like a NYPD detective, you're heading in the wrong direction. Last time I say this. You have any second thoughts, go home when this plane touches the runway. If you're still here, you better have your head in the game."

"He killed twenty-three people the last time," Owen reminded Miller, "Tremaine Bull, the last one, was my best friend. A six-man Black Ops team dropped on his head yesterday and he massacred them, plus their pilot. Ex-Special Forces. All dead."

"He killed my partner," Owen told Miller a second time. He didn't tell Miller the rest, how the case had messed up everything: career, family, everything that mattered.

"I've scanned the reports," Miller quipped. "Funny. He seemed more like the type to hole up in a tower and blast away in blaze of glory. Now he's got wannabes showing up in these Dimitri Vosilych clubs."

Miller found it interesting, engaging; he felt a rush like nothing he had sensed in months. With $2.5 million bouncing along a dead-cover trail outside the prying eyes of the IRS and NSA both, Afghanistan was already in his rearview mirror.

"Criminy," Owen exclaimed.

"Criminy?" Miller questioned.

"Something my father used to say."

Miller's eyes squared on Owen. "You need to get focused. We're keeping this one cozy, not bringing too many people to the party. This is going to be handled discretely, Irish."

I'm good," Owen affirmed. "All good."

"I had Spencer working on special assignments for me," Miller explained to Owen. "Not a friendly guy, certainly no conversationalist, but after six months you get to know things about a person. Spencer likes his habits. He did what I told him to do and he went about it meticulously, examining every tiny detail. He sticks to the formula, practices it like a religion, hours and hours and hours.

Me, I could never be in the military. I need to make sense of things, even when they boil down to the basics, greed and ego. I need that global picture. The military is about compartmentalized thinking; that's how you run a war that makes no sense to the men fighting it, men like Spencer learn to do their job and leave the thinking to others. That's how he got squared away for the next mission; he didn't think, he just did it. Thinkers contend with fight-or-flight; soldiers don't get to choose, ergo, soldiers better not think."

Not thinking holds a whole lot of appeal. Owen got that. Just accept the Lake Success bullshit and make life easier. *Keep ordering fake strawberries that taste like a thousand real strawberries put together into one.* Because real isn't good enough.

"He was in love with being the perfect army tool," Miller continued. "He worked his ass off to be all he could be, like the army was going to love him right back if he did that. Man... looking for love in all the wrong places..."

He leaned and looked up the airplane's narrow aisle. "What is this crap? No drink service?" He leaned back hard, shifting his attention back to Spencer.

"Get yourself ready for I Kill Rich People two," Miller told Owen, who was staring at his tray table.

Bishop was gone. Now Miller was in charge. And nothing about Miller added up. The drinking and the hookers Owen could understand; a government guy with an expense account. But the gourmet stuff, the diction, and Miller's clothes... none of that connected.

"Those couples next to us were saying they waited six months to get reservations," Owen commented. "How did you get us in?"

Miller chuckled under his breath. The plane flew through some bad air, getting bumpy. "I'd tell you," he started, "but--"

Owen finished the sentence for him: "But then I'd have to kill you."

He shook his head. "I never knew food could be like that, turned inside out and controlled. 'Magic,' my mom used to say. Magic." He loved it and it pissed him off; he was there for Jonathan Spencer. For Tremaine. What the hell did fancy food have to do with anything?

"Molecular gastronomy," Miller corrected. "Getting in there is simple math, by the way. That maître d', the guy at the restaurant podium, probably brings down fifty-K, tops. He takes in another Benjamin a night, tax-free, even one, and he's almost doubling his take-home pay. It ain't rocket science."

"Should food even be like that?" Owen asked. "Make your brain get all fired up? It's still just food, too, you know?"

Miller leaned again, on autopilot, looking up the aisle. "What kind of airline doesn't have drinks?" he grumbled.

Owen checked his watch. "It's six-thirty in the morning," he replied.

Miller shook his head. "Not in Afghanistan, pal." He threw up his hands and turned back to Owen.

"Take me through the attacks. Not the facts; I have ballistics, autopsies, victim profiles. Walk me through what distinguished your investigative approach. At least six state and federal task forces were after Spencer and nobody except you and your partner ever got close. How did you pull that off?"

Owen strained against his seat belt and looked around the tight airplane. "Not in here. Too many people."

"Secrets are overrated," Miller philosophized. "You want to know why secrets stay secret? It's not because people don't talk, it's because people don't listen. Oh, they care about gossip, celebrities and all that, but 99.9 percent of people don't understand and they don't give a shit about things that really matter. That's why."

Miller leaned his seat back and closed his eyes. "Keep your secret. If I can't get a fucking drink around here, I might as well be sleeping. Wake me in Jersey."

*****

Nobody shouted "Draw," but the second the airplane's wheels touched ground Dilip, Kip, Dale, and Stephen were a split-second apart in firing up their cell phones.

Stephen was checking texts when a new one came in. Jonathan Spencer had crossed the intersection of the 80 and 287, Parsippany-Troy Hills, New Jersey, at 04:51.

He planned to forward it to Bishop, and then realized that Bishop was off the project. He had no numbers for Miller and Cullen, the new consultants.

Each of the six received a text message with the address and their individual lock codes to open the doors into a non-descript tilt-up warehouse building.

Owen looked again at his watch. Just about then, the boys were leaving for school and Callie was heading to work. For Doctor Marc. They were less than forty-five minutes away, just cross Lower Manhattan and head up the Expressway.

Inside the stark interior, motion sensors automatically turned on the lights inside a secure lobby the size of a big elevator. Red LED lights turned to yellow when the outer door closed. Concrete floors, office space bolted together within a cavernous outer shell, generic furniture, glass offices along one outside wall. The singular distinguishing feature was a full-wall AV hub with a digital, multi-channel projector. Single green lights attached to cameras circled them on every wall. At the center of the open space was a bullpen.

The four techs had already checked broadband speeds and set up shop before Miller and Owen arrived.

"Last sighting was fifteen minutes ago," Stephen announced by way of greeting when Miller and Owen entered. "No," he corrected, "sixteen minutes ago.

"Twenty-three miles from here." Nussbaum plugged his laptop into the media hub and projected a huge map onto the white wall. A few keyboard taps later, he added in both the car and where Spencer's average speed would have taken him in sixteen minutes.

"Traffic density rises 40 percent coming into the city," Dale volunteered. Using his cursor as a pointer, he corrected for traffic and pinpointed Spencer's probable location. "He could be right here in a half-hour. That would make things easy."

"Be careful what you wish for," Miller muttered.

*****

The whole West Virginia episode had left Bishop's stomach queasy. Seven men dead, the two women, and no trace of Jonathan Spencer. The airplane ticket was a welcome relief. He appreciated that Jeffers had thought ahead. Jeffers was right, too. The flight from D.C. to West Virginia was booked in his name; the car rental was in his name. He had used an alias with the mother and with the private detective, but that one degree of separation wasn't nearly as good as the nine-thousand-mile flight he was on board.

He had never been to Thailand, but he had heard plenty. Everyone knew about middle-aged men traveling there.

He didn't have a wife to cheat on anymore; nothing at all was stopping him from enjoying whatever the country had to offer. The Marriot had a pool and a spa, but first thing on his agenda was sleep. He felt exhausted, wiped out straight to his core. Sleep for days maybe.

Delta. Thirteen hours and forty-five minutes to Narita, then another six-and-a-half hours to Bangkok. His hips barely fit between the armrests. The seat in front of him was reclined so now his tray table pressed into his gut unless he reclined, too. He read the in-flight magazine cover to cover, followed by the Sky Mall Catalogue, followed by five movies. He didn't follow a single plot.

He stood up and retrieved his bag out of the overhead compartment then made his way sideways to the toilets. Once inside, he slid the lock and the fluorescent lighting came on. Bishop took out his electric shaver and ran it across his face, shaving on autopilot while he followed in the mirror blankly through drooping, bloodshot eyes.

He undid his belt and unbuttoned his pants, tucked his shirt down deep, then sucked in his sour belly and buttoned again. He smelled his armpits, stopped, and pulled his shirttails out before opening up his shirtfront to apply deodorant.

The plane had bumped onto the tarmac and stopped before he realized that passengers were unbuckling their seatbelts and standing up. He shuffled after them as they herded out the ramp toward immigration. Immigration to baggage claim. Baggage claim to customs. Beyond customs, he saw his name written out in large capital letters: BISHOP. An Asian man wearing a black suit caught sight of him and reached out to take hold of his luggage.

Bishop didn't remember making arrangements for a driver, but followed the man out to the curb where a black Toyota Alphard luxury minivan with darkly tinted windows was waiting. The driver opened the sliding side door and put out a step stool. Bishop got inside and shut his eyes for a moment while the driver put his luggage into the trunk. The trunk hatch shut and then the driver got inside, seating himself behind the right-side steering wheel.

Bishop told him to drive to: "Radisson Hotel Sukhumvit."

Before he could react, another man jumped in beside him and slammed the sliding door and a third man got into the front passenger seat.

The man in the front passenger seat turned around as the van pulled into traffic. He pointed a revolver a foot in front of Bishop's red eyes.

"What is this?"

"You shut you mouth!" The man beside him screamed. "Hands in front of you!" He twisted a thick wire around Bishop's wrists and then stuffed a sock into Bishop's mouth. Bishop's eyes opened wide when he saw the black hood. He snapped his head side-to-side to keep the hood away. His futile effort brought an elbow cracking at the base of his skull.

*****

Spencer flipped license plates outside Harrisburg, Pennsylvania, and then again with New York plates he took from the lot behind a body repair in Suffern before getting on the Thruway. After driving the bridge across the Hudson, he pulled into the drive-through line at Jack-in-the-Box. He tugged the hood tight around his head and slouched below the dashboard, watching for anything out of place, any anomaly that might be trouble.

They killed Mercy and Mouse, he thought. *They had thrown me into hell. Right in Washington, D.C. No rights, no lawyer.*

Power. Raw, morbid, rotten power. He had recognized all along that he couldn't get them all; his random attacks impacted their entire category; it was the logical strategy, making for more target range, fewer ways for them to protect themselves, and more ways for him to hit them and get out alive. But he was a just a moth circling a flame, never attacking where the real power was centered.

That approach was all over. He was done with nipping at their flanks. Now, he wanted to see that one bullet, clean and true, hitting straight at the biggest snake of all of them: Vision Partners' founding member was so rich that he built bogus institutes to legitimize his own greed; he bombarded legislatures across the country, tying them up with hatred-breeding bills; he manipulated news and politics and even science. *One bullet!*

"A system that moves toward imbalance always needs to correct or it crashes out of control," Spencer recalled the captain saying, word for word. "We lose fairness, we lose faith in the system and, like the poet said 'things fall apart, the center cannot hold.' Johnny, somebody needs to stop them before we turn back to the Dark Ages. That's the main truth of our time."

"I'll do my part, Captain," Spencer promised.

"Excuse me?" the voice crackled through the speaker. "Can I take your order please?"

"Um…a steak and egg burrito," Spencer told the plastic clown. "And a fat-free mango smoothie."

He woofed down the burrito while he drove past Sleepy Hollow out toward the trailer park. You'd never know it was there, tucked behind a mini-storage in front, a warehouse store behind, and forty-year-old arbor vitae hedges running down both sides that kept it entirely hidden away from the view of wealthier neighbors in every direction.

Outside the chain link fence surrounding the trailer park he pulled the 4Runner off the road and lifted the HK onto his lap. He had a fresh mag loaded inside; the trigger was set to 3, fully automatic.

Spencer studied the trailer park for a full hour, and then he slowly drove the three lanes between trailers. The cars were right: older rigs with faded paint, lots of cracked windows; dusty, dirty Detroit relics with big back seats for when that was the only option for a night's sleep. No anomalies, nothing to indicate a trap.

He finally drove alongside his trailer, the one he had rented before they captured him at Citi-Field. Yellow curtains in the windows; a red charcoal barbecue was tucked underneath his awning. Different, but not different like law enforcement had gone through it. They would have torn it apart.

Spencer parked and got out of the 4Runner, fast-jogging around the Winnebago sitting on blocks. The on-site manager lived out there with the storage containers at his back. Spencer's lock was there, along with an even bigger padlock, painted yellow, hanging on a second hasp. Spencer lifted the yellow lock, reading "MGMT" written in black felt tip on the side. He grabbed the lock and pulled hard, then slammed it back against the steel container.

"Hey!" A gruff voice shouted angrily from out of the old box-shaped motorhome as the brown curtains parted above a faded army green W on the front side.

"Oh, it's you," the manager called, recognizing Spencer after throwing open his door. He grabbed the side, turned sideways, and let himself down to the packed dirt, wearing only blue jeans held up by a single suspender. A sleeveless undershirt failed to cover a prodigious belly. He waddled, favoring his bad hip, and extended his thick, tattooed arm toward Spencer.

"Thought you might show up," Ollie said as he took Spencer's hand in his thick mitt and squeezed. "Been six months."

"I had to give up your trailer," he explained. "The park is totally full. But nobody touched your locker. I put the second lock on it. I expect you saw that. Come on over and I'll buy you a cup of coffee. I still got your clothes and stuff. Meant to give it to the Goodwill, but if it's not one thing it's the next. Glad that worked out your way. Let's figure the numbers, and once you get squared up, I'll pull that padlock."

"I don't have the key to my lock," Spencer explained. "Lost it."

"Got a toggle-joint bolt cutter. Take it off no problem. I'll fix you up."

"How about a flashlight I could borrow for maybe an hour?"

Ollie had that, too.

"You got it, Sergeant. Just as soon as we have that coffee and get what you owe squared away."

*****

Miller moved through the building fast, looking important for dramatic effect, and leaving behind Owen and the techs, who were watching the digital footage showing Spencer clean-shaven and clearly moving more fluidly, his body flowing with an efficiency that defied the record for his injuries.

Owen looked on, captivated; he had seen Spencer only as a distant flash on a metal roof and two still photos on Facebook. Seeing Spencer pumping gas, buying a burrito, getting himself a coffee and stirring in powdered creamer, viewing him functioning like a free man, had Owen straining like a skinny redheaded Hulk ready to attack the life-sized projection.

"Bastard!" Owen kicked at a plastic chair, sending it flying.

"Dude!" Kip called out to him. "That is from yesterday. You know he can't hear you, right?"

Owen pointed at the image while in it Spencer took a bite from the burrito, blew the heat out of his mouth, and then licked at cheese dripping over his lip. He wanted to reach his hands through the monitor and strangle the life out of the sonofabitch. Callie was fed up with North Corona, the house, and the boys' schools before the attacks ever started. But they would have worked it out. He knew they would have worked it out. Losing Tremaine was what broke their backs. The shooter whose image projected across the whole wall broke their backs. *You did that. You motherfucking bastard!*

"Arrg!" Owen growled. "I can't stand it! Seeing him looking all normal, like a regular guy." His closest friend was dead, his marriage was fucked up, and he had fucked up on the job, too. Now the new captain was about to replace him.

So long as Jonathan Spencer walked the face of the planet, he was never going to be able to make things right.

*****

From inside Starbucks on Tonnelle Avenue, Miller absently sipped at a double tall mocha while constantly eyeing the mobile app on one of his cell phones, waiting for the confirmation. When it pinged, he tapped and snatched thin air inside his fist. A two, a five, and five more zeroes.

"Yes!" he called out loud. After recounting the zeroes, he walked outside and dropped the phone and the drink together into the trash. No phone contacts, no papers, no wire trails, no trace whatsoever. An army of forensic accountants couldn't track the funds.

"No more penny-ante skimming," Miller smirked. "This is how real business is done."

Continuing up Tonnelle, his next stop was Chase Bank. "How much would it take to buy into a hedge fund?" he considered.

Miller's posture and gait, his entire persona shifted; he stepped up and took charge. He was a different person when he returned to Owen, Stephen, and Dilip. First thing, he slapped a banded stack of fresh one hundred dollar bills on the table.

"Any one of you can take that for yourself today, ten grand cash money. Be great at what you do. Simple," he said.

He waived his arms wide, his forefingers pointing in every direction. "Listen up. The client, through me, is going to be very generous, gentlemen. Think big. Think about tropical islands. With success, you might well be there. We are engaged in a private-public partnership.

"Gentlemen, start your computers. Enter the sanctum sanctorum. The Gods have given us the Ark of the Covenant, the keys to every technology you've only ever talked about in whispers. But the tools and the data come at a price. There is always a quid pro quo. You get the tools, you get highly remunerated, and we handle this on the deep DL. We are about to do remarkable things, gentlemen, and you can never breathe a word about them."

Miller's eyes locked on Owen's face. The challenge floated like bloated ghosts hanging heavy in the dead air. Dilip eyed Stephen, but said nothing. Fifteen seconds passed. It felt like days. Owen blinked first. When the moment passed, he was still there.

"Good," Miller announced crisply. "We all can be certain that our client knows everything." He scanned the walls and ceiling tiles, certain they were under observation at that moment. "I mean *everything*. You do not want to be on the wrong side of this, not now, not ever. You will never speak about this, you will never write about this, and you will never bear witness to any of this. There will never be a circumstance when you are better off talking about this, not ever, not ten years from now. I don't care what you get caught up in doing, you'll be better off in prison than ever trying to trade on what we are now going to do here."

Dilip glanced again toward Stephen, who was riveted, totally engaged in being the composer within a real-world conception of the perfect gaming thesis. Miller's description brought Spencer to life; up until that moment, Stephen and the techs had never connected the images to flesh and bone.

Owen followed intently while Miller detailed Spencer's arrogance, describing the sociopathic void that the military had programmed, the perfect Triple Threat.

"We are tracking an escaped prisoner. Jonathan Spencer. A year ago Spencer was an elite soldier. He went bad. Spencer was captured, unconscious, with two shattered legs. The same day his casts came off, he took out two guards and the doctor and walked out of high-security segregated detention."

Owen questioned in disbelief. "Spencer was caught?"

"Caught and broke out," Miller reiterated.

"How did he break both legs?" Owen demanded confirmation as the pieces fell together. *A long fall onto concrete.*

Nussbaum turned, looking sideways as Owen talked to himself.

"Dimitri Vosilych!" Owen explained, answering his own question. "It *was* all bullshit! Everything! Motherfucker!"

"Are you done, Lieutenant?" Miller asked sarcastically. "Gentlemen, I kill people."

Nussbaum's jaw dropped. Stephen, Dilip, Dale and Kip exchanged glances. "That is one hell of a line," Stephen whispered tensely. Layer upon layer, the reality was sinking in.

Miller's stark statement pulled Owen's focus back to the immediate while a tidal wave massed offshore inside his head, roiling and tumbling.

"More precisely," Miller continued, "my regular work, my *oeuvre* if you will, is tracking and elimination." He scanned their faces as he spoke. "I know Master Sergeant Jonathan Spencer. I know him well. In fact, he worked directly for me. I also saved his life. Not to my credit, I see. So let's fix that, shall we?" He matched his eyes into each of theirs, holding his stare until one by one he held their riveted attention.

"With his hands and with all hand-held weaponry," Miller continued, "Spencer is a nearly perfect killing machine.

"Call it like it is: hell, he was my star. But after six straight months soloing for me, he was just as cold as Day One. He has no friends, no relationships, and he trusts no one.

"Let's be clear. We aren't going to drag it out; bonus money will more than offset your consulting fees. We have one goal here. Our roles terminate with Jonathan Spencer dead.

"We are going to keep this simple. We are not here to capture; not that he will let himself be caught again. We are all here, unequivocally, to kill the burrito-munching sonofabitch up on that screen. You find him, I send a hot team, and they kill him.

"Let me paint a more vivid picture, just in case escaping from confinement straight out of full-length leg casts hasn't painted a clear picture. The drug cartel firefight yesterday in West Virginia? Spencer. A tactical team closed in on him. Spencer destroyed a helicopter, killed the pilot, and executed six experienced, heavily armed Special Forces-trained ex-soldiers. That is who you are up against. Don't forget it. On the bright side, it was your tracking cameras that enabled that assault. You succeeded. Failing is on the dead commandos. Price of failure. Bishop put together those commandos. I'll be vetting professional replacements; my hot teams will be serious killers. There are no rules of engagement. If it means killing everyone in a room, they'll do it or I'll get another team. That may be tough for you to digest, but that's what you're into, boys."

Miller's glare dared them to look at one another for support. Each one of the techs gulped. Owen Cullen's only tell wasn't fear; Cullen looked ready to charge forward.

"Spencer is that good," Miller resumed. "But he is no thinker. He didn't come up with this. Somebody is telling him what to do. You find that somebody and we find Spencer."

Miller sat down and swiveled his chair in front of Stephen. "Your team, these young men, have the keys to the Formula One racers of technology. Impress me and you get the chance to be made men. This is your IPO, gentlemen. Get it done! Nussbaum, I'm expecting to see the tightest net in history around this motherfucker."

He turned to Owen next. "Detective, you found him once. Do it again. Show us what to look for."

In quick staccato, Miller laid out directives that would have overwhelmed a floor covered with techs working around the clock. "Find the hatred. Sift the entire goddamned internet and boil it down for repeated messaging that shows fervent hate for the rich."

Dilip looked over to Dale and Kip, who both looked to Stephen Nussbaum, once again at a complete loss. "There will be millions of entries, tens of millions," Nussbaum protested. "That would take thousands of programming hours to create our own filters and then we'll be constantly impeded by every search engine." He pointed around the room. "We're four guys."

"You're four guys with the backdoor key to the NSA's whole piggy bank," Miller corrected. "Look through the lens you've been given! Dig into it and find out what this system can do. The facial recognition piece is only the beginning. Get behind the wheel and run this through the paces. Push the pedal, gentlemen!"

"Every shooting, he used a long rifle," Owen offered. "What about screening for objects, long objects, in cases, inside duffle bags? How about that?" He eyed the stack of hundreds. What would Callie like better, going somewhere special for a real vacation, or jewelry? Ten thousand dollars could buy a legitimate engagement ring. He could replace the speck he had bought when he asked her to marry him.

Dilip shook his head. "We can't write new programming," he cried. "They will know we are corrupting a federal system. That is espionage."

"You're not getting it!" Miller shouted. "They let you in! Nobody wants to prosecute, so nothing is illegal!"

"Ok ok ok," Owen interrupted. "If we are right that he is returning to resume attacks, then I may be able to shift the odds in our favor." He thought about explaining about how Callie found the websites. He also thought about the website that went in and published their Citi-Field trap days ahead of time. But explaining all that was too much.

"Stay with me here. If I can give you three or four or five probable targets, can you concentrate filters on just those spots, looking for long objects, and people in scarves, lots of things? This guy is precise. We know that. He plans meticulously down to every detail.

"If we know high-value targets and we screen for many more variables ahead of time just on these targets, can we raise our percentages? Could we screen and watch for males around six feet tall with big feet wearing scarves and hats and hoodies, anything that covered their faces?"

Owen's red scalp trembled; he suddenly realized that it wasn't losing Tremaine that broke him. He had broken down because nobody was on his side. He knew he was right! Jonathan Spencer, always Spencer. So why did he need other people to believe him? Why was that so important?

"By limiting the data volume," Dilip interjected excitedly. "With limited data volume, we can direct pure feeds here and apply our own filtration criteria. It can work."

Owen snapped back into the moment. "Fix me up with one of those extra laptops," he told Dale. "Let's find out who and where and when he might attack." If Spencer was planning IKRP2, he had to first find the rich before he could kill them.

"Point each for you two," Miller scored. "Three for our detective. Time is fleeting. Get on it." He left them in the bullpen, leaving the bundled cash behind.

Owen couldn't help looking at the stack of bills.

I'm in the lead, he told himself. *I'm winning this ten grand. I'm getting you a real diamond ring, Callie. This time, I'm doing things right.*

*****

Spencer counted out four hundred-dollar bills into Ollie's thick paw and was onto a fifth when Ollie closed his fist around the bills. "That'll do. Let's get under my trailer and find that bolt cutter. I know I've got it somewhere down in the belly boxes."

Ten minutes later they were standing at the metal container with Ollie holding a flashlight on the padlocks. Spencer opened the pincers and set them first onto the larger yellow padlock when the manager pulled them back. "Hold on. Cut yours and give me minute. I'll find the key for mine."

Ollie took out his thick key ring and worked his way until he found the right one to open the padlock. He took the bolt cutter back from Spencer and waddled toward the Winnebago.

The scorched image of Mouse's lipless mouth came back to him through the darkness. It had scored into his psyche. Spencer needed to get past that, to push it down. In the cool air he worked his controlled breathing techniques. He puffed through tiny breaths for minutes and then exhaled until his lungs were collapsing. He drew air back in so deeply they felt like they would burst.

When he finished, Mouse and Manchester United and all the ghosts were locked away and his bowels were left turning into cement.

He tugged the container handle out a quarter turn, opening up the hooks holding the doors shut tight. Then he pressed his back to the container and shouldered the steel door open just enough to turn sideways to get inside. His electric lamp was still there, right beside the door, just where he left it. He flipped its switch and the LED bulb shined onto two large chests carefully covered by a canvas painter's tarp. The careful folds were undisturbed. He also found the heavy nylon strap, hooking one end to the outer door then hooking the inside end to a steel eye along the container wall. He locked down the tension lever to shut himself inside securely.

Yanking back the tarp and throwing open the bigger of the two chests, he saw the long broad lines of his most trusted companion beneath the blue blanket in which he had it swathed. He lifted the thirty-one pounds, hugged them to his chest, and appreciated the satisfying heft. He ran his right palm underneath the smooth rail. He reached up inside the magazine and wiped his fingertip against the oily spring. Transferring the weight, he moved his left palm up the barrel, extending his arm to reach over the muzzle brake before stroking back down to the top of the rail then reversing his hand and gently fingering along the bipod's legs down to its spiked feet.

Spencer pushed his back against the wall and slid down the cool metal until he was seated on the floor with his legs extended in front of him. He held the Barrett upright between his legs.

"A hundred-ten more, Captain Sam," he whispered softly. Then he smiled for a second, for Mouse. *Probably should use a Dragunov,* he kidded himself. *I am Dimitri Vosilych.*

Inside the first chest he unpacked ten fully-loaded ten-round magazines, the Leupold scope, his Armasight PVS-7 Night Vision Goggles, Kevlar vest and body armor, a Sig Sauer P226 semi-automatic pistol along with six ten-round mags, .40 caliber bullets and three full fifty-round boxes.

A variant of the HK inside the 4Runner was inside the second chest, the semi-automatic version of the military rifle plus an M24 custom-equipped with quick-breaking lock pins. He could dissemble the weapon in twelve seconds, rebuild it in twenty. There was his laptop, too.

Spencer stood on the tips of his toes, reaching his fingers deep into the crevice where the container's wall and ceiling were joined together. His fingertips touched cloth, which he pinched tightly until he was able to withdraw enough to grip the pillowcase inside his fist. Pulling one hand over the other, he reached the whole sack up and out from inside the double wall.

Inside the pillowcase were five carefully folded and rubber-banded wads of cash, one thousand dollars apiece. He touched the U.S. Army Sniper School Merit ID beside them. He had earned it at twenty-one. Ranger ID a year later. U.S. Army Special Forces Patch. Skull and Crossed Arrows—Motivated-Dedicated-Lethal.

Growing weed? What the hell were you thinking?
Own it. This is who you are.

*****

Thirty-two New York websites listed the upcoming social calendar. Owen drilled down to four; two of these were now members-only sites requiring registration and login. Stephen stepped in to assist; with several keystrokes Nussbaum created a false identity and email trail. Owen was in.

"It's that easy?" Owen commented.

Nussbaum shrugged. "Standard anonymizer."

"Jaysus, Mary, and Joseph," Owen muttered. "What chance do the rest of us have?"

Scrolling within the sites, he began creating a list of the most likely targets, a seemingly impossible task given the number of venues. He started by trying to go out for a full month, then backed it down to two weeks and finally just ten days. The charities alone packed in two hundred events.

Dilip said, "We cannot monitor for concealment across twenty to forty events per day." The social calendar was back in full swing. At Kip's suggestion, they ran a double filtration based upon the financial rankings of those names tied to past events and current.

"It's simple enough," he claimed. "Most of it is public information."

He had the overlay built and populated inside a half-hour. "AIPAC, the American Israel Public Affairs Committee, is drawing the wealthiest and powerful players," he showed. "At least three billionaires, potentially double that, plus seventy-five with net worths north of one hundred million."

"Israel-lobbying?" Owen asked. "Doubt it. The only time he communicated at all, 'I Kill Rich People,' was to distance himself from the Jew-haters. He also prefers longer-range shots in open settings. AIPAC is deep inside the Convention Center."

"Not at the auction house," Miller countered. "He was sixty-one feet from the nearest victim."

"You do your homework," Owen observed, "so you know he's not going after Jews."

"Touché. So what else?"

"Perhaps we should consider targets based on degrees of visual security," Dilip suggested. "If he is choosing, why would he not opt for the lowest security values? He might avoid anything we have covered."

"Hello?" Nussbaum interrupted. "And how would he know coverage matrices? Exclude targets based upon that assumption and we might as well exclude the entire city. Manhattan is out for sure."

Owen zeroed in on Phillip Black's birthday gala; the description sounded eerily reminiscent of Morris Levy's party at Sands Point. Black, running the most successful M&A firm in America, was throwing himself a black tie bash at his six-acre Scarsdale estate, which was currently listed for sale at $12,500,000 and included a three-story library and gallery, "Italianate Gardens," two three-bedroom twin guest houses, indoor and outdoor swimming pools, and a Victorian tea house, an authentic scale version of London's late Crystal Palace. According to the gossip blogs, insiders were already speculating about the menu; catering was to be under the supervision of Marcel Sert, whom Black was flying in on a private jet from his eponymous Michelin three-star Right Bank restaurant for the event.

Owen cut and pasted the selection to a Word document. Nobody seemed impressed at his computer skills.

Four hours later, Owen's head was exploding. He had drilled down to nine high-value targets and was only beginning to get into the second week moving forward.

"Fucks sake," he kept cursing. The ten thousand dollars lying six feet from his grasp seemed to be getting farther and farther away.

He handed the nine high-value targets to Dilip and Kip, who looked over the list together. Kip's nervous tic reflected Owen's uncertainty. The last series of attacks averaged six days apart. At that rate, the data avalanche was going to drown him.

Miller, meanwhile, had sourced multiple commando squads and was vetting those available for hire. Two were comprised of retired 1st SFOD Delta Force F members, both contracting through a retired Joint Special Operations Command army colonel. Miller considered submitting his own clearance, then decided against registering any presence in the systems.

"Can you get me inside?" he asked Nussbaum.

"Don't need to," Stephen explained. In several keystrokes, he walked Miller straight in through NSA's back door.

Miller focused his attention on reviewing dossiers of domestic and international operators along with their mission histories: hostage rescues and hostile extractions, limited strike-force fixed-target eliminations, opposition command-structure disruption. Assembly and deployment were guaranteed on-site inside sixteen hours within the contiguous lower 48 states. Six national distribution centers. In-house MH-6 helicopters available at each center.

A half-page list of standard materiel was included in the base pricing; a six-page menu of optional large ordinance and missiles was attached as an addendum along with transportation add-ons and replacement fees due as a front-end deposit, refunded if unused. A retail army.

Israeli squads comprised of Mosad and Sayaret were available in San Diego and Ft. Lauderdale. Their emphasis and productivity clearly slanted toward fixed-facility work. Miller recognized several of their claimed successes; work at refineries, power plants, and server centers that had been accomplished without any hint of their involvement. But Delta, ex-Delta, was the better fit for Americans for Patriotic Action, Miller decided. Fee-clarity and guaranteed deployment turn-around times helped seal the decision.

"Okie-dokie. Let's get us some firepower."

*****

Screen colors reflected onto Spencer's face inside the dark storage container. He scanned through the social calendar websites he kept bookmarked; the laptop still had enough power to turn on and connect, piggybacking onto the web through a half-dozen unprotected Wi-Fi connections in the trailers. He also scanned articles written after each attack. That was how he learned, for the first time, the black detective's name. *Detective Sergeant Tremaine Bull.* But not a single article mentioned how Bull got there not once, but twice? Nothing explained why he let go.

"I would have pulled you up! Why did you let go? To kill me? To protect billionaires? Would they ever die for you?" Spencer moaned. "I would have pulled you up."

Spencer looked over the array of potential targets; even more than before Sands Point: charity functions, birthdays and anniversaries; events by the dozens every day, in hotels, country clubs, and private homes.

Did it achieve anything? He hadn't pushed over any dominoes. The rich didn't spontaneously start falling. Nothing spread at all, just a few embers that drifted and died out.

Nobody had stepped up to carry the cause. Dimitri Vosilych was dead and gone. As soon as the all-clear sounded, the rich had re-emerged in their tuxedos and designer clothes and went right back to their parties.

"I sparked a bad tattoo on your neck," he groaned. "And if I never showed up, you would be alive now."

Push it down!

Shifting amongst targets could make it harder on law enforcement to stop him, but there were no sustainable strategies left.

"They have my name, my face, my DNA." Kevlar couldn't save his ass. He had one mission left, maybe two, before they closed in on him. That was what he could rationally hope to accomplish. What he couldn't figure out was why was there nothing on the radio? How could thousands of police officers have his name and description and keep that secret?

"And how does that connect to Dimitri Vosilych?" he wondered. *Ok*, he thought, *they violated my rights.* But if that ever came out in the news it would be a hiccup, not an earthquake.

Captain Sam was right; the snakes were connected… like that monster with all the snakes coming out of her head. The one you couldn't look at without turning into stone.

Money was the real connection, money beyond anything they could spend in ten lifetimes.

A bomb would go much further, take more of them out at one time; he recognized that. With a bomb he could strike more deeply. But that's not who a sniper is, not what a sniper does, not what he would ever do. He could not bomb Vision Partners into oblivion.

"You're a sniper, not some bomber scumbag. You set your aim and you kill who you aim for. *A clean way to kill, a clean way to die.*"

He returned to the laptop, virtually walking along Google Maps, taking in street views along Park Avenue and Central Park West. Just two Manhattan residential structures, two buildings with a few dozen units apiece, held more net worth than half the nations on Earth.

He imagined the billionaires, each seated on the top of pyramids of grain, miles and miles high. Grain enough to feed the world, more grain than they could ever possibly consume, and all of it spoiling while they hoarded it beneath them.

The image surprised him. Satisfied him, too. He had never thought about it in that way, not until that precise moment.

CHAPTER TWENTY

"I won ten thousand dollars."

"You what?" Callie screeched. "How did you do that?"

He wanted to keep the secret, but what was the point? "I want to buy you the diamond, Cal. I want to start off fresh and do it right this time." Owen fanned the edge of the bills and looked at them. He still couldn't believe it. "I'm making real money."

"Slow down, Owen. You're getting way ahead of yourself."

"I'm in Jersey now, not far. A couple miles from the stadium." A chill ran through him the minute the word came out his mouth. *Stadium.* "Cal, I want to see you and spend some time with the boys."

"How did you suddenly get ten thousand dollars?"

"It's a bonus. I'll explain later. Let me spend it on you."

"We'll talk about that," Callie said. "Next week. I'm away this weekend."

Owen swallowed hard as she hung up the line. Suddenly, he needed to set the money down and step away from it.

*****

Their task felt impossible. Owen pored through the target options, speculating over Spencer's selection criteria and assigning weight to each one. He raised attention to anomalies, the Central Park shootings, the auction house. Not everything was a social event and Spencer's next target certainly did not have to be one of those.

Ten thousand dollars didn't change his reality or Callie's; Owen recognized that, but he had a win in his column, his first win in way too long.

"He's coming off two badly broken legs," Owen reminded Miller. "He might decide to lay low."

"You've seen the footage. He's moving around just fine."

Miller considered and rejected Owen's thinking. "Spencer has no imagination," he countered. "He takes orders. That's what career sergeants do. You're a lieutenant, right? Is it any different in the police department?"

The comparison annoyed Owen. "I came up through the ranks."

"What is that supposed to mean?"

"It means that rank and IQ don't correlate. Neither do service rankings. I'm a detective lieutenant; a navy lieutenant is like an army captain; in the department, a detective lieutenant is roughly equivalent to an army major."

Miller wasn't interested; Owen could see that his attention had already drifted away.

"Stephen, can you pull maps for each of these event locations?" Owen asked. He purposely turned his back to Miller.

"Get them up on the wall so I can visualize them."

"Where are you going with this?" Miller wanted to know.

"Egress," Owen answered him. "It's easier getting in than getting out, but he always manages to escape. I want to eliminate locations that impede escape and see what we get."

So far, what Owen knew about Miller is that the man hit the booze hard then switched it off instantly. Miller loved fancy food and liked his fancy words. He announced that he was a "Kill Manager" like that was a normal job. And he talked a hell of a lot more than he listened.

The word "stadium" still lingered in Owen's head like a foul odor. That and Callie spending another weekend… with Doctor Marc?

"Well?" Miller wasn't asking rhetorically after all. "Who does the thinking at NYPD?"

"Look, I'm not a spokesman for the department, ok? But we're up against way too much here. I don't care what sort of technology we've got; we can't cover the Tri-State area with six people!"

"We'll do precisely that; we're blanketing from Queens to Jersey and north to Connecticut," Nussbaum claimed. "You cops may be the face of law enforcement, but this software is the new brains and the backbone, too. I have 150 cameras for every law enforcement officer in the Tri-States Area; 500 cameras for every set of police eyeballs on duty, and that is only scratching the surface. I'm only starting to get the feel for what we have. There's a protocol called Minerva here. DOD and NSA stuff, dealing with responses to internal terrorism and social upheaval. I've never seen anything like this except theoretical stuff. What we're into here is real. We are only into tracking; the enterprise side of this interfaces with DOD drones and all sorts of futuristic scalability. If I'm right, and I'm pretty damned certain I am right, four people and this software can support national coverage. These capabilities make 'feet on the street' a meaningless anachronism."

"For fucks sake," Owen argued, "you can't trust this to computers!"

Nussbaum and Miller seemed lost in their own imaginary worlds. "Miller, Spencer is going to attack and we're going to be counter-punching," Owen insisted. "We need manpower! There are 50,000 cops within fifty miles of this spot. You're not utilizing them and you're jeopardizing lives by keeping them in the dark!"

Miller smiled. "An hour ago you looked happy enough," he told Owen cynically. "You get many $10K bonuses with NYPD?"

*****

Spencer followed a Craigslist ad to a basement room inside a decrepit Victorian that was chopped into fourteen cash-only rentals. Paid by the week. The hard-luck housemates aside, the space was warm, when he turned on the shower water came out, and he could join shared Wi-Fi for $15.

Web maps and real estate sales information provided reams of information on the target location, everything from the other residents in the building to layouts of most of the units inside it. The place may have looked like any other pre-war Manhattan building, but behind the brass and glass doors, the simple understated awning, the classic marble surrounding the doorway and the air conditioners hanging out the windows, the building was a fortress. There was even a book written about the building and its famous residents. The richest one was reputed to regularly work the door staff harder than anyone else and gave just $15 dollars, begrudgingly, for an annual Christmas tip.

Their Park Avenue address was for early mornings and mid-week. They all had other residences. Spencer noted that. *Early mornings. Mid-week.*

He would have shot anyone who could afford to live there, but that strategy did no good. Spencer studied the face on the laptop monitor. "That's a snake, Captain," he murmured.

The real estate sites shared prices, layouts, and amenities. Whether it was described or just implied, every unit had internal security systems: alarms, reinforced entries, cameras, safe rooms. The building had no resemblance to Central Park West; these were not people who spared security costs. For all he knew, they could have evacuation tunnels with high-speed trains.

Impediments were everywhere. Their parking was hidden. Big trees in front interrupted sight lines.

"You need to get on-site," he confirmed aloud. All the mapping software in the world couldn't replace fundamental reconnaissance. "Put your boots on the ground."

"It has to have an emergency safety plan. How do I get it?"

An outline was starting to take shape. If he could get inside disguised as a first responder, he could freely mix in the stairwell and get out again to the street through the side door. But how many stairwells? What if they shut down the whole structure with him inside?

"No good," he concluded. "Get them outside. Hit while they're outside."

He had to make them evacuate, on foot, to channel them to a location that he chose. He needed to keep them out of the garages.

"What's your fire position?" he asked himself. "And how do you get out afterward?"

Spencer snapped vectors covering front of Park and 71st. Just one open convergence: the open terrace, seventh floor. *There*. Sight lines on Main and Side, functionally equidistant; range 120 meters, down angle from sixty-five feet elevation. Piece of cake provided they evacuated through either door.

"Wanna have a party?" a high raspy female voice interrupted him through his thin door. "Hey. I'm real good, baby."

Spencer shut the laptop and put it on top of the stacked index cards, then froze and listened.

"Baby, I do it all. I mean everything." After thirty seconds, she smacked the door with a resounding thwack. "Fuck you, man. You think I need you? Shit. I don't need nobody." Her voice trailed off down the dark hallway.

Spencer waited then went back to examining the street directions, the closest subway stations, alleys, and parks, everything that went into supporting survival. There were still plenty more snakes. But this one was a python squeezing the entire country.

*****

"Got a hit!" Stephen shouted. "A copy/printing company in Yonkers."

Owen knew the area. It was only twenty-five minutes away from North Bergen driving against incoming morning traffic. He bobbed on his toes anxiously as Dilip projected Spencer's image onto the wall. It looked like they could reach out and touch him.

"I've got people I know on Yonkers PD," Owen called toward Miller. It was Spencer, confirmed. He was calmly making color copies; the screen image was black and white, but with white paper all around for contrast, Spencer was clearly using a darker shade.

"I can call in a bench warrant!" Owen pleaded. Miller seemed detached, like he was in another world.

Why was he exposing himself just to make copies? Miller wanted to know. Color copies. When he was done at the self-service copier, Spencer took the four copies off the tray, pulled a thumb drive from the machine, and then walked to the cashier.

"He's going to leave!" Owen argued. "We need to call Yonkers PD!"

"Show me visuals outside the store," Miller barked over Owen. "Get them on the wall. Now!"

Kip displayed a map screen in the upper corner of the wall projection, centered on Saw Mill River Road, and then opened a one-mile outward radius. Thirty-eight active cameras showed, but just four exterior cams, traffic-monitors located at thoroughfares and highway entrances. Nothing that would display Spencer, his mode of transportation, or where he was headed.

"Shut up!" Miller snapped. "Nobody is calling PD. This is internal assets only. You are being well paid to keep this low-profile."

"This is Yonkers, not Pennsylvania," Owen griped. "He's right up the road. For fuck sake! He's about to walk out of there and vanish again and we're sitting on our asses. We sit on our asses and that bastard gets away!"

"Spencer will kill your Yonkers PD," Miller stated bluntly.

Owen fought the urge to scream. "Tell me how we're going to stop him then! Your phantom commandos aren't there! He's right there, in real time!"

Spencer's live image was cast across the long wall. "That piece of junk killed my best friend. That guy—right fucking there!"

But Spencer didn't pay the cashier and didn't walk out. He was directed toward the print center's computer stations and sat down facing directly toward the security camera they were all watching.

"Can you pull up what he is doing?" Miller asked Stephen.

"If he is online and if we can get an IP address." Stephen turned toward Dale and the others. They were already on it.

Owen brought his 9mm out from its holster, released the clip, checked it and reloaded in a continuous fluid motion. "Watch your show, I'm going!" he shouted.

"Hold up!" Miller ordered.

Owen ignored him. On the run, he slammed his hand onto the bar mechanism and shoved the door so hard that it slammed against the outside wall of the building.

"Turn around!"

Owen accelerated. "I can't do any good here!" he yelled behind him. "Keep me posted!"

He drove seventy-five miles per hour. At the Fort Lee Bridge, he took out his gold detective lieutenant's medallion and rubbed his fingers on it for luck. He was onto the Hudson Parkway heading north when Miller phoned. "He's gone. You should thank Christ you never took him on. You'd die."

Miller went silent while he considered. "You're up there now. Keep going and do some police work. We're trying to find out from here what he was doing on the computer. See what you can get on your end then call me back," he told Owen.

"And Irish," Miller added, "that was your mulligan. Don't pull that twice."

*****

Owen was pulling into the parking spot across from the copier store when he realized that he couldn't remember anything between the George Washington

Bridge and where he was sitting at that exact moment. Five or six miles of driving, a complete blank.

He crossed the parking lot and entered the glass double doors and then he was in front of the same cashier, the cashier Spencer was speaking with in the video.

"May I help you?" the man asked. He was a twenty-something overweight version of the techs, Kip and Dale.

Owen looked back at the glass double doors, swept his eyes over the copy machines and the people using them, around past the computer area, and back to the cashier standing in front of him. He registered the signs: COPYING/COMPUTERS/PROJECTS/PAPER/CASHIER.

"NYPD," he announced. He broke PD rules, not giving a damn and displaying his gold medallion during a suspension. "There was a man here a few minutes ago, six feet, slim, light brown hair cut short. Used the copy machines then was on the computer."

The cashier nodded.

"What can you tell me about him?" Owen asked.

"Um," he stammered. "This isn't New York City. Are you supposed to be here?"

Owen looked at him incredulously, repeating to himself to keep it together and tensing as though he might go off.

"Would I be driving all the way here if it wasn't important?" Owen yelled back. Eyes turned to look at him from every corner of the store. "Let's start again," he whispered. "What did he copy?"

"I should call my manager."

"I can call Riverdale Avenue and bring in Yonkers Police right here," Owen threatened. "You want to talk at the stationhouse or you going to cooperate?"

"How would I know?" the cashier answered. "Five sheets: a couple canary, a couple pale sky, and a rose petal. I don't know what was on it. He made copies. Then he used the computers for a few minutes. Doing business cards. He did a minimum order of 250."

"Show me."

The cashier shook his head. "It's all online. I just rang it up. Cash payment."

He looked up on his screen and scrolled down to the receipt then spun the monitor around toward Owen. "Five sheets color, 40 cents; 250 two-color basic cardstock, $12.95; overnight delivery, $17.70; one pack of 3 X 5 index cards, $1.19; plus tax, total $34.93."

"Where?"

"Where what?"

"The shipping address! When they're finished, where are the business cards going?"

The cashier spun the monitor back around and clicked through, while Owen waited anxiously for that address.

The cashier turned the monitor back to Owen. <u>Privacy Policy: MagicPrint, Inc. is not responsible for online security during or after customers utilize our services. We acknowledge that you may provide personal data or other information to its site via the Internet. No system is 100% safe. Despite the use of security software and other precautions, customers are advised to take care to minimize exposure to third parties. MagicPrint does not share or sell personal information to any outside parties. Your information may be shared or re-printed as required by law, rule, regulation, or court order.</u>

"Unless you have a court order, we don't share customer information," the clerk said. "But it's not here anyway. Once they click send, it's sitting in the production queue on a server someplace. Cleveland, probably. That's the nearest print facility."

Owen called Stephen Nussbaum from the car. "He placed an online order for business cards to MagicPrint. Can you intercept it? We need to know what is going to be on those cards and where they're heading!"

*****

Google Maps showed every street and building, every doorway with line of sight to Park Avenue. Spencer spotted three possible overviews. On the NYC building permit site, Spencer trolled until he located an electrical permit issued on E 71st. Zillow displayed Terraza's recent sales. Several more clicks produced key details: one apartment per floor, rooftop deck common area, and building management. In fifteen more minutes he had photos and plans for all twenty-one floors.

Not quite as much specific data on Park Avenue: number of units, board information, residents, limited floor plans.

Spencer dialed the management company. "May I speak to your agent for Terraza?" he asked reception.

"She is away on vacation through next Wednesday, I'll forward you to her assistant," the receptionist offered.

"Nothing urgent," Spencer replied. "I'll email it. Can you give me her email address? Oh, does she have a direct line?"

He thanked the receptionist for her direct line and email address before hanging up.

Check. *Now I need those business cards.*

*****

Owen watched anxiously while meaningless chains of information flew down Dilip's screen. Within two minutes, the sides of his mouth had turned up.

"I have not seen this before," Dilip announced.

"What does it mean?" Owen asked.

"Well, it means that I would be quite secure using MagicPrint, at least for the next month or maybe two, until somebody cracks this newer encryption. I can do nothing with this. Nothing at all."

"Then why are you smiling?"

"It's very, very good work. Even using the NSA supercomputers, this mixed-symbol fifteen-digit encryption would take up to a day to break," Dilip explained admiringly. "I won't go into elaborate detail, but this system is designed to be constantly morphing. Essentially, it changes the data and inherently passes along the simultaneous interpretation code to approved end users. Mark my words, more and more entities will be using this technology and many of these billion-dollar government systems we are using will made be totally redundant."

Owen looked to Miller, who seemed calm, bored even.

"This client of yours won't let us call in extra resources, won't allow us to run an APB or utilize Yonkers PD or even call a sympathetic judge for a warrant for MagicPrint and do you even care? He was right there, right in front of your eyes, too," Owen ranted.

Stephen, Kip, and Dale all stopped to enjoy a screen-share with Dilip, who was salivating at some other nerd's handiwork.

"Leetness," Dale mouthed in total awe.

"Sweet," Kip agreed.

"Miller, I'm a Detective Lieutenant in the Intel Division," Owen reasoned. "We need to get a warrant. Right now. Client or no client."

"And do what with it?" Miller shot back. "Where's your evidence tying Jonathan Spencer to a crime? Unless you know something I don't, you can't even tie him to what happened in West Virginia. Not with anything admissible. Tell me what you are going to do, take this jigsaw puzzle outline to your new captain? Are you going to go higher, FBI? Al Hurwitz retired. It's noise, detective. Don't get yourself all pumped up for nothing."

"Why are you doing this?" Owen wanted to know. "You're CIA, right? You flew halfway around the world to be here. Why? I don't get it. Do you even care that he killed two dozen people?"

"You're older than I am," Miller spat back. "Grow up, for Christ's sake."

"What is that supposed to mean?"

"It means every two minutes two dozen people are getting killed somewhere or another. Unless you're one of 'em, what's it matter? But you sure tried hard to be one today. Fool."

"Yonkers PD should be staking out that place," Owen griped. "This is insane."

"Cullen, your old boss Christiana Dansk is getting seven figures for supplying drones to your precious police department. My unofficial official assignment in Afghanistan was to shut down competition for the heroin cartels our U.S. allies run so they can keep pumping their supply over their northern border straight into Russian veins. Are you getting my point?"

"Screw you," Owen said. "And screw your money, too. You don't own me. I'm not here for you; I'm not here for the money. I'm here for Tremaine and I'm here because I was right! All along. I'm getting right with the department and I'm getting right with my wife, too. I owe that to my partner. I owe it to myself. As long as Spencer is out there, I'm not stopping. I'll never stop! You couldn't stop me if you tried!"

"Are you done?" Miller asked sarcastically. "You think you can get to Spencer without me, walk out the door. Without this operation, my operation, you're on your own."

After a long silence, he continued. "Wise up. Read your Nietzsche. Men cooperate when cooperation furthers our individual desires. There's no such thing as a common cause. Mankind has no greater purpose. I take care of me and you take care of you. We're animals. That's all. Only a dead idiot jumps on the grenade to save the other guy."

Miller ran his fingers through his thinning hair and turned his back on Owen. "I'll get Jonathan Spencer," he said. "My way. Jonathan Spencer disappears, the client pays, and you and I move on with fat wallets. That's how the grownups roll. Don't bullshit yourself, detective. You'll take the money. I saw your face when I handed you the ten grand."

*****

The weather turned wet and cold, forcing Spencer to purchase clothes. He bought comfortable Timberland work boots in his right size and left the smaller running shoes at the store. He also purchased underwear, socks, undershirts, work shirts, one pair of Lee jeans, one pair of tan work pants, two more sweatshirts and a heavy orange-brown canvas work jacket with a thick woolen collar. He couldn't find Emporio underwear.

Inside the changing room, he slipped out of the sweat pants, pulled off the hoodie, then stared at the dirty pile that represented everything left from XMercy and Mouse; a filthy heap of worn-out cotton. Mouse's struggles, Mercy's dreams, dead on a scratched-up linoleum floor.

The stick-thin pale-skinned figure in the Emporio underwear did not appear prepared to strike a blow for anyone.

"You look like ready for the last act of a Passion Play," he told the image looking back from the mirror. He turned away, then dropped the briefs and stepped out from them before putting on replacement clothes.

Men were coming for him. He knew it. He could sense it in the deep aches along every fracture. Snakes have fangs. Snakes can strangle.

Selecting specific, high-value targets lowered the already lean odds. *But no more rich women in green dresses.*

He picked up a blue baseball cap before paying. Oddly, the cashier didn't say anything about his wearing the merchandise. She asked him to turn around, scanned the tag on the back of the new jeans, and bagged the dirty sweats.

With the undershirt, sweatshirt, and the jacket with the collar upturned, good footwear, and the cap shedding rain, he was good. Standing outside and looking back at his reflection in the dripping store window, he could have been anybody.

*****

Spencer descended the delaminating plywood steps at the back of the Yonkers Victorian to get to his rented basement room. Under the bare bulb he looked over the work order, now both yellow and pink copies seated inside the plastic report binder he had picked up at Staples. Inside it, he placed a copy of the blue work permit along with one of the business cards. He also bought a 5 X 3 pocket notebook out, from which he tore the first twenty pages then worked at the cardboard cover until it looked well worn. On the top page, he wrote out the agent's name and direct dial number from memory.

Electronics proved harder to find. RadioShack had nothing to offer. It would have been easy to get everything online, but online purchasing required him to supply a credit card and a delivery address. Using credit cards would leave a direct trail. Even if he held onto them, he couldn't risk it. He finally located Micro Center, which carried the webcam he wanted. He also picked up a drill-driver and long sheetrock screws to go with it. But buying the unit was no answer in itself. There were a dozen pieces he still needed to work through.

Sound carried through the thin plywood walls that separated the makeshift rooms. He could hear the junkies, the nutcases. That left him able to practice all night long if that's what it took to get it right.

Lying wasn't his strong suit. "Pretend you are talking to a dog," his course instructors had taught. "It's all in the tone. Be confident. Be natural. You can get away with murder, just as long as you say it in the right tone."

Spencer hoped they were right.

Intel drives mission success. Reconnaissance drives intel. Recon is mission one. Reconnaissance-Diversion-Attack.

"Hi. I'm here to check the roof," he practiced into the mirror. He thought it came off sounding weak.

He tried again, this time more casually. "I'm supposed to check on the roof."

*****

Miller approached AlliedHamilton to get his sniper teams moved up and the helicopter ready at the airfield in White Plains. The line dropped before the call went through. Before he could redial, a text came across.

Locate alternative resource.

The text was a quick reminder. Jeffers and APA monitored his every phone call, every text, and every keystroke.

OK, Miller texted back, acceding to the checkbook. It was all a game of chess, really. He who thinks ahead of the opponent wins. APA might be close with AlliedHamilton. Fine. Commando talent was fungible. He'd bring up two squads from another resource. As long as the money was wired, that would take Spencer down. Then the entire issue disappeared out over the Atlantic inside a weighted body bag. The end.

"Well I hope you enjoyed my dinner at Per Se, all nine courses," Miller remarked, thinking of Jeffers and the APA. "You paid for it."

$2.5 million in hand, $2.5 million ahead.

*****

"Gentlemen," Miller announced with high energy following his successful telephone calls to North Carolina. "Let's summarize what we know."

Per Miller's order, Nussbaum had improvised a quick PowerPoint, now playing behind Miller's shoulder.

"A six-man team was annihilated, along with their pilot, here in southeast West Virginia," Miller narrated as the slides covered the projection wall behind him. "West Virginia State Police have called it drug cartel violence and called for forensics help from both the FBI and DEA. Feds have no clue except that the deceased include two females suspected of being drug dealers and the aforementioned team, apparently all killed by the identical type of weapons they themselves were carrying. Said team, comprised of former members of U.S. Army Special Forces and using fully-automatic military assault weaponry, was hired through an off-shore middleman who could not be located.

"We alone know the connection to former Master Sergeant Jonathan Spencer. There is no evidence to indicate that Spencer had assistance in taking out these seven ex-soldiers. This would seem implausible, but I know him, remember? He has a history of solo operations with at least one hundred military kills that have been confirmed on record. We also know, from sighting here, here, here, and here, that he moved five hundred miles to get from West Virginia to the latest sighting in Yonkers, New York, home town of Horace Vandergelder. So, is the loner acting alone? What is he doing in Yonkers?"

"He is planning to attack?" Dilip offered, his voice rising on the last syllable.

"I can't find any indication that there are upcoming events in Yonkers involving rich people," Dale remarked.

"Of course he's planning to attack!" Owen barked at the techs.

"Yonkers has to be his staging area," he insisted. "He's preparing to attack someplace else."

"Give the man an award!" Miller chided back. "I'll have to get another bundle of Benjamins. He only sent the index cards after speculation about killing Jews. So why buy more ahead of time? What's he planning to make clear?"

"Why do you think he bought the index cards?' Owen responded. "He's going to mail them out, just like he did before. Is there any way you guys can scan U.S. Mail, locate where he mails them?"

Stephen stood up and slammed his foot down under the table. "We're four people! Four! You want us to map out the richest people in New York. You want us to track all these events. You want us to program facial recognition software for tens of thousands of cameras. Now you want us to scan the U.S. Mail? On the chance that he sends out index cards from a particular mailbox? Fuck it! Just fuck it! You're fucking nuts!"

Miller intervened. "Take a breather," he told Stephen. "Chill out. Never mind the postcards, the Postal Service. It's off the table." He pointed at the map and Dilip followed Miller's arm with the cursor.

"West Virginia, rural, middle of nowhere," Miller narrated. "That's a man going to ground. But he tried that and he failed, even though he succeeding in killing the six men who came after him along with their pilot. He isn't hiding now. He's back on familiar soil, his hunting ground."

They could all see the pattern of attacks from upriver on the Hudson to the Connecticut shore, attacks in Manhattan on the Upper East Side and Central Park West, Long Island attacks at Sand Point and all the way out to Sag Harbor. It resembled a fishhook.

"So, why business cards?" Miller wanted to know. "How do business cards fit in?"

"Access," Owen suggested. "Getting inside a security perimeter."

"Crazy," Kip quipped. "You can't even get inside clubs unless you're on the list. What good is a card going to do?"

"That's your next bonus," Miller told them as he walked toward one of the offices. "Figure it out. Isolate the top twenty events and the top twenty fixed targets. Get every camera in every location and every subway station in the vicinity. Get ahead of him. If it takes all night, get ahead of him."

"Top twenty in terms of attendance, in terms of gross income, by median income—what criteria do you want to use?" Stephen called after Miller.

Owen stared, debating and groping for answers. The objective seemed simple enough, but leave it to a tech to parse it into a weeklong debate.

"Median income," Owen decided. *Fuck it.* He looked around for Miller, who had disappeared behind a closed door. "This is still bullshit. One detective and four techs. We might as well be sifting a beach to locate a single grain of sand."

*****

Spencer double-parked outside 110 E 71st, leaving the emergency flashers blinking while he rang the doorbell outside Terraza.

"Where do I park?" he asked, dropping his tool chest at the doorman's feet. "I can't afford more parking tickets."

"What are you here about?" the doormen wanted to know. He was dressed in full livery: black police hat with gold band, full-length wool overcoat with more gold at the collar, gilded buttons and gold sleeve ribbons, crisp white shirt and gray tie, gray trousers, shining black shoes. His square stance said it all. That was his door; nobody was getting past it without his say-so.

Spencer thrust a pink copy at him and ran back to the car while he perused the work order. "So, where to?" he yelled back. The doorman produced a blue handicapped placard, ran it out to Spencer and pointed toward Madison Avenue. "Walter" was printed on his gold nametag.

"Watch my stuff, will you?"

"Grab a spot, then come back and register with me," the doorman said.

Once he got inside the building, Spencer was startled. The building went far beyond the older-looking structure he saw on the online images. An entire modern new building had been added that towered over the original structure.

"So what's this about?" the doorman demanded. Early forties, Spencer guessed. Protective. The leather thong and handle-end of a black nightstick dangled at the edge of his desk just behind the bar-height countertop.

"The roof deck. Regular six-month check-up. Got to get a look at the membrane, see it isn't going to start leaking again. Ounce of prevention or a pound of cure." He fished into pockets, coming up with a business card. "Jay Spender. That's me." Spencer pointed at the name and back to the work order in the doorman's hands.

"You're not on the list."

"So that's my problem?"

"You're not on the list," he repeated.

"Ok. I did my job, you did yours. So I come back in six months. Maybe it don't leak." Spencer picked the toolbox off the floor, turned toward the door, stopped, and pulled a small notepad from his pocket, then thumbed until he came to the right page. Returning to the doorman, he offered the pad and pointed.

"She's your management agent, right? How 'bout you call and then she can send a right list."

The doorman lifted his telephone in one hand and rested his other hand onto the nightstick while he pressed in the number. Voicemail picked up. She was on vacation. The doorman hung up, looked Spencer up and down, and then ordered him to place the toolbox on the counter, take two steps back, and hold still.

He hefted the toolbox off the counter down onto his desk. Inside the toolbox Spencer had a selection of used pawnshop tools along with the brand new drill-driver and the electronics. The doorman lifted open the lid, moved his gloved fingers through the various drill bits, safety goggles, screws, earplugs, and bits and pieces inside the upper tray, then lifted out the tray and examined the large compartment below. Box knife, wire-strippers, hammer, drill-driver, and electronics. He held up the electronics, turned them side to side and upside down. When he reached out his arm, Spencer caught sight of the crossed black powder pistols tattooed above his wrist.

"What's that?" the doorman asked, still moving and examining the round black ball, tapered base, and tail antenna.

"Infrared moisture meter, sarge," Spencer answered as he had practiced. "Looks for leaks where we can't see 'em."

The doorman put the camera back inside Spencer's toolbox then looked Spencer up and down and came from behind the desk carrying a security wand.

"Take off the hat. Collar down. Arms out, legs spread." Spencer obeyed as ordered. While he was passing the wand, the ex-MP patted along Spencer after each tone.

"Army?" Walter asked.

"82nd. Bragg."

"988th. Benning."

Spencer thought of Harmony Church, but didn't mention the Sniper School. "Combat MP, huh? Saw your stamp. When did you serve, Walter?" Spencer asked.

"Name's not Walter, its Vince, Vincenzo. Every doorman here since '82 has been Walter, so here I'm Walter. Makes it easier on the residents. Deployed in Desert Storm, Sierra Leone in '97, Kosovo in '99. Ten years. Staff sergeant."

"I'm only out a year. Not much." Spencer pulled out another business card and read, "Maintenance Technician.

"I used to destroy IEDs, now I fix toilets."

Walter gave him a gentle pat on the back then stepped back behind the counter.

"Come over here," Vince said apologetically, lifting up a digital camera. "I got to do it." After taking Spencer's photograph, he pointed to the resident elevators instead of making Spencer trek to the service elevators in back and then around again to the front roof deck.

"Seventh floor," Walter indicated. "Wait a second." He ducked down behind the counter and came back with a fresh pair of black booties. "Put these on inside so one of them doesn't shit themselves over the carpet and go nuclear on me."

"Tough place," Spencer remarked.

"Naw. Rich people. There's a few assholes lighting me up over every fucking thing just 'cause they figure I'm the whipping boy. But most are ok. They leave me alone. The worst is the ones who act like they're your best friend. Ask me have I ever seen one those guys one time outside the job. Have they ever had me up for a meal? A beer even? No fucking way. They're not my pals.

"But I stay dry. We got the union. Sundays when I work I bring my iPad and watch the games."

"Oh hey. That reminds me," Spencer said. "It takes me forever to send the images back to the office over the phone. You think I can use your Wi-Fi, Vince? Sure would save time."

CHAPTER TWENTY-ONE

All four techs were fidgeting more than their normal hyperactivity when they excitedly displayed their accomplishments. As they were getting more familiar with the huge enterprise system, they kept peeling back the onion to discover more and more functions. In less than two hours they had mapped primary and secondary events in order of the median incomes of known persons attending. They had every camera feed and all public transportation geo-linked in association with each specific event.

At the onset, the entire screen looked like a jumble of flags superimposed one upon the other. Stephen opened the map view outward until each was differentiated, yet the concentration of wealth remained staggering.

"Are you understanding this?" Dilip asked Owen.

"You see, we applied color intensity to coincide with the median wealth represented at each venue," Stephen explained.

"Wow," Owen agreed. "It hits you when you see it like this. I mean, you know the money is here. It's New York. But holy crap."

"I also wrapped each flag in those circles, with the width of the circle corresponding to a public exposure metric," Dilip added eagerly. "The more each event appears online, the wider the circle."

Dale opened the mapping tool wider still, exposing black camera icons. He suggested that Owen come closer and take the mouse. "Click on one of the cameras. Any one of them, just pick one."

Owen did as instructed and instantly a live view appeared in the upper corner of the monitor. He moved the cursor, clicked again, and a new view popped up.

It was Kip's turn now. Jumping in ahead of Dilip, he excitedly insisted upon showing the second side of the equation. "I correlated the Forbes 400 list with physical addresses here in NYC. Let me show you."

Dale interrupted; they acted like gleeful children during show-and-tell.

"Here are their residential addresses; I backed out post boxes and commercial zoning."

The map showed another confused concentration of flags, green and purple this time. Owen assumed that one color represented addresses, the other cameras, but he would have been incorrect. Dale opened the geography outward so that smaller areas of concentration displayed as distinct flags, sometimes as many as sixteen flags in single key buildings.

"Each of the purple flags is a Forbes 400 individual. Purple was, of course, the emperor's color in Ancient Rome."

"I did the green," Dilip chimed in.

"The cameras," Owen thought out loud.

"Not at all," Dilip corrected him. "Green flags represent foreign nationals, known billionaires with residences here. I derived these by filtering State Department and IRS records and supplemented high net worth private client logs within investment banks, hedge funds, and private equity databases."

Once he had the floor, Dilip continued frenetically, shifting to another screen wherein the black camera icons were so densely-packed that individual apartments had to be mapped room by room. As he moved the cursor over the icons, a graphic displayed the individual's face, his ranking on the international wealth list, and net wealth in two digits—billions and hundreds of millions.

Dilip placed the cursor over a particular camera within a large room at the top of the sixty-eight story building occupying a whole block on 5th Avenue between E. 56th and E. 57th and began giggling uncontrollably before he clicked.

"No," Stephen shouted, "not The Donald!"

"Oh yes," Dilip confirmed. "The Donald!"

Dilip bowed and continued. "This is excellent," he promised. With a right click, he opened a radius out to twenty feet, superimposed on top of the live feed. A number 4 flashed then moved to the upper-right corner.

"Four devices," Dilip explained before moving his cursor over one of the small red earphone icons on the screen.

A valet appeared, with his back to the camera and a rack of gold ties from which The Donald, standing in his underpants, made his selection.

"You tell them," the voice ordered, "if their security people won't do the job, then I'll get up and leave."

Stephen beamed. His techs, Dilip especially, looked like three baby birds gaping for their momma. "Audio!"

"Audio!" they shouted in chorus.

"I don't give a damn if they put up a Purell dispenser," the voice affirmed. "I don't shake hands. It's filthy! They pick their noses! How hard is it to tell them in line before they get to me and up they come, reaching out?"

Dilip scrolled through until he found the mayor's office.

Miller shut them down, the minute it appeared, scolding them all. "Jesus! Tools, not toys. If it isn't Spencer, don't put it up. Not on monitors, either!"

"Can you imagine how much the tabloids would pay?" Dale muttered. His mind was abuzz. "Even for the clips! Holy crap…there's billions sitting there for the taking in this technology."

Kip expanded the thought. "Board meetings. Getting ahead of every corporate announcement. Getting the inside track on product releases, mergers."

"The person who controls this conceivably alters economies," Dale confirmed, synthesizing all their thoughts. "Wicked shit."

"The end of privacy," Nussbaum murmured. He took over the program and moved his cursor around, doing a 'fly-over' across Manhattan.

"They've got security cameras everywhere, even in their toilet rooms," Stephen explained. "We can see right into every room in their places."

"And we can hear," Dilip added. "And not just in New York. The fundamental architecture scales to Beijing, Berlin, London, Delhi."

"Spencer!" Miller shouted at them, clapping his hands. "Stop with the Masters of the Universe. This is about one target. One!"

"Filter out the apartments and drill down to exteriors and public areas," Owen told them. "Everything in and around the primary targets on my list."

"Easy," Stephen responded, "but thousands are still left. The system is built to spot any person we're seeking across millions of cameras. It isn't able to get inside his head!'

Owen threw up his hands and turned to Miller. "We need assets in place, here, now! The second we get the next hit on camera we need to move! Right away! The moment Spencer attacks again, it is going to be all over the news and there goes your low profile. This makes no sense!"

*****

Spencer stretched his legs out on the basement floor and sat, munching on peanut butter and Saltines, while he studied the camera feed until his eyes felt like they were ready to explode out of his skull. Individual recon always meant either boredom or terror, but it was necessary and no one else was handing him prepared intelligence data.

He awakened at 04:00 and studied the front and side entrances non-stop until 11:30. Middle of the week, yet he counted only eleven residents departing the front doors all morning long. The doorman walked them out under his umbrella to waiting sedans where drivers held open the doors. He had key faces committed to memory from photos off the web.

Even the lowest-grade spotting scope had better resolution than his wireless webcam. Not pretty, but it was sufficient; he could still recognize his target. This wasn't Afghanistan; he had no satellites or drones to confirm target presence.

Mercedes, Daimler, Rolls Royce, Bentley, and one Mercedes Sprinter Van passed the front doors. He wanted to tie his target to one of the vehicles. Get some kind of an edge.

One drop of drizzle and the doorman's umbrella obscured their faces; all Spencer could see were legs and shoes. "You'll get one chance," he observed. "You can't miss it. That's it. One chance."

Eighty-five people have as much wealth as the poorest 3.5 billion. Let's make that eighty-four.

Through the morning, he watched the screen off the feed from the camera he had mounted; it was fixed at 42-degree angle looking diagonally across the street to the corner of the Park Avenue structure. He counted thirty-one domestic employees entering off E. 71st. He also counted nineteen deliveries—FedEx, UPS, and DHL vans stopped in a nearly constant succession.

Bingo. Big box vans. Big enough to carry a bomb that could level a city block.

"Now make them believe it. Don't leave them time to think. Get them running. Out the doors, straight into the line of fire."

*****

Using a prepaid cell phone, Spencer dialed the Terraza.

Vince answered, "Terraza, Walter speaking. How may I help you?"

"Vince, Jay, calling about the roof deck. Good news and bad news, which you feeling like first? Ok. The good news is that the deck membrane isn't too bad overall," Spencer explained. "Bad news is there is a section along the southeast corner where the whole sub-structure is sopping wet. No good. Good news is we caught it before it soaked into the apartment underneath, but more bad news, too.

"Vince, with this wet weather I have to tent the whole thing, protect the ceiling below it when I cut out the wet plywood, and then get it good and dry before I come back and recoat it. Won't get adhesion if it isn't dry."

"When you coming out?" Vince wanted to know.

"No promises, I can try for this afternoon late or at least by noon tomorrow."

"No problem either way. None of the residents go out on the deck in the rain except to let their dogs go, and that is against the rules anyhow so they can't bitch about anything. Thursday I'm off, but I'll put you on the list."

"Thanks, sarge."

Spencer then made a second call, this time dialing 9-1-1.

"Emergency services. What are you reporting?"

"There's some black dude with a pitbull dog that he just set loose on this guy. Can you hear that? He's chewing his arm off! "

"What is your location?"

"Outside the restaurant. The Italian place. East 71st Avenue near Park."

"What is your name sir?"

"Whoa. I'm just calling. I'm not getting involved. Oh man, he's bitten an artery or something."

Spencer hung up the phone and removed the sim card and battery. 11:43. At 11:46, a patrol car screeched to a stop on the curb directly below the camera. *Three minutes.* Spencer watched the ambulance follow at 11:50.

Quality information, but he wasn't convinced. It wasn't going to work, not by itself. The sort of people living at Park Avenue won't march to anyone else's tune. They couldn't be given a choice. The city had to be on edge. They had to be afraid, really afraid, before he could make them march out the doors.

Spencer noted the response intervals, then pulled up the events calendar file he had been building and massaging.

"Something easy, flashy." He needed an easy target first, something to set the tone. Put the city on edge. "Then everyone at Park will run straight out those brass and glass front doors."

He turned back to the index cards. He still had the contact points and addresses in a file; all the television and radio stations and newspapers where he had sent out "I Kill Rich People." He had tried seventeen different phrases, but none of them got across what he needed to say. The Captain would know the right words, but he couldn't come up with anything.

"Crap!" he shouted. The Barrett had to speak for him now.

*****

Past 10 p.m., the techs were still working. Stephen, Dale, Kip, and Dilip had six primary events and eleven bracketed venues. It should have felt like an incredible accomplishment, but Owen was at the point of trying to ask a Ouija Board.

"Still way too many targets," he complained.

"This will help," Stephen offered. "I have the system set to an automatic function. It constantly scans through more than a quarter-million frames. The second it picks up Spencer, you and I get texted with the time, the camera footage, the location."

Owen nodded, too tired to argue. So many empty pizza boxes and soda cans were scattered around the place that it looked like a fraternity house. "Ok," he told the techs. "Back here 7:45 tomorrow morning. Get some sleep."

He had a room at the Super 8 in North Bergen. Tired as he was, he couldn't sleep. He wanted to get into the car and drive straight out to Long Island, but just showing up would be worse than drunk-dialing and he'd already done more than his share of that.

"Go when the job is done," he told himself. "Then drive out there and get your family."

At least he had Miller agreeing to put all of the SWAT team on the clock immediately when they had another sighting. That was something, but they still hadn't even considered commercial venues: the Stock Exchange, the

Goldman Sachs Tower, or even one of the high-end restaurants catering to the city's elites.

The task was fucking impossible. The whole thing. He might have stayed up all night, every night, forever, and still done no better than guesswork.

Miller, with his ten thousand dollar prizes, was staying at the Mandarin Oriental at Columbus Circle. Whatever Miller was doing all day was unclear. They must have been paying him hourly, Owen griped to himself, because Miller was on vacation again.

Miller came on like the leader, but where was he when everyone else was doing the heavy lifting? Owen was the one who waded through hours upon hours of looking at sidewalks through webcams. Too much information to wade through and not enough eyeballs.

Forty thousand law enforcement officers in the city and five people were doing this thing, him and four nerds looking inside rich people's bathrooms.

God help us, he thought. *We need more people.*

*****

Vince's part-time replacement looked like Lawrence Taylor, big as a house and still looking able to put the hurt on any quarterback. He wasn't looking to make new friends, either.

"Mister, my handicapped placard is for loading and unloading cars for residents," he informed Spencer. "Period."

Spencer tried to break through, tried to find some common ground, but no-go.

"You call me 'Walter,'" the doorman instructed him. "You don't need another name."

Spencer was forced to haul the tent all the way around the building, that along with the six heavy sandbags he needed to hold the tent in place. Down long interior halls to the rear service elevator and then back again in the reverse order up on the seventh floor. By the time he made it to the service elevator he was fighting to stifle back the searing pain shooting from his legs and his back.

One step forward, two steps back.

It was the first time he had humped a load in over a year, he realized. His Barrett and ammunition weighed about the same as the tent and sandbags: fifty-five pounds. Two hundred yards had him aching; he used to handle bigger loads over mountainsides.

Sixteen months ago he made double-time across five kilometers carrying the Barrett and a full field pack holding ten days' rations and water.

As the service elevator opened on the 7th floor, the realization hit hard; he wasn't a Tower of Power. That was something he used to be. All over.

The legs were improving, but they would never be there again. Once a Ranger, always a Ranger? *Nope.*

Before, when it was just about having the one kidney, he could prove to the Physical Evaluation Board comprised of officers in his United States Army that they were wrong. Now, it really was over. Nothing in the world was going to give him the tools, not now, not ever again.

Now, it was about Captain Sam. And XMercy and Mouse.

"Finish it," he told himself over every trudging step back. "Finish."

At the seventh floor rooftop doors he set down the load, closed his eyes, holding them closed until his mind had cleared the pain. He wiped tears out of the corners of his eyes and lifted.

"Get your head straight," he reminded himself. *Limitations are load-factors; you don't whine, you calculate for them. Get right. Mission mode.*

Thirty minutes later he had the full-height green tent tied off on one side against the railings along the southeast corner of the rooftop; on the interior side, he knotted the sandbags to the stake lines then added additional bags inside the tent to keep it in place. The flap doors opened to the rooftop.

Spencer opened the zipper window at the back of the tent and set his feet in firing position, then stretched his empty arms before bringing them back into firing position; the fat of his thumb fit just below his right cheekbone. The webcam was three feet above him and ten inches forward; he had the scene imprinted into his memory.

He sighted the invisible weapon at the side door of Park Avenue then rotated his shoulders ten degrees right in a compact movement that required no change to foot position. His left forefinger pointed straight at the brass-and-glass front door. Again and again he lifted and sighted the imaginary weapon. BRASS. Shift to the front door. BRASS. Every shot inside a twenty-degree lateral motion, three degrees rise and fall.

Satisfied, Spencer unzipped the tent, emerged, and hung a laminated sign on the side of the tent facing toward the building. It read: Maintenance in Progress. Thank You for Your Cooperation. We Deeply Apologize for any Inconvenience._

*****

Owen was still putting the pieces together. West Virginia made sense to him. Spencer was laying low, recovering, and avoiding trouble. But now that the trouble had come to him, he wasn't returning to Yonkers to fit into the crowd. "He knows his identity is out. He has no more cover," he said. "He's back because there is nowhere to hide. He's back to finish what he started."

Owen watched the techs with their fingers flying over keyboards. Stephen had the wall projection set up with a separate corner window flashing the micro-analysis on Spencer's face and alternately scrolling through the array of cameras scanning for convergent data points.

Miller had seen Spencer in action. He explained Spencer's meticulous approach. "He will scout his target, pick his location, know his exit strategy; he did it in Afghanistan, he had done it in every other attack. Master Sergeant Jonathan Spencer is always thorough.

"Your partner stepped right into the middle of Spencer's preparations," Miller told Owen. "We're going to take him down that same way."

He looked up, addressing their foe: "Only this time nobody is underestimating you, Spencer. You never hear the shot that kills you."

"We've got a hit!" Stephen yelled from the bullpen. Dale immediately shifted the live camera feed onto the big screen while Kip and Dilip applied mapping overlays for physical location, public transportation, events and fixed targets.

Spencer was up on live video, covering the long wall. Dilip boxed a street map into the corner showing his location, direction, and the camera icons around him.

"He's on Madison," Stephen called. He looked like any other New Yorker: a baseball cap hid his eyes and he had his collar was upturned, but the software gathered enough data from his jaw, cheekbones, and partial sections from Spencer's nose to trigger a match-alert.

"The Whitney," Owen and Stephen shouted in unison.

"Tomorrow night," Stephen continued. His fingers raced along the keyboard, highlighting the event site at Madison and E. 75th.

"Fundraiser for Whitney Museum of American Art," Dilip read excitedly, cutting in on Nussbaum, who looked annoyed. "Live auction of Mid-Century Masters including notable works of Andrew Wyeth, Grant Wood, Edward Hopper, Man Ray."

"That's it!" Miller shouted. "That's five thousand dollars for each one of you!"

Miller studied the satellite photo put up by Dale, one of the twenty-something techs. The Whitney was smack in the center. "Give me an attendance list and cross-reference it for Forbes 400 attendees," he ordered. "I want daily calendars, maps, public transportation, and camera coverage. All right, Lieutenant. Now we call in the heavy artillery! I'm putting a blanket over the Whitney Museum. A dozen military-trained snipers are going to be waiting there to blow Spencer's head off. Satisfied?"

Miller watched Spencer's steady pace as he maneuvered through the pedestrians around him.

"Do unto others as you would have others do unto you, Spencer," he told the screen image.

"You overreached, Jeffers, but I'm preserving your career," he whispered under his breath. He moved stridently toward one of the private offices. "Get my next two-and-half-million dollars ready, Jeffers."

*****

"I'm looking at your guest list," Jeffers told Miller. "A Rothschild, a Rockefeller."

He read, scanning for associates. Not one APA member was on it. "Take him down afterward," Jeffers instructed.

"Say again," Miller responded.

"Let him get off some shots, then kill him," Jeffers reiterated.

"He kills anybody and that brings in every cop in Manhattan," Miller argued. "I'm going to have twelve men with rifles on rooftops, in windows. How do you explain that away? Pretty far-fetched for a coincidence."

"That's my piece. That can be handled. Nobody questions heroes," Jeffers said. "Let him get off two shots, then take him down."

CHAPTER TWENTY-TWO

Miller slapped two bundles of bills against his palm. "Heads up," he told Dale, before tossing them underhand.

Dale's arms shot out and missed the catch. He had the cash trapped against his stomach before it slipped out onto the floor. Dilip, Stephen, and Kip stared at it, frozen like dogs looking at a treat and not sure if they would get scolded for eating it.

"Divide it between you," Miller told them to their communal relief. "Great job."

Owen followed him back to the office and shook his head in disgust. "Sunset is 7:42," he protested. "They start seating at 6. What if he attacks afterward? He'll be shooting from darkness. Everyone he targets will be lit up like Christmas."

"We'll handle that," Miller countered calmly.

"Cameras," Owen grumbled. "Ok, what is near the Whitney? Get me every visual and every means of transportation. Taxis, ride-shares, subway. We need to cover every angle. He'll have to carry a large satchel or duffle, something that conceals his weapon."

"And night vision," Owen realized. "Tell the snipers."

"Chill," Miller responded. "Cullen, this is your own plan. It's an exact parallel to Citi-Field; we draw Spencer out and take him down."

"This is nothing like our plan," Owen protested. "No way. We had Major Gonzalez, our sniper team leader, with a practiced team in place. At Citi-Field we had police officers behind bulletproof glass.

"We had a controlled environment with acres of open buffer. We could hit a switch and light everything. Gonzalez spent days planning and training until they had every conceivable wrinkle worked out. He still killed Tremaine. Don't tell me to 'chill'!"

Miller wasn't deterred. "I have that piece under control. These men aren't Bishop's rejects. They don't miss."

"We can't dangle eight or nine hundred private citizens as bait. Don't bullshit yourself. There's traffic. Darkness. Things don't go as planned!"

"All right, fine," Miller conceded. "I'll ask for drone feeds along with the cameras. Let me contact the client."

"The client. Right! We know the client is the government!" Owen shouted back. "Why not say so? One look at these systems says it all. We were just watching The Donald in his bathroom, for God's sake."

Miller leaned back then squared his intense focus straight back at Owen's comical freckles. He was obviously enjoying peeling back the curtains from Owen's eyes.

"I listened to your position, detective. I made my call. Get this, loud and clear. We're not giving up our best shot to bring in your precious NYPD. Spencer worked for me, remember? I know how he thinks, how he plans. You apply your standard police procedure and you get a lot of your officers killed.

"Now, I have assets to put into place and building plans and response models to work through. Have Stephen set you up with a tablet and run you the live feeds. When the drones are online, we'll jump them in, too," Miller said. "Get in close to the Whitney. Keep running through the exterior camera feeds. The minute he's spotted, our assets get the green light."

Miller turned back toward the techs, announcing, "I'm setting aside a hundred grand for the man who takes Spencer down.

"You too, detective," he told Owen. "A hundred-thousand-dollar bonus. That's a long way from bankruptcy for ten days' work."

Miller tossed his car keys at Owen, who snatched them out of the air. "Now get moving!"

Owen looked down on Miller's bald spot while Miller walked away. "Asshole," Owen grumbled after him. "That bankruptcy had nothing to do with you. You weren't there. You don't know a fecking thing about that."

But a hundred thousand dollars. Owen was afraid to repeat it out loud, like he might jinx it and make it go away. A hundred thousand dollars would mean a fresh start.

*****

Spencer searched the websites for something simple and flashy, one quick, low-exposure strike where he could get in and get out safely, something with enough visibility to stir the pot, to get the city on edge. Unless the residents believed the bomb threat was real, Park Avenue wouldn't succeed.

He also knew that he had to be sure Vince was working the door at Terraza; the second "Walter" wouldn't let him through without a search. He could sink the scope and magazines inside five gallons of roofing sealant. He needed the ladder to hide the rifle and the 4Runner to transport the ladder, but there was no foolproof means to conceal the five-foot-long Barrett rifle.

"You'll have to leave the Barrett behind afterward," he told himself. That hurt.

The 4Runner had to be abandoned, too. NYPD would box down the whole city after Park Avenue. *Public transportation. Blend in.*

This is for you Captain Sam, and for XMercy and Mouse.

He looked at his hands and in the craggy palm lines he saw the kid, the red Manchester United t-shirt. His dark head moving into line with his mother's burqa when he shot. One shot, two heads.

"You did that," he murmured. *One great shot for Man, one fucked up evil for Mankind.*

All the training, all the conditioning and planning and proficient execution. A hundred and sixty-five dead people. Not targets, people. One hundred and sixty-six, he corrected; he missed counting Stocky.

"Killing fifty or eighty or a hundred snakes might give the whole country a new start, Captain, but I'm one man. I can't set a Controlled Burn, not alone," he said aloud. "The rich can keep squeezing. I can't change that. But I just might shut Vision Partners down. That's something, Captain. I can try."

*****

After Stephen walked him through a short tutorial, Owen left the tablet screen set on the coordinates surrounding the Whitney and familiarized himself with the program. Each icon represented a different camera view.

Stephen tapped one of the buttons along the control bar. "This scrolls through all the cameras on the map view," he explained. "Up here is the speed function to make it scroll faster or slower. If you move the cursor to a tighter area then hold down on the right click, you can spread whatever radius you want." He demonstrated twice until Owen nodded.

"Got it." Not that it lent him much confidence. He knew the area; too many places where Spencer could be.

"We need to narrow the field," he told Stephen.

"Working on it," Nussbaum replied. "You'll have a lot more capability coming out of that tablet than anyone could ever have with feet on the ground."

Owen was already focused on a slow scroll. He glanced into the corner of the screen and noticed that the icons on the map lit up to coincide with the camera feed.

Stephen picked up on Owen's attention.

"I set it up so you can tie the view to the location," he explained to Owen. "Not always easy." He took the tablet and scrolled to a larger map scaled out to a mile radius, then pointed to a number at the lower left of the screen. "There's 72,136 live feeds in that mile. I can handle looking at twenty before they all start to blend together. Fortunately, most of those are interiors. You can pull those up by going to the toolbar. They're listed under References."

"Take me back to the Whitney," Owen snapped.

"No worries," Stephen responded. "Move the cursor to the back arrow and tap. Or you can also shift to a street view; just put the cursor into the map and right-click."

Owen cupped his hands beside his eyes to concentrate as the scroll moved through eighty exteriors. The shots didn't blend together so much as they broke repeating categories. Most of the views were obviously set above doorways; the people moving in and out were dead giveaways. Others were on the transit grid, set above traffic. Owen stopped the scrolling and concentrated on an odd, brightly lit motion view. He watched for two full minutes before realizing he was viewing the inside of the New York City Sewer System.

He moved the cursor to the ticket office directly in front of the Whitney and restarted the scrolling from there. More doorways. Alleyway shots looking at dumpsters. More traffic along Fifth, Madison, Park, and Lexington. Owen stopped again, holding the feed on an odd down angle looking diagonally across a corner with a blurry visual onto the corner of a residential building. There was no other view quite like it. He shifted to the map to identify the location right when Miller shouted at him.

"Why are you still here? Traffic is going to be brutal. Get going!"

Owen moved out of the inner office toward the door, and then stopped before opening it. He reached up underneath the back of his jacket and came out with the 9mm in his hand, looked at it and dropped the clip, confirmed it was a full ten, then slid it back up into the magazine, where it seated with a reassuringly solid click.

One clip was not enough.

"Guys," he called out to the four techs, "where's the nearest gun store?" Then he realized he already knew a gun store nearby. He and Tremaine had gone through half the gun stores in North Jersey.

"The tablet is set up as its own mobile hotspot," Stephen called behind him. "If that goes down, go to the toolbar, scroll down from Network, and select 4G."

*****

Owen bypassed the ticket lines by flashing his gold medallion. It felt good to be back on familiar streets, good to have his medallion hanging from the pocket of his jacket. He felt right, useful, a lot better than he had felt in months. The contrast startled him, showing him from the inside-out what a bitter pill he had been. Everything wasn't on Callie; he knew that all along. But now he could feel it; he was back on the job, back to his old self. The billion cells throughout his body were renewed.

He trotted through the Whitney Museum carrying the GoPro camera that Kip had lent him. At the entry and every door in and out of the cavernous room where the auction was going to be held, he photographed outward, looking through the entry doors and out every window until two security guards walked toward him and quickly held up their hands to signal for him to stop.

"Sir, still photos only. I'm going to have to ask you to stop filming," one said.

After Owen showed his shield a second time, the museum's Chief of Security rushed out to give him the royal treatment. Owen's back cracked as he straightened up to his full height.

The man seemed delighted to walk the Detective Lieutenant through their security arrangements; theft deterrence systems in place for every item on display, along with multiple cameras in each gallery. Special events? In addition to the chief and the full-time security staff, they supplemented with off-duty officers, all NYPD and Parks Police. Most of them had worked their events for years.

"Why do you ask? Is there something I need to know about?"

Owen deflected his response with another inquiry. He wanted to know about parking.

"We offer valet parking for evening events through a service," the Chief of Security explained. "The formula is one valet per eight cars, roughly a valet for each thirty arriving guests. There is some foot traffic, then some multi-passenger cars and some solo-drivers, and guests arriving with drivers, of course. There's guesswork, but the formula serves us well. We've used the same company for nearly three years; that allows us to add valets or subtract, as needed. More are needed after events since the guests all tend to leave at about the same time."

Owen made a mental note of that disturbing observation. The entire guest list would be stacked up outside, under the lights like sitting ducks. He looked at the slender security manager and bit his tongue. The other man's slim fit suit was definitely not hiding any weapon.

"Where do they park the cars?"

"68 East 80th or 35 East 75th. We contract with both garages."

"Show me your roof."

"The roof?"

"You hard of hearing? The roof."

They accessed the roof by interior stairwell; the door to the stairwell was tied to an alarm that could be bypassed only by entering a code onto an electronic pad. The security chief showed the security fob clipped onto the inside pocket of his jacket then discretely placed himself between Owen and the pad to keep the code from Owen's view. He had to repeat the process at the top of the stairs to get onto the rooftop.

Both buildings from across Madison looked directly onto the Whitney's street-level entrance. Owen scanned the exposure. "How do you secure this?" he asked himself. At least half a dozen buildings offered a direct line-of-sight.

As the security chief scrambled to answer, Owen realized he needed Gonzalez. Gonzalez would shoot a dozen holes through Miller's thought process.

Looking over the edge to the ground level, Owen pictured a crowd being channeled into the narrow entryway down below like cattle going to a slaughterhouse. He looked up and immediately spotted six-dozen windows, all easily within Spencer's proven attack range.

Counting them one by one, it suddenly occurred to him that at least half the windows were fixed windows that couldn't open. That was something. Miller's assets needed night vision.

Would Gonzalez's thermal imaging machine be able to tell at night when a window was open, he wondered?

Gonzalez had had his men out at Citi Field drilling and practicing for hours. What the hell was Miller thinking, that he could pick up snipers like day laborers and everything was just going to work out? Miller wasn't a sniper. He didn't get it. Look at what just happened in West Virginia. Bishop sent in commandos and Spencer killed them all.

Owen thanked the Whitney's security chief then jogged outside at a fast trot, looking toward the highest point that he could see from the entrance. At the door to 23 East 74th, the fiftyish balding doorman looked apprehensive about opening until Owen pressed his medallion against the glass. "Roof," was all he said, looking to the ceiling for emphasis.

The doorman swiped Owen into the elevator and swiped his identification again, pressing 18. "Sixteen floors, but no thirteen," he explained. "Eighteen is the roof access. Hold on." He ran back to his desk and returned with a rubber wedge. "You'll want this. Don't let the door close behind you." Before the elevator doors shut, he reached inside to make them open again, asking Owen, "Should I dial 911 or do anything?"

"No. I need to look at your roof. That's all."

From the rooftop, Owen looked right down at the Whitney. From that acute angle he could only see the tops of heads. It didn't feel right, not for shooting at anyone on the street. His eyes ran to rooftops lower, better placements for visuals on the Whitney entrance. Nearly every rifle shot he had made in his life was with a BB gun, but he found himself lifting as though he had a rifle in hand and aiming to one roof, then another, and another, and another, every single one a possibility. One of Millers' snipers needed to be positioned exactly where he was standing. More had to be on the roof of the Whitney, scanning outward.

He came out shaking his head. *"Jaysus. Who ya trying to kid there, boyo?"* he could hear Eamonn calling him on this. Hundreds of targets bunched together under lights and Spencer in the dark with the choice of dozens of places.

It was overwhelming. Impossible. Like scanning an ocean for a single swimmer. He went into Via Quadronno to use the tablet to catch up with Miller and Nussbaum and absently ordered a coffee and the first sandwich on the chalkboard.

The waiter set down the cup then gave it a half-turn so that the handle was positioned perfectly. They both looked good. He realized how hungry he was but stared down at the creamy foam and the ham inside the fancy bread. He wished that he could just eat and drink without having his brain racing.

He sipped at the coffee, tasting the rich bitterness on his tongue and licking the creamy foam off his upper lip. The tablet sprang to life with six live views per page, every exterior view between 68th Street Station and 77th and between Fifth and Lex: looking out from residential entrances, street cams looking out to traffic, security cams covering retail door fronts; dozens upon dozens of views, so many that they made all the windows looking down to the Whitney seem digestible in comparison. He bit through the flakey crust into the salty, thick-sliced ham and scrolled through page after page as his tongue reached out to snatch back a gush of mustard dangling at the corner of his mouth.

Again, he had that feeling that he was missing something. *What?* He wished he could just talk it through with Callie. She was good at that, seeing the things he missed when he got into his head too much in a case.

A hundred thousand dollars would be amazing. Callie couldn't ignore that, he told himself, picturing her reaction if he walked up to the door with it in both fists.

"But there is no way to do this," he griped aloud. "People are going to die."

He stuffed a huge bite into his mouth and tapped his fingers on his chest as he chewed through it like a masticating cow, then swallowed it all, choking it down when it came to him. At the auction house, Al had found a microphone that Spencer had put into a bouquet. What would keep Spencer from using a camera?

Nussbaum answered Owen's call. "Is there any way to find out when the camera feeds came live?" Owen asked intently.

"That data point is inherently compromised," Stephen told him. "These cameras are resetting constantly. I suppose we could deduce when a current feed initiated, but I doubt that it would be of any value."

"Humor me. Call it a hunch."

"'Humor you'? What do you think we do here twelve hours a day, longer even? Dale, one of my techs, is developing keywords to screen web traffic from Yonkers and every place north and south for ten miles. Right now, I have Kip identifying every use of mapping technologies for Manhattan from the same area. Can you imagine how many people are looking for a restaurant or mapping for a business appointment? Now I need to apply a filter for every search for the ten blocks around Whitney Museum. Humor you!" Stephen said sarcastically.

But a moment later, he called out begrudgingly: "Dale, take the area ten blocks around the museum and try to find out when the camera feeds went live." There was a pause, and then Stephen responded to a question someone on the other end had asked: "How am I supposed to know? I have no idea why. You get to humor the lieutenant."

*****

Spencer knew that they wouldn't be scouring the hills of West Virginia forever. They would find him eventually, whoever they were. What he did to them on the farm was just prolonging the inevitable. Killing one team was going to bring on more; the next time it would be better-trained units coming in wary. No used-up gimp was going to get through that a second time.

"You're a dead man walking," he acknowledged aloud. That was ok. He had gotten right with death a long, long time ago.

Sleeping in a stinking basement. Living on borrowed time. He flashed on the roof of the tower at Walter Reed. At least with suicide you control the time, the place, and the method. But suicide was a parasitic disease; he wasn't letting it creep inside his ear and dig into his brain or let it swim up his dick hole and breed in his guts.

Suicide by cop? Going out in some blaze of glory? That was even more pathetic than curling up in the 4Runner, pushing a hose inside the tailpipe and huffing carbon monoxide.

If you're doing it, just get it done. If he ever pulled the plug, he knew the method—a 661-grain brass jacket from a .50 BMG.

"Nobody is taking me. Not ever again," he promised.

All the training, every jump, every desert, every action against superior force—white guys, black guys, Mexicans, kids straight out of high school, college graduates—warriors always had one thing in common: the ones who got through, the men who earned their patch, they would die before they would give up. No matter how hurt and how low and how fucked the situ gets, you don't give up. You never give up!

He might make it north to the Saint Lawrence; he might find a way across to Canada. Then what, find an empty spot on some mountain and fight the elements instead of fighting people?

Canada. *Right.* Borders didn't matter to the men who were coming after him. "People with their own prisons don't care about borders," he reminded himself.

Spencer looked over the fresh roll of fifty self-stick stamps, the black felt-tip marking pen, and the 3 X 5 lined index cards on the floor in front of him. He tried and couldn't remember whether last time he had written it out in all caps.

"What the hell does the font matter when you don't know what to say?" he scolded. What did it matter if he still couldn't find the words?

KISS, he told himself. Keep It Simple, Stupid. But the more he worked on it, the less he said anything like what it was that he wanted to get across.

"What do I say?" he grumbled in frustration. "I'm an instrument of God?" That sounded like a schizophrenic hearing voices.

"God ain't talking to you, Johnny Boy," he told himself. "All you've got is raging tinnitus."

Maybe I can just leave my thumbprint, he thought. But what would that do? Prove he existed? "Nobody is going to rush out for Jonathan Spencer tattoos."

*****

Emerson Elliot could do it again, Spencer thought. Speak to the city. Let people know that he was alive. Get the city agitated, get those rich people Park Avenue primed and ready to run for their lives. With all the radio stations and television and newspapers, Elliot was the only voice to look at *why* anyone would attack billionaires. Everyone else wailed about 'leading citizens' and how the city was losing its critical philanthropic leadership.

It took him fourteen calls, but Spencer stayed with it until he got through to the call-in line. An automated voice told him, "At the tone, clearly state the topic of your comments, then hold the line."

"This is Bullets," Spencer told the machine. "I'm back."

Crazy Thumbs, Emerson Elliot's producer, read the transcription and disconnected the line. "Not cool," he said.

Spencer listened to the disconnected line, figuring that it must have been an error. Emerson Elliot had made "I Kill Rich People" into a media phenomenon.

He dialed again. Busy. He dialed again. This time he was luckier and got through.

"The prior call from this telephone number was screened and rejected," the machine puked at him. "Thank you for listening to the Emerson Elliot Program." Then it disconnected again. Spencer looked at the phone in disbelief.

After a minute, he pulled another cell phone out from under the mattress, one of the phones he took off the six-man team. He inserted the sim card and connected the battery, dialed and waited.

When he finally got through again, he told the machine, "You were wearing bright purple with frills. You kissed the little bald man on top of his head."

Crazy Thumbs felt chills down his spine when he read the words. He switched over to commercials during the middle of an interview.

"EE, what were you wearing that night of the shootings?" he asked. When Elliot paused, he switched on the booth microphone and asked overhead, "Were you wearing purple?"

The blood ran out of Elliot's face. He didn't need to say a thing. Thumbs didn't need to hear. He could see his answer through the glass.

"There is no Dimitri Vosilych," Spencer told them. "I was at the stadium. I didn't kill the detective, either. He unloaded on me. If I hadn't been wearing a vest, I'd be the dead one. We both fell. He died; I broke my legs and got caught. They put me in a secret prison. No lawyer. Torture. Right here, right in Washington, D.C. But I'm out. I escaped. They came after me in West Virginia and murdered the two women who helped me."

Thumbs used hand gestures to tell EE that he was calling the police, but EE waived him off.

"What do you want from me?" EE asked.

"Tell them I kill rich people. Tell them I'm back."

Elliot looked frantically at Thumbs and shook his head. *No way.*

"I can't help you," Elliot insisted. "Don't call here. Ever." Elliot slammed down the line. "I'm not going there. Never again. Its bullshit, Thumbs. The whole thing. Delete it. Right now! That's never going on the air. You hear me! Delete it!"

*****

From the top of the highest roof, at 23 East 74th, Owen watched with binoculars, scanning the constant flow of delivery vans, florists and liquor vendors, caterers, musicians, and furniture rental companies passing below on Madison with frenzied staff barking orders and pointing directions as men and women rushed to offload. He counted sixteen of them, trucks and vans both, in just a half-hour. Nearly every one of them had boxes and tables and rolls of linens large enough to conceal a long weapon.

"Hell, Spencer might already be inside," he muttered.

Using the tablet, Owen emailed Dale, questioning him about the timing. "When did the cameras come online?"

The reply was succinct. At least one-hundred-ninety-three had come on during the prior two weeks. It was therefore impossible for Spencer to have set the others up.

Dale sent the links. The first displayed the sidewalk looking outside from a building that could have been anywhere. The second was inside the subway station at 35th; Owen didn't need a flag for that one since the camera looked straight onto the platform and a pole that said "34th St." He tapped the third link, the one that had caught his eye. He glanced at the odd street view below, then saw it was all the way over on 71st. Zip. A dead end.

After the vans were offloaded and pulled away, young men in black pants and athletic shoes, all carrying daypacks, started showing up on the sidewalk, greeting one another and congregating in small groups. When another van pulled up, three of the closest men recognized it and trotted over to open the doors. The driver stepped around and shouted greetings then pointed to where he wanted the men to position the podium and the key rack they had just dragged out from the back of the van. All at once, they dropped their backpacks and peeled out of their various sweaters and hoodies, revealing white shirts underneath. They pulled black vests from their packs, pinned on nametags, and fumbled with black clip-on bow ties, helping one another to get these straight before jamming their other clothes into the packs and tossing these inside the van.

Three men who looked like the Road Warrior walked past with knives and ammunition hanging from their thick black vests and black helmets with dark visors, each obviously carrying a rifle inside a soft case in their black-gloved hands. Miller's snipers. All the way from the rooftop, Owen could see the outlines of their weapons through his binoculars.

They calmly deployed right past the valets and all the people walking down the sidewalk on Madison. None of these New Yorkers seemed bothered or flustered or even curious. They emerged onto the Whitney's roof a few minutes later, positioning themselves behind sand-colored fabric shields that looked like full-length kites.

Are those supposed to fool Spencer? Owen wondered.

More two-man teams came out onto the roof tops all along the west side of Madison where there were the best vantage spots looking down onto the Whitney. They were unzipping their rifles before they were out the rooftop doors. The first man, carrying the longer weapon, positioned himself kneeling along the short wall at the edge of the rooftop while the second man, carrying a shorter weapon, dropped into a prone position aiming back toward the rooftop access door. Owen saw nine of them deploy. He heard through the headset fourteen chill voices calling off by number. It came off like just another day at the office for them.

Hearing them left Owen's heart pumping even faster.

Owen turned around and was nearly blinded. The sun reflecting off the lake inside Central Park shocked his retinas. He squinted to see rowboats before turning his eyes back to the Whitney. The casual efficiency playing through his earphone left the upsetting impression that he was the only man there with any sense of urgency. One after another, he spotted places where a shooter could be hidden right now; huge HVAC units were on every roof, at least three vehicles were parked illegally across the street. Spencer could be inside a moving vehicle. He could be standing behind the curtains in twenty, thirty, fifty windows!

Below Owen, the valets drilled on their lineup and rotation to the cars, over to the garage, and back to the keyboard. While Owen paced back and forth with the binoculars, he could tell that the valet manager was instructing a new hire about tearing the tickets and attaching the matching stubs to the key rings before hooking them onto the board. Then the manager gathered the whole group to bring them out to the curb, where he pointed out the second garage on East 80th. He looked like a coach settling down his team with last-minute instructions before the big game.

You have no fucking idea, Owen thought. *Bait.* Miller might as well be tying them all up like sheep. *While you stand and watch, boyo. For money.*

Owen watched as down on Madison a black Cadillac limo arrived at ten minutes to six. Four more limousines arrived directly behind that first Cadillac. Valets ran to the doors while the drivers stood at the front of the first and second cars, waiting until their passengers were safe before ducking behind the wheels to pull away. Owen's hand reached out unconsciously to pat the leather wallet holding his gold medallion as women in fashionable evening gowns looked up from their phones to waive at other guests.

Owen tried to spot Spencer, knowing that it was impossible.

He clearly remembered watching the "Bigfoot" camera footage taken from the Central Park West attack. He could smell the gasoline that had been all around their speedboat and sensed the black smoke and the fire. "Jesus."

More people were arriving now. The valets opened doors for the drivers and passengers then took the wheels and pulled out onto Madison with practiced efficiency. In two minutes there were already dozens of guests bunching on the sidewalk in front of the Whitney.

Owen swept down Madison Avenue, where a steady stream of traffic was bumper-to-bumper along the east-side lanes. He counted the cars. There were New Yorkers inside every one of them; people out to have a good time. He was supposed to protect them!

Owen scanned the windows and rooftops another time. At least a hundred people were gathered into smaller groups below him, kissing cheeks, shaking hands.

"The old man would knock you out of your socks!" he yelled at himself. "You don't think twice. Nobody buys you! You do what you were trained to do. You do the fucking job!"

The medallion came out of his pocket as if on its own while he sprinted for the elevator. His eyes were glued to the numbers while it took forever getting down. He turned his body sideways to get through and leapt into the ground floor lobby, then charged toward the center of Madison with his medallion held high above his head.

Waving his arms, he stopped traffic then curled his lower lip to let go the loudest whistle he'd blown. Two of the off-duty rental cops looked up.

"Sniper!" Owen screamed. "Shut it down! Get these cars out of here!"

He snatched the walkie-talkie from the closest officer.

"This is Detective Lieutenant Cullen, Intel," he called in. "Level Three! Repeat. Level Three! 10-31 at Whitney Museum, Madison at East 75th. Live sniper."

Miller's team spotted Cullen below and broke off from their positions, hustling down their egress routes in lock-step as sirens joined into a cacophony for blocks around.

"Block Madison," Owen ordered the off-duty patrolmen. Grabbing one of them by his sleeve, Owen ran down the center line the half-block to the front of the museum.

"Inside," he shouted. "Everyone off the street and away from the windows!"

The guests stood still initially, staring at him and looking around for the source of the sirens. Owen slammed his hands onto a black tuxedo jacket and shoved the man and everyone in front of him toward the interior courtyard.

Women were screaming. Several lost their footing and fell out of their high heels as the rush Owen triggered swelled into a stampede. Owen dragged one fallen woman behind him while pushing and herding them all under the cover of the museum's entryway.

An unmarked police vehicle turned south on Madison, jumped the curb and screeched to a stop on the sidewalk. The uniformed driver opened his door and crouched behind it, gun drawn, looking up at the windows above them. Owen recognized the passenger, a captain from the 19th Precinct.

The captain turned his eyes upward toward a police helicopter that appeared, hovering high above the street then walked quickly and confidently to put his arm around Owen's shoulder.

"What have we got, Cullen?"

"Sniper, Cap," Owen yelled into his ear. "Getting ready to attack the event. We need to set a perimeter and lock down every building along the west side."

He pointed at each of six different buildings. "We need to go through them floor by floor."

*****

"Goddamnit!" Miller shouted. The second the snipers reported it, he knew. *Cullen.* They didn't need to mention "red hair."

Miller threw his cell phone at the wall, exploding it into fragments. After the outburst, he inhaled deeply, held his breath, then exhaled and looked for the phone to get out the sim card.

"It's a setback," he told Jeffers over the phone, "not a catastrophe." His sniper team was all secure and accounted-for. But Spencer would likely get out through the chaos. "If they catch Spencer, we'll deal with it."

"How?" Jeffers voice came off breathy and strained.

"Let's cross that bridge if we come to it," Miller told him coolly. "I didn't bring that nut job into this, you did," he reminded. Triage didn't leave room for diplomacy.

"And what about Cullen?" Jeffers demanded.

"He's got no evidence. Cullen has told his Spencer story all over town. He just made a few thousand NYPD cops deploy on his say-so. He's already on suspension. They don't catch Spencer, would you want to be Cullen? He's still the loser who left his partner to get killed."

Jeffers weighed the consequences. His own phone calls had opened the doors to NSA's vault. If they got to North Bergen, it could lead back to APA. "Cullen leads back to everything!" he said.

Miller looked out to Nussbaum and the techs. They knew. The live scene was splashed across the projection wall.

"It's under control," Miller answered hurriedly. "I'm cleaning house now. Cullen leads them here, there won't be anything here to find. This is going away."

He hung up and shouted orders. "Listen, we're shutting this down."

He grabbed a garbage can and ran toward them. "Cell phones and hard drives. Get them out. Now!"

All four of them stared, frozen in place.

"This place is compromised. I need cell phones; I need the laptops. You hear me?! Now!" He snatched Stephen's phone, cracked it open, pulled the sim card and dropped the phone into the can. "Laptops and phones. Do it!"

Nussbaum shut the laptop and leaned his weight onto the clamshell. "There's business plans, applications in development. No. You don't get the laptop. I didn't sign on for that. Fuck that."

"You got that shit backed up somewhere," Miller yelled, spitting his words into Stephen's face. "Don't play innocent.

"What? You think all this is kosher? There are enough felonies here to put you away for life. Right this minute, I'm the best friend you have."

Their faces paled. *Life in prison* got their attention.

"Wait outside for me," he ordered them. "No going back to the hotel. I'll buy you new clothes." He fanned money at each of them, counting out thousands into their hands until they acquiesced.

Miller was already grabbing wads of paper towels and beginning to wipe down the desktops as they shrank toward the exit. All except Dale.

"I need to go back to my room," he complained. "My meds are there. Even if I replaced them, my names are on the prescriptions."

"We'll sort that out. Go!

Miller ran to the sink and reached out every cleaner there, gallons of it, then ran sprints across the inside bullpen, along the sink counter, and all through the inner workspace until these were empty.

It was ridiculously inadequate. Nowhere near enough to spoil DNA and cover fingerprints.

"You saw it in him and you let it happen!" he screamed at himself.

Cullen couldn't keep it together and now he was forced to scramble for options.

Miller looked for answers in every direction. Then he spotted his answer. Above.

No ladder around. Miller looked at the swivel office chairs. Those wouldn't work.

He ran inside the windowless space and returned with a solid chair that he lifted on top of what had been Kip's desk. He ran back again to get the hot bulb from his desk lamp.

With the hot incandescent bulb fizzing inside the moist paper towels, Miller climbed up onto the desk and then stepped carefully up onto the chair. Once he had his balance, he straightened himself to reach the hot bulb up against the sensor on the ceiling and held it there against the wax seal.

Even though he was expecting it, when the fire sprinklers let loose the forceful spray blasted him off the chair. He bounced off the desk and landed on the floor face-up with the wind knocked out of him and a cascade drenching him from above. He picked himself and dizzily zigzagged toward the outside door before remembering to drag the garbage can out with him.

Stephen, Dale, Dilip, and Kip were waiting inside Miller's sedan. He couldn't hear them, but the security light threw enough light to show the shapes of their heads through the rear window. It was obvious that they were arguing and agitated.

His head ached. He had to close one eye. Somehow, that allowed him to organize his thoughts. He combed his hand through his wet hair. A clump of loose strands laced his fingers afterward.

He stared at them then forced himself to snap out of it. *I might have a concussion,* he realized, but there was no time available to devote to any concussion.

Adding Owen Cullen to the team was on Jeffers. *It's on Jeffers to gather resources now,* he decided.

He called Jeffers back. "In two minutes, there's going to be fire engines all around here," Miller said. "I have their cell phones and hard drives. We need a safe house until this blows over. I need you to do something. Have a call placed to 293-459-2200. Tell them Miller needs SH and EXX for five."

"SH and EXX," Jeffers repeated.

"For five. I'll be on 95 South," Miller told him. "Reach me in the car."

"No loose ends," Jeffers reminded Miller. "That was your own emphasis. I have adopted it as policy." Jeffers went silent on the other end of the line for what seemed like minutes as Miller expected to hear sirens at any second. By then, all four techs had turned back, watching while Miller dragged the waterlogged garbage can.

He popped the trunk and splashed laptops and cell phones inside then slammed it closed. The car keys shimmied in his hand as he looked at them. He couldn't get his eyes to focus.

Miller opened the passenger door where Stephen had his seatbelt on. "You drive," he ordered Nussbaum. He needed to raise his voice to be heard over the approaching sound of fire trucks. Stephen fumbled nervously, unable to get out of his seatbelt. Miller pressed the release for him and slapped the keys into

Stephen's gut. All three terrified techs in the back seat looked like they were verging on tears.

"Where are we going?" Stephen asked insistently after getting behind the wheel.

"The venue is compromised, obviously" Miller replied succinctly. "We'll set up at a new location."

The sirens were getting close. "They're coming here. The fire sprinklers must have set off a silent alarm. You need to start the car, back up, and drive."

"I am not signing up for this," Dilip whined from the middle seat. "I am a software engineer!"

"Don't be naïve," Miller growled, glaring back through his one open eye before shouting into Nussbaum's right ear.

"Start the fucking car! Listen, geeks. Your clean fingernails don't mean anything. You're in this and you've been well-paid for it.

"Drive," he ordered Nussbaum. "Go out the parking lot and turn left."

The fire engines passed them going in the opposite direction. Miller sighed and calmed down to a focused, level pitch. "The freeway entrance will be coming up on the left, three blocks ahead. Get on 95 South. Slow and steady. Don't speed."

Miller's phone buzzed and lit up in the dark car. The new text read: **95 to 78W. 12m. More to follow. SCP. (Secure communication protocols.)**

"What's it say?" Stephen demanded as the three rear passengers strained to see.

"I'm having anxiety," Dilip insisted. "I don't belong in this. I have a 1st from IIT Chennai! I am waiting on acceptance for my master's degree!"

"Shut up!" Miller snarled back at the software engineer. "Just f-ing shut up!"

Stephen was calculating alternatives even as he constantly checked the rearview mirror for the police lights he expected to see behind them at any second. Bishop flew to Thailand. Was that what they really expected them to do? *I can't just up and disappear*, he told himself. He had two new apps in beta. Could he coordinate everything online?

"I want to get out!" Dilip demanded. He tried to climb over Dale's lap to get near the door.

Dale shoved him back to the middle and Kip raised his knees instinctively to corral Dilip's panicked shifting.

"We're going at sixty miles an hour," Kip told Dilip. "I'm with you, but you have to chill, dude."

Miller's phone buzzed again. This time he made the point to hold it close to his chest, away from probing eyes. **Follow directions to Reservation. Yellow boat hull at top of driveway. Barn 300m in. CCX en route.**

Miller read it twice. The inside of his mouth felt suddenly dry. CCX. Collection crew-deceased.

"What's it say now?" Stephen wanted to know.

"We're going to a transfer location," Miller, said, coughing to get the words out. He shifted in his seat to try finding a comfortable position. "Fifteen minutes," he told them.

They turned off the highway onto the Indian reservation, where the only light came from the car's headlights and a few dim houses off away down long dirt driveways; no stores, not a single streetlight.

"Turn in here," Miller told Nussbaum. Twigs crackled under the tires as they turned past the wrecked shell of a fishing boat.

Stephen stopped the car. "What is this place?" he asked Miller.

"How many cameras have seen this car?" Miller countered. "We're dumping it," he told them, pointing toward the old barn in the dim distance at the edge of the beams.

"A van is coming," he added as Stephen continued toward the weathered building. He didn't say for what.

"I'll wait in the car," Dilip whimpered.

"Me too," Kip agreed.

"Get out and open those doors up," Miller told Stephen. "They can wait in the car." *Better in the car.* He looked around him, quickly realizing that they could bolt twenty feet into the black darkness and be gone. Nothing he could do about it.

"I don't think so," Stephen said, refusing.

"We don't have time for this," Miller hissed. He reached over, turned off the engine, and jerked out the car keys. "Open those doors," he repeated. "I'll get a flashlight."

When he opened the passenger door, Stephen opened the driver's side door and followed around to the back of the car. Dale also got out.

Kip and Dilip still sat frozen in the backseat.

"Why not use the headlights?" Stephen asked suspiciously.

"Go turn them on."

Stephen didn't move. He watched in the darkness as Miller raised the trunk lid. Miller felt along the upper edge inside the trunk's left side well, patting into the black hole until his hand was around the weapon and the flashlight both.

He brought the flashlight out first, scanning it toward Stephen and Dale. "Come on out," he told the two techs, shining the flashlight onto them through the rear window. "We need to wipe down this car."

The flashlight was in Miller's left hand. Stephen spotted the object gripped in his right. "Stay put," Stephen told Kip and Dilip in open defiance.

"Why the gun?" Stephen asked quietly. "We're in this together! Cullen knows you more than he knows any of us."

Miller began to hyperventilate. He couldn't help it. He had assigned a thousand kills; this was the first time he'd had to do the shooting on his own. It was intimidating, but undeniably stimulating, too.

"Detective Lieutenant Cullen knows Miller," he announced. "My name's not Miller."

Nussbaum's reply stunned him. "We know that, Leonard," Stephen said. "You're Leonard Korn. Born in Tempe, Arizona. Mesa Community College and BYU. Communications major. 3.44 GPA. Don't go bragging about being a professional killer. You were the first thing I checked on the system."

Stephen got in Miller's face. "I'm a data guy! You think I wouldn't build an insurance file? What? You think we're idiots? Your face, your fingerprints, your DNA, a log of everything we know about you, about Jeffers, and about Jonathan Spencer, is sitting on the cloud. Unless I log in to stop it, the file distributes automatically. You'll be all over the news wires at 8:01 a.m."

He turned back to the other techs. "Dale, you get back into the car. Leonard, I'll take back those car keys. Now!"

"Oh my God," Dilip exclaimed. "I have to pee!"

Stephen's knees shook. He expected a bullet was about to kill him. In the rearview mirror he could make out Miller's face lit by the cell phone. Miller was urgently punching his finger at the screen as Stephen sped up the dark driveway.

Dale pounded on the dashboard as the four of them passed the boat hull and Stephen accelerated toward the freeway. "That was so fucking badass!"

CHAPTER TWENTY-THREE

Madison Avenue was closed to traffic until after 11 p.m. Owen watched from inside the back seat of a squad car as K-9 units and bomb squad vans pulled away. The commanding officer of the paid unit detail remained on the sidewalk, pointing his finger at the assistant chief, commanding officer of the detective unit, and arguing with the assistant chief of patrol borough Manhattan North, whose captain of the 19th had been the first other officer on scene.

"You don't tell me to come along," the Paid Unit captain argued. "I take orders from the chief, the commissioner, and the mayor, not you! Don't put this clusterfuck on my guys!

"What do you want my guys to do, ignore emergency orders coming from a gold medallion? Nobody is laying this on Paid Unit Detail. This is on you. Suspension doesn't change anything; Cullen's your guy! He called the fucking Level Three."

The Assistant Chief of Detectives rode in to One Police Plaza in the front passenger seat. Owen sat like a suspect in the back seat behind the cage. The assistant chief looked out the windshield without engaging while they were driven south toward police headquarters.

Word had already come to the assistant chief that the department spokesman had 50 reporters waiting for a statement.

Seven hundred officers, five aviation units, counterterrorism, shutting down traffic to a quarter of the Upper East Side, causing the cancellation of one of the biggest charity events—what was he going to say? "Whoops?" Or just, "Sorry"?

Nobody spoke in the police garage or in the elevator, either. The hallway went silent as Owen and his top direct commanding officer emerged and walked toward the main conference center, their footfalls clacking along.

It was 11:30 at night, but the room was packed with more senior officers than Owen had ever seen in one place. The Deputy Commissioner of Intelligence was at the head of the huge table. Behind him were two aids wearing earpieces and carrying tablet computers. Owen's bureau chief of Intelligence, the chief of the Counterterrorism Bureau, the chief of the Internal Affairs Bureau, the commanding officer of the Real Time Crime Center were seated on both sides of him. At least six other senior department officers were distributed around the table. The captain of the 19th Precinct stood mid-table on the opposite side.

"Detective Lieutenant," the Deputy Commissioner began. He had already been there for two hours, waiting and readying himself to grind Owen to a pulp. "I've been around here thirty years and I still have fingers and toes left to count the Level Three alerts over my career. I didn't see any planes hitting towers. I don't recall any hurricane. So explain what motivated you to damage the reputation of the New York City Police Department? You just cost this city hundreds of thousands of dollars. More importantly, you scared the crap out of half this city! Plus what happens the next time there is a real emergency? How many people will ignore warnings because of what you did? People may well die because of you!"

One of the aids leaned in to whisper into the Deputy Commissioner's ear. "Well why the hell was he on duty?" the Deputy Commissioner reacted sharply.

"He has been on unpaid medical leave," the chief of the Intelligence Bureau responded, anticipating the question. "Detective Tremaine Bull was his partner. *Dimitri Vosilych?*"

"I know who Bull is," the Chief barked back. "What the hell was he doing running up and down Madison Avenue with his Lieutenant's medallion calling in a goddamned Level Three if he's on leave?"

The Deputy Commissioner stared down the Intelligence Chief then shifted his glare toward the Captain of the 19th, who shrugged and raised both open palms; the detective had nothing to do with the 19th division.

The Commanding Officer of Detectives offered a symbolic defense, reluctantly suggesting that this was a briefing, not a disciplinary hearing. "Detective Lieutenant Cullen ought to be heard, and if he needs to defend himself, he should have ample time to get representation and to prepare."

"There are over a hundred reporters out there and after I leave here, I'm going to be on the hook to brief the Commissioner of Police and the mayor of New York. So thank you, Assistant Chief, for the procedural niceties, but let's get back to what the hell is going on," the Deputy Commissioner said. "Detective Lieutenant, are you on unpaid medical leave?"

"Yes, sir."

"Why?"

"Sir?"

"Why are you on unpaid medical leave?"

"IAB interviewed the Detective Lieutenant's immediate superior, Deputy Commissioner," explained the Chief of Internal Affairs. "There was an altercation between the Detective Lieutenant and the new partner assigned to him. The other detective declined to file on the event, but was himself out a half-day following the altercation and was seen wearing a protective nose bridge. Detective Lieutenant Cullen was placed on paid leave for a period of four weeks and that leave was extended for an additional four weeks, unpaid."

"So he popped his partner."

"Sir," the Assistant Chief of Detective interrupted. "We need to cut this off. If formal charges are proffered, none of this statement may be admissible."

The Deputy Commissioner shouted: "I don't need a department lawyer right now, Assistant Chief. You said your piece, now sit the fuck down!"

"Why did you do this?" he growled, spitting straight into Owen's face when his words came out.

"There is no Dimitri Vosilych," Owen blurted. "Jonathan Spencer killed my partner. Jonathan Spencer attacked Sands Point and Central Park West and Mamaroneck. He shot a boat out from under us on the Hudson. He was captured at Citi-Field and held in a special security prison from which he escaped almost a month ago. I was hired to locate him and kill him. Me, a CIA operative named Miller, and Stephen, Dilip, Kip and Dale, the four technology guys. We were in D.C. first, working for a man named Bishop. Then Bishop was let go because there was an attack in West Virginia that went bad. Spencer killed six commandos and brought down their helicopter. The client moved us to North Bergen. We were tracking Spencer from there. That's how we found out about he was planning to attack the Whitney."

"Christ!" the Deputy Commissioner griped. "And Martians are landing in Central Park!"

Everyone at the table suddenly imagined the shit storm that was about to rain down. The Deputy Commissioner motioned toward the chief of the Intelligence Bureau, and the captain from the 19th.

"Take him upstairs. You keep him the hell away from those reporters. They hear this cockamamie BS and this city will be paying out millions," he warned.

As his chief rose and the two men approached him, Owen looked around the room, searching for someone to believe him. "Sir, I was doing my duty! I was saving those people! He's out there! But they don't want a celebrity trial. They don't want to give publicity to 'I Kill Rich People.' You don't understand! Jonathan Spencer is a trained killer, the best the Army had. You have to believe me! Somebody, believe me! Sir," Owen stammered. "Sir, I can prove it. They're right there! In Jersey. North Bergen. Right across the bridge. Sir, these guys have everything, surveillance like nothing you've ever seen. I just saw Donald Trump in his bathroom!"

The chief groaned. One of his aids had scanned IAB notes on Owen and leaned in close to whisper details. "Looks like depressive psychosis. Cullen could be manic. But he's been refusing psych-counseling so no meds, no treatment."

The chief threw his hands in the air. "Donald Trump in his bathroom," he griped.

"Hell. Take him over to Jersey. Chase rainbows. Just keep him the hell away from those reporters. You hear me? Keep this nutcase away from those cameras."

*****

Spencer dragged an eight-foot section of scaffolding inside the storage container; he lowered it to the floor and then shut the metal door behind him before turning on the battery-powered lamp. He moved straight to the inside corner and lifted out the drag bag containing his Barrett. He carefully unzipped the tan canvas and hauled out the forty pounds of pure effectiveness. He took a long moment to admire it, the one sure companion that never let him down.

He hit the release, dropped the magazine, and admired the glinting reflection off the brass bullet, the 661-grain full metal jacket, before setting the full mag down and continuing the weapons-check routine. He had the Leupold scope inside a separate protective foam case that also had to be well hidden.

Spencer placed a flat sheet of cardboard on the metal floor and laid the Barrett on top of it and then folded the cardboard around the Barrett until nothing indicated it was a weapon. From the stock up past the pistol grip and all the way along the rail, he was going to have to carefully wrap every identifiable part inside the length of scaffolding.

He admired his work. The parts might plausibly be tools for floating sealant. There was no reason to think otherwise.

In case he was searched, he wasn't going to risk that a police officer might feel the weapon. He especially didn't want Vince to feel it. He knew that his actions would be costing Vince his job; killing the guy was the last thing that he wanted to do.

But he didn't have to contrive a separate event because the city was already on edge. Something that happened on the Upper East Side had the entire city put on edge. Hundreds of policemen, reporters, helicopters; all of Manhattan was on high-alert. Even the news helicopters were being forced to hover outside a square mile of restricted airspace.

Spencer felt along the weapon, adjusting his wrapping until he couldn't have identified it himself. Next, he worked duct tape around the cardboard then wrapped the entire 57-inch length of the rifle inside clear plastic wrap and duct taped it again inside the aluminum scaffolding. Then he wrapped the rifle and scaffolding inside a brown plastic tarp, fusing everything into one conjoined piece that he could carry under one arm.

He lifted the heavy bundle and felt it for balance, then practiced stepping forward with the six-foot, fifty-five pound bundle held against his right armpit. His left hand had to be free to carry the five-gallon plastic bucket of roofing mastic with his ammunition.

He retrieved the mastic and set the bucket down, then put a tight grip on the tab and ripped away the plastic loop that kept the lid seated tightly. He caught his finger on the plastic, tearing out a nick that started bleeding. Exactly where the thorn had gotten him, he remembered. He sucked away the drip that was forming then made a fist to apply pressure. It didn't work, so he tore away four inches of duct tape and wrapped the finger tightly until the bleeding stopped.

His plan was take the Leupold scope and the magazine and the semi-automatic pistol he was bringing, put them into Ziploc bags, and sink these into the mastic. He lifted the lid, and then placed it off to the side, being careful not to spill the sticky contents. Looking inside, he recognized the weakness in his plan and became frustrated with himself for overlooking the obvious—the contents would overflow, plus he was going to need to fish his tools back out while he was inside the tent.

He powered up a cell phone and checked the time. It was nearing 02:30. By his calculations, Spencer determined that he was going to need to unwrap his Barrett, load up, set the Leupold, tape it to the scaffolding, and then wrap everything up all over again in ten minutes or less. Having done it once, he hoped he would be faster the second time.

Two hours were left to get in some shut-eye. He had to sleep right where he was or he wouldn't get any at all.

The steel container reminded him of the back of an army personnel carrier; it was better than listening to working girls and junkies in the basement room.

*****

"I need your medallion, Cullen," a captain from Internal Affairs Bureau ordered.

"You think it's a coincidence?" Owen pleaded. "You think the fire sprinklers just happened to go off in an empty space with no fire anywhere?" Owen's fingers squeezed around the leather, holding tight to the medallion he had earned.

"Give it to him," the captain from the 19th demanded. The whole thing disgusted him, too. Internal Affairs guys always left him feeling like he needed a long shower.

"See your rep in the a.m.," the captain said reassuringly. "There's more here than meets the eye. Suspended or not, you're a police officer acting in the interests of New York City. We've got your back."

"Your weapon, too," the IAB officer demanded.

"Unless it's department-issue, you don't have to give him nothing," the captain told Owen. "You are unarmed, right? Detective Lieutenant? Right?"

"Right," Owen agreed.

IAB and the captain stared one another down. Three in the morning and the captain from the 19th wouldn't give an inch. "You try to frisk this man and I'll file charges on you myself," the captain said. "I guarantee it."

*****

His medallion was gone. No matter how many times he replayed it in his head, the weight of it leaving his hand remained unreal. He drove alone through the darkness, still hearing their anger. Suspended. Investigation pending.

Spencer is out here and they won't listen. Nobody believes me.

They would have taken his service weapon, too. He had to lie to keep it. They nearly treated him like a suspect. They would have stood him against the wall and forced him to spread his legs for a pat down. "I'm a detective lieutenant!"

Six detectives from Intel Division, five guys and one gal, people who knew him well, had all gone out to North Bergen. Two detectives and four uniforms from North Bergen PD came along. All by itself, Intel Division was bigger than North Bergen's entire police department, but everything was done formally; every protocol was observed. There was nothing there. Just a soggy warehouse.

Suspended. Investigation pending.

Owen drove out to Lake Success and pulled up to the curb. For a long time, he sat there staring at Mike and Shelley's new house from the car. They were supposed to be his friends. Now they're protecting Callie and the boys from me, he wondered? Why? How did that ever happen?

He didn't have a plan; he only knew that his family was inside. His family, not theirs. Shelley putting herself in the middle and Mike letting her coach Callie without saying a word. What was that about?

Owen wasn't seeing a dark house. He wasn't thinking about the time, four o'clock in the morning. Callie and Liam and Casey were close enough that he could reach out and have them in his arms.

A few minutes were all he was going to ask for—just a chance.

He walked along the side yard to the back door. He could see the red light on the security system. He knew their old code by heart. He figured he would take the key from under the mat, enter the code, and go in. Not bother Mike and Shelley. He wasn't coming to see the two of them.

He checked under the mat. The key wasn't there. He ran his fingers across the top of the doorframe. Nothing. He thought about knocking, but he tried the knob first. Locked. The security system came on when he touched the knob. The system bleeped and flashed red. A 20 appeared on the control pad, then counted 19 and down through a twenty-second delay. He looked at the glass; he could punch right through and try the code for their old house, but as the numbers descended, he froze.

It hit zero. The shrill, repeating whirl sounded like it had to be waking the entire neighborhood.

"It's just me," Owen shouted over the piercing intensity. "Shut it off!"

Mike's face appeared behind the glass.

"Jesus, Owen! It's the middle of the night." Mike turned his back to the door, obviously hiding the pad from Owen's view as he punched in the code. "Are you nuts? You shouldn't be here, man," he told Owen firmly. "All the drunk-dialing, now this. You're making things worse. You don't want to force Callie to get a court order."

Owen looked around Mike's frame. Callie was coming down the stairs. She stopped at the doorway into the kitchen, twenty feet away from him.

"I'm not drinking, Cal," he pleaded. "I swear! Please, Cal. I need you."

From behind, Shelley came down the stairs and put her arm around Callie's waist.

"Do you know what time it is, Owen Cullen?" Shelley screeched.

"Please," Owen asked her. "Just let me kiss the boys goodnight. Then I'll go. I promise."

"I'll call 9-1-1," Shelley threatened. "You leave here! You leave us alone!"

The 9mm was pressing into his back. Owen reached behind him then immediately pulled his hand away like he had touched a hot stove.

Mike waved toward Shelley with both his palms open, then spun back to the door. "Buddy, you need to go," Mike told him firmly. "Go and I'll call you in the morning."

Callie looked for a moment like she wanted to be angry, but she looked at him standing there, so pathetic, and her anger faltered.

"They took my medallion, Cal," he cried. "I messed up. The thing on the news? That was me."

Callie took a step toward him, but Shelley grabbed her by the arm and pulled her back. "You've moved on. You've got to tell him."

Callie shook herself free and ran to the door, Shelley chasing. When she fumbled to open the deadbolt, Mike opened the door for her and put his bulk between Shelley and the door.

"Damn it," Shelley hissed at him.

Callie reached her arms out to stop Owen from wrapping his arms around her but she grasped hold of Owen's forearms and squeezed.

"I'm helping her rebuild her life, Michael," Shelley argued. "We're putting a roof over her and her kids." Shelley eyed the telephone. Mike read her mind and gestured repeatedly for her to settle down. She shook a fist at her husband and cussed under her breath then turned to listen.

"He's back," Owen told Callie, speaking slowly. "And nobody in the department believes me. Cal, they had Spencer caught.

"He got away, that's why they called me. To catch him. We were right, we were always right, you, me and Tee," he said. "That job I had, I was in D.C. because I know about Spencer."

Owen slumped down onto the concrete porch, taking Callie down beside him. They leaned their backs against the door. Callie's hand stayed on his forearm as both his arms flopped limply at his sides. His long legs stretched out in front of him. He looked exhausted. "The department doesn't believe me. They took my medallion," he explained. "I went to North Bergen. Remember I said I was there? There's nothing there now.

"I have ten thousand dollars, Callie. New bills. If I'm lying, how would I have that? How?"

"I don't know, O," Callie told him, petting her hand down his shoulder. "It will be all right. You do the right thing. It's going to be ok."

"What is a guy supposed to do? I worked my ass off. All the time!" he insisted. "Did I ever hit you, Cal? Did I ever once hurt the kids?"

Tears rolled down his cheeks as he pleaded for answers.

"I'm not drinking, Cal. You can tell that, right?"

She nodded yes. "What is a man supposed to do? Tell me! What's a man supposed to do anymore? Just tell me what's good enough, because I don't understand! What am I supposed to do?"

Callie wrapped her fingers in his big hand. He lifted her fingers and held them to his lips.

Shelley watched through the door, growing more agitated.

"There are children in this house, Michael," she hissed. "It's four a.m. Drunk or sober, he's raving.

"I don't care what you think. I'm calling the police!"

"Damn it, Shelley!" Mike shouted at her. "Put down the phone!"

There was fear in his voice. Behind him, Shelley had the phone in her hand.

"Owen, you have to leave. You need to go."

"There is a man at my back door," Shelley reported. "Owen Cullen. He's a police officer. He carries a gun."

She paused, listening. "Because his wife and kids are staying here," Shelley reported. "Yes, Lake Success. That's the address. He's acting crazy."

"Owen, get out of here!" Mike shouted. "Callie, let him go and you come back inside.

"Owen, you need to go. Now, before this escalates! Callie, tell him you'll talk in the morning. Really! Callie, come inside. He's not going to leave unless you come inside!"

*****

It was all a continuation of the same bad dream. The whole night. Everything since Tremaine got killed.

Owen drove in the dark along Horace Harding Expressway. He turned on the police band as he got onto the Long Island Expressway, listening to

Manhattan North dispatch and thinking about his medallion as he headed west toward FDR Drive into Lower Manhattan. All quiet.

"You feckin eejit," he scolded. "Where is your brain? Acting like a fucking crazy person. Think! You didn't make up Miller or Bishop or Nussbaum or any of them. The warehouse was flooded. That was no coincidence! You need to figure this out! Think!"

He wanted to call. Apologize for setting off the alarm. But Callie promised she would phone. She promised.

When he entered the Midtown Tunnel, he switched the radio to 77WABC and waited for Imus to come on at 6. He thought about going to morning Mass and then he thought about how weird that sounded. Except for Christmas Eve, he hadn't been to Mass for longer than he could remember.

The DJ on the radio was talking politics. "Ed, what do you think of Americans for Patriotic Action's new so-called anti-discrimination legislation? Do we need laws to protect the rich? I mean, we have laws protecting gays, laws protecting the handicapped, laws that make it a hate crime to attack people because of their race or their religion. We have laws protecting people who have no legal right to even be in this country! So why do we let everyone take free shots at our most successful, our most philanthropic citizens? What sort of liberal insanity is it that we just let class warfare rage unimpeded? Isn't attacking people because of their economic status just as much a hate crime?"

Owen groaned and switched back to Manhattan North dispatch. *God, I'm so tired,* he thought. *How did they just disappear so fast, like Miller and the techs never existed?* There were all those snipers deployed. People had to have seen them. Doormen, the valets, the caterers.

Pulling his medallion? Suspension pending a hearing? For what? For working while on suspension? If they didn't believe anything he said, then how could he be working? How did that make any sense?

"Nobody is dead! Maybe you should be thinking about that. Huh, Commissioner? Think about that!"

*****

Spencer used several of the index cards to make meticulous notes: directions and travel time from Yonkers to Park Avenue, time needed to dress and pack supplies and to load the 4Runner. Everything that he needed was set into carefully arranged piles: boots and water, underwear/socks/pants/shirt/vest/jacket, Barrett/ammo clips/Sig Sauer/ammo clips/monocular, roofing mastic/scaffold/plastic wrap/duct tape/tar brush/rollers. He reviewed each stack and then set out two pallets and rolled a canvas tarp for his pillow. After setting his alarm, he had two hours to sleep, provided that he could get to sleep.

His juices were rushing; he felt the warmth moving through his chest. He knew the building, every balcony, every ledge, the elevators, the stairwells; every ingress and every way out was committed to memory a hundred times over. Park would be shut down, so west on 71st. If 71st was shut down, back alley to 72nd. If 72nd blocked, failsafe shift to boiler room 72nd apartments where he had pre-cached two gallons of water, electrolytes, twelve power bars.

Clear the mind. Sleep. Breathe. You're in a hammock, swaying gently. Breathe. Waves are tumbled into the sand. Breathe. The breeze is warm. Feel it move across your neck. Breathe.

Spencer awakened stiff and aching. Sacking out inside the storage container proved to be a bad call. Lying on the cold metal left his neck stiffened. The cold had penetrated his jawbone. A dead, dull, mind-numbing pain pulsed from his right ankle up through his leg, hip, and into his guts. Every screw and plate inside him displayed like constellation points, each of them gnawing away at his operational capabilities.

He inhaled deeply, focused, and steeled himself. He had to reach out against the container wall and used his upper body muscle groups to spread the load and pressed through up onto his knees, forcing his body upright through the agony.

This is just you. No pack. No weapon. Just you. Stand!

Spencer swallowed the pain, blinked repeatedly until he had it together. Had other members of his unit been dependent upon him, he would have been obliged to stand down. His condition diminished the opportunities for mission success. Running the hill above Mercy's farm had pumped him up, but now he knew better; he was bullshitting himself. In comparison to the mountains he used to run on regularly, that incline was nothing.

Then he laughed. "This is as close to feeling old as you're ever going to get."

"This is the preview," he chuckled, gritting his jaw against the hurt. "You're never seeing the movie."

The scaffolding, bucket, tool chest and gym bag were neatly positioned, ready to go. He stared at them; each one represented anguish.

Spencer acted out of character, slowly dressing himself layer by layer, procrastinating. He had devised a way to sink the pistol and three additional loaded clips inside doubled Ziploc bags within the five-gallon bucket of roofing mastic using clear monofilament fishing line tied to the teeth of the lid. He could retrieve the pistol by lifting the lid and reeling the line taut, but he could still open it for inspection without revealing anything. Now he stared at the sixty-five pounds and passed it over, permitting himself to load the lighter supplies first.

Every noise seemed exaggerated by the dark silence in the sleeping trailer park. Even the hiss from the rear tailgate sounded cobra-like as it lifted up. The dashboard clock showed 05:10. He had already set the back seat down the night before and made sure the scaffolding fit inside, but now he doubted that he could get it in without making noise. He managed to get the bucket lifted inside, then tilted it and rolled it into place rather than pushing it and scraping along. He tried to lift the scaffolding and lean it deep inside in order to softly let down the end he was carrying, but the effort was impossibly agonizing. He had to stop or he would risk blacking out. With no other choice, he had to accept the noise and slide the aluminum inside the cargo area. Turning immediately, he shut and locked the container, ignoring the noise. Ollie, the trailer park manager, wouldn't like it, but it couldn't be helped.

He pulled through the park without turning on headlights, then cranked the heater up to its highest setting and directed the air down at his legs. The morning news programming replayed the police department spokesman, who was indicating that the initial reports of a potential terrorist event had been discounted.

"Department investigators are now reassuring a frightened public that there was no actual threat," the reporter said. "According to police, 'the Departmental coordination and rapid deployment we have just witnessed offer absolute confirmation of the extraordinary dedication, readiness, and professionalism of the world's finest police force.'"

As he drove, the warm air helped; Spencer alternated driving and massaging his knees and thighs. 05:25. He was making good time and decided to drive south along the Harlem River to the East River, taking the longer route instead of driving the Hudson to avoid having to cross Manhattan on surface streets where there might well be a heavy police presence. Between the buildings, the sky was turning a beautiful rich dark blue wrapped by a thin ribbon of gold as he pulled in front of 110 East 71st at 05:52. But it wasn't Vince inside; Spencer could see Walter, the Lawrence Taylor look-alike standing huge behind the front counter. He put the 4Runner in neutral and bobbed his feet on the floor. If he went ahead, would his legs carry him? He assessed the weight and the distances. Could he make it all the way down and around to the service elevator hauling a hundred-fifty pounds?

Could he wait? Would there never be a better time?

Exhaling hard, he blew out the negative air and stood in front of the glass doors until Walter looked up, folded his newspaper, and ambled forward looking menacing. Spencer knew he was recognized, but that made no difference to Walter.

"Walter, I need to offload before I park. Any chance I can use the placard?" Spencer beseeched. "Five minutes?"

The doorman looked at Spencer, checked his watch, then poked his head out and looked up and down East 71st. "Fifty bucks," he said.

Walter's stoic expression said "take it or leave it" loud and clear. Spencer gave in, grabbing the cash out from his front pocket and handing it over. Walter walked back to his desk and remained there, waiting for him to walk over to retrieve the handicapped placard.

Spencer got back inside the 4Runner, hung the placard from the rearview mirror, then reached inside the gym bag and retrieved kneepads that he strapped into place. With the kneepads on, he returned and opened the 4Runner's rear hatch, pulled up the bucket, then moved it to the building, using it against the base of one of the front doors to keep it propped open. "I'll just be a minute," he called out to Walter. Two minutes later he had the gym bag, the tool chest, and the scaffolding out, and was moving the bucket inside to let the door close behind him.

Walter walked over with the metal detector wand and had Spencer stand with his legs spread and arms extended while he went through his routine, even making Spencer empty the keys out of his front pocket. Spencer caught him eyeing the roll of bills.

"Open 'em up," Walter ordered, standing over the gym bag and the tool chest. Spencer complied while Walter took his time.

"What's that?" Walter grunted, looking toward the scaffolding.

"Work platform, trowels, stirring wand." Walter looked at the kneepads and put two-and-two together. Details make the difference. "Uh huh."

"Man, I came in early to get done before your residents are inconvenienced. You can see how heavy this is. Can I just use the front elevator? I'll be in and out," Spencer said.

"Heavy." Walter stood stone-faced, revealing zip while Spencer waited, envisioning himself struggling to carry that load along the hallways in one trip. Back to the service elevator, and then around again, all the way to the rooftop.

"Fifty bucks," Walter concluded.

"Twenty," Spencer countered, almost involuntarily.

"Go around or use the stairs."

Spencer counted two twenties and a ten into Walter's paw. It was better that Vince wasn't working. It took the sting out of paying, thinking how in a few hours this a-hole was probably going to be losing his job.

Spencer squared himself, blew out the anxiety, and prepared for the first of three heavy trips up to the roof deck where he had the tent anchored. The city lights were starting to give way to the first rays of sun creeping up over the Atlantic.

*****

Once inside the tent, Spencer dropped the thick jacket then worked on unwrapping his Barrett, taking special care not to jar the scope when the duct tape came off. He recalled the sound of that first shot when they killed Mercy—XMercy. *Screw it,* he thought. She was Mercy for thirty years. XMercy for less than a month. He'd remember what he wanted.

Spencer cleared the elaborate wrapping off the long weapon. He was going to have to leave it behind. *More and more being left behind, a kidney, my legs, and now the Barrett.* But this wasn't the time for extraneous thinking.

When he lifted it out, the familiar heft of the Barrett in his arms shifted him into another gear.

He shook off the emotional attachment and went into his routine. He dropped the magazine, fingered the metal jacket on the top round to confirm the full load, then flipped the bipod and cleared away the wrapping debris with his shoe before setting his weapon on the tent floor.

The bucket lid fought back again, nearly reopening the nick that he still had duct taped as he tried to pry it open. When it came free, he lifted the lid up high then spun it to wind up the invisible monofilament until, with a sucking sound; the plastic bags separated above it and dripped glops of material back into the bucket in heavy splots.

Spencer pulled on plastic gloves and retrieved the inner bag carrying his 9mm semi-automatic and extra clips, smudging only a little mastic when he set it down. He peeled off the gloves and dropped them inside the bucket then replaced the lid before precisely opening the nearly clean bag to reach for the pistol inside.

After dropping the magazine and checking his load, he racked the slide to chamber a round, set the safety, and pressed his right index finger under the slide before pressing the Sig Sauer into his belt. He slid the additional clips in his pockets, and looked down again, taking a moment to appreciate the Barrett. It was long and bulky, heavy too, yet it was a thing of beauty, solid and dependable, capable; all business, with nothing extra or showy. He and that weapon were one and the same, the ultimate extensions of the warrior's truth.

Spencer unzipped the window at the back of the tent. Park Avenue showed as a gray outline emerging from the darkness below. He lifted the Barrett, scanned the imagery through the Leupold4 scope, and internalized the subtle sighting window, the thirty feet between the front doorway and the sidewalk that translated to a one-and-three-quarter-inch barrel shift. *One-inch lateral shift between the trees along the curb to either side of the doorway.*

His legs throbbed again. He stood the Barrett up on the rifle butt and held his hand around the suppressor, steadying himself until it passed. The blisters on his left hand had dried out, leaving skin peeling. Less than a week ago he was cutting rounds with the chainsaw on Mercy's farm. *Mercy and Mouse.* On his palm, just below the middle finger, the biggest blister was now a hardened flap over soft new pink skin. His fingernails were getting too long.

*****

Owen passed Via Quadronno, thinking about getting coffee; it was dark inside, nobody even beginning yet to get ready. Six a.m. He hadn't slept a minute for the past twenty-four hours.

Owen considered shifting on the radio to Imus again, then left on the police radio instead. The routine call codes: 10-14, License Plate Check, 10-67s as double-parking delivery trucks stretched their welcome, the uniforms on patrol calling in 10-63s as they stopped at Best Bagel the minute it opened; these sounds were as familiar to him as sitting in the dark listening to Liam and Casey sleep.

"They fucking took my medallion," Owen repeated for the hundredth time.

It had to get reversed, he figured. It just had to. Like the captain from 19th had said, his union rep would make it right. *Maybe its better that they couldn't find Miller,* he told himself. Without Miller, how could they prove he was on unauthorized work? Whatever he said last night they couldn't use. He was entitled to have his rep present. Even the Assistant Chief said that!

Nobody died. Spencer would have killed those people, only he didn't!

"They're alive 'cause of you, Owen Cullen! You didn't sell out. You did that!" he told himself.

He punched the ceiling, hard, and then shifted his throbbing fist over the empty spot where his medallion should have been.

"It was good that Callie came out," he told himself. "She came out and she wasn't mean." She came out. She touched him. She knew he wasn't drinking; he was sure she knew that.

If she were all into Dr. Marc, would she have come out? *No way.*

"10-33," the radio crackled. "10-33. MTU en route to Park Avenue. All available units respond."

Bomb threat. Park Avenue.

Then it hit him, like one of those pictures you can stare at for a month before you shift your focus just right and a whole picture appears that was right there in front of your face the entire time. All the blood drained from Owen's face.

"Oh Jesus."

That was the camera angle. The weird one, not like any of the others. It was looking straight down onto the corner. Park Avenue.

Spencer. I Kill Rich People.

A second chance.

"Yes!" He slapped the dashboard and raised both his clenched fists. "I knew. I knew!"

Owen reached his red globe light out the car window and set it on the roof in one fluid motion. The tires screeched as the car tore away from the curb. He was moving at fifty miles an hour when he hit the corner at Fifth Avenue, then spun hard left alongside Central Park and gunned the engine. He hit another hard left onto 72nd, sliding around and butting the high curb. Sparks flew onto the sidewalk as he punched the pedal, the metal rims grinding. He accelerated east toward Park Avenue.

*****

The first delivery truck, a dark brown box van, turned onto East 71st and pulled to a stop. Spencer watched the driver run around the front to drop his package and ring the door at the side entrance to Park Avenue. The tent flashed at the same time as the bullet burst one of the rear tires and shifted the van into an obvious tilt. Spencer fired again, easily taking out the opposite rear tire and dropping the van like a true shot collapses a buck's hind legs. Both rounds boomed and hissed like a launching rocket. The sound that only a Barrett can make.

Spencer had already fired when he realized he hadn't used ear protection. The tinnitus raged.

He dialed 9-1-1 at 05:58.

"Emergency Services. What are you reporting?"

"One thousand pounds of military munitions are inside the disabled box van parked beside Park Avenue. You have nine minutes to evacuate. If police or the bomb squad gets within twenty feet of the van, I detonate it that second." Spencer disconnected the call and then pried open the back of the cell phone; he removed the sim card and the battery, and tossed the pieces into the corner of the tent.

*****

"All units be advised," the police radio crackled. "Do not approach the box van. Repeat. Do not approach box van at Park Avenue building."

Through the Leupold scope, Spencer watched the doorman and nighttime building security men run outside, first checking the van then sprinting back in. They can't press the alarm, he thought. Nearly every apartment had panic rooms. If the owners locked themselves inside, they would never come out in time to evacuate.

Up and down the Park Avenue building, lights blinked on as police units arrived. Uniforms trotted around the side of the building, leaning into their shoulder mikes to report. Their movements shifted noticeably; after they spotted the van, the adrenalin pumped through their systems.

"10-33 is confirmed," Owen's radio crackled.

"No!" Owen yelled. "It's Spencer!"

He reached to call it in and pulled back his arm. "They'll never believe me."

Multiple uniforms tackled a man wearing a brown shirt and brown short pants. They wrenched his arms in the air and forced his fingers open, pinning his hands against the granite stonework on the side of the structure. More uniforms kicked open his legs before a police officer patted one leg up to the driver's crotch then down the other. Then they pulled his arms behind his back, handcuffed him, and then pushed him again, face-first, into the side wall of the building. Both his feet were kicked out from under him. He fell and was dragged, half-conscious, east on East 71st.

Eight officers from the 19th poured into Park Avenue while the doorman held open the front. He fumbled, throwing his hands into the air.

"We need a detailed list of the names and numbers of people present within the building," the squad commander shouted.

"I've only got workmen and guests," the doorman stammered back. "Nobody's working at 6 a.m.," he told them. He handed over the names on the short overnight list.

"What about the residents?" the police demanded.

Their tone scared the doorman. It had a 9/11 sound. He couldn't think; he'd worked there since 2003, but he couldn't remember a single name of anyone who owned the building. Why was he there? Why wasn't he getting the fuck away?

"I've got kids," he responded.

It took a moment before he remembered his clipboard. He could see his chest pounding, physically see it, while his finger shook over the names.

The building's security detail rode with the uniforms up in the elevators. Floor by floor, they sprinted against time, fanning out. 9/11 was on every one of their minds, too.

Not a single face looked up in Spencer's direction.

"Five minutes thirty," crackled through every walkie-talkie as dispatch clocked down in fifteen-second instruments. "Four minutes to evacuate, then all responders follow FD directions."

Inside Park Avenue, where one hundred million dollars liquid net worth was the baseline to even be considered for approval to own, residents who were accustomed to giving orders sensed the need to obey, no questions asked. The police never mentioned the deadline; their brusque mannerisms conveyed volumes.

Additional units rushed inside the adjacent building to the north, across East 71st and spread down the street in both directions. A fire engine pulled to a stop along the east side of Park Avenue.

A roof-mounted loudspeaker sounding as loud as a rock concert announced, "All persons take nothing and immediately leave your building." More sirens approached as emergency services personnel directed people to safety. Some fled in pajamas; others were shirtless. One woman was wearing nothing but her panties and her four little white dogs clutched to her chest.

"All persons hearing this, move to the nearest exit immediately. No messing around, people. We need you to move now! Emergency services will direct you to safety."

*****

The first sets of residents trickled out of Park Avenue, older residents mainly, with assistance from uniformed officers. Many were crying and hurriedly carried their pets. None were using umbrellas.

Spencer watched their faces carefully through the Leupold, waiting. If the target wasn't there, it would all be for nothing.

Since when was that anything new? That was being a sniper.

Spencer fed on every siren, every announcement, concentrated, his mind moving toward the calm zone. He felt the serotonins surge. The high.

*****

Owen braked hard and jumped out at the northwest corner of Park and East 71st, leaving the engine running. On the opposite corner, butlers and maids and personal assistants moved out the side door of Park Avenue and ran in a long pack, single-file, behind a uniformed patrolman heading east down the middle of the street.

He grasped the view immediately; it had been rattling around his brain for days. Owen turned 180 degrees and threw his head back, looking upward for the exact perspective. His eyes hit on another anomaly; his feet were churning in the direction of the tent before his mind caught up.

That was it. That was the viewpoint.

He was around the corner in seconds, pulling on the locked doors at Terraza.

Walter looked up from his desk and moved to the door.

"NYPD," Owen shouted inside. "Police emergency!"

He shouldered past the doorman. "Don't you hear what's going on?" he demanded. "Where's the roof?"

Walter looked Owen over. "Up there," he answered, "on eighteen." He didn't like being moved out of *his* doorway.

"No!" Owen shot back. "Directly above here. What floor?"

"How I know you're a cop?" Walter countered. "Show me a badge."

Owen reached behind his waistband, drew his service weapon, pulled back the slide, and held it down at his side.

"What floor?" he screeched, his eyes wild.

Walter glanced toward the telephone.

"The floor!" Owen screamed.

"Seven. Terrace is on seven."

*****

In front of Park Avenue, a white paddy wagon rolled up, double-parking beside a black Daimler waiting for the owners of 3A. The van narrowed Spencer's field of vision to just six feet between the box van's roof and the gray-green awning in front of the doors. His inch-and-three-quarters vertical melted to a quarter-inch.

Spencer raised his right shoulder and sighted in on a slightly more acute angle. A wave of occupants moved fast out of the building, surrounded by a phalanx of police and private security.

Spencer watched, recognizing faces from their photos on the web: all billionaires. *BRASS.*

"Not today," he muttered, allowing one after the next to pass.

A cop standing with his back to the street waived them urgently up the steps and inside the rear door of the paddy wagon and then directed the others to hold inside the doors.

Owen ran out the elevator. His thumb double-checked the safety as he lifted the Glock and held it fully extended, aimed and ready, rushing forward with eight-foot strides.

Spencer followed the faces as a second group was ushered out the glass-and-brass Park Avenue doors. One face looked up. Spencer fired. Instantly, the 661-grain round boomed. A hiss issued from the barrel as Spencer absorbed the recoil's heavy punch without losing sight of his target through the Leupold.

The hissing mixed with the plastic-bag popping impact noise as the brass bullet struck across the street, piercing the Vision Partners founder symmetrically between his gray eyebrows. The impact lifted the man's body off its feet as bone, spraying blood and brain matter running down the glass doors.

Within the tent, Spencer gently set down the Barrett and forced himself to breathe and mentally adjusted for the real-time positions of the first responders. *Inside right, around to service elevator. Loading dock at rear, through alley onto East 70th, left to Lexington.* He stepped toward the tent flaps, pushed aside the flaps, stopped, peeled and dropped the nitrile gloves, then withdrew the Sig Sauer and glanced downward. He still had the kneepads on.

Owen had the fingers of his left hand around the bar on the glass door opening onto the rooftop deck when he heard the booming report. His peripheral vision captured the flash illuminating the inside of the tent like heat lightning.

Owen ripped back the tent flap and fired. The Glock's first round slapped hard against Spencer's right shoulder. The force spun him around and paralyzed every nerve in his right arm. Spencer's brain told him to reach his beltline, to draw the Sig Sauer, but the arm hung useless. A tall silhouette was framed in the doorway backlit by the lights on inside Terraza.

Owen grabbed his left hand around his right wrist and squared his aim in one fluid motion. He quickly fired three more rounds. Each of his shots struck home dead center within a narrow killing diameter just below the breastbone.

Spencer saw the bright flames come out the gun barrel lighting the forearms and hands holding the weapon. His arms jerked side to side before his legs collapsed out from under him. He looked like a marionette left behind by a bored child; his limbs fell in a twisted heap. He dropped without ever registering a face.

The sharp gunpowder scent filled his lungs when Owen finally inhaled. He turned sideways and swept back the tent flaps to let in light. He saw the 9mm semi-automatic remaining in Spencer's belt and jerked it free then sent it skidding behind him across the roof deck.

Spencer's chin was dug into chest, but Owen leaned in and easily identified the face. "Fucker," he swore. "We got him, Tee."

He couldn't wait for crime scene investigation. Seeing the Barrett, he grabbed up the rifle. It felt like he was holding a cannon.

He stepped out of the acrid scent lingering inside the tent. The morning air outside was crisp and fresh. Owen's arms shook from the adrenalin rushing through his system, but he lifted his trophy high above his head and howled. He howled for Tremaine, howled because it was done, and he howled because he had done it.

"I did it, Tee!" he screamed, gripping his right hand vise-like around the huge weapon and pumping its barrel up and down. "They took my medallion, but I did it. I did this! Owen Cullen. Detective Lieutenant!"

Tears welled and then ran freely down his face and wet his shirt. He let them. The Glock was locked so tightly in his left hand that he couldn't open his fingers. In his right he held up that Barrett like it was the Statue of Liberty torch.

"I did it, Callie," he said with the noise of a dozen sirens coming up from below. "They can't take this away. I did it!"

*****

Inside the tent, Spencer's eyes opened wide. His lungs demanded air. His fingers and feet flexed spasmodically. He tried to press his torso upright, cringed, breathed, and listened.

Owen used his back to press open the glass doors to get back inside just as both elevators opened. Six black-uniformed, black-helmeted SWAT officers surged out of the doors and fanned to the sides.

He tuned and stepped toward them, smiling, starting to laugh. The big gun shook above his head.

"Gun!" they shouted in unison. HKs were up at their cheeks, all on setting three, all leveled at Owen.

Owen's eyes opened wide. Someone had fired. He felt the bullet burning in his gut.

But I'm on the job, he thought, as his arms came down.

The second bullet struck his jaw. Then four weapons fired, their bullets ripping through Owen's heart and lungs and spine. The last image he saw was an orange sunrise. He saw it from the floor, looking up through the shattered glass doors.

Two of the officers pounded forward, leaping over Owen's body and crunching glass beneath their boots. They split directions, sweeping the rooftop. The first moved up to the side of the tent while another knelt and secured the Glock. The others took positions and froze, statue-like, ready to fire as more police troops followed.

The one nearest the tent looked behind him, verified readiness, and nodded.

The others, in unison, raised their aim.

He reached out his HK and used its barrel to whip the tent flap open and then he raised a black-gloved fist to signal "Hold Fire."

"Clear," he shouted from inside the helmet.

"Clear," the others echoed.

AFTERWORD

Carlton Jeffers, president of American Patriots for Action, released the following statement:

This nation has lost a great patriot and an ardent freedom fighter, a founding Vision Partner and the soul and spirit of Americans for Patriotic Action.

His death will not dim the causes that he and tens of millions of us hold dear. I call on all of us to make his murder count for change, to produce change.

We are a nation of laws. We have laws to protect lesbians and gays, bisexual and transgender individuals, laws to protect handicapped people, laws for all races and religions, laws to protect our elderly. We have laws to protect people who stay in this country illegally. Yet we tolerate attacks on our more successful Americans.

How can it be right to allow our most successful citizens to be maligned and abused in ways we would never tolerate against minorities ten times, twenty times, a hundred times larger? Where are the laws to protect the people who work hard and strive for success, the people who create jobs and through their achievements lead our young men and women to aspire to better themselves? Surely, the most successful amongst us deserve the same protections!

Real Americans celebrate success. We strive to emulate the drive and perseverance that produces success.

The APA, along with the American Legislative Council and Vision Partners, will not stop pressing for legislation in all fifty states and in our nation's Congress, to secure the rights of all American citizens to be free from all forms of discrimination based upon their economic status.

Class warfare is a hate crime.

*****

Spencer waited a day and a night, the entire time squeezed inside a dark utility closet inside a basement off the alley running between 71st and 72nd. Uncontrollable drowning flashbacks left him wet with perspiration and shaking long after the terror passed.

After twenty-four hours, he could still just barely inflate his lungs. Babe Ruth swinging a ball-peen hammer. Again.

He made his way back to Yonkers. Subway, then train. He had planned to move again. Get out that day. But he was too busted up. First he had something to say. He took hold of fifty pre-addressed and stamped blue-lined index cards. One by one, he wrote it out carefully, all in black caps.

FIGHT

SPECIAL THANKS TO MY COMMUNITY OF READERS.

Gypsy Courtois, Jerome Soismier, Melissa McClintock, Sylvan Selig, Joel Geffen, Ali Daniali, Cassandra Goduti, Tyler Hurst, Zina Timoney, Hugo Cerda, Rhian Gibbs, Paul Collins, Steve Kilisky, Lisa Cox, Jack Prober, Tanya Kolosova, Melissa McClintock, Sue Nikiel, Betsy Bogin, Shane Bogin, Brian Coltrell, Jinglan Wang, Janet Frink Ann, McClusky, Ric Mangialardi, Gaerda Zeiler, Randy Zeiler, Cori Josias, and Albert Sarfati.

ABOUT THE AUTHOR

Mike Bogin lives in the Pacific Northwest with his wife of twenty-eight years. He has three grown children. His parents traveled extensively and worked abroad; taking him to sixty countries by the time he was ten.

Mike completed his undergraduate degree at the University of California, graduating Phi Beta Kappa with Honors and Distinction. After spending a year on an island in Greece working manual labor and writing his first novel, he went on to complete his graduate studies at the University of Cambridge in England at the Institute of Criminology within the Faculty of Law. His Master's Thesis focus, Anti-Terrorism, would not turn into a major industry until after the 9/11 attacks.

In addition to writing novels, Mike has been active in real estate, farms wheat, and grows grapes, from which he makes several distinctive red wines.

Mike has written five novels and a screenplay.

www.MikeBogin.com